Naythorn Blackmane Unicorn

And

The Seventh Prince

Book 4

G. D. Hanson

G. D. Hanson

Naythorn Blackmane Unicorn and the Seventh Prince

G. D. Hanson

This is the fourth part of a story that takes five parts to tell:

Briarburr Blackmane and the Unicorn Hold

Naythorn Blackmane Unicorn and His Animal Band

Naythorn Blackmane Unicorn and the Gift of the Winged Horse

Naythorn Blackmane Unicorn and the Seventh Prince

Naythorn Blackmane Unicorn and the Ghost Wolf

canst thou bind the unicorn...
Job (Authorized KJV)

CHAPTER 1

STORM

"Blast and Ruin! Since there is little more for me to lose... rope me to what remains of the forward mast!"

"You ask me, Admiral, to do... *what?*" responded Captain Avalcar with a look incredulous.

"You *heard* what I said! If this storm tonight breaks apart my flagship barge, I will with her descend to the bottom of the sea."

"Alright, I will reluctantly obey my admiral's order," replied the captain. "But be advised, Sir, that because daylight shortens, the coming cold and wet night will for you be very long. According to my calculations, this evening's fall of darkness brings the longest night of the year."

"Hmpf! I *will* be miserable. But at least so restrained I will not by monstrous winds be washed overboard before my barge capsizes."

Upon securing Zoumar, the captain lingered.

"So bound, Sir, every member of this crew will be impressed by your dedication to this vessel and the magic blue gold treasure carried in its hold. Only this immense sea could spawn a gale so intense, and of such long duration. It was the worst luck for your fleet to be caught in these crushing south winds."

"With masts broken, and sails unmanageable, our only chance to survive is to let the waves this night and tomorrow drive our prow more northward, opposite the direction of our return to Phoenicia."

"I agree, Admiral."

"The force of the gale *lessens* as morning approaches," encouraged Avalcar found again at the side of his rope-restrained admiral. "From the moment you were tied to the mast, if only by a little, the storm began to subside."

"If that is the case, Avalcar, you should have secured me to the mast five days before."

Another new morning found strong, but not gale-force winds, still blowing out of the south.

"It is come time to unbind my admiral!" exclaimed Avalcar.

"My other four barges... *are to me gone,*" lamented Zoumar as he rubbed the rope burns on his arms.

"Sir, although your other barges are not found, that does not mean one or more of them do not remain afloat. As for me, I am proud that the barge I captained survived seven days of ferocious winds. And, I continue sure that blue gold magic shall come to deliver your flagship home to Phoenicia."

"Where in heaven's name do we now sail?"

"All I can say, Admiral, is that the storm drove us very far north of where we wanted to be. Unfortunately, we have come by no islands where we might replenish supplies and timbers. Until our three great masts are replaced, this barge will by oars alone be powered."

"Can something, can anything be today done, Avalcar?"

"Do not lose heart, Admiral. We will soon find harbor."

"Having lost four of my five barges, how can I *not* lose heart?"

New Day

"If we do not presently sight land, we will starve. That said... remain you positive, Avalcar?"

"Yes Admiral, I do. My heart does not doubt that we will survive this voyage. By the way, I am pleased that following the awful tempest the stomachs of Hammereins and Lucareins quickly resettled into the roll of sea waves."

"I still cannot believe that your two horses were not by the tempest hurled into the sea."

The admiral and his captain moved to sit with backs against a splintered deck rail.

"Speaking of equines, Avalcar, after traveling so far to find the unicorn hold in the shadow of the fiery volcano, and then freighting the white herd through many adventures on the high sea, it is to me a cruel twist of fate that the unicorns departed the peninsular camp without waiting to bid us farewell."

"Our sailors were disappointed that they could not mark the departure of unicorn favorites that they shall never again come upon," replied Avalcar. "In their lives as mariners, the time spent with the white herd was most compelling."

"In their presence, one could not but sense magical goodness. You and I were privileged to come to know Aneilee and Elianor the two matriarchal leaders,

Cabalblade the captain of the unicorn guard horses, the courageous half-horned Belfloralex..."

"She spun her body around so fast that she made the wind to obey her," said Avalcar.

"When you once said that she could *harness* the wind... you described her magical gift perfectly."

"Unlike the arrogant Hoovefort, Haltervor became a favorite of the sailors on this vessel," added Avalcar.

"He was the unicorn for whom they made a halter, right?"

"And a very nice halter it was, Admiral. The stallion liked it so much that he changed his name from Vor, to Haltervor. Is it possible that you and I shall one day again escort Haltervor and the white herd?"

"That would take... a miracle. I was just recalling that in several conversations with Aneilee and Elianor, the name Naythorn Blackmane loomed large."

"Hammerclaw and Lucars told me," continued Avalcar, "that without the unrelenting quest of the blackmane to unlock and solve the mystery of the pyramid-crested peaks, the deposit of magic blue gold would never have been found within the mountain of spires."

"I very much wanted the blackmane to refind the white herd before my fleet's departure from the camp of the unicorns."

"It is strange, Admiral, but I do have the feeling that there will come a day when I again share adventures with the magical white herd. In fact, something tells me that I shall one day chance upon Naythorn himself."

"If your intuition is correct, Avalcar, you will come to know firsthand the nobility of the blackmaned war unicorn. Huh! Perhaps you wanted to stay behind with Hammerclaw, Lucars, and Marsand, the three Phoenicians that do not with us return."

"I dared not make that request of my admiral."

"You knew that I depend on you too much, Avalcar. Without your exceptional leadership and superb navigational skills, this barge would not have survived the storm."

Upon the approach of evening Avalcar was accustomed to do something that most of his crew thought to be strange. The captain would bridle and mount Hammereins, or Lucareins, and upon the back of a horse watch with tranquility the set of the sun. From time to time he would have his horse to prance in place, or move smartly from side to side. Then he would relax while he combed and rubbed the hide and mane of his horse.

Amidst the grandeur of billowing clouds, endless skies, and azure seas the companionship of the two horse stallions permitted Avalcar to commune with perfect *Beauty.*

Zoumar approached Avalcar and his horses.

"In spite of being stranded on high seas with hope sparse, I will to my captain admit one thing. When I think on the sheets of magic blue gold still secured in the hold of this barge, like you, I am made *hopeful.*"

"Thank goodness, Admiral, that before we cast off in return voyage my platoon found Hammer, Lucars, the black bison, and the brown and white cattle freighting the gold sheets toward your fleet. A thousand years is a long enough time for Phoenicia to wait to replenish magic swords and armor.

"By the way, Sir, while some sailors are poor horsemen, and others do not like horses, for me there is no disharmony in sitting astride a horse that stands upon the deck of a great barge. The act of hitching a saddle and bridling a horse melts away my worries."

"If that is the case, then I need to mount my captain's second horse. Hmph. When last we crossed this great ocean the voyage was not so hard. Too long on half rations, I worry that my sailors scarce possess the strength to pull oars."

"When last year we sailed forth from Phoenicia," replied Avalcar, "the nobility of our quest to rescue the white herd of unicorns brought the blessing of continuous blue skies and fair winds."

Pacing later that night the deck, Zoumar felt himself to be completely alone. The creaking of planks loosened and splintered by turbulent winds was the only sound that kept him company. For one of the few times in his life at sea, he felt afraid. The fear was not for himself; he had lived a large enough life. His fear was that, along with his sailors, the priceless blue gold secured in his hold would soon sink into unknowable depths of sea water.

His countrymen were beset by Hittites on one side and Egyptians on the other. In that regard, the store of magic gold carried in the hold of his flagship was required to arm and protect soldiers and sailors become more numerous over a thousand years of Phoenician history. The protective blue gold in his hold would not only save the lives of soldiers confronting belligerent armies, the magic would also inspire bravery among his countrymen.

"Where are you, dolphin pilots, when I need you!" exclaimed Zoumar. "Come and again guide my vessel!"

As the prow of the flagship bounced against contrary waves, the admiral was sure that he could hear to groan every part of the decking.

Rainbow Hope

"Against this wind, Admiral, your vessel scarcely moves."

"Before our crew has rowed fifty more leagues eastward we will all have starved," responded the admiral.

"Hmph! Sir... to the north... is that the making of a rainbow?"

"But, Avalcar, how does a rainbow form when the sky is everywhere clear and the wind feels dry? Be assured that the rainbow colors will soon vanish."

In middle night the admiral approached Avalcar and observed, "I have never before seen a rainbow of the night. How can a rainbow persist into darkness?"

"Sir, for the unusual rainbow I have no explanation, and I cannot take my eyes off of it. The top part of the compact rainbow begins to point in sharpness upward. To be honest, the rainbow calls to me."

"Once again your intuition, Avalcar?" As Zoumar walked away he muttered, "Strange... strange."

"The clouds that present to the north render an appearance benign," observed the next morning the captain to his admiral. "It is unfortunate that in return voyage this vessel needs to sail south."

Nodding his head in agreement, Zoumar turned and walked away.

That afternoon found the admiral and his captain standing at a rail observing the persistent rainbow.

"I am sure you noticed, Sir, how the clouds that today overlay the northern horizon color themselves in hues of reds and purples," observed Avalcar. "While clouds caress the exterior of the rainbow, curiously none are found within its interior. As the growing bank of fulgent clouds shifts more northward, their unusual look fully engages the interest of the sailors."

"What good does that do us?" muttered Zoumar with exasperation toned in his voice. "You and I require clouds to hint of land... to our south. In that regard we need the wind to blow out of, rather than into, the north."

"Sir, as this night approaches the rainbow arches higher, while its sides remain compacted," observed later Avalcar upon refinding his admiral. "Once more no clouds form below the layered bands of purest colors. I do not recall ever before seeing a rainbow take that form, or remain so long stationary. It is as if the rainbow beckons us to sail through its vacant arch."

"Funny that you should say that," replied Zoumar. "Something inside me wants to do as you suggest, and sail right through the rainbow doorway."

"Your intuition, Admiral?" responded a smiling Avalcar.

"About that rainbow there is a thing unusual, perhaps even magical."

"Admiral, with a distinctly pointed top and persistence through both day and night, that rainbow is without a doubt magical."

"Huh! I was, Avalcar, more than once told by the high escort of the white herd that I should ever listen to my heart."

"Speaking of Aneilee, she neighed to both of us that the power of the unicorn horn brought love, and that the protective magic of blue gold required the presence of truth in one's heart. Perhaps in addition to love and truth, there are other things magical. Saying that, Admiral, makes me to recall a conversation I had with Hammerclaw on the night that he and Lucars delivered to my scout party the blue gold they had mined.

"Finding himself to be in a very good mood, Hammer that night recounted the things that had happened to him and Lucars while from us they traveled apart. For example, the blacksmith said that he could not enter the canyon that shines of blue gold without feeling its magic. And later, at the end of a desperate battle where the blackmane's band was made to flee, he and Lucars placed a newborn foal on the back of the winged horse Rayalas. Attempting to deliver her precious foal across an unimaginably deep river gorge, the mare tragically did not succeed. Hammer said that when the flighted unicorn crashed into the far cliff of the gorge her magic armor exploded in a display of dazzling lights, and glass-like bits of blue gold burst upward in colors that lined horizontal.

"The colors transformed into columnar shafts of vertical light that Hammer called the Rayalas Borealis. I myself saw shine down those unforgettable colored lights. The point I am getting to, is that Hammer concluded that the magic of the Rayalas Borealis brought a kind of celestial grace to those below found bathed in its light."

"So, Avalcar, you are telling me that to the magic of unicorn love, blue gold truth, and the heavenly grace of the Rayalas Borealis, we can add..."

"It may be, Admiral, that the doorway-like rainbow that you and I now observe, that seemingly invites us to sail under its pointed arch, brings to us... *a heavenly hope.* Many times on the field of battle the only thing that kept me alive was the hope that came to me from above."

"Avalcar, on this I am going to trust you. We change course to pass right through the doorway rainbow of heavenly hope. Saying that reminds me of a poem."

"I think I remember that poem, Admiral. It is about a benign spirit that makes a way in the sea, a path in the mighty waters... the spirit is mightier than the noise of many waters."

Blown by south winds toward a miraculous rainbow that two days and nights stayed before his barges, the flagship of Admiral Zoumar came upon an island, actually a cluster of islands, with pink sand beaches. Set between reefs, a perfect harbor was there found. Fruit trees were abundant, and the cedar trees on the island would well-serve to repair and rebuild masts and decks.

"Sails!" shouted the lookout standing on a bluff above the harbor. "There are sails! Although half destroyed, they are our sails! Four ships approach!"

"My barges did not founder!" exclaimed the admiral as he turned to grasp hold of Avalcar's arms. "It is a miracle!"

"Through the storm your other four vessels stayed together. More than that, your captains did not give up on you. Following also the rainbow of hope, they cast about this sea until they regained their Admiral."

"It will take much time to repair and resupply all five barges, Avalcar. This storm that blew us northward, and damaged our ships, will by three moons delay our return to Phoenicia."

"My admiral cannot but be disheartened by the costly postponement of return," replied Avalcar. "Still, I will choose to think that for this suffering and long delay, there will be a recompense."

"Do you mean to say that from this tragedy can come something good?"

"That thinking provides me comfort. You see, Admiral, in the past I have found that when I open my heart to learn from suffering, loss, and misfortune, then a benefit is always found."

"What kind of benefit?"

"Sometimes, Admiral, a very valuable benefit that I find to be... purposed."

"Well then, Captain, we shall hope that this terribly costly storm-provoked delay brings to you and me some future thing advantageous."

G. D. Hanson

CHAPTER 2

FOUR TROYAN PRINCES AND PRINCESSES

Egyptian soldiers rampaged long into the longest night of the year, and in a burning palace the bloodied Troyan king lay dying.

The city of Troy was, or had been, the capital of a nascent kingdom established in a dangerous part of the world. The twelve years of labor and sweat to build the new capital had been for naught. By the time the next day's sun stood high in the sky, warring Egyptian barges would be loaded heavily with gold, grain, and Troyan men and women with hands bound.

Knowing full well that this night of destruction could someday present, the king had taken one extraordinary covert measure of precaution. Section by section a long escape tunnel had been built, with no one permitted to work on more than one stage of the subterranean passage. The pretext for the long and difficult digging was to provide improved drainage for the growing city. However, no drainage flowed through the tunnel that began under the floor of the palace and coursed far beyond the walls of the city to end in a rock strewn place at the shore of the great sea.

About to be overwhelmed by sword and fire, four young people of royal descent fled into the hidden tunnel. The oldest and tallest of the four, the dark-haired Prince Ermir, emerged first from out the tunnel to see against the shore many Egyptian barges. As the broad-shouldered brother with an auburn tint to his hair, Prince Ermal, and his two trim and fit sisters Princess Admira and Princess Resi huddled at the side of their oldest sibling, a plan of escape was formed.

There was no time to mourn a father now from them departed, nor their many friends now held in bondage, nor the loss of their palatial home. There was, however, time enough to seize the last barge in the line of anchored Egyptian vessels. For some unknown reason that conveniently situated barge, with a hull formed in a particularly sleek way, had been left lightly guarded.

Four swords were drawn. As the two princes dispatched two sentries posted in front of the target vessel, the two princesses trespassed the ship and without a fight seized the one man minding its decks.

With two swords at his throat the captive said quietly to Princess Admira, "This unique vessel requires a skilled pilot. I am he."

"Give us your name," ordered Ermir as the four royal siblings gathered round the slender, clean-shaven captive with penetrating eyes that shone a dark shade of brown.

"Bashkeem."

"How is it that you speak our language?"

"Born in a mountainous land found to the west of here, I am a slave of Egypt that speaks many languages and does many things. I have piloted this vessel since it was built. Because I also designed this barge, I know its lines like the back of my hand."

"What must four princes and princesses do, Bashkeem, to be quickly launched?" inquired Ermal.

"Cast off the lines and help me pull up the sails," answered Bashkeem. "Fortunately, the wind strengthens."

Turning to a young lady that had just held a sword to his throat, Bashkeem ordered, "You with red hair, take hold of the rudder and turn the barge. The wind favors our departure."

With the quickness of a cat Bashkeem sprang about the deck of the vessel seemingly able to do the work of two heavier afoot men. Just as he said would happen, the wind caught firm the sails; soon the flaming city of Troy receded into night darkness. First light of a chilly new morning found a barge carrying four royals and an Egyptian slave surrounded by nothing but seascape.

"My turn to steer this vessel," said Resi. After tightening shoulder-length dark hair close to her head, the taller princess replaced her red haired sister Admira. Grasping firm the handle of the rudder, Resi watched captivated as Bashkeem continued to adjust every scrap of sail to fill with wind.

"Brother Ermir," observed Resi at midmorning, "I say that Bashkeem is ten times more naval captain... than slave."

"He is at that. Come Resi, let us discover if we can make Bashkeem loyal to the four of us, and as well make this the first ship of our new navy." To hold firm the rudder, Ermir helped Resi adjust two looped ends of rope to hold the steering handle in place.

"Come and sit with the four of us," directed Ermir. "Have no fear, Bashkeem, of honest pirates."

"Prince Ermir is oldest of all of us, and Prince Ermal comes next," said Resi nodding toward each sibling she introduced.

"May I inquire the ages of the princes?" asked Bashkeem.

"I am twenty-six," responded Ermir, "and my brother is twenty-three."

"Third in line," continued Resi, "is Princess Admira who is..."

"I just turned twenty-one," interrupted Admira. "My sister Resi is only eighteen..."

"Almost nineteen!" exclaimed Resi.

"You told us your name is Bashkeem," began Ermir, "but who really are you?"

Sitting stiffly, the tall man with thinning jet-black hair answered, "I was born in Illyria. Until last night the Egyptian to whom this ship formerly belonged, was my master."

"Speak on," said Ermir.

"As befell you yesterday, when I was a boy of ten Egyptian raiders attacked the place of my birth. After trespassing into our mountains they carried away captives young and old. For twenty-five years since I have been an orphan possession of Egypt."

"When we were very young we four also lost our mother," responded Resi nodding her head.

"But until yesterday we still had our father," volunteered Admira with a sigh. "So that his children might survive, he perished with sword in hand."

"Prince Ermir, here is an information about myself that is essential to who I am. Since I could not command my physical being, as I grew into manhood I chose to command my mind. What I set about to know, I learned. If I came upon a companion who spoke a new language, I persuaded him to teach it to me. When another companion knew to build a pyramid, I prevailed upon him to teach me to engineer upward four lines of rock to meet in one point. For the last three years I have piloted this vessel." A slight smile crossed the face of Bashkeem as he added, "Stop me if I talk too much."

Bashkeem paused, but no prince or princess chose to say a word.

"I have yet to come upon an Egyptian barge as fleet as this one," continued Bashkeem. "Although this vessel is not particularly large, instead of two masts I made three. The sails that billow above your heads are of my design. Cut more square than is found on other Egyptian vessels, the tightly woven cloth shakes off the dampness of sea spray. The set of the sails is integrated, so that a wind that passes over one can catch in another. Because the captains of the vessels with traditional designs derided my innovations, this barge was yesterday made to moor last in the line of Egyptian warcraft."

"Fortunately for us," observed Ermir, "the end barge is the most isolated and the easiest to turn about."

"I find it curious that no other barge ventured after us with intent to recapture this vessel," offered Ermal.

"Upon noticing our departure, the other barge captains probably said *good riddance,*" replied Bashkeem. "Until last night I never had occasion to show to anyone how much speed these sails possess. The modifications I made to the design of this vessel will make it well-serve as a pirateer."

"With not one oar being pulled, this barge moves fast," observed Resi.

"I am a man that observes, learns, and builds," continued Bashkeem. "In my hands broken things become better than they were originally made.

"From the exquisite design of your armor, and your refined speech, I last night saw that the four of you were indeed of royal blood. By your actions I quickly determined that you are fair-minded. You now know more about who and what I am, than the man that owns title to my name."

"Bashkeem, from this day onward you are no longer a slave, but a nobleman," prompted Prince Ermir. "I say to you, kneel!"

The Egyptian placed a knee on the deck, lowered arms to his sides, and bowed his head. Ermir touched the flat of his sword blade to one shoulder, the other shoulder, and then to Bashkeem's bent head.

"Rise, *Sir Bashkeem!* You are made a noble citizen... of the one day to come new kingdom of Troy! Because your superb seamanship rescued last night our royal lineage, I further appoint you captain of this ship and commander of the Troyan Navy, which the five of us now comprise."

Because the little ceremony happened without foresight or plan no one knew how Bashkeem would react to the gift of his freedom, appointment to the nobility, and designation as commander. The new nobleman offered not a single thank you. Instead, Bashkeem stood and in return offered a simple salute accompanied by a trickle of a few tears down one cheek.

"Hah! Look at us!" exclaimed Ermal. "We four muddy royals, and a slave made to be an admiral, are truly a sight to behold."

"An admiral that happens to possess more dignity than my younger brother," chided Ermir.

Undeterred, Ermal smiled wryly as he added, "If they could see us now, would not the Egyptian barge captains laugh loudly at the prospect of our new navy?"

"Admiral Bashkeem," offered Admira, "please tell me that found today on this fleet vessel we four brothers and sisters are presently made safe."

"It is my pleasure to inform Princess Admira, that she is *made safe,*" responded Bashkeem forming for the second time a small smile. "Young lady, if ten vessels appeared in the distance intent on capturing us, my hands on these sails would leave them all wondering to where we had disappeared.

"Ahem, Princess, you bear the lofty name of Admira. Since we five comprise a very small and intimate collection of sailors, grant me the honor of calling you by your given name, and please do not call me admiral. An admiralty must through many hard battles be earned. By your leave, and that of your sister and brothers, I am pleased to become the captain that commands what shall soon become a flotilla of pirate barges."

"Captain Bashkeem, I am most satisfied to be by you called, Admira." Smiling wide, the older princess added,

"Consistent with my name, my service to you shall in every way be... *admirable.*"

"I value a smile from you that is most congenial," answered the newly made captain.

"Hah! Although Resi's teeth are straighter than mine, I am proud to possess a smile that is to myself exclusive."

"Bashkeem," interjected Resi, "our father the king is now forever gone from us. We pleaded with him, but like the captain of a sinking ship he would not abandon his burning palace. Last night we lost everything but our lives. How can I know that you will never become a traitor to four unfortunate princes and princesses?" After breathing deeply she added, "I want to trust you, but possessing a character more skeptical than my sister, I am afraid to."

"Do you believe, Resi, that I am a man of logic, an engineer, a builder?" answered Bashkeem without hesitation.

"Sir, having seen with my own eyes how well you designed the performance of these sails, that much I can clearly tell."

"Only a short-sighted man of dismal intelligence would turn his back on four royal siblings that rescued him from a lifetime of slavery. Just as you were by this vessel last night vouched safe, your theft of this vessel in the midst of terrible battle rescued my life from disdain. I thank all four of you for giving me the freedom to fully employ the intellect the heavens gifted to me. With you four at my side, I will faithfully build future things that are sure and worthy."

"I apologize, Bashkeem. My earlier attempt at irony, or perhaps it was both irony and sarcasm, was in bad taste," offered Ermal. "From this day forward the four of us that from the royal household of Troy endure, will place our trust in your steadfast service. I anticipate that someday you, Bashkeem, will erect imposing buildings in the future rebuilt city of Troy."

While they ate bread together Ermal broached the question that all were considering, "We this day need to form a plan, to decide what steps to take next. If we do not have today a clear strategy to guide us forward, tomorrow might be too late to begin well the difficult road of return to Troy."

"Because we are only four," cautioned Resi, "we must recognize that overwhelming odds prevail against us."

"Sister we are not four, but five," affirmed Ermal. "I am confident that Bashkeem is, or will soon be, a more valuable part of our team than am I."

"On that score, Bashkeem," interjected the oldest of the four royals, "you have far more experience on the high seas than the rest of us put together. How say you that we proceed?"

The former slave did not right away answer. Instead, he rose and slowly paced the deck from fore to aft. Upon returning he sat himself down and answered Ermir.

"Although difficult and dangerous, there is one strategy that holds promise."

"Whatever your plan, we four will consent," replied Ermir.

"Our two strengths are that we today ply these seas in a very fast barge, and that the four princes and princesses aboard are well-trained to wield a sword. Recognizing those advantages, I will make Ermir, Ermal, Admira, and Resi to become master ship captains. Because the fledgling navy of Troy must seize additional vessels in future battles entered of our own volition, let us make to be our goal the capture of four more ships, one to be captained by each of you. With five ships refitted to my designs for speed, we can become a small armada that strikes fast, and after quickly escapes. I will wager that five fleet and well-captained ships, like this one, will vanquish ten slower ships captained in the old ways.

"Time cannot be wasted. Our best prospect for success is to build rapidly our small armada before Egypt knows who, what, and where we are. Within thirty days we will find, recruit, and train a crew to take the oars of this ship, and on this vessel form a formidable company of attack. Now, every vessel that we capture will require some modifications to promote speed under sail... and that will take time to accomplish. But if together we shoulder the heavy burden of piracy, in one hundred twenty days forward from this shortest day of the year, we will multiply this one barge into a small navy of five superior vessels that can begin to acquire the gold and wheat needed to rebuild your city of Troy. Since Egypt to Troy brought destruction, it is fitting that Egyptian vessels contribute the ransom that finances the rebirth of your city."

Four princes and princesses stood to clasp upraised hands in a show of agreement with the strategy laid out.

Bashkeem stretched hands to grasp those of his new comrades in arms.

"I would that we could recruit sailors in our city of Troy," offered Ermal upon reseating himself. "But few, if any, able-bodied men there remain. Those not taken away into slavery lie lifeless; their bodies corrupt."

"Prince Ermal," answered a confident Bashkeem, "sailing westward I know many islands and inland places formerly devastated by Egyptian raiders, where we can recruit first rate sailors with tough hands forged hard in fighting, and with hearts intent on revenge. A man whose village was burned by Egyptian soldiers will welcome service that holds the promise of retaliation."

"Then, Sir Bashkeem," answered a smiling Ermal, "lead on the Jenelisa!"

"Why is your ship so named?" inquired Resi. "It is such a pretty name."

"Ah, yes, Sir Bashkeem," interjected Ermal. "The younger of our two sisters is the more romantic one who would think to ask you that."

"The brightest flower in the village of my birth, Jenelisa was my age. Warmed by rays of the summer sun, strands of her brown hair turned golden. She was witty, her smile was infectious, her laughter was music to everyone's ears, she could run faster than I, and every day I heard her to sing. Someday I will discover to where she has gone."

CHAPTER 3

DISCONTENT

N aythorn is *no...* fun anymore!" After Featherspark's complaint was hronkked so loudly that it awakened still sleeping members of the band of the blackmaned unicorn, goose wings launched upward.

"I would rather work hard my wings than to be found putting up all day, even though it is about the shortest day of winter, with a gloomy Naythorn Blackmane, a bothersome Webstir duck, and a dreary herd of unicorns."

On this morning's routine scout mission the long-necked gander with black cheeks scarfed in white feathers found invigorating the mix of blue sky, brilliant sunshine, and chill north wind. Blood racing through sinewy bird muscles combined with a thickly feathered coat to warm him. For the goose whose back was marked by arcing bands of purple and gray feathers, flight provided a sense of athletic exhilaration.

Featherspark promised he would no more dwell on things negative, and that especially included the blackmaned unicorn's notably sour disposition. However as his thoughts shifted to Naythorn's sire that had long captained the unicorn guard horses, the goose soon broke his promise to himself. No one understood why Cabalblade had been dismissed, or could identify exactly who had removed him from the leadership of the unicorn guard stallions. That fact that not even the high escort Aneilee could explain how and when had happened the ouster of Cabalblade, made Naythorn to feel even worse for his sire.

Looking about, the distracted goose found he had completed the outward half of his routine scouting mission.

"If you return now, Sparksy, you will land webbed feet to find everyone bored, restless, and in dismal moods. Each and every one of the five members of the razorback pig family will look like they have a stomach ache. By taking a little liberty with your orders to change southward your flight, you just might glimpse the yellow-mottled wolf Danseyelono, and at his side the big mountain lion named Lianvil. After all, you cannot help but wonder if the returning Dansey will still be shackled to the vanquished monster wolf Albarochk."

The gander's elegantly feathered body angled leftward. Sparksy, a nickname given to the goose because his feathers wanted to sparkle and glow when he alerted to wolves, settled into a wind-aided southward course.

With a mischievous grin spreading apart his black bill, Featherspark flew on and on. Behind the steady progress made by his big wings were left several places he knew well. The place of the great battle that defeated, and incapacitated, the monster wolf Albarochk now lay under a thin blanket of snow. Wind-hardened snow drifts laced the summits of three mountain ranges that together fingered northward. While separated band members searched for the rest of their band, each of those mountain tops had been walked by one or another group of Naythorn's military company.

As the sun shifted more and more westward, in the far distance Featherspark came to glimpse the profoundly deep river gorge where the winged horse Rayalas crashed into a cliff. Her demise occurred during the battle in which Danseyelono and Lianvil changed loyalty to join the band of the blackmane, and then the same wolf and lion sowed much confusion among Albarochk's army of fierce wolves and warriors. The treason against the monster wolf committed by the small wolf and the big lion had permitted Naythorn's company to finally escape, with hides intact, that place of ferocious fighting.

The fast-flying Featherspark had traveled ten times more distant from Naythorn's camp than he had been instructed. With the sun accelerating its decline, it had become past time for the goose to return to deliver that same day his scouting report to Naythorn.

"Listen to me, wings! You have flown too far! Turn around, now!"

Although his wing speed slowed, for some reason stubborn goose wings resisted the idea of obedience hronkked by the black beak of Featherspark.

"Hmpf! Rubbing too many times my wings against the feathers of Webstir permitted the duck's stubborn streak to penetrate into my own feathers. Again I order my feathers to turn around... *right now!*" Nonetheless, the wings of the gander flew slowly on southward.

"Long return flight into the freezing cold of coming night, would be very uncomfortable and very reckless," hronkked the goose. "After all, since my instinct tells me that this night is the *longest* of winter, I best find a safe place to light down and through the deep darkness nest warm."

When a ground movement, of some sort, caught his eye the curious goose would investigate. Featherspark shifted course toward the place of movement.

"Now, where precisely was the motion that I saw?" The gander began to fly a pattern of circles, each new one inside the last. Focused on his purpose, he did not notice that his wings had begun to glow.

"Grawwaarrrll!"

"Yipe! Yipe!"

"You rascals almost gave me a heart attack!" fussed Featherspark as he touched webbed feet to ground. "On a freezing cold day I was nice enough to go looking for you. And for that all you can think to do is scare me half to death!"

Goose wings that still sparkled from alert, extended to embrace first the wolf and then the lion. Between the backs of the closely huddled Danseyelono and Lianvil, the goose plopped down a very tired big bird body.

Featherspark noticed something held in the grip of Lianvil.

"Naythorn has *not* been the same since that very same horn shard was lodged in the monster's heart. Tell me lion, what happened to the giant wolf? Where is he? Did you scratch a big hole in the ground and with dirt cover his dead body? Well?"

"Settle down, Goose," yipped Danseyelono. "Give us a chance and everything will be satisfactorily explained."

"You big lug heads!" the impatience of Featherspark persisted. "Tell me right now what happened on your long travel! All of us in Naythorn's band have been worried *sick* about you!"

"While Lianvil and I escorted southward our monster wolf prisoner," began to recount the yellow wolf, "we had plenty of time to reflect on all the evil that not only Albarochk, but that we two had also committed against unicorn goodness. After much distance had been traveled, the big lion and I finally came to find peace within our chests.

"We at last led Albarochk to the place that marked the beginning of the long and bloody war between a grayback wolf and a blackmaned unicorn. Upon reaching the box ravine where began all the trouble and consuming hatred, Albarochk bared his innermost heart and cried uncountable tears.

"When on the following night we arrived at the side of the mountain that destroyed Wittanor, the thousand-year hold of the unicorns, the unusually bright light cast by the Rayalas Borealas seemed to shine down directly upon us. We three slept on ground still warmed by volcanic heat. In fact, that night both Lianvil and I slept more soundly than we ever remembered to have before done. In the morning we awoke to find that our prisoner had melted into a narrow new flow of steaming lava.

"Molten rock melted through the links of Albarochk's golden tether, and the shard of unicorn horn lodged in Albarochk's heart was that night covered by hardening lava. After clawing down to find the unicorn horn shard, Lianvil decided that it belonged with its other half that still crowns Naythorn's head."

"So by digging through hardened lava, *Li... anvil* proved that not just his muscles, but his claws are also anvil-hard," observed the goose.

"Carrying with us the shard of unicorn horn," continued the yellow wolf, "Lianvil and I undertook the return journey to refind Nay..."

"So then it was lucky that the once touch of Cabalblade's horn made the lion to walk on hind legs," interrupted the gander. "Otherwise, it would have been very hard for Lianvil to walk on four paws and at the same time carry the horn shard."

"For my part, I am very glad that the blackmane is now only some days distant from the spot where Sparksy goose this night came upon us," answered Lianvil.

After a very long flight followed by intense conversation with a small wolf and a big lion, the eyes of Featherspark struggled to stay open. While his beak muttered something about how wonderful it was to think that the evil monster wolf had both died and disappeared, the piled feathers of the goose with a black neck could no longer resist the idea of sleep.

The next morning Featherspark woke up with a brand new idea.

"Dansey, Lianvil, can you imagine that we in Naythorn's band are to remain the rest of the winter cooped up... *like pigeons?* I am too big to be a pigeon in a coop. Geese are supposed to migrate south to avoid snow. I will return to the band and tell Naythorn that you can be found at the bottom of the middle range of the finger mountains. I will hronkk that you are too exhausted to more travel, and that you insist that the band comes out to meet the return of the yellow wolf and the big mountain lion. Your presence here provides the perfect excuse for the blackmane's band to depart the discordant camp of the unicorns, where we are presently as good as imprisoned. The entire herd of unicorns only complains. They care not to move, and they do absolutely nothing to find their new hold!"

"So, Sparksy... now it will be the blackmane that obeys *your* command," yipped the yellow wolf as he nodded to the goose.

"Because I all by myself came up with such a brilliant plan, for once Naythorn will *have to* go along with me.*" Stretching long his neck and fluttering his wings, the goose added, "It is no fun to winter with unicorn horses that are lazy, stubborn, and what is worse... arrogant. Wait right here for the soon arrival of the company of Naythorn. This gander wants to fly south for the remainder of winter!"

"Do not, Sparksy, mention Naythorn's half shard," barked Dansey. "That will be a big surprise!"

"Hronkk! Hronkk!" Goose wings launched upward.

Away from Unicorns

The blackmane's insistence, that in search of their new home the white herd should travel in the direction of the fixed star, had been to no avail. With Naythorn's band there to protect them, unicorn horses felt no need to brave snow and cold winds in order to leave a valley that adequately housed and fed them. Unicorn mares and stallions had come to be in agreement with the view of Hoovefort, who saw Naythorn as his bitter rival, that it was easier and safer to remain stationary and not risk further travel in quest of a new unicorn hold.

A year older than Naythorn, the big-bodied Hoovefort had since colthood delighted in tormenting the blackmane, the only colt that staunchly resisted his bullying. For his part, the blackmane wondered if Hoovefort's refusal to search for a new unicorn hold arose more from his antipathy to Naythorn's contrary coloration, than from any other reason. The fact that Aneilee and Elianor supported Naythorn's view of things made Hoovefort to resist even more the departure of the white herd. Because of the impasse that centered on Hoovefort, for the blackmane and his band time had been made to drag.

All four of the razorback sow's offspring complained everyday of boredom. The very same thing could be said of Buckwhite bison, Taurington cattle, the two big-horned sheep Rambuncture and Ewelissas, the two dogs Trackler and Blackler, and the green-head duck Webstir. Every member of Naythorn's band, including the two warrior-blacksmiths Hammerclaw and Lucars, would support almost any reason to leave behind the bickering and malaise permeating the camp of the horned horses.

Featherspark's report, that Danseyelono and Lianvil waited not so far away, enlivened the dreary camp of Naythorn's band.

Mrs. Razorthwacker missed the yellow wolf that she had come to value as a first-rate conversationalist known for his original and insightful thinking. Each of her four wild boarlings, grown now so big that they weighed more than most grown men, admired the solemn dignity of Lianvil who spoke little, but whose grrrs and growls always carried a certain majesty of tone.

At the news brought by Featherspark, Naythorn's first inclination was to gallop away in the lead of his band, with no forewarning given to the two unicorn leaders. But, upon reflection Naythorn decided that galloping away without telling Aneilee and Elianor to where he was off, or when he would return, was not a very mature thing for a three year old unicorn stallion to do. He, Naythorn had been through enough grown-up adventures fighting for his life, the lives of his band members, and the very lives of the mares and foals in the unicorn herd to know that the guide matriarch and high escort merited prior notice of his departure.

Naythorn shook his head and decided. *"Nyeerrrhherrhh!* I am going to leave behind this valley and embark on a brand-new... *adventure."* Made to be at peace with himself, Naythorn trotted to find the two leaders of the white herd.

"I see from his smile that the blackmane woke up this morning in a noticeably buoyant mood," neighed Aneilee in greeting.

"That is because new journey awaits me. I and my band make ready to meet the return of the yellow wolf and the captain of the mountain lions."

"What if I do not give you permission to leave the white herd... what then?" replied Elianor with a sly smile curling her muzzle.

"While moon after moon comes and goes above this mountain valley, I provide no service to anyone. I have instead become a source of contention. I know that in fairness, you two will not detain me. My departure is the best solution for all of us, including for two gracious and esteemed unicorn leaders."

"But, Naythorn, I greatly value the protection that you and your band afford the white herd," responded Aneilee.

"That thinking, High Escort, is not shared by the unicorn stallion that for all practical purposes now directs the white herd."

"You speak now too forthrightly, Naythorn," chided Aneilee.

"Hoovefort insists that the brokenness of my horn renders me unmagical."

"Naythorn is not mistaken," offered Elianor shaking her mane. "The self-serving Hoovefort everyday pushes the limits of unicorn propriety. He has become a very difficult problem for me, the guide matriarch, to contend with."

"Elianor and I cannot permit any unicorn, no matter how willful or strong, to dismiss our authority. Since the very first unicorn herd came to be, matriarchal mares have always led the horned horses."

Elianor's long horse face changed to wear a small smile, "I remember when you were the only colt that would stand up to his bullying. Unlike the other colts you did not run away from bites authored by the sharp teeth of Hoovefort."

"Withstanding his punishment prepared this blackmaned stallion to stand on his own four hooves."

"When then, will you return?" inquired Aneilee.

"Perhaps after the passage of thirty suns. High Escort, if upon my return you are not in this place to be found, I will send Featherspark goose and Webstir duck to climb the wind and find to where you have departed."

With nothing more to neigh, Aneilee and Elianor moved to rub cheeks against the blackmane's shoulders.

After enjoying some last few moments of sentient togetherness, Naythorn turned and trotted away. The unicorn stallion with the severed horn and unfortunately colored mane did not stop to neigh anything to any unicorn he encountered. He wanted that his departure from the white herd would be a quiet one.

After rearing and batting front legs toward the south, Naythorn began a slow trot. One by one, members of his band joined behind him. Upon their departure from the white herd Naythorn's band numbered himself plus fifteen.

Accustomed to having led bison and cattle herds, Buckwhite and Taurington soon moved to the front of the blackmane. Webstir and Featherspark enjoyed the challenge of using their wings to maintain balance while hitchhiking on the backs of the two bovines. Mrs. Razorthwacker was followed by her offspring Hamilton, Practicia, Roothyford, and Timidthy. Released from their oaths to the Phoenician army the two blacksmiths Hammer and Lucars trotted easily at the sides of the mountain sheep Ewelyssis and her pessimistic mate

Rambuncture. As they moved forward, backward, and from one side to the other of the band, Blackler and Trackler bounded about in the fashion of dogs. Although few in number the disparate members of the band were proud for the speed, agility, prowess, and valor possessed by each and every follower of the blackmaned captain.

From time to time Naythorn turned his head to glimpse the animal and human person soldiers in his company. The eyes of the unicorn stallion conveyed how much he valued the friendship and loyalty that he could always count on.

"After trotting all morning, can we slow to a walk?" solicited Timidthy drawing alongside the blackmane. "Since your band is not now at full force, I also think it would be well for us to not get too far ahead of any latecomers trying to catch up with us."

At an easy walk the band proceeded onward.

When to the rear noises were heard, and then grew louder, the bison and cattle bulls halted their steps. From the considerable height of their raised heads they saw that they were being followed. Rainsnow, the uncle horse of the departed winged mare Rayalas, Isabayas the winged unicorn foal that had survived the death of her mare, and the half-horned unicorn Belfloralex galloped together toward Naythorn's band. On the back of Rainsnow rode Marsand the Phoenician youth, and Scarlet Point the grandson of Chief Walking Tree. Scarlet Point's sister Amaluna, and the island maiden Alexzana, shared the back of Belfloralex. The four young people were the noise makers.

"Wait for us, Naythorn!" shouted Alexzana whose eyes that hinted of green always gleamed bright. "We also want to refind Dansey and Lianvil!" The seven more recent additions to the band drew next to the blackmane.

"Where my sire leads, I follow," neighed Isabayas. "Besides, now that my mane has begun to color both black *and* gold, the other fillies make fun of both my wings, and my new color."

"How dare you leave us behind!" scolded Belfloralex shaking her head. "I now also belong to your band! Where you lead, I with you go!"

"Besides," interjected Amaluna, "sitting in one place for so long bores us to tears. For a new adventure we are more than ready."

The four riders dismounted. With seven more recruits the company of Naythorn had grown to count twenty-three. Naythorn nodded his head approvingly at the thought that with the addition of a big horse stallion, a tried-and-true battle-tested unicorn filly, a fast-growing unicorn filly with wings, and four young warriors his band could better defend itself.

"Each and every one of you knows that you are most welcomed," neighed the blackmane. "Since it was time and again made clear that the unicorn herd does not want me to dwell with them, we will for now seek a new place apart. Our band moves southward as a military company with scouts and patrols, and sentries walking perimeter at night. Stay watchful and remember that if in this vast wilderness we are to survive, we must act in a coordinated fashion, and quickly come to the defense of one another."

With a tight formation established, the band continued a southward path.

The uncle horse moved to accompany the burly blacksmith. After taking some silent steps together, the horse stallion inquired, "I notice that no smile is worn on your face. What troubles you, Master Hammer?"

"No, no, Rainsnow... it is just that I do not understand... why Shawnee did not join also to us. Will she not miss dearly her daughter Amaluna and her son Scarlet Point? Her absence makes me uneasy. I also wonder why Cabalblade does not with us travel. Because the sire of Naythorn no longer serves the unicorn guards, he has too much free time on his hooves."

"Master Hammer," responded the horse stallion, "you may rest assured that absenting herself from Naythorn's band, Shawnee will also much miss your presence. Now that I think about it, I also wonder how Aneilee and Elianor will handle Naythorn's departure. The blackmane not only provided protection and security for the herd of unicorns, he strongly supported the guide matriarch and high escort. Hmpf! Mount up Master Hammer. You and I are going to do some scouting on our own."

"Hammer and I are going to double-back on our trail," neighed Rainsnow to Naythorn. "Before nightfall we will rejoin you."

"Since this day well enough proceeds," answered the blackmane, "do as you find fit to do." With that Rainsnow and Hammer turned heads back to the north.

After traveling several leagues Hammer touched his hand to the horse stallion's tautly muscled neck and said, "Something moves on our right. It is a... unicorn and rider." As he drew closer to the galloping unicorn the beat of Hammer's heart quickened, and a big grin grew to cover his wide-angled face.

"Halloo Sir Cabalblade!" shouted Hammer. "Halloo Shawnee!" The horse and unicorn drew together. Jumping off the back of Rainsnow, Hammer affectionately rubbed rough hands along the neck of Cabalblade.

"We were on our way to find out why you two absented yourselves from our company," declared the blacksmith. "Why you did not depart the unicorn camp with the rest of Naythorn's band. Encountering you here saved us more travel."

"You see, it is important for me to keep my figure trim," responded Shawnee. "With that in mind I decided on such a splendid, albeit chilly morning, to take exercise with a long walk. I returned to find much commotion among the unicorn horses. I could not believe what they were neighing... that Naythorn and his band had deserted them!"

"Shawnee, you know that Naythorn did not and would not desert the unicorn herd," answered Hammer matter-of-factly. "It was made clear by the unicorn guard horses, of course at Hoovefort's behest, that the blackmane and his company were no longer welcomed in the presence of the white herd. Because most unicorn stallions and mares chose to agree, or at least to not overtly disagree with Hoovefort, Naythorn tired of the animosity that was every day demonstrated against him.

"Hmpf! Since the white herd no longer has any fear of the evil monster wolf vanquished by Naythorn, unicorns have decided that they no longer need the protection offered by the blackmane and his loyal friends. That circumstance frees our band to begin a new adventure. I hope that Shawnee is come to join us."

"Certainly I shall join to the blackmane and Master Hammer!" responded Shawnee with conviction.

"I as well join to the band led by my colt," neighed Cabalblade.

"That... is exactly what I wanted to hear from both of you!" exclaimed the big blacksmith whose mood noticeably brightened.

Rainsnow began to nervously pace back-and-forth. Cabalblade stepped to block the pacing of the uncle horse and neighed, "Something wrong?"

"*Nyeerrarrragh!* I do not know that anything is actually... wrong. It is just that I suddenly feel in my chest that something does not set right with the high escort. I have come to well-know Aneilee, and to prize her kind words and actions toward us outsiders that came to dwell with the unicorn herd."

"As an outsider, Rainsnow, you perhaps notice things that I do not," reflected Cabalblade. "We unicorn horses too often take for granted the work and worry of the high escort. Do you want me to return with you to make sure that everything is well with Aneilee?"

"No, Cabalblade," answered the golden-maned roan stallion. "Leave now with Master Hammer and Shawnee to follow the trail southward. Tell Naythorn that after I make sure that the high escort is fine, and extend encouraging neighs to her, I will rejoin his company."

"Rainsnow, before Hammer mounts to ride on my back with Shawnee, I have a favor to ask of you," neighed Cabalblade. "You remember the unicorn sentry Haltervor?"

Rainsnow nodded up and down his head.

"I need for you to give Sergeant Haltervor an instruction from me, his former commander. I want him to keep close tabs on Lieutenant Hoovefort, who I think is up to something nefarious. Ask Haltervor to spy out what Hoovefort does when he is not with guard unicorns found. There is one thing more. Tell Haltervor that when spying on the new leader of the unicorn guard horses, he needs to be subtle and careful."

"The part about being careful around Hoovefort is important," agreed Rainsnow. "For my part I do not trust the ambitious usurper unicorn that took over your post."

Naythorn was truly delighted that his sire had joined to travel with the band. At the arrival of their mother, the joy of Amaluna and Scarlet Point was exuberant.

"I see that the master blacksmith is massaging his legs," remarked Lucars seating himself.

"They ache," responded Hammer. "It takes more and more time for me to accustom myself to the strenuous activity of new march."

After pausing to look about, Lucars answered in a voice made to sound more loud than needed, "I *do* wonder which of all of us has this evening the most hurting muscles."

"That is me!" proclaimed Hamilton.

"No, brother pig," grunted Roothyford, "my muscles hurt so much that I shall have to change my name. I am too out of shape to ford a stream, and I have no energy to root for worms to eat."

"Then I shall also have to add *Im* to the start of my name," groinked Practicia. "It was very *imm*practical of me to not discipline myself to exercise so that my legs stayed strong."

"I am ashamed to admit that of all the animal persons here present," grumphed the mama sow flopping down her big body, "it is me that is the most out of shape. If I do not start a diet, for my excess weight my poor legs will give out on me."

"Mama, after a few more days of travel you will be thinner than ever," affirmed an ever kind Timidthy in an attempt to cheer his mother sow. "I guarantee it!" That said, one wild boar after another was heard to snore.

Guardian Horse

"Do I find you unwell?" inquired Rainsnow upon encountering the matriarchs of the white herd standing together with heads down.

"It is Rainsnow!" exclaimed Elianor.

"You came back!" neighed Aneilee. "You have no idea how glad I am that you are returned to us."

"Because we did not know how much we would miss Naythorn and his band, you find us anxious," informed Elianor. "Now we are delighted to see you."

"I think the blackmane will be absent longer than he neighs," offered Rainsnow. "He may not return for the remainder of the winter. Naythorn thinks, no he is certain that the white herd resents his presence, and is also unwelcoming of his animal person band."

"Be that as it may, I was so hoping that Naythorn would soon return to us," responded Aneilee. "After he and his band departed this morning, Hoovefort became even more insufferable. Something tells me that before too long Elianor and I will here require the strong and supportive presence of the blackmane."

"With each passing day the high escort and I find that the leadership of the white herd slips more through our hooves," lamented Elianor. "The guard unicorns, and now the colts and young stallions, at best only pretend to obey us. I do not know what is to become of the purity and beauty of our herd of unicorn horses."

"Both you and I, Elianor, abhor the arrogance that here grows daily," added Aneilee. "While easily forgotten, it cannot be doubted that humility and obedience are essential to preserve unicorn goodness."

"Since Naythorn does not right now require my presence, have I your permission to remain close to the white herd?" inquired Rainsnow as he touched lightly his muzzle to the necks of the two leader unicorns. "Should I not feel welcome, I would not presume to remain nearby. However, given your consent I will climb the south ridge and from there daily surveil the unicorn camp."

"It would be kind of you, Rainsnow, to keep near to us," affirmed Elianor. "One can never know when the protection of the roan horse stallion will come to matter. Your strength will compel new hope to come to Aneilee and to me, and your presence will be a gentle reminder of the blackmaned unicorn that I hope to again see soon."

Into the night walked together two unicorn mares and the big uncle horse with a golden mane.

Returned to Naythorn

The meeting up of Naythorn's band with Dansey and Lianvil provoked a rousing display of pure animal joy. At the news that the yellow-mottled wolf and the big lion had brought back the missing half of Naythorn's horn, animal persons jigged feet, hooves, and paws.

"The horn shard is undamaged," muttered Hammer as his fingers felt each and every speck of the shard.

The bovines sniffed from end to end the shard cradled in Hammer's big hands. "You know what, Sir Cattle?" brayed the bison. "I am convinced that this piece of unicorn horn still maintains its magic intact."

"I will bet... that about that you are right," responded the cattle. I think this shard carries even more magic than is possessed by your impressively thick white bison hide."

Overhearing the bovine banter, Amaluna approached. Tugging at Buckwhite's floppy beard, Amaluna offered a thought, "Because I can grasp in my hand the beard of the sacred white bison, I am the most fortunate young lady in my entire tribe."

"Do not," ordered Buckwhite shaking his head, "spread the rumor that I am the sacred white bison of the native sagas."

On that night of reunion Marsand and Scarlet Point rustled up a great fire; the band gathered round to soak tired bodies in the warmth of fire light.

"Naythorn," inquired the mama sow, "now that we have reunited with Dansey and Lianvil, to where do we go from here?" Because the answer to that question would matter much to each and every one there gathered, Mrs. Razorthwacker's question had the effect of making many ears to prick up and necks to straighten.

"Hmpf," interjected Hammer once again gripping the unicorn shard in his hands. "Mrs. Pig, do you know that since I found that Lianvil brought back this shard, I have thought about one thing only? When can I bind this half to the remaining half of Naythorn's horn? After all, it was my hammer and chisel that cut in two his horn. While what I did was a needed thing, there can be little doubt that cleaving the horn in two lessened its magic. I had never thought that I would have the opportunity to again make whole what I had undone. Now I cannot wait to do so. Only... a problem has arisen. To fashion a spiral binding for something as precious as a unicorn shard, I require the purest blue gold unsullied by the grime of usage. None so pure is in my possession found."

"That comment, Master Hammer, reminds me of something," mrawed the brown cattle with a white face. "I would be much obliged if you could increase the girth of my blue gold armor. It seems that since you fashioned for me the gold plate, my sides have somehow grown... more muscles."

"That, Sir Cattle, would also require additional blue gold that this blacksmith does not now possess."

"And my frame has grown taller," added the bison.

"Aye," added Hamilton. "The armor I wear, along with that worn by Timidthy and our sister wild boars could use extending to fit fast-growing pig bodies."

"Master Hammer," interjected Timidthy, "there is one place where you could find all the pure blue gold needed to make whole the unicorn horn, as well as to refit the armor plate of unicorns, mountain sheep, bovines, pigs, water fowl..."

"And to as well forge magic armor for the newest members of the blackmane's band!" interjected Alexzana.

Come to relish the direction that the conversation had taken, Lucars added, "I, for one, would like to show Lianvil, Dansey, Scarlet Point, Marsand, Amaluna, Alexzana, Shawnee, Belfloralex, and Sir Cabalblade the wondrous canyon that shines of blue gold... which is as splendid a place as exists in this wide land."

"You do recall, Lucars, that I before protected Shining Canyon."

"Of course I do! You were the lion captain that commanded all of Spire Mountain. But rather than guard its rims from above, I want Lianvil to enter the canyon through the cave door to be there fitted with incomparable armor."

"Our lion would look even more regal in blue gold armor," asserted Dansey. "And that would make me even more proud to be Lianvil's best friend."

"For the precise needs required to rebind your horn, the forge and bellows that are still to be found in Shining Canyon would serve perfectly," directed Hammer to Naythorn.

The blackmane rose to stand on four hooves, stretched high his neck, shook his head, and began to pace about. He paced first by the campfire, then he paced away from the fire.

"I am made to change my thinking," neighed Naythorn upon his return. "If the magic of my horn can be fully restored, then I will have that to be done. I will not worry myself about a soon return to defend the white herd that resents my presence. And because I am no longer compelled to protect the unicorns, there no longer remains a reason to travel in pursuit of the fixed star. We will travel in the opposite direction toward... Shining Canyon.

"Since some of you have not before traveled far with me, I will caution you that our journey to Spire Mountain will not be easy. And, I do not want to hear any future complaints that the trek is taking too long, with mountain passes too high to scale, river gorges too deep to descend, and deserts too hot to pass over."

"You, Sir Lianvil, are going home!" chortled the yellow wolf butting his head against the side of the lion captain.

After shoving with a friendly paw his yellow-hided friend to the ground, the big lion raised himself to stand on hind limbs, sprung himself upward, and while suspended roared his joy at the prospect of returning to the mountain of spires that he had before commanded.

CHAPTER 4

Matriarchs Apart

Worn inside, the self-satisfied horse smile did not show. Hoovefort wanted his guard unicorns to instead notice his mouth set in a sneer, and hear his whinnies sounding sharp commands.

Events had succeeded exactly as planned. He, Hoovefort, had stirred up dissension over the presence of the unicorn he hated, the misfit stallion with the unruly black mane and the severed horn shard. That animosity eventually led guard horses to ostracize Naythorn's sire. It was whispered throughout the white herd that both Naythorn and his sire Cabalblade were forever departed from the herd of unicorns that Hoovefort now controlled.

The reputation of the standoffish Cabalblade had been felled by the accusation that when the unicorns had most needed him to fight against wolf packs and enemy warriors, he had abandoned the white herd to instead defend his misfit offspring Naythorn. It was further alleged that the war with the monster wolf Albarochk was entirely the fault of Cabalblade's blackmaned colt. It took some conniving, but so disgraced, the formerly powerful Cabalblade had been pushed aside. His remaining friends, mostly older stallions and mares, discovered that it was hurtful to suffer kicks and bites as a result of their unpopular support for the sire of Naythorn. The guide matriarch

Elianor, and the high escort Aneilee, had proven powerless to restore Cabalblade back into the good graces of the white herd.

New morning found Rainsnow standing motionless in the tree line of a ridge overlooking the unicorn camp. The big uncle horse knew that only sudden movement on his part would permit guard unicorns the chance to spot him, and so recognize that a spy was looking down on the white herd.

Rainsnow's heart dropped each time he observed the upstart Hoovefort push his considerable weight around. The new captain of the unicorn guard horses seemed to relish biting, kicking, or even knocking down unicorns that did not concur with his unrelenting grab for power. Truth be told, rather than watch this morning broken-spirited unicorns succumb to the bullying of the new captain of the guard stallions, the big roan would much prefer to be trotting at the side of Naythorn.

From afar Rainsnow saw Hoovefort berate and kick out at one, then the other unicorn leader mare. When Hoovefort ratcheted up a notch the art of his bullying, rather than escalate more the altercation Aneilee turned and trotted head down away from Hoovefort. The younger of the two unicorn leaders, however, showed her mettle. Elianor stood firm, and without complaint suffered Hoovefort's kicks and abuse.

Rainsnow reflected that of course he was angry at the bad behavior and arrogance of the new captain of the guard stallions. But more than angry at Hoovefort, Rainsnow was dismayed at the cowardice of the adult unicorns in the white herd. Not one horned horse had moved to stop the abuse that had just happened against the two matriarchal leaders. The leadership of the two renowned mares counted for something. They had led the white herd away from an exploding volcano, across a great sea, and then through plains and mountains to a valley with a sparkling brook and grass that beneath intermittent snow cover still sprouted green.

Should Hoovefort cross a line, if his bites drew blood from either Elianor or Aneilee, Rainsnow would step in and stop the big arrogant guard commander. The way things had gone today it was only a matter of a few more suns before he, the uncle horse of the deceased Rayalas, would place himself between Hoovefort and the two elegant mares that were the rightful leaders of the white herd.

If only by a little, Hoovefort was the bigger of the two; he might even be faster. No matter. The uncle horse promised himself that in a violent confrontation with Hoovefort, the body of the haughty unicorn stallion would feel the hardest knocks and deepest hoof cuts he had ever known.

Seeing more commotion come to center on Hoovefort, Rainsnow pricked up his ears and focused his hearing on the loud whinnies of the guard captain standing on the south edge of the white herd.

"I, Hoovefort, am alone tough enough to lead the magic white herd! Aneilee is weak in spirit! Her body is not hard enough to withstand a few bruises dealt by my hooves! As for Elianor, her mind is too slow to get out of the way of my kicks and bites! The time for the old leadership has come and gone! Without my leadership, from this new and dangerous land the white herd of unicorns will soon come to vanish!"

The next morning awoke to a drizzle of raindrops; rain turned to snow. The uncle horse smiled at the thought that this day's change in the weather offered fulfillment to his name. Nestled in a dry nest of fallen leaves Rainsnow rested late. North winds blowing down from the mountains made it convenient for horned horses to clump cozily together. Rainsnow guessed that by afternoon the big flakes of snow would become driven, thick, and grainy.

Deception

Glad for the concealment provided by wind-driven snow, the new captain of the unicorn guard horses walked early in the evening with one thing in mind, to find Aneilee.

Hoovefort had accomplished the first two parts of his plan. Cabalblade had been rendered powerless, and the blackmane had been forced to abandon the white herd. From what Hoovefort could tell, Naythorn and his vexatious band were forever gone. That would allow to transpire the third part of Hoovefort's plan. The final part he purposed was to displace entirely the two mares that for too long had walked in the lead of the white herd.

"Nyeerrarrrgh," snorted Hoovefort, "Aneilee and Elianor do not know that in the lapse between this sun and the next, they are to be rendered powerless."

Since most unicorns had never known the white herd to be led except by the two leader mares, Hoovefort felt constrained to devolve stealthily to himself their authority. In that regard the guide matriarch and the high escort would both fare better if they quietly acquiesced to their destitution from power. After all, Aneilee was only interested in ideas of purity and beauty, not in the concept of command. And although Elianor well-understood power, she was not a violent unicorn. She was certainly not a warrior unicorn like himself. Long past their prime, at least in the opinion of Hoovefort, the two matriarchs were worse than useless. And now that the blackmane had been made to go away, he, Hoovefort, was the dominant unicorn in the white herd. Toppling Elianor and Aneilee from power would take a decisive act, a great push delivered by one and only one stallion... that being himself.

The usurper stallion did admit one thing. He did not relish having the blood of one, let alone two leader mares come to stain his hide. Still, if he was clever enough that would not happen.

Upon finding Aneilee standing apart on the east edge of the camp of unicorn horses, Hoovefort neighed to her, "You and I need to clear things up between us so that we can work together... for the betterment of the unicorns that we both serve."

"That would be more advantageous than you constantly fighting against me," replied Aneilee shaking her head tentatively from side to side.

"*Nyyeeerrryeeesss!* Better for you, for me, and for our herd of magic horses. Come with me and let us neigh from the depths of our hearts."

Not waiting for an answer, Hoovefort began trotting toward a far ridge. Aneilee turned and followed, but at a distance of several horse lengths.

Rousing himself from a late afternoon nap, that had snuck up on him, from his ridgeline Rainsnow's eyes began to search back-and-forth across the camp of unicorn horses. He did not spot Aneilee anywhere. Then Rainsnow noticed a mare moving rapidly through the camp seemingly in search of... another unicorn. It was Elianor.

The uncle horse put two and two together. Both he and Elianor were at the same time looking for Aneilee, who among the herd of unicorns was apparently nowhere to be found. The golden-maned stallion, whose brown hide was flecked with white markings shaped like raindrops and snowflakes, realized that another prominent unicorn was also from the herd missing. Hoovefort was not there. And Rainsnow knew that Cabalblade would want not just Haltervor, but himself as well to keep track of the new captain of the unicorn guards.

Leaving his place of observation Rainsnow shifted his pace to a gallop. Drawing near to Elianor he whinnied for her to join him. From the way Rainsnow held his nose and eyes close to the ground as he trotted, Elianor sensed immediately for whom the roan horse stallion was searching.

Rainsnow found something. Imprinted into white snow two sets of hooves tracked eastward.

"Wait, Hoovefort! To where are we headed? Where do you take me?" After following Hoovefort for nearly three thousand paces, Aneilee was impatient to know.

"There is a close by a promontory, that when seen under a snowy night sky presents a scene of rare beauty. There we can talk in a way that is better than on this trail."

"Let us get there soon. I do not like leaving the herd without letting Elianor know where I have gone."

Set high above a precipitous drop, the promontory offered a view of a long and deep rocky ravine.

"This same view can be had closer to our camp," neighed Aneilee. "Now, Hoovefort, what were you going to neigh to me?"

"Aneilee, you would be more comfortable and relaxed... if you simply gave up your leadership of the white herd."

"Why would you *neigh* such a thing?" inquired the high escort arching up her neck. "I accomplish every day the work I was born to do. I cannot suddenly become... not responsible for the unicorns that I love so dearly. I cannot become lazy, and for the rest of my life stay that way."

"I brought you to this far place because I knew that was precisely how you would answer. Found in a new and dangerous land, the white herd needs not a gentle old mare, but a powerful stallion general to lead it forward. More than anything, unicorns require discipline! Whether they like it or not, I will make an end to the soft and old-fashioned leadership to which you always aspired. *Nyeerrrrrrragh!* If on a future day a unicorn disobeys me, that unicorn will be *banished* from the white herd!"

"What you neigh is all wrong! But if the white herd did require new leadership I would do the only thing that would make horse sense, and appoint Naythorn to guide us onward. The blackmane is a proven leader stallion."

To show his animus for what Aneilee had answered, Hoovefort jumped several times front hooves while shaking vigorously back-and-forth his head.

"No! Never! Never Naythorn! The shameful coloring of his coat and the grotesque cleavage of his horn will not ever permit him to lead the white herd, at least not while I live and breathe!"

Hoovefort advanced threateningly; Aneilee stepped defensively backwards. Before Aneilee knew to prepare herself, it happened.

Hoovefort sped hooves and crashed shoulders into the chest of the high escort. As she was pushed back, moist ground under her rear hooves gave way. She scrambled to regain her footing, but before she could reset her hooves Hoovefort whirled around and with his hind quarters kicked out; for a moment Aneilee tottered precariously on the edge of the precipice.

Into the deep rocky ravine plummeted the body of the unicorn high escort. As she fell she whinnied, *"Elianooorrr!"* The last thing Aneilee would later recall about that moment was the pain of hooves kicking hard into her.

As thickening darkness overgrew daylight, Rainsnow was certain that he and Elianor were still on the trail taken by Aneilee, and most likely Hoovefort.

"Do you hear them, Rainsnow?"

"Yes, I hear the approach of hooves. I hope it is Anei..." The approaching hoof beats sounded too heavy to be those of the high matriarch who moved with lightness and grace.

"Hoovefort, where is she?" neighed sharply Elianor. "Where did you leave Aneilee?"

When the big stallion tried to move around Elianor, Rainsnow blocked his chest.

Elianor moved her head close to the cheek of Hoovefort and neighed with authority, "Where... is... she?"

"*Nyeerrhaahaahharrghh!* I no longer answer to Aneilee, and much less to you! The high escort ran away and deserted her responsibilities to our herd. In the presence of unicorn horses her name is forever... tarnished!"

With no forewarning Hoovefort jabbed his horn into a heavily muscled shoulder of Rainsnow. The force of the hurt made the uncle horse to fall to his knees. By the time Rainsnow raised himself again on all fours, into swirling snow Hoovefort had vanished.

"Hoovefort will pay for that!" neighed the uncle horse. "My cut is but a prick from the horn of a coward. Elianor, follow me!"

Rainsnow knew what he had to do. Disregardful of his hurt, he would make all speed to find Aneilee, no matter to where she had run. The tracks of horse hooves led the horse stallion and unicorn mare to a high place.

"Here ends the trail, but the high escort is not here found. Elianor, this light fallen snow cannot have covered up hoof prints showing that she from here departed. Aneilee did not retrace her tracks, and no set of hoof prints veered off from the trail."

"I have been wondering," replied Elianor, "just how perverse beats the heart inside the chest of Hoovefort. Had he wanted to be forever rid of Aneilee, this place would have served well his purpose."

Rainsnow and Elianor peered over the steep drop.

"The ground here is disturbed. For the darkness and the falling snow I can see nothing down there. Find a way, Rainsnow, to lead us to the bottom of this precipice."

Through treacherous terrain a way was found for hooves to descend to the bottom of the steep-sided ravine. Into a bouldered place a horse stallion and a unicorn mare slowly picked their way. Half covered by wind-blown snow, in a small open area sprawled the crumpled body of Aneilee.

When Elianor touched her muzzle to the cheek of her dearest friend, the unconscious mare did not move. Elianor sparked her horn to the forehead of Aneilee; in response the neck of Aneilee quivered ever so slightly. After horn-healing had been sparked for one hundred horse breaths the high escort found strength to raise her head.

"Rainsnow, dear horse," neighed Elianor, "your blood has dripped onto the back of Aneilee."

"I count it a mark of honor to have my hide stained red by the blood of the noble Rainsnow. But he must not lose too... much..."

Many more horse breaths came and went before Aneilee gathered enough strength to stand. Meanwhile, the touch of Elianor's horn made to quickly close Rainsnow's wound.

"The ground gave way beneath my hooves," whinnied Aneilee softly. "No... wait... I recall hooves batting into my side."

"Hoovefort made this to happen!" neighed Elianor with anger in her voice. "That is the only explanation for him leaving you here alone to die. Along with yours, his hoof prints are at the top of the promontory. Hoovefort was there when you fell, and it was he who pushed you. The fact that he returned alone, proves his guilt. We must return to the white herd and force him to leave. From the fellowship of unicorns... he must be exiled!"

"Elianor, the time may not be right to displace the usurper," neighed Rainsnow. "Among the stallions, and even among the mares of the white herd, Hoovefort has managed to attract many followers. If Hoovefort were to say that it was Aneilee's clumsiness that made her to fall, who knows how many unicorns would believe him.

"During a long life I have witnessed strange things to happen in a herd of horses. I have seen proud stallions gain leadership, and then left to their own devices, soon lose it. But know that whatever you and Aneilee decide to do, and whenever that happens, you have my allegiance."

"Rainsnow is right about this," concluded Aneilee. "Elianor, instead of you, me, and other unicorns shedding blood to be rid of Hoovefort, we will permit the arrogant conniver stallion to all alone himself destroy."

The horse and two unicorns found a rock wall that rounded inward. With horse bodies lying touchingly close to one another, they there rested during what remained of night darkness.

CHAPTER 5

A CRY UNEARTHLY

Two days after having been pushed off a cliff, Aneilee found herself hobbling behind Rainsnow and Elianor along a path that from the ravine of treachery meandered south. Without a neigh being spoken, each of the three knew why they southward journeyed; that direction was now traveled by Naythorn and his band.

"Hmpf. It is hard for me to believe that the sturdy magic of our esteemed guide matriarch did not make me to be again... *good as new,*" sighed Aneilee.

"The fall you suffered would have ended the life of a normal horse," observed Elianor. "I know you are discouraged that your limbs move painfully, but the perspective of how fortunate you were to survive, should give you heart. Combined with your innate strength, your notable magic will soon return you to perfect health."

"Aneilee will soon be galloping with nary a pain or worry," affirmed Rainsnow with further intent to cheer.

The increasing cold of midafternoon made to condense and harden the flakes of falling snow. Aneilee coughed once, a second time, a third time. Once begun, her bout of coughing did not stop.

"Are you thinking, Elianor, what I am?" inquired Rainsnow.

"Yes I am. We need to take shelter and nestle beside Aneilee to keep her warm until morning." A shallow cave with a narrow opening lent itself to their purpose. Absorbing full the body heat of her two companions, Aneilee rested quietly.

Out of a deep sleep Rainsnow stirred himself awake. The stallion stood to stretch his back, and then decided his legs could use stretching as well. Rainsnow moved to stand at the entrance of the cave. While the night was bitter cold the snow had ended, and the moon shone bright. At last he remembered what had awakened him; it was the distant howls of predators on the hunt. But what could wolf teeth and paws find to overpower on a night when for the harsh cold, no prey animal was moving? Perhaps he had only been dreaming of wolves.

"Rrrawwrrraaoo!" There it was again.

Focused intently on the howl, Rainsnow froze. The sound carried a sense of uncommon meanness. Rainsnow retreated back to where rested the guide matriarch.

"Dame Elianor... *wake up.*"

The sound came again. At that Elianor scrambled to her hooves and with Rainsnow walked outside the shallow cave. In no more than twenty swishes of a horse's tail the sound, this time made more distinct, was again heard. As they came closer and closer the menacing growls of more than one wolf were identified.

"Do you see the three big shadows, Elianor? These particular wolves are almost as large as bison."

"While I see their size... I cannot believe my eyes."

Aneilee hobbled to join Elianor and Rainsnow. No more than thirty paces from Rainsnow and the two former leaders of the white herd, three huge wolves sat down rear haunches and broke into a round of savage barks that were more like cruel laughs than normal wolf talk.

"I have waited long to meet the two... *former* leaders of the white herd," growled in the uniform animal tongue the biggest wolf whose hide was the color of rust and whose cheeks, chest, and legs were marked white. "It is my pleasure to inform that you two, and the stallion, are trapped. I see that Aneilee limps. No matter! For you and your kind, both unicorns and horses, everything is finished."

"When Albarochk came no more to be," snarled next the black-hided smallest of the three big wolves, "you mistakenly thought you had beaten us."

"Be gone with you while you can!" threatened Rainsnow waving front hooves high. "Still magical, the guide matriarch and the high escort remain very powerful!" Upon hearing that, another round of cruel wolf laughter ensued.

"You cannot expect us to pay heed to your drivel," growled again the largest wolf. "Which of you three could stop even the smallest of us monster wolves? Because of our enormous size, we three wolves fear nothing."

"I find it amusing," continued the smallest huge wolf, "that one mere stallion, with no sharp teeth or long claws, could even imagine vanquishing me in a fight. Now there, Rainsnow, for the new leader of the white herd said that was the name you answer to, why not call the renowned Naythorn to come to your aid? Where is the blackmane anyway? *Grrarrrhhaarrrrhaa!* It is for you unfortunate that he and his company abandoned the white herd. What a *coward* the blackmaned freak turned out to be."

"Rainsnow," neighed Elianor quietly, "what can we do? Because Aneilee limps we cannot break away without her being caught in wolf teeth, and we will not abandon the high escort. I can think of nothing that will free us from this trap."

"About one thing these wolves are not wrong," neighed quietly Rainsnow. "We right now need Naythorn to charge into this place."

"There always lingers hope for magical horned horses that persist pure in spirit," answered Aneilee with her neigh sounding strangely confident. "I am taken with the idea that this is not to be the place of my demise."

"You are right, Aneilee, to give us hope," replied Elianor moving her head slightly up and down.

"Nasty wolves!" exclaimed Rainsnow as he sideways pranced back-and-forth. "Just think on what you do! The surviving unicorns are few. Their dwelling with us makes this to be a more abundant land to feed deer, bison... and consequently wolves. While it has been prophesized that external evil will not vanquish the white herd, were you to succeed in destroying the magic of these unicorn matriarchs, you would bring down upon yourselves the revenge of fate."

At this comment the bodies of three enormous wolves shook hard with laughter.

"The horse stallion only tries to delay what here tonight *has* to happen," replied the biggest wolf. "When a cloud passes over and hides the moon, your fate will no longer be delayed. We will be quick about it. For you it is better to have your suffering to be done and over with."

"You two matriarchs are not the first unicorn flesh we have devoured," continued the smallest of the three huge wolves. "Recall that before Albarochk was killed a unicorn colt ventured into the magic shield, and was promptly eaten by three wolf brothers. That colt was our first kill."

"What you growl is... not true," answered Elianor. "While Albarochk's evil was ended, his life was by the blackmane spared."

"No matter!" responded the smallest wolf brother. "Aneilee and Elianor will be only two of the many unicorns that serve to satisfy the hunger awakened in our bodies by the trespass in this land of the white herd."

"You see we made... a deal," growled once more the largest wolf as he made a show of pawing the snow. "To save himself, the new leader of the white herd... what is his name again?"

"Hoovefort," grrrd the smallest of the three wolves.

"Yes, Hoovefort it is. You see he has agreed that on the night of each and every new full moon three big strapping colts, one for each of us, are to satisfy our lust for the blood that flows in the veins of horned horses."

For the unimaginable monstrosity of what the wolf had just growled, Aneilee was overcome; she collapsed onto snow covered ground. Upon seeing the high escort's vulnerability, Rainsnow instinctively broke from where he stood and charged at the three big wolves. In spite of the hard blows landed by his hooves, the fearless stallion was soon driven back.

Standing before the body of Aneilee, Elianor reared high to menace three slowly advancing wolves. The guide matriarch settled her hooves back to ground and neighed to Rainsnow, "Strange as it seems, I now also feel that Aneilee is right. Somehow this night will for us finish well."

Elianor turned back her head and gazed upward. She sensed that something up above was spying, observing how unfolded the confrontation against the three huge wolves.

A large stone fell to land on the ground between Rainsnow and the monster wolves. When a second huge stone flew down knocking over the smallest of the three monster wolves, yelps of hurt filled the night air.

From the cliff above came an eerie screech that was unlike anything ever before heard by Rainsnow, Aneilee, Elianor, or three huge wolves.

"You see and hear what Aneilee foretold would happen before this night ended," neighed Elianor as she moved to stand beside Rainsnow. "Something with paws that can grasp and throw great stones has come to protect us. Now be off with you! Bother us no more, or you will by stones be destroyed! Be gone! Now!"

The two largest wolves stepped to the side of the wounded wolf. Bewilderment spread to cover the faces of three enormous predators.

The middle-sized wolf that wore a gray colored hide took his first turn to growl, "This is not... *over!*"

With an expression of puzzlement, Rainsnow watched as three monstrously large wolves slunk away. Dripping blood from where he had been gashed by a big hurled rock, one of the three overgrown predators moved painfully his hind limbs.

"What on earth made that cry?" neighed Rainsnow. He could not stop wondering what manner of beast could make a sound that would curdle a stallion's blood; the shriek had frightened the big stallion down to his very hooves.

"Whatever it was," answered Elianor, "the enormous wolves knew immediately that the strange cry came not from an ally of wolf terror. Do not for now worry, Rainsnow, about what it was that wailed out to gain for us the night. Perhaps we will one day again encounter that cry."

The following morning broke brilliant with the sun gifting chillingly pure light. By midday the horse stallion and two unicorn mares were on the move, their warm breaths making steam puffs to float on freezing cold air.

"Your limbs, Aneilee, move noticeably better today," observed Rainsnow.

"Because my spirit is revived," answered the high escort, "my body insists on fast recovering from the wounds left by the punishment of Hoovefort's kicks and a fall off a precipitous cliff."

"Aneilee, do we now return to make sure that Hoovefort does not abide by his evil sacrificial agreement made with three monster wolves?" inquired Rainsnow.

"No!" Aneilee's surprising reply came with conviction. "Hoovefort knows better than to do that. He cannot, in order to preserve his power, sacrifice even one unicorn to wolves. That evil is too great for even Hoovefort to bear upon his brow. A hard trial is to be borne by the white herd. The time has come for unicorn stallions and mares to by themselves reconcile with the ideas of humility, purity, and obedience. If the white herd is unwilling to follow, I and Elianor cannot lead. I can only believe that the unicorn horses, that I know so well, will soon decide to rightly act.

"Actually, on this day I find myself more troubled about what made that terrible cry in the night, than I am about the white herd. Just like Elianor before neighed, something tells me that we will one day learn much more about the creature that intervened in our favor."

"You, Rainsnow, are a noble and majestic stallion," commended Elianor. "Not once thinking to desert us and thereby save yourself, your guardianship carried us through to this day. Do you not want to return to the valley of the mountain horses? I suspect Aneilee wills us to travel to that far place where you were born and bred."

"While Hoovefort's drama with the white herd plays out, we do find ourselves with extra time on our hooves," affirmed Aneilee.

"Why, Dame Elianor," answered the stallion with a big smile spreading across his muzzle, "a return in your company to the valley of the lost pavilion would for me be a singular benevolence."

Two unicorn mares and a horse stallion began to walk with hearts made confident.

"By the way," neighed Rainsnow, "I also think it was no coincidence that in our moment of dire need the phantom creature that cried in the night, and heaved rocks the size of my head, arrived to rescue us. Could it be that not only me, but someone else was lurking in the hills keeping watch over the white herd? If so, was the specter also regardful of me?"

Naythorn's Band Marches and Plays Tag

As if each were trying to demonstrate that he could outmarch and outlast his bovine friend, the forward movement of the bison and the longhorn cattle was unflagging.

Having finally had enough of the one-upmanship of Buckwhite and Taurington, the mama pig grumphed, "Sir Cattle, Master Bison, I say that rather than a race between two bovines, tomorrow shall be a day of rest. I absolutely need a day to relax and so recover my strength."

"Captain Naythorn, you do know that about things like this my mama is always... *right!*" squealed Practicia in accord with her sow.

"We today traveled far enough," agreed Naythorn. "Mrs. Razorthwacker has earned the luxury of a lazy tomorrow. After all, in only a few suns the two bovines have led us far beyond a deep river gorge."

"A rest will suit well my legs," asserted Hammer sitting down next to his two bovine friends. "Still, if my vote counts for something, I say that tomorrow afternoon when well-refreshed, we should address tactics."

"As a newly organized military company with many new members, we could use practice on our formations of defense," seconded the younger blacksmith.

"A morning of rest will be followed by an afternoon session intended to shape up military form and fitness," neighed Naythorn. "It seems that we are never allowed to be too long at peace before we are by enemies set upon, and time previously spent to organize our company always served us in good stead."

New morning light warmed the beds and bowers of animal persons that awoke to eat, rest, and eat and rest more. Patches of snow began to melt. As the afternoon progressed it became apparent that band members were less than keen to form up and drill on defensive tactics.

Thinking it was time, past time, to commence training Naythorn walked over and nudged a shoulder against the side of Cabalblade. Rather harder than necessary, the former leader of the unicorn guards bumped back Naythorn. At that Naythorn reared high, waved hooves at his sire, and was off running. When the staid Cabalblade raced after his colt everyone knew what was up.

The bison tore after the cattle, and the duck and goose batted wings at the two dogs. Within moments it seemed that everyone in the band was playing tag with everyone else. The game grew rough with pigs tumbled about, dogs tossed in the air, the rumps of Hammer and Lucars butted by mountain sheep, and Scarlet Point and Marsand jumping on and then being bucked off by not one, but two bovines.

With one exception the roughhousing proved contagious. The only animal person in the band not challenged to participate in the tumultuous game of animal tag, was Lianvil. No one chose to tackle the sinewy muscles of a huge mountain lion with long claws and sharp teeth. For his part it was clear that the big cat disapproved of being tackled, grabbed, or jumped upon in the spirit of play.

The games moved to the stream the band followed southward.

The first challenge was who could make the biggest splash. The next challenge became who could dunk into chilly water another animal person. The two dogs were the first to start mud wrestling with each other. Slipping and sliding in the mud, band members rediscovered the joy of... *youngness.*

"Just look at me, Sir Cattle. With my hair and armor muddied black all over, I am no longer the sacred... white... bison."

"*Mrrooowww...* you are right!" exclaimed the cattle whose brown hide and blue gold armor were now thoroughly dirtied. "Rejoining the rest of us, the bison is again become unsacred."

"Do you not see, Lianvil, how it is best to sometimes relax and not take ourselves too seriously," brayed the bison.

"Even if I once knew how to play, I have forgotten," grrrd the big cat in reply. "If I am made a lion that is too serious, then that is what I am come to be."

That statement made Lianvil began to walk, on hind legs only, away from creek banks sprawled with muddy animal persons of all kinds and sizes. The lion stopped, reached down, and grabbed a clump of mud. He returned to address the bison.

"There is a spot on your shoulder that still shows the new white color of your hide." That noted, Lianvil rubbed mud about Buckwhite's white spot. The lion turned and again walked away, this time with an even more majestic two-legged stride.

"You know what, Sir Cattle? I kind of like my old blackness of hide. I am not going to take a bath, but wait for a rain to turn again my coat white."

"That, Master Bison, is not a bad idea. Until it rains the smell of your hide will be thankfully muted by caked mud."

As a bonfire that evening flamed high, twenty-six disheveled and muddy animal persons had paradoxically become a more true military company where fun and good will had renewed hearts and minds.

Naythorn, Belfloralex, Isabayas, and Cabalblade stretched together along the ground. For the first time ever, the four unicorns felt they formed a true equine family within the band.

Scarlet Point, Marsand, Amaluna, Alexzana, and Shawnee lounged with Hammer and Lucars. The bison and the cattle lay back to back with one horned sheep situated on each side of them. The pig family and two waterfowl went so far as to sleep together that night with a big lion, a yellow dancer wolf, and two dogs.

The magic of a unicorn with a black mane embraced a company that from big to little, arm to wing, and leg to horn had become truly united one with another. However, the absence of Tristanbear and Rainsnow still made vacant two heart-corners in the chests of a company found ever loyal to Naythorn Blackmane.

CHAPTER 6

BETRAYAL

" Every unicorn feared the cruel sounding name of the first monster wolf," grrrd the rust colored biggest of three bison-sized lupines. "So just like Albarochk, I need a name... my own name. Three terrible wolves require three fearsome names."

A huge gray wolf and a huge black wolf tilted quizzically their heads as they waited to hear more.

"And, I just thought of a name for myself," continued the biggest wolf. "When he would take a deer kill away from other wolves, the most mean-tempered wolf that I ever knew would make a *grrruuullkk* sound. To honor that cruel throaty cry, I am to be called... Grulk!"

"That name does suit you," grrrd the smallest of the three wolf leaders. "Erhrrmm. Now it is my turn. So, the trickiest wolf I knew as a cub clicked his teeth, *trqqq, trqqq* when he stole rabbits from the wolves that had killed them. So in honor of that slippery and devious wolf, call me... Trike!"

"That is *not* a terrible sounding name," responded Grulk.

"But I promise that unicorns will come to dread the sound of it!" barked back the black-hided Trike.

Grulk and Trike looked at the gray-hided second largest wolf, who took his time to reply.

"*Grarr...* I too had a favorite mean elder wolf that was a frightening bully. Before he attacked other wolves, he always cleared with a *claqqing* sound his throat. In honor of his cruel tyranny, you will call me Clak!"

The three had sated their large appetites on the meat of an old unicorn mare that had wandered away from the white herd.

"You two can be glad that there was plenty of unicorn meat for all of us," growled Grulk, "else I would have done what my favorite mean wolf used to do, and take the carcass all for myself."

"Clak and I would have ganged up on you and reclaimed for ourselves the unicorn carcass."

"You two would have ended up with cracked bones and bloodied hides," answered the big rust colored wolf. "*Grarr,* after sating my belly on unicorn flesh and blood, I should be made even bigger. Strangely enough, I do not feel more grown."

"My incisors are longer than they were yesterday, right?" inquired Trike of Clak.

"Not that I can see. Something is not right. For eating the flesh of the unicorn, just like Grulk and Trike, I am not made bigger and fiercer."

"Hoovefort cut out a very old, you might say ancient mare for us to prey upon," snarled Grulk. "When she saw us coming she fell over from fright. Was she dead when we tore into her flesh?"

"Since I run the fastest, I got to her first," barked Trike, "and when my teeth bit into her she did not even flinch in pain."

"Before Trike sank teeth into her throat," grrared Clak, "I saw a blue mist rise up from her frame. I think the vaporous mist was magic departing her body."

As the wolves grew pensive their ferocious semblance became less so.

"Just look at us," grrrd Grulk, "our appearance is no more frightening now than it was yesterday. By giving us a decrepit unicorn, that was as good as dead and had lost her magic, Hoovefort tricked us."

"Do you remember how great and fierce was the body of the monster wolf Albarochk?" queried Trike.

"His gigantic size and jagged teeth frightened even me," observed Clak.

"Why then are we not made equal to the monster size of Albarochk?" inquired Trike.

"It was in hard battles against the fierce blackmaned unicorn that Albarochk garnered his transformation," gruffed Grulk. "Unless we triumph in tumultuous battles against the perverse goodness represented by Naythorn, our bodies will never grow to match the size of Albarochk."

"Something tells me that about that, Grulk is right," grrrd Trike. "I wish Albarochk were right now here to lead us into an all out battle against the white herd."

"Albarochk is *no more!*" snapped Grulk. "Such talk does not help us to vanquish the white herd."

"When we had trapped the two unicorn leader mares and the horse stallion," continued Trike, "what manner of beast cried out of the darkness at us? What beast threw a big stone down at me?"

"Leave well enough alone," ordered Grulk. "What we heard was just the howling of wind, and Trike was in the wrong place when a whirlwind loosened rocks to fly off the cliff. We were foolish to think that a great beast crawled above us."

"But... I... felt the beast," whimpered Trike.

"And we all three heard his cries," seconded Clak.

"I just told you two dull wolves that a perverse wind played tricks on us," growled Grulk as he assumed his most menacing look. "Now go to sleep and rest your weak minds so that you can tomorrow help me develop a plan to triumph over Hoovefort and the white herd. I will make Hoovefort, who is a sly one, suffer for his treacherous dealings. Hoovefort will soon learn that I am no wolf to be played with, or to be dealt a decrepit and as good as dead unicorn mare."

Hoovefort

Daytime sunlight was lengthening. Notwithstanding the continuation of inclement weather, springtime was surely not far off. Newborn unicorn foals jumped about kicking up hooves in play. Yearling unicorns were become frisky and mischievous. Stallions wanted to be on the move to somewhere, and mares wanted to settle in a permanent hold, wherever that might be found. While in the place where they found themselves unicorns could not complain about the taste of the green grass matted beneath snow, a mare could complain that there were no caverns broken into the faces of cliffs where on cold nights she could feel warm, safe, and protected. Hoovefort would soon have to come up with a better answer than his standard... *from here we are not ready to depart.*

Hoovefort approached the spot where he had given Aneilee a nasty shove to propel her over the side of a steep cliff. As the moon lit in white cleanness the yet snow covered landscape, the unicorn waited. At last, in the distance he saw the approach of the three oversized wolves.

"Tonight, I will tell a good story," neighed to himself the captain of the unicorn guard stallions, "and these vulgar wolves will believe every lie they hear."

Before the muscular stallion three huge wolves formed a semi-circle.

"You gained weight since the last time we met," growled Grulk. "The grass must be excellent in your valley."

"Since you three look to have put on weight as well, the hunting must be good," returned Hoovefort the compliment.

"With the exception of your ancient unicorn mare, the hunting has been excellent," answered Trike. "Her old meat did us no good."

"By leaving us a unicorn that was already half dead, you tricked us!" exclaimed Clak. "In the carcass of a dead unicorn remains *no magic.*"

"How clumsy of you," replied Hoovefort shaking reprovingly his head. "It is your fault that you arrived too late to hunt her down."

"If it happens again," growled Grulk as he several times bit the air, "it will be you that becomes our next meal!"

"I can see that you are angry... but you big wolves need to calm down," responded Hoovefort taking another tack to the conversation. "To show my good will a substitute sacrifice will be provided, an arrogant big-bodied yearling that will give you a real fight. You three will enjoy the challenge of subduing him. In fact, I am certain that before you finish him off, each of you will come to be... bloodied.

"After the passage of seven suns, return to this very spot as the great orb descends to touch the mountain tops to the west. The next morning I will bring you the yearling, you will have your feast of unicorn flesh, and I will be rid of a problem young stallion. There is one thing more. Until the next sacrifice takes place keep your distance from the white herd. I do not need for you, or any other wolves, to scare the unicorns and cause them to question my leadership. Both you and I need for our mutually beneficial arrangement to long continue."

As three disgruntled wolves snarled menacingly, Hoovefort calmly stood his ground.

"You do not scare easily, Hoovefort," growled Grulk. "I will grant you that much. When we in seven suns fall upon him, for your own good that yearling unicorn had better be fit in body."

"Wolves found on every side of your valley will be ordered to keep their distance from the unicorn herd," added Trike.

"I am always ten steps ahead of unclever wolves," neighed Hoovefort as he trotted back toward the unicorn camp. "Those three will never outsmart me. The old mare wandered away to die, and I am glad she was dead before the monster wolves got to her. During passage of the next few suns they should learn to relish their hunts for deer and rabbits, because for many moons that is all they will have to eat."

"There you are!" saluted Haltervor standing on the trail where returned his leader. "I wanted to make sure Captain Hoovefort was alright. When we could not find you, we guard horses became worried for your safety. What are you doing way out here?"

"That is none of your business," neighed Hoovefort brushing against his sergeant guard horse. "You are not to follow me around. Understood?"

Gotten well-past his sergeant, Hoovefort muttered to himself, "How long was Haltervor watching me? Surely he could not have seen me neighing to the huge wolves?"

Hoovefort assembled his guards and announced that the white herd was now ready to depart upon a northerly course. Early the next morning the horned horses found themselves on the move. While guard unicorns had been sent ahead as scouts, the confident new leader placed no stallions to trail as rear lookouts.

As Hoovefort led the herd across the gently rising valley the excitement of the foals and yearlings became contagious. In spite of the lingering cold, with the approach of springtime not so far distant it suddenly felt right for unicorns to search in earnest for their new hold.

The climb that followed an ice-encrusted stream bed up the neck of the canyon, became difficult. Still, no unicorn horse stumbled and fell to become bruised or broken. With each league traveled by the white herd, Hoovefort's spirits rose. He was proud that he had played both ends against the middle. Haltervor and the guard unicorns were clueless as to his clever machinations. And when the three huge wolves returned to an abandoned unicorn camp, the horned horses would be nowhere to be found.

As a frowning Haltervor walked on one side of the white herd he was certain that he had the previous night glimpsed, under the light of the moon, big moving shadows close to where Hoovefort had disappeared.

"What last night compelled Hoovefort to go to a far place and endanger himself with fierce wolves nearby?" whinnied the guard stallion to no unicorn in particular. "Since the matriarch and high escort departed the white herd, there is something about Hoovefort's behavior that does not smell right. What can Hoovefort be up to?

"He would not be so arrogant if with the white herd Naythorn was still found. Should the day come that I have to stand up to Hoovefort, will I be brave enough to fight him? He *is* bigger than me. If Hoovefort needed to be stopped, would any guard horse stand with me?"

Haltervor looked up at ridges looming over the white herd, *"Nyerrraghhh!* If in this place packs of wolves fell down on us, they would scatter unicorns to the winds."

Travel during the passage of several suns served to harden unicorn muscles. As Hoovefort's mood became more and more relaxed, the guard horses cut back their forward patrols. Every report to Hoovefort indicated that all was well. That is, with one exception. The reports from Haltervor always pointed out reasons to exercise caution and care.

"Relax, Haltervor. There is nothing to worry about."

"Yes, Captain Hoovefort. Only that... something does not feel right to me."

"Exactly what does not feel right to you?"

"We should be coming upon lone wolves," neighed Haltervor shaking his head. "I do not understand why among the many predators that inhabit these valleys, we arouse no curiosity."

"Afraid of my powerful guard stallions, wolves know better than to bother us," answered Hoovefort.

"But wolves hereabout have never before seen a unicorn. They should at least be interested in finding out what kind of animal persons we are, and where we are headed."

"Let it go, Haltervor. Do not worry that the present lack of trouble means we should anticipate future problems."

"Still, Captain, it might be well to send out more and deeper patrols to our sides and rear, scout out places of refuge for the white herd in case we were to be attacked, and quicken our pace of movement through these mountain valleys."

"I tire of your whining, Haltervor. Go station yourself at the back of the herd... and stay there! While everything is under my control, I will not have you spreading malicious rumors about imaginary wolf attacks. The next time I hear you neigh about nonexistent wolves you will from the white herd be exiled, and you will *not return.*"

Head lowered, Haltervor walked disconsolate toward the rear of the unicorn column.

CHAPTER 7

GRULK, CLAK, AND TRIKE IN PURSUIT

On the eve of the appointed seventh day three enormous wolves arrived at the place where they had been instructed to await the unicorn sacrifice pledged by Hoovefort. At first morning light the enormous wolves occupied themselves with old and subtle scents that lingered in the now empty valley where had wintered the white herd.

"I have had enough of Hoovefort neighing out of both sides of his mouth," growled Grulk. "Curse that split-tongued unicorn!"

Unable to control his temper Grulk clawed, bit, and quickly destroyed a small white-barked tree. He next scratched front paws at his two companions. Smaller but quicker, Trike and Clak dodged the assault by Grulk.

"Control your temper, Grulk!" barked Clak. "There is only one thing to do: summon wolf packs to a war council."

"A wolf army will have revenge on the deceitful Hoovefort!" howled Trike.

"Go, you two, and recruit wolf packs," growled Grulk sprawling down his big belly upon incongruously relaxed limbs. "Three suns from now I require them to gather at this very spot. With my teeth I will break the heads of wolves that do not obey me."

Three days later many wolves converged.

"The war unicorn Naythorn deserted the white herd," howled the biggest monster wolf. "The two mares that formerly led the one-horned beasts, abandoned their responsibilities. And the stallion that now presumes to lead the unicorns... *is a mere pretender.* Attacking now and destroying the entire white herd while they are as good as leaderless, will make their magic to be ours, and ours alone!"

From previous battles with Naythorn and his band, many of the gathered wolves bore deep scars, and even deeper resentments. That being the case, the brigade of wolves exploded in howls of support for Grulk. In a rough demonstration of enthusiasm for a fight against a now weakened herd of unicorn horses, snapping wolves jumped upon and chased one another about.

The wolf army formed into three battalions.

Led by Grulk, the battalion with the most and biggest wolves marched at the front. In the lead of the older wolves, Clak commanded the middle of the wolf army. As befit the smallest of the three huge wolves, the members of Trike's closing battalion consisted of the youngest and most inexperienced recruits. Traveling both day and night at a run, the wolfly army chased after the white herd.

Time and again Grulk howled, "Unicorns hearts are deceitful!"

Each time the wolf brigade responded, "Horned horses are desperately wicked!"

Just as every wolf knew would happen, it was only a matter of days until scouts located the slow moving white herd. The place selected for attack favored the three wolf battalions. The climb at the far north end of the narrow valley, in the direction to where the unicorns were moving, was rocky and sheer. Fast escape there would be difficult, and next to impossible for very young and very old unicorn horses. With the place where the white herd directed made precipitous by steep terrain, the three wolf battalions deployed to block unicorn escape to the west, east, and south.

Trike and his battalion of young wolves climbed the summit of a long ridge on the sunrise side of the valley. The older wolves led by Clak arrayed in heights on the sunset side of the unicorn herd. Grulk and the strength of the wolf army would from the south pursue and bottle ahead of them the unicorn horses.

As three hundred wolves moved stealthily into position the thoughts of Grulk, Clak, and Trike were the same. The moment of revenge upon the unicorn that had played them for fools, was at hand.

As the grayness of evening set in, both Trike and Clak spied the captain of the unicorn guard stallions walking relaxed at the front of the white herd. It was evident that Hoovefort did not have the slightest idea that he was about to become entangled in all out battle.

At the fall of dark Grulk launched the ambush.

"Attack! Attack! *Wolves Attack!*" neighed excitedly Haltervor the rearmost guard stallion.

As the hindmost unicorns in the herd stampeded, crowding and pushing those before them, equine bodies shoved everywhere about in confusion.

"Stand, and with me fight the oncoming wolves!" neighed Haltervor to the guard unicorns found close to him. As wolves closed fast, for long moments that seemed to be without end Haltervor stood alone.

"I am *Haltervor!*" neighed the sergeant guard unicorn to the approaching giant wolf. "You will *not* pass by me!"

"You are no more than a meal for wolves!" howled Grulk in answer.

As ten guard stallions joined to fight beside Haltervor, wolf bodies crashed into unicorn hooves. Become surrounded by wolves, Haltervor and his desperate platoon struggled mightily to hold their ground.

Hearing on all sides the sounds of howling wolves, Hoovefort turned to see the entire white herd rushing toward him. With wolves cascading down upon the flanks of the unicorns, too late the captain of the guard stallions realized... that he was trapped.

Hoovefort fought harder, faster, and fiercer than he had ever before done. However, when two giant wolves joined to the circle of the lesser wolves that had cornered him, his destiny was sealed. The stallion neighed in pain as long incisors grabbed into his flesh. Onto Hoovefort's mane fastened the powerful teeth of Clak. Into the soft underside of Hoovefort's neck clenched the sharp teeth of Trike. The elegant body of the captain of the unicorn guard stallions crashed to ground.

As he continued to kick and struggle Hoovefort came to reconcile himself with the thought that everything he had planned, was lost. Fighting for each breath, Hoovefort neighed the name he had long despised, "Naaayyyythorrrnnn..."

Since Lianvil, Buckwhite, Taurington, Hammer, Lucars, and the rest of the blackmane's battle-tested band were not there to parry and fend off the brunt of the wolf attack, the fight of ordinary unicorns was the last and only resort. Unicorn stallions kicked, stomped, and bit to protect their mares that in turn fought to protect their colts. Flight came not to be an option. As the defensive perimeter of the unicorns was pushed inward, thick darkness came to envelope a place of harsh battle.

Above the tumult of wolf howls and whinnied screams an otherworldly cry sounded, and at the same time the cry was felt. The terror embedded in the throat of the shriek gave fright to animal persons both equine and wolfly. An enormous thing, as much shadow as substantial, swathed through files of wolves. Someone, something else, had entered the battle to bring loss to the wolf brigade.

Ranks of wolves were left and right mown down. Crushed and crumpled wolves on one flank, and then on the other flank of the white herd, filled the night with cries of abject anguish and fear. On the darkened battleground wolves found they could not stand against a force greater than Grulk, Trike, or Clak.

"Curse the great beast that joined cause to the white herd!" howled Grulk in desperation.

"What is this thing come to our aid?" neighed Haltervor to the guard stallions about him. "In the darkness I cannot see it pass! All I can see are the bodies of wolves being batted about!"

Finding that his wolf soldiers could not withstand their new enemy, Grulk howled the command for retreat. Wolves at the rear and on both sides of the unicorn herd tucked tails between hind legs, and abandoned as fast as they could the field of battle.

"We must collect the herd!" neighed Haltervor to the guard stallions gathered about his position. "There is no time to lose! We do not know if the beast next comes *for us!*"

"Unicorn horses scatter every which way, and Hoovefort is *dead!*" whinnied loud a guard horse returning from the front of the unicorn herd.

Driving hooves toward where Hoovefort had walked at the front of the herd, the sergeant guard stallion found his captain's fallen body washed in blood. Pausing to look about, Haltervor saw fleeing unicorns dismayed at the sight of their fallen leader, pass at a far distance from his bloodied hide.

Muzzling the nostrils of the collapsed stallion, Haltervor detected a faint gasp of breath. When the guard sergeant touched his horn to Hoovefort, at the intersection of two horns sparkled blue light.

Hoovefort revived enough to cough weakly in an attempt to clear his throat.

"It is I, Haltervor. A stronger magic than I possess is required to shut your wounds. If only Aneilee were here."

"Haaalterrrvorrr... I lied to you... I am... sorry..."

"The strongest unicorn must hold onto life. I will assemble what I can of the sage council to bring healing to Captain Hoovefort."

"Too late... for me... protect the unicorns... the... blackmane..."

The body of Hoovefort stilled.

After briefly pawing dirt to cover bloodied ground, Haltervor galloped toward the north end of the valley where unicorns in two's and three's were scrambling up the rim of the canyon.

"Stay! Hold together!" ordered Haltervor. "Do not scatter about and become lost!" His cry was picked up by the guard horses about him. Here and there unicorn horses turned heads, and reversed course to rejoin what remained of the white herd.

By the light of new morning Haltervor counted the unicorns gathered close together in a defensive ring at the north end of the valley.

"More than one hundred unicorn horses are here unaccounted for," neighed Haltervor to guard horses. "We now have a double charge, to make safe the unicorns that with us remain, and to find and bring back those that fled. As quickly as possible we must lead the herd to the nearest place that offers defensive protection. Once the herd is safe, we will organize and send out patrols to search for every unicorn that remains to us lost."

In agreement with the neighs of their sergeant, guard stallions nodded vigorously up and down their heads.

Three Wolves After Battle

"We were last night so close to victory, that I could smell it," lamented Grulk to the two huge wolves walking at his side.

"At least we three survived," growled Clak.

"And I and Clak ended the life of our hated former ally, the traitor Hoovefort," yipped Trike grinning slyly at Clak.

"*Grarrarr!* His blood tasted ten times better than the blood of the old sacrificial mare!" answered Clak. "For the feast of blood from a very powerful magical horse that in the prime of his life fell to the cuts of my teeth, I feel myself grown bigger."

"My teeth are today grown longer and sharper," added Trike baring wide his jaws.

"With his teeth clenched to the base of Hoovefort's neck, Trike had the upper paw," growled Clak. "He drank the lion's share of the unicorn's magic blood."

"For that Trike is now grown almost as big as me."

"You are mistaken, Grulk," responded Clak. "If only by a little, Trike is now made huger than you."

"If it had not been for the guard horse that calls himself Haltervor," growled Grulk, "I would have tasted much unicorn blood. I will refocus my hatred of Hoovefort to become hatred for Haltervor."

"Grulk," grrrd Trike, "was it a spirit that stopped us?"

"All I can answer is that I do not know what passed like a rushing wind through us wolves."

"Whatever it was, its two glinty eyes burned black!" barked Clak.

"Now that you say that, Clak, I do recall two burning eyes glaring down at me," grrrd Trike. "Those eyes truly frightened me."

"If the beast's intent was to promote terror, in that he succeeded," responded Clak. "More than cut them and break their bones, he scared wolves half to death."

"We do not give up!" howled Grulk springing up to land on all fours facing Trike and Clak. "From our army we will gather what wolves we can find. With three battalions each made strong by seventy or eighty wolf soldiers obedient to our commands, the three of us can take down isolated unicorn horses one or two at a time. We will surely find the unicorns that ran away into the wilderness, that are now become lost and alone. Before we are done, last night's defeat of our wolf army will for unicorn guard stallions prove to have been a very costly victory."

"It already proved calamitous to Hoovefort," yipped Trike.

"So what if I lost eighty wolf privates?" snarled Grulk. "Plenty more wolves are every year born, five or six in a litter, to replenish my army."

"If Clak and I continue to devour more unicorn blood than Grulk, we will become the strongest," offered Trike with a smirk. "Then two enormous gray and black wolves will command the wolf legion. *Grarrarrrwwarr!* Not the bossy and overbearing rust colored Grulk!"

To dispute what had just been barked, Grulk jumped to sink teeth into the hide of Trike.

"My black hide is grown so tough that it withstands your biting," snarled the bitten wolf as he shook off Grulk. "That *proves* that I am now stronger than you."

"Trike, you numbskull!" growled Clak stepping between the two snarling wolf leaders. "Grulk still possesses twice the intelligence that you do. You and I will do well to follow Grulk's commands."

"That is a good fellow," grrrd Grulk approvingly to Clak. "Without my leadership my two brother wolves will fail... and fall. To be a leader one must think ahead and plan for all the many unpleasant things that happen to wolves in this vast wilderness. Speaking of which, have either of you thought about what became of the two matriarchs and their protector horse Rainsnow? If with their powerful magic those two mares return now, the white herd will fight twice as hard against us."

"I had not thought more on them," answered Trike. "Where can they be?"

"See there," growled Grulk with a salacious grin spreading to cover his huge face. "That demonstrates why it is me that commands. Several suns ago I sent out two wolves to pickup and follow southward their trail. Once found, they cannot be permitted to rejoin the white herd."

"I blame both of them for the hurled rock that almost broke my back," barked Trike.

"Of course they are the ones to blame," replied Grulk nodding his big head.

"The destruction of the unicorn matriarchs would be acclaimed as the greatest victory ever achieved by a monster wolf," replied Trike slyly. "Whoever destroyed the two leader mares would be forever famous in the annals of wolf lore."

"Maybe we are missing something," barked Clak. "What if the specter that defeated us continues to protect the white herd? Because our diminished army is not now big enough or strong enough to stop that evil force, all our efforts to destroy the white herd would be doomed."

"We already decided that we are going to attack the stragglers that abandoned the white herd," growled Grulk.

"Since the specter is here now," continued Clak, "why not first destroy the unicorn leaders, and after reattack the white herd? Ending the sorry lives of Naythorn and the two matriarchs would cut off the roots that nurture the unicorns."

"Like I grrrd before, if I killed the matriarchs it would be the greatest wolf victory ever!" exulted Trike.

"I think that a victory over Naythorn would be even greater," barked Clak. "From the battle that ended the life of Albarochk, I remember the blackmaned unicorn only too well. The first time the shield fell his hooves scarred my hide. For that I hate him with all my heart. Hmpf. It will not be difficult for me to recruit wolves to pursue the blackmane."

"For once you two make a good argument," responded Grulk. "Trike will gather wolves to track down and kill the two matriarchs. Clak will lead a wolf battalion against a soon to be refound Blackmane. We know that he also travels toward the south.

"As for me I want only one thing... to kill Haltervor. He stopped me last night, and specter or no specter, I vow that he will not stop me again. Once you two have destroyed the two matriarchs and the blackmane, return here to me. Together we will make certain that not a single unicorn in the white herd escapes our claws."

"*Grarrharharrrr!*" laughed Trike. "Upon drinking the blood of the matriarchal mares, I will be bigger and fiercer than was Albarochk!"

"If Grulk kills Haltervor and drinks the blood of twenty more unicorns, he will also be bigger than was Albarochk," snarled Clak.

An enormous gray wolf loped away in search of Naythorn. An even larger black wolf loped off in quest of two matriarch unicorns. Behind remained a huge rust colored wolf.

The Matriarchs and Rainsnow

"Have you noticed the two wolves that this day came to follow us?" neighed the high escort to Rainsnow.

"I did at that, Dame Aneilee. Early this morning the wind brought whiffs of them to me. The two spy wolves right now sit above looking down at us. I would wager a bite to my side that they were sent out by the three huge wolves to find us."

"That is the most likely conclusion to draw," agreed Aneilee.

"Once the leader wolves are told where we travel, they will send many wolves after us," opined Elianor. "The survival of we two matriarchs threatens the quest for lupine victory over the white herd. Strangely enough, I find the way the white patterned markings finger into their black hides, makes them to be about the two prettiest wolves I have ever seen."

"You know what, Dame Elianor?" responded Aneilee with a smile encompassing her muzzle. "Having the same thought, I did not share it. I did not want you to scold me for commenting something about the appearance of our wolf adversaries... that you would tell me was trivial."

"By tomorrow morning they will have departed from us to report back to their captains," neighed Rainsnow. "I do hate to think that each of the three huge wolves that accosted us will continue to grow to achieve the size of the monster Albarochk. I cannot imagine how Naythorn and his band could at the same time and place contend against not one, but three monster wolves."

"Listen closely, Rainsnow," neighed Aneilee. "Do you hear the faint cries coming from somewhere far behind us?"

"I hear nothing. What is it that you hear?"

"Inside my head I hear quiet reminders of the eerie sounds we heard the night we were saved from the three monster wolves. The disquieting, distant, and almost imperceptible vibrations that register deep in my being tell me that the direct route toward Naythorn is troubled."

"Those two spy wolves will report to their ferocious leaders that we travel southward," replied the stallion.

"In that case," answered Elianor, "it will be safer for us to detour before we at last come upon Naythorn and his band."

"I, for one," neighed Aneilee, "have a longing to again gaze upon the tranquility of the sea."

"Then in the company of the high escort and the guide matriarch, this horse stallion leads eastward to the coast."

CHAPTER 8

TROYAN PIRATES AT SEA

"She again sings!" exclaimed Princess Resi pointing at the figurehead maiden that embellished the prow.

"More than sing, the bow maiden whistles," answered Bashkeem. "I designed her so that as the wind changes direction or force, the figurehead flutes different sounds."

"I would never have thought to do that," remarked Prince Ermal. "It must have taken you many days to perfect the design of the whistling maidenhead."

"It proved to be a harder invention than I thought it would be. I had to fashion my own styles of flutes to make her tell a story about winds caressing sails."

"The Jenelisa sings more loudly now," added Resi. "As the wind strengthens, her voice rings clear like the cloudless sky above us."

As had said Bashkeem, the islands and coasts to the west of the place that once flew the flag of Troy had many harbors where a ship could land and piracy could be discussed, if not openly then almost so. The way a seemingly transparent comment about the weather was phrased could signal that something else was afoot.

The Jenelisa lowered sails in a harbor holding promise of recruitment. Bashkeem brought out cloaks for the princes so that no notice would be drawn to their beautifully forged swords and breast plates. As the three men walked about the town, from time to time Bashkeem would pause long moments to inspect, and then offer a greeting to likely candidates for the crew of the Jenelisa. Besides the salutation, no other words were with any stranger shared.

"It is better if our eyes tell the story to *only* the men that we want to learn of the opportunity that we bring," muttered Bashkeem to Ermir and Ermal.

That evening a small group of men joined Bashkeem and the royal offspring on board their barge. While Bashkeem succinctly summarized the quest of the Jenelisa, a bottle of strong drink distilled from plums was passed around. As Ermir expected the commander to do, Bashkeem matter of factly pointed out the improvements he had made to the design of his vessel. Forthcoming to a fault, Bashkeem instilled trust in the men gathered round listening.

A slender but muscular sailor of thirty or so years at last spoke for himself, and as well for the other men invited on board, "So you newly made pirates are going to reclaim what was taken from you?"

"That is so," answered Bashkeem simply.

"Will you take back more than what was from you taken?" persisted the man's questioning.

"That is also so. There is interest calculated both in coins and blood which the Egyptians must pay. The share for the crew is half of the spoils. That half will be well-earned."

"But you are an Egyptian." observed another sailor. "That makes you a traitor to your people."

"I was for twenty-five years possessed by Egypt. For that, my head is trained to think in the way of my Egyptian masters. I am convinced that Egyptian learning is the most advanced anywhere. Out of respect for all that my masters taught me, for as long as I live I will wear the dress of Egypt. While on the outside I look to be an Egyptian, to me alone belongs what dwells within."

The potential crewmen huddled to speak quietly among themselves. Their answer was finally delivered, "Before first light we will here assemble."

"Take this coin," said Bashkeem to the youngest of the seven. "Yet a sapling tree, you do not tomorrow report for duty. If a year from now you remain willing to enlist, it will be different."

To the other six men Bashkeem said simply, "Very well. We cast off at break of dawn."

At the next port of call ten candidates for the crew were identified. Eight of the ten were chosen by Bashkeem to serve aboard his ship.

Ermal asked why with a crew so small all ten men were not selected to serve aboard the Jenelisa.

"Young prince," answered Bashkeem, "the secret to winning battles at sea is about far more than the genius of the captaincy. The deciding factor is the skill and valor of the sailors that in turn carry out both good and bad orders. More than anything, the mettle of individual sailors matters to our success. If we do not exercise the greatest care in recruitment, our endeavors at piracy will not come to fruition."

"You make a good point Bashkeem, but we really need sailors, and soon."

"More times than I care to count I have observed that the decay of a promising enterprise be it business, construction, military, or government is brought about by the recruitment of the wrong people."

"Very good, Sir," answered Ermal. "By posing the question I was made to learn something that I shall not forget." After only a few more days the crew of the Jenelisa was made complete.

"When will we be ready to do battle, Bashkeem?" inquired Ermir. "Our remaining food supplies are meager."

"Ideally, I could use twenty days to train and prepare this crew to fully comprehend my orders for the management of sails and oars, and to learn to fight as one company. How long can our food supplies be stretched?"

"At the most, fifteen more days."

"Then, Sir Prince, you have my word. In fifteen days this crew will be transformed into one of prowess."

The day for action dawned in strikingly bright sunlight. When the Jenelisa closed on a convoy of Egyptian barges laden with the spoils of pillage, excitement lit the hardened faces of Bashkeem's sailors drawing on the oars. The Jenelisa began to close on a trailing barge, with noticeably clean lines, that had not maintained a tight formation with the other vessels in the convoy.

"They will welcome our arrival," said Bashkeem to the members of his crew, "and not think that a ship of

Egyptian design and flying Egyptian standards will seek to do them damage. We will hail in friendship the target ship, draw next to it, and then seize it in the time it takes me to count to one hundred. Do not shout or make noise. We want the other Egyptian vessels to be slow to realize that we are, in fact, the enemy.

"Egyptian sailors thrown overboard are to splash down on the side of their ship away from their fleet. Some of the slaves on board the vessel we attack may be from your lands, and speak your tongues. If so, recruit them to our cause.

"Under the command of Ermir, half of our crew will sail the captured ship northward, with this barge trailing the prince. The other half of my crew that returns to man the oars of the Jenelisa, will bring back supplies of food. If on the high seas we are separated, our two vessels are to individually proceed to the deserted harbor on the western point of the large island we sailed by two days ago."

"Listen!" exclaimed Bashkeem to his crew. "The maidenhead of the Jenelisa breaks forth in whistled song, telling us the wind begins to change from north to south. Now is the time for us to strike. When you feel the touch of our vessel against the hull of the Egyptian barge, spring to the fight and dispatch the enemy. Do not forget that complete surprise is our ally. If each of us executes our duty, victory will await. Today we glory as loyal pirates of the new kingdom of Troy!"

The Jenelisa closed on the target barge. Arrayed in impeccable Egyptian attire Bashkeem excitedly shouted orders to his crew... as if to prevent a collision. When the hulls of the two barges bumped, surprise engulfed the faces of the sailors manning the preyed upon Egyptian vessel. The fighting immediately grew fierce.

Blood began to wash the deck of the Egyptian vessel. When a second time the Jenelisa knocked against the commandeered ship twenty five sailors, some clutching loaves of bread, bounded back to the deck of the barge commanded by Bashkeem.

The Jenelisa turned to follow the captured Egyptian ship.

Rowers were unchained. Ermir, the new captain of the seized barge, immediately observed that the freed oarsmen gave everything they had to row away from the Egyptian fleet. Ermir grabbed water flasks, bent over each rower, and provided refreshment to replace the sweat dripping off brows.

The remaining Egyptian captains in the convoy were confused. Some became afraid that if they turned in pursuit of the taken ship, they would fall into an ambush. How else could they explain to themselves the brazen and reckless display of courage shown by the crew of one barge willing to compel battle with a seven vessel convoy?

While Ermir placed more distance between his barge and the Egyptian fleet, one of the remaining six Egyptian vessels turned to pursue the pirateers.

Not willing to be followed, Bashkeem ordered the Jenelisa about and took on a course of collision with the Egyptian ship intent on rescue. The Troyan barge would have to outmaneuver its Egyptian adversary that had the advantage of size, but not of speed.

Bashkeem maintained a head-on course centered on the closing Egyptian ship. Moments before the collision should occur Bashkeem feinted a course to port, as if to avoid hitting the Egyptian pursuer. As Bashkeem knew would happen, the bigger Egyptian ship veered right to block. Once the Egyptian captain took the bait, Bashkeem signaled to turn sharply starboard. Prepared for the maneuver, the crew of the Jenelisa scurried to adjust sails and rotate the pull of oars. The iron-tipped ram protruding from the prow of the Jenelisa struck into the enemy vessel, jolting Egyptian sailors into the sea. Every attempt to board the Jenelisa while it was briefly joined to its adversary was thwarted.

Bashkeem's rowers reversed the pull of their oars, and disengaged an Egyptian barge that had begun to list badly. Undamaged, the Jenelisa followed northward the stolen barge commanded by Ermir.

With the desired landing gained, Ermir had the ship's cargo unloaded and spread in two lines on the shore so that the two crews could closely inspect the spoils of war. Upon finding that more plunder had been taken than anticipated, a big smile lit the older prince's face. In celebration his brother and two sisters embraced Ermir.

Hoisted onto sailors' shoulders, and paraded so that from a high perch he could see exactly what was secured from their first foray into piracy, Bashkeem would underplay the moment.

"Can there be about us anything of *real* value?" inquired Bashkeem gesturing with his arms. "Here are a few trinkets of gold. Over there lie a few bars of iron for smelting. Some paltry swords, spears, and armor scatter about over there."

"Liar!" "Liar!" rang out shouts directed at Bashkeem.

"There is one hundred times more plunder than Bashkeem admits!" yelled a crewman.

"I find here what matters most to us," proclaimed Bashkeem smiling wide. "These barrels are filled with dried fish!" As if to command the fish packed therein, the commander was set down on a barrel head.

"Sir Bashkeem," spoke Resi, "it was not long ago that four frightened and homeless princes and princesses crawled through a dirty tunnel toward a future permitting no hope. You changed that. At great risk to yourself you rescued us, and taught us to willingly obey and fight for you. For all that you have done, we four have decided that our share of this first treasure rightfully pertains to you."

"You give me back something much more valuable than this plunder," replied Bashkeem. "You return to me my dignity as a free man. I have no need for more than the thoughts that spring from my mind, bread for my stomach, and the privilege of deciding who will assist me and become my friends in this work of life."

"Alright, it is time to decide!" said Bashkeem turning once more to the crew. "Which of the two lines of treasure will you take as yours?"

The crewmen from the Jenelisa chose, and then drew lots to individually distribute their half of the spoils of piracy. Most realized that they had on that day become wealthier than they had ever before been, or could have hoped to become.

"Commander Bashkeem," spoke the oldest member of his crew, "come the next battle you will find us to fight even harder for the new Kingdom of Troy."

"Loyal sailors," responded Bashkim, "even now the Egyptians endeavor to learn who we are and from where we sail. They will come looking for us. With a few new surprises we shall receive them."

Given the brilliance of the sky on the day of her capture, the new barge with notably sleek lines was renamed the Sun Flash. More than once Bashkeem wondered who it was that had designed the Flash, for her slender figure was in marked contrast to stodgy Egyptian barges built for freight, and not speed. Under the direction of Bashkeem the refitted Flash would be made to be... indeed fast.

The next fifteen suns were spent on a construction project. The captured barge received another mast; iron sheeting was added along the water line. The naval ram was lengthened and made more sturdy. To lessen the draft of the vessel the deck was cleared of benches, stalls, tables, perches, and a cabin.

The mind of Ermal thought much like the mind of Bashkeem. Both were born builders. Ermal took on the task of designing the maidenhead for the prow of the Flash. When finished, from the sounds of the flutes embedded in the figurehead the crew could well-distinguish changes in wind direction and velocity.

As the renovations progressed Bashkeem took the time to motivate crew members. The commander of a fleet now comprising two ships wanted his sailors to feel that they were listened to and understood as individuals, each one with his own ways. Bashkeem told the men that he expected them soon to be coming to him with their ideas for how to better trim a sail, or better place a rope. Invariably the crewmen shook their heads in agreement with what Bashkeem had to say.

"We sail west!" proclaimed Bashkeem upon completing the refitting of the Flash. "A deserter from an Egyptian ship, that I before treated well, found us. He wants to join our crew, and I will have him. More valuable than his service is the warning he brings. If a deserter can locate us, then so will soon the Egyptian captains that search for us in this part of the sea. With every league that we travel west, the chance of happening upon Egyptian warships lessens.

"The capture of our third barge will be fifty leagues west of where we are now anchored. Seizure of our fourth barge will take place one hundred leagues to the west of our present position. Capture of our fifth barge might well be one hundred fifty leagues to the west. When our fleet numbers five fast ships manned by seasoned crews, we can then upon our return to the coast off Troy challenge Egyptian fleets with eight, nine, or ten barges... and stand and fight them all day long."

Bashkeem led the little fleet of two ships to obscure trading ports where the Jenelisa and the Flash took on food, oil, wine, and supplies of rope and canvas cloth. There was always demand to trade for gold and armor.

"Do not give anyone the satisfaction of recognizing who you are," insisted Bashkeem. "Our greatest allies are secrecy and surprise." To that end, individual sailors were instructed to not trade more than one item of their personal store at a time.

At every stop Bashkeem went immediately to search out those he called hoopers, the craftsmen that fashioned the barrels used to store all manner of foods, liquids, and other goods aboard ships. Bashkeem was intent on designing the tightest barrels ever made. The commander applied his knowledge of shipbuilding to the knowledge he acquired in hooping. The concept of minimizing the penetration of water, the same notion that applied to the hulls of ships, was applied to keep the contents of barrels from leaking out through vertical slats of wood clasped tight with metal hoops. The Jenelisa and the Sun Flash came to carry the tightest stave barrels that could be anywhere found.

"Sir Bashkeem!" exclaimed Ermal upon examining several newly made barrels. "Please do not waste any more of our precious time theorizing about the perfect barrel... in which to stow dead fish!"

Without a Fight

The Jenelisa and the Flash happened upon a solitary Egyptian trading vessel. Wanting in seamanship, the very young captain of the lightly armed trading vessel had carelessly allowed himself to become separated from his maritime convoy. Despising the young captain's haughtiness, his crew did not lament his downfall. Without so much as raising a sword in defense, the ill-led ship captained by the scion of a powerful politician, surrendered.

Because the youthful ship captain, Olsi by name, decided that responsibility for the loss of his ship could be charged entirely to the disloyalty of his crew, his pride was undamaged by the fiasco he had endured.

"Swearing that he will no more put up with his unjust treatment," reported Admira to her commander, "Olsi rejects his oar. Because the other hard-working rowers are fed up with Olsi, if he persists in his arrogance something unfortunate will come to happen."

"This captain, Admira, does not tolerate violence among his crew."

A fuming Olsi soon stood with arms crossed before Bashkeem.

"I was in a *palace* born! Even the pharaoh has heard my name! A former slave of Egypt, one that tomorrow will be hunted down as a pirate, can do nothing to me. Treat me well, Bashkeem, and perhaps I will intervene so that upon capture you will not for days be tortured before your life from you is taken."

"Son, you look weak to me. Without disciplining yourself to pull hard at an oar, I do not know how you will add heft to your muscles. Life has taught me that an Egyptian needs to be strong, and strength requires hard work and discipline."

"Admira, have this young Egyptian nobleman tied to a mast," instructed Bashkeem. "No, wait. I will first have Olsi to dine with me."

"I did not see you to scold Olsi while you ate with him," commented later Admira.

"It would have done little good, at this time, to chastise the arrogant young Egyptian. Instead I asked a few pointed questions of Olsi, that he will have more than enough time to reflect further on," responded Bashkeem.

The next day Bashkeem directed the Jenelisa toward a small uninhabited island. With hands bound, a kicking Olsi was boated by Admira and Resi to the island, and there deposited with only a knife at his disposal. As the sails of the Jenelisa filled with wind, Olsi ran along the sand beach screaming at Bashkeem. Sailors lining deck rails taunted the highborn former Egyptian captain.

"If some day we pass this way again," said Bashkeem to the two princesses, "we will stop and find out how fares the arrogant Olsi now found with only himself, a knife, and the rocks and boulders of an inhospitable island to command. The youth is not unintelligent. Someone believed enough in Olsi to place him in command of a valuable vessel. I hope there proves to be more to that young former barge captain than conceit and false pride. Humbled by adversity and the threat of mortality, some people come to learn vital lessons about the hardships of life.

"Not to change the subject, but we are presented with a major problem. Our third vessel, the newly captured ship, is too slow to keep pace with the Jenelisa and the Sun Flash. The ships in our little navy must all be fast so that in post-battle flight not a single barge falls behind, and not a single crew member is abandoned."

"Why not sell or trade her for a faster vessel?" responded Admira.

"It will be difficult to find a buyer for a barge stolen from the great empire that dominates the shores of this sea," reflected Bashkeem. "Hmpf. I know a small port that sits two days sail up an obscure, but nevertheless navigable river. The shipwrights of that isolated port have established a reputation for craftsmanship. The remake would be challenging. But, if I had a moon to disassemble our newest ship, lighten her, and rebuild her thinner and longer I am sure that with the help of Ermal's aptitude for design we could make her to be much faster."

It was decided that while Bashkeem, Ermal, and talented local shipwrights refitted and reconfigured the newly captured vessel, Ermir in command of the Jenelisa, and Resi and Admira sharing command of the Sun Flash, would continue acts of piracy.

After nearly a moon had passed the prince and two princesses, and with them one more captured vessel, refound the river port where Bashkeem and Ermal had been hard at work making a barge... to be not slow.

"Well done Ermir, Resi, and Admira!" exclaimed Bashkeem. "The fourth capture will require only a few modifications. She looks right now to be almost as fast as our other three ships."

"Because we were selective, it took more time than we thought it would. But, for our fourth vessel we finally found exactly the barge we wanted," answered Resi.

"It is a miracle!" exclaimed Admira. "Bashkeem and Ermal have remade our third capture, a stodgy wide barge, into a sleek and long vessel. And, she is at the front rounded. I never before saw a rounded barge prow. That is genius! I think that the redesigned vessel is no longer a real barge, but has instead been made to be an elegant ship."

"We used the same wood from the barge to remake her," offered Ermal with a tone of pride in his voice. "We wasted nothing. She is faster, lighter, and tighter than before. We even thought of a pretty name to give her. The Wave Rider will be as fleet as a winged unicorn that gallops the waves."

Before recommitting to the sea, the pirate leaders that now commanded a fleet of four fast barges met to plan their next course of action.

"While I am the older sister, I know that my character is sometimes too spontaneous and brash," acknowledged Admira. "By her tireless diligence, and also by the respect accorded to her by the sailors, Resi has earned the right of captaincy."

Bashkeem commended the unselfishness of the older sister for insisting that her younger sister be given command of the fourth capture, that only some days previous had sailed into the small harbor. Bashkeem next informed his captains Ermir, Ermal, and Resi that the Egyptians had surmised the strategy of the Troyan pirates to sail westward in order to stay beyond the grasp of Egyptian naval strength. The pursuing Egyptian navy was not far away.

"We have two options," offered Ermal. "We can continue our strategy to stay to the western side of Egyptian patrol ships, or we can reverse course and sail back towards our homeland."

"We are not yet ready to return to the east where Egypt has a vast number of vessels, and Phoenicia plies actively the seas," replied Captain Resi who had renamed the fourth capture the Star Sheen. "It is said that in a dangerous part of the world Phoenicia counts on no alliance and recognizes no friendship. We would confront not only Egyptian power, but also Phoenician war barges. It is better to stay with our plan to grow our navy to five ships, improve our seamanship, and only then sail back to Troy."

In agreement with Resi's analysis Ermir, Ermal, Admira, and Bashkeem nodded heads.

When at high tide the next morning villagers helped to knock out the struts that held the Wave Rider, the rebuilt ship with a rounded prow slid into the river. The Jenelisa, the Sun Flash, the Wave Rider, and the Star Sheen floated out to sea.

When the island where had been stranded the brash young Egyptian captain came once more into view, Bashkeem made an unplanned stop. The sighting of the island had piqued his curiosity about how had fared Olsi. And, the commander told himself he could always use another set of arms to man the oars. No persuasion was this time required to entice the no longer scowling young Egyptian nobleman to rejoin the crew of Bashkeem's barge.

"Do you recall, Bashkeem," said Olsi upon gaining the deck of the Jenelisa, "that every oarsman on the ship I before captained was chained to his bench?"

"As *you* recall, Olsi, on this ship there are no chains," replied Bashkeem. "What we do have is hard work, food, and plunder. Being myself a former slave, I require that everyone be treated with fairness. Hmpf. While you lost some weight, I commend you for adding muscle. To continue that plan, pulling at an oar will provide good discipline."

"No ship passed close by the island. I was certain that on that miserable spit of land my days were numbered. If you had not come back for me, I would have soon died. You, Bashkeem, hold power over me. Nothing remains for me but to accept that my lot in life has irretrievably changed. It may as well be on a ship, commanded by a former slave, that I am abased and made to pay for my carelessness and arrogance. But, know that especially in battle when the risk of ships sinking is ever large, I greatly value not being chained to my bench."

Ermal began to escort Olsi to his oar. The rescued young Egyptian wrested himself from the grasp of the stocky Troyan and returned to stand before Bashkeem.

"I once before met a man that like you, Bashkeem, spoke with two layers of meaning to his words. While the first layer could be interpreted to minimize or trivialize the import of what he said, the second layer of meaning was what mattered. The man I refer to would with a few words say a thing, look intently to see if one grasped the full significance of what he had said, and then by the comment made back to him ascertain his listener's depth of comprehension. Your measured words, Commander Bashkeem, are always worth paying heed to, and that is because there is often a partially hidden thing to be learned in what you express."

"Olsi, I am puzzled by what you say," responded Bashkeem.

"Because I almost starved to death, my arms are most definitely not stronger now than when you exiled me to the island. Since you do not indulge in gratuitous flattery, I can only think that the added muscle you commended was not the physical kind. So I conclude, Bashkeem, that when you before told me that the discipline of pulling an oar would add muscle, you were really telling me that in order to be a true Egyptian I needed to become strengthened in mind."

The act of mercy to rescue Olsi appeared to bring bad luck in the form of an unusually violent storm. Day after day strong winds carried four pirate vessels westward, and more westward. When at last the skies shone blue, there were no Egyptian ships of commerce found to prey upon. The far western waters they plied were unknown to Bashkeem and the crews of the Jenelisa, Sun Flash, Wave Rider, and Star Sheen.

"There is a legend, Admira," commented Bashkeem, "that at the place that marks the terminus of our sea a great mountain stands in salute. In the far distance, framed against the setting sun, I glimpse the shadow of a tall mountain. Perhaps we are arrived... at the end of the world."

CHAPTER 9

MANY SHIPS IN BATTLE

"I count *fourteen* war barges!" exclaimed Admira with disbelief sounding in her voice. "*Why...* do we happen upon such a large Egyptian fleet at the very end of the known sea?"

"In a place where they can have no business sailing, it is unimaginable that Egyptian vessels would expend so much energy and expense to hunt us down," replied Bashkeem. "But, to be safe we will turn away our vessels; I am confident that we can outrun them."

Four Troyan pirate ships broke northward.

"The Egyptian vessels continue passage westward. They do not turn to follow us. Captain, you were before correct; we are not the prey that the Egyptians pursue."

"Hmpf. Mark my words, Admira, those many ships are on the hunt for something... big."

"Would not you say, Captain, that those barges are the most impressive we have anywhere seen? Not only large, they are very sturdily built. How is it that our vessels hold no interest for the admiral of those fourteen ships?"

The eyes of Admira lit large as she added, "My curiosity is awakened. I want to know what new conquest has drawn this powerful Egyptian fleet into the unknown waters of this far place, where no vessels trade."

"You are... right Admira. Something fateful is soon to happen. We will at a safe distance follow the flotilla that here presents, and at the same time prepare ourselves for combat. It may be that a handsome pirate's pay awaits.

"By the way, I much value your presence on board the Jenelisa. The older Troyan princess is observant, listens closely, and learns fast."

"For my part, Sir Bashkeem, I am glad my younger sister commands the last barge that we captured. That gives me the opportunity on this barge to learn more from an exceptional sea captain."

Attack on Phoenician Barges

To the west a convoy was sighted. When the line of fourteen large Egyptian barges formed into a wide blocking crescent, it was made clear to all that the five barges sailing eastward lacked the opportunity to turn their vessels right or left to escape impending battle.

After crossing an immense sea on the return voyage from the land of the white herd of unicorns, Admiral Zoumar's fleet confronted an overwhelming force. On the masts of five Phoenician barges battle flags unfurled.

Captained by Avalcar, the admiral's barge repositioned to follow behind a wedge made by the other four Phoenician vessels. The precious sheets of blue gold carried in the hold of the flagship, were at any and all costs to be protected.

"I ask you Avalcar," inquired the admiral, "since they surely came out to meet us, how on earth did the Egyptians find out that a Phoenician fleet was now returning from across the unknown sea?"

"I *cannot* explain their presence here," responded the captain. "I can only presume that Egypt declared recent war on Phoenicia; that is the only reason for them to attack us. If not at war, why would they challenge our freedom at sea... when our country has always sought only peaceful trade with Egypt?"

"The four ships to the north of the Egyptian fleet fly pirate flags!" alerted the watch.

"First Egyptians, and now pirates," fumed Zoumar. "Can this day get any worse for us?"

Egyptian vessels engaged in battle the Phoenicians.

Zoumar's barges could turn more sharply than the larger and more heavily weighted Egyptian vessels. With the benefit of more experience and seasoning, against long odds the captains and crews of the Phoenician barges at first held their own. Although the Phoenician sailors rowed hard and fought valiantly, there remained little doubt that for the badly outnumbered fleet of Admiral Zoumar, the day would inevitably come to be lost.

"Bashkeem, the encroachment by Egyptian vessels upon the Phoenician flagship barge tells us something," said Admira.

"I agree," responded Bashkeem. "It is apparent that the Egyptians know what they are looking for; their intent is to rob the cargo carried on the Phoenician flagship."

"What do you think Prince Ermir?" inquired Bashkeem as he met with four Troyan royalty. "Do we stand by and only observe? Once they have beaten the Phoenicians, will the Egyptians turn on us?"

"Victory over the Phoenicians will only strengthen Egyptian resolve to destroy Troyan pirates," answered Ermir. "If we do not do something now, surely the Egyptians will hunt us down with the same aggression they demonstrate against the Phoenician barges. I say that we have no choice but to sail in support of the Phoenicians. Committing our four vessels to the fray will better the odds of battle from fourteen ships against five, to fourteen against nine. The Egyptian vessels will have to worry about fighting a battle on two fronts. Hah! When we have triumphed, we will lay claim to the best Egyptian barge left afloat!"

"And the one captured will be mine to captain," observed Admira.

"Just remember, sister," observed Resi, "that in a fierce naval battle where mariners on each side know too well the consequences of defeat, ships on the losing side are often unsalvageable. Rammed ships tend to sooner or later... sink."

"Do we all concur with Ermir's call to action?" inquired Bashkeem. Agreement was unanimous. After a strategy was decided, Troyan pirate captains returned to their vessels and readied quickly their crews for battle.

The songs of bow maidens signaled that the wind had changed direction, and increased in strength. With filled sheets the Troyan fleet would from the north smash into the Egyptian formation. In the lead of three following pirate ships the Jenelisa sailed into battle.

Bashkeem happened to glance at the youthful former barge captain pulling hard at his oar.

"I must say, Olsi, that your arms look well-muscled."

"For the first time in my life I possess both physical and mental strength," responded Olsi.

"You and I this day wear the same uniform, the dress of an Egyptian sailor. On this sea who does Olsi fight for?"

The reply took Bashkeem by surprise, "I fight for the best sea captain. I fight for the winner!"

"On this barge I have seen the young Olsi develop into a strong and disciplined man." That said, Bashkeem turned and walked away, but not before smiling big at the youth.

Upon seeing the fast approach of newcomer barges sailing directly at the line of Egyptian warships, captains on each side guessed what awaited. Since for their overwhelming numerical superiority the Egyptian vessels neither required, nor wanted assistance, the four interloper barges presenting pirate standards would in battle take the side of the Phoenician vessels.

"We have allies!" shouted Admiral Zoumar. "The addition of four friendly vessels brings us chance of victory!" The crew of the flagship broke out in a loud cheer that became contagious and spread to the other Phoenician ships.

When six Egyptian barges turned to face his pirate fleet, Bashkeem muttered to himself, "I shall now see of what are made my princes and princesses."

Commander Bashkeem and Captain Resi joined the strength of one vessel to another. Together their two ships clipped both fore and aft an Egyptian barge. When the barge began to list the rowers on one side of the Egyptian craft had to extend their oars three times over for each rowing motion from the other side. Upon seeing the enemy craft crippled, two pirate crews cheered with enthusiasm bred by accustomed victory, and as well by the anticipation of eventual plunder from the listing Egyptian vessel.

Ermir and Ermal worked a strategy where their two barges feinted an attack upon one vessel, and then broke away to ram the true victim of their tactics. When the targeted Egyptian barge suffered piercing hits on both sides, timbers broke. The enemy vessel came to flounder in the water.

"That barge no longer accosts us!" shouted Ermir to his crew.

Bashkeem was elated that his fleet of four pirate ships had so quickly garnered victory over two Egyptian war barges. Surely he had taught well the art of sailing to the princes and princesses. However, upon finding that Ermal's barge, the Wave Rider, no longer remained seaworthy, his elation did not sustain. To make matters worse, after the Phoenicians crippled three Egyptian war barges, two rammed Phoenician vessels were fast sinking.

Upon seeing that, Bashkeem nodded gravely his head and muttered, "It is a terrible loss for the Phoenician commander to so soon lose almost half his fleet. But at least the sinking of his two ships is offset by his fleet's destruction of three Egyptian vessels."

The Jenelisa took on Ermal and his crew.

Three Phoenician and three Troyan ships now faced nine Egyptian vessels.

Bashkeem signaled to Ermir and Resi to keep fighting the rearmost ships in the Egyptian fleet; the Jenelisa would penetrate the fierce inner part of the battle. As he threaded his way toward the Phoenician barge that had become the focus of the fight, Bashkeem could see little that made the flagship to be more valuable than the other two remaining ships bearing the Phoenician standard.

"The flagship's precious cargo is not mounds of grain or anything stored in barrels," muttered Bashkeem. "While not in any way visible, the cargo carried in that ship must be extraordinarily valuable to have become a magnet for the Egyptians. Hmpf! I say that the treasure that the Egyptians covet has to be gold more pure, or jewels more precious, than any found in lands bordering this sea. If through our actions the treasure of the vessel is not lost, by heavens we will lay claim to half of what is held in the hold of the Phoenician flagship."

Bashkeem turned to the sailors on board the Jenelisa and shouted, "Once we save the Phoenician flagship, we will demand a payment of gold and silver greater than you can imagine! Fight hard and do not relent!"

Three enemy ships achieved the position of the Phoenician flagship. Two pirate and two Phoenician vessels positioned themselves to prevent the remaining six Egyptian barges from entrancing the inner part of the battle.

Admiral Zoumar could not believe that only a short time past his heart had soared at the sight of the great mountain that entranced his home sea. Now, in spite of the destruction of five Egyptian barges, all looked to be lost. While Egyptian ships continued their attacks the one consolation he would carry to a watery grave, if he must succumb, was that against overwhelming enemy forces his men had fought with no lack of courage and no stop of strength. As battle engulfed his flagship, Zoumar was riveted with one thought... was this day to mark the end of his illustrious career in the navy of his homeland.

When Egyptians boarded the flagship, Avalcar lost control of the barge containing in its hold the priceless sheets of blue gold. The Phoenician captain quickly found himself besieged by four Egyptians slashing swords. The thrusts and parries of his own blade bought him precious moments, but his attackers were unrelenting. Backed into a corner Avalcar waited for the worst. Of a sudden the Egyptian soldiers readying to pounce upon him, were dislodged.

"We two horses will not permit our captain to falter!" neighed Lucareins.

"I find now that my great equines are both pleasure *and* war horses!"

"Climb upon my back!" ordered Hammereins. "Together we will fight to save the precious blue gold!"

The crews commanded by Captain Avalcar and Commander Bashkeem linked together. In the Phoenician tongue Bashkeem yelled to Admiral Zoumar, "Sir, we need a miracle to hold on and sustain!" Alerted to a commotion, Zoumar looked around to see the advance of Avalcar and the two horses.

"Avalcar," the admiral yelled loud, "I am told we need a miracle. You and the hooves of your horses must provide one!"

"That we shall!" exclaimed Avalcar.

Bashkeem swung himself onto the back of Lucareins. Egyptian sailors fighting on the deck of Avalcar's flagship now faced two mounted warriors. While one kicked with rear hooves, the other smashed into enemy foot soldiers with shoulders and front hooves. An Egyptian warrior that menaced one horse and rider, was by the other horse and rider cut down.

The fighting of the horses and their mounts came to be worth dozens of ordinary fighting men. What is more, the gameness of the horses in battle became infectious; Phoenicians and Troyan pirates took heart and began to surge forward. Bashkeem smiled when he found Olsi with sword in hand defending the side of his horse.

"I told you I would fight for the winner of this battle!" shouted Olsi. "Mounted on a war horse, Bashkeem is winning!"

Pushed back, the Egyptians were at last cleared from the deck of Zoumar's flagship. That accomplished, the two horses and their riders jumped to Bashkeem's vessel and sowed destruction into the ranks of the Egyptians that had forced their way onto the Jenelisa.

The battle was carried to the decks of all three Egyptian vessels. By the time the shouts of battle died away, three Egyptian barges had been set afire.

Sinking to his knees, Admiral Zoumar gave thanks for deliverance procured when all looked to be lost.

"The flagship breaks apart!" shouted Avalcar. "The magic gold will be lost to the depths!"

Grasping immediately that the situation was dire, Bashkeem raced to clear space to pile the precious sheets on the deck of the Jenelisa. There was scarcely time for the last sheet of gold to be moved and stacked before Zoumar's flagship was by pounding waves broken in two. Along with two horses, the crew of Zoumar was compacted tightly onto Bashkeem's barge.

When the Egyptian commander found that his fleet's three largest barges had been sunk in the fight with the flagship of Zoumar, and two more crippled by the Sun Flash and the Star Sheen, he abandoned the fray. Under the pallor of defeat the four Egyptian barges that remained seaworthy began long journey back to the great port of Egypt. They would report to the pharaoh that their downfall had been the powerful magic possessed by the Phoenicians.

Clinging to boards and timbers, Egyptian survivors paddled toward where stood the pillar mountain.

At the end of the day the magic blue gold had miraculously been made safe. Calm restored to a sea beset by much havoc and bloodshed.

Two Fleets Made One

No matter how the admiral thought to organize his sailors that had survived the fierce sea battle, they would not all fit onto his two remaining vessels. Every available space on Bashkeem's three barges came to house Phoenician sailors.

Deciding it was advantageous, Zoumar and Avalcar requested to sail on Bashkeem's ship instead of on either of their two over-crowded vessels.

"Princess Admira, her brother Prince Ermal, and I will be delighted for you to sail with us," responded Bashkeem to the petition. "And, I insist that your two brave war horses remain as well on this vessel."

"If I had a captured Egyptian vessel to command," added Admira smiling, "I would be delighted to have Phoenician officers to sail with me."

"You will get your own vessel, Admira," responded Bashkeem, "unfortunately, that does not today happen. The urgency to quickly transport the magic gold to Phoenician shores precludes any salvage operation of a crippled Egyptian barge."

"Oh well," sighed Admira, "the Egyptian barges are anyway too big for me to steer."

To prepare themselves for the voyage to Phoenicia, Bashkeem and the four Troyan royals met on the Jenelisa with Zoumar and Avalcar.

"The cup of water I hold is drawn from the tightest barrel I have ever come upon," remarked the admiral. "Not a single drop of water seeps out."

"I am a sailor that thinks tight barrels are the most important freight that a barge can carry," replied Bashkeem.

"You *just* might be right about that," agreed Zoumar.

"Sir Bashkeem," spoke next Avalcar, "your barges recently plied these waters. Do you think we shall confront more enemy ships before we reach Phoenicia?"

"We are now a fleet of five ships manned by tough, experienced, top-notch sailors. Because Egyptian naval officers cannot so quickly ready another powerful fleet, they find themselves unable to pursue us more. During the past one hundred days we have seen few pirate ships, and none that would dare to attack this fleet. I am confident that on this voyage of return we will confront no more warfare from either Egyptians, or *true* pirates."

"Your words give comfort, Commander Bashkeem," responded Zoumar with his smile broadening. "Having traveled thousands of leagues beyond the imagination of the people on the shores of this my home sea, I now want nothing more than to deliver the blue gold to my king, and then to enjoy a long respite from the responsibilities of command."

"Sir, I am sorry to inform that your king will conclude you have become far too valuable to be given leave of rest," cautioned Ermal.

"I like that you have a sense of humor, Prince Ermal, or perhaps it is rather a gift for exaggeration. Yet if that should turn out to be the case, I will immediately inform my king that Captain Avalcar is twice as valuable a sailor as am I."

"And if that is what my admiral is found to answer to our king," interjected Avalcar, "then I will set the record straight and tell his majesty that the most valuable combatants that fought on many decks of battle... were my horses Hammereins and Lucareins."

To Admira this statement sounded less than fair. "Hah! Captain Avalcar, did not my sister Resi and I fight valiantly against the Egyptian navy?"

"I am quite sure that it was I who fought the hardest," quipped a grinning Ermal.

"To be sure, brother, we all know that the loss of the Wave Rider was the fault of its rounded prow, and not your captaincy," needled Admira.

"I had before much hope for that innovative concept," replied a frowning Ermal.

"Ermal and each of his three siblings fought with courage and brilliance," offered Avalcar.

"And for that I will recount to my king the fierceness with a sword shown by the two royal sisters and their brothers," affirmed Admiral Zoumar. "Still, try as I might I cannot fathom the information source for the Egyptian spymaster. How could the Pharaoh's Navy come to know that we were at this time to be found at the narrow entrance to this sea? Not even our Phoenician king has any idea where we now sail."

"Admiral Zoumar," mused Avalcar, "the explanation I have for the start and finish of yesterday's conflict is two-fold. Magic was first used to discover our presence. Magic then secured our rescue."

"Avalcar," responded the admiral, "when you find out what strange magic led our fleet to battle against fourteen Egyptian barges, and then came to our salvation in the form of Troyan pirates, by all means please share it with me."

Zoumar brought the conversation back to Bashkeem, "Commander, I still cannot believe the fineness of the wooden barrels that service your craft."

Bashkeem and four royal brothers and sisters decided that the honor of command must go to the most senior naval officer; the five vessel fleet of Phoenician adventurers and Troyan pirates came to sail under the command of Zoumar.

Bashkeem and the four Troyans quickly won the admiral's trust. The friendly way a few words of conversation were phrased carried much meaning to the officers and sailors of the combined fleet.

Even more than the honor of command, Admiral Zoumar relished the satisfaction of teaching the art of seamanship to the promising young naval officers of Troy. Bashkeem and the royal personages made a class of five students that did the one thing a good teacher always requires, they asked questions that made Zoumar think new thoughts and develop new approaches to better connect concepts together.

"I was certain that the sea was to receive my body," reflected Avalcar as he one evening stood with the two horses that had helped to win victory. "Amidst the fray of battle I gave myself only moments to live."

"Two horses, long ago touched by the blackmane's horn, combined well with the magic of your blue gold sword," neighed Lucareins in reply.

"I was told that unicorn magic rewards selfless love, and that the benefit of blue gold magic directs to hearts that are ever truthful. But I find it paradoxical that love and truth should excel on a watery field of battle where torrents of blood are made to flow," responded Avalcar.

"Had you and Bashkeem presented your swords of blue gold in the valley where I was born," whinnied Hammereins, "my horse herd would have survived. I cannot express how saddened I am that great evil caused the destruction of so many mares and colts."

"From this battle I will learn that no matter how high the cost in blood and suffering," responded the Phoenician captain, "love and truth must come to bear on matters of power, avarice, and boundless hatred. Otherwise just like your horse herd, all true hearts will come to be vanished from the earth."

"There is one thing else to consider," neighed Hammereins. "Being to us neither friends nor allies, it would have been convenient for the Troyan pirates to have disregarded our distress. Knowing that we were outnumbered by fourteen vessels to five, they still chose to risk their lives to better the odds to fourteen ships against nine. That shows that no matter what the cost, love and truth do not stand aside when great evil is perpetrated."

"The Troyans had before seen the destruction brought to their homeland by Egyptian raiders," added Avalcar. "With that foreknowledge they risked their very lives and took a stand so that our Phoenician mariners did not come to share the same wretched fate that befell Troy. In so doing, the consequence of love and truth was to bring justice."

Night after night newly hung curtains of stars sparkled delicate descendant light on five barges sailing eastward a great sea.

CHAPTER 10

PHOENICIA REGAINED

Throughout a long military career the admiral had worn a serious cast to his face. No longer could that be said; the personality of Zoumar had... warmed.

Having sailed year upon year under the command of the admiral, Captain Avalcar had never before observed his leader to enjoy days aboard ship more than on the last part of the voyage that crossed their native sea in direction home to Phoenicia. It took some time for Avalcar to become used to being treated by the admiral, as fondly as a son.

One day a new realization came to Avalcar. This last chapter of good cheer, the closing days of sail on their long voyage to a new continent and back, had come to change not only Zoumar, but also to change his own sense of fate and destiny.

"Admiral, as I watch how well the royal four of Troy learn from you the art of seamanship, I think that there is to become written another chapter in our friendship with them."

"I had, Captain Avalcar, not thought on that. But now that you raise the possibility, I would not disagree with you. After all that has happened since the pirates of Troy sighted our returning Phoenician ships, you and the royal four are young enough to long remain connected to each other."

News of the combined fleet's arrival preceded them. With bugles sounding, and colorful banners waving in the sea breeze, an escort of a dozen Phoenician barges welcomed home their admiral. Phoenician dignitaries found that the decks of the barges bearing the admiral and his crews had been made to shine; the five vessels absolutely sparkled with cleanness.

Zoumar and his sailors found their home port thronged by cheering Phoenicians.

A color guard and drum corps escorted the admiral toward the main gate of the capital city. With Hammereins and Lucareins at his side, next walked Avalcar in the lead of four yoke of oxen pulling two wagons laden with sheets of blue gold. After followed five Phoenician barge crews. Bashkeem, Prince Ermir, Prince Ermal, Princess Admira, and Princess Resi came next. Because the story of the heroic rescue carried out by Bashkeem and the Troyan royalty had immediately become everywhere known, the crowds lining the parade route cheered loudly. When a voice that carried well shouted, "The princesses are *beautiful!*" the cheeks of Resi and Admira colored rosy. Behind Bashkeem and the four royals walked four companies of mariners representing each vessel in the Troyan fleet, including the one lost to the sea.

Upon entering the western gate of Byblos the beat of the drum corps began to sound a celebratory rhythm that signified victory in battle. In response to the joyful drumming Avalcar gave Hammereins and Lucareins nods of encouragement. With heads and tails held high, two riderless horses began to prance.

"Horses dance!" was shouted. "On their own the two horses are dancing!"

Craning their necks to better observe, people applauded the sight of Hammereins and Lucareins prancing to the exact beat of the drum roll. Feeling his spirit moved, Avalcar matched his paces to the stilted cadence stepped by the hooves of his horses.

Upon reaching the royal palace the procession condensed and reformed. Standing on the raised terrace fronting the plaza, and wearing a robe decorated in fine blue gold, the monarch addressed the gathered throng.

"Your king gives thanks for the safe return of our valiant sailors! I congratulate Lord Admiral Zoumar for the successful accomplishment of all that I had commanded of him. Across waters unknown the admiral traveled unimaginably far. Upon providing rescue to the herd of magic unicorn horses, our fearless admiral brought back to Phoenicia the blue gold needed for armor and swords to protect our soldiers in battle. So long as Phoenicia rules the depths of the sea, this great voyage shall not be forgotten!"

The tall king that looked to be about fifty years old, with thinning shoulder length dark hair and an unthinning waistline, motioned for a pillowed sword to be brought to him.

King Barsuna beckoned Zoumar to approach, embraced the shoulders of the returned hero, handed the beautifully wrought sword to the admiral, and proclaimed "Accept this elegant sword which signifies the love and esteem that I and my people bear for you and your courageous mariners!" When Zoumar turned to face the people massed in the plaza, and bowed low, the roar of the crowd grew intense.

The admiral signaled to Avalcar to lead the two horses up the steps, and join him. More cheers sounded as one by one the sheets of blue gold were carried up the steps of the palace and displayed for all to see.

The admiral next motioned for his friends from Troy to approach.

After climbing steps Bashkeem, Ermir, Resi, Ermal, and Admira bowed to the cheering crowd. Without asking permission, Admiral Zoumar presented to Bashkeem the precious sword he had only just received. At that gesture an unmistakable frown was seen to pass over the face of the king.

"My king," said the admiral in loud voice, "without the military aid provided by these princes and princesses of Troy, and their commander Bashkeem, I would not now be here with you. My body would instead be corrupting in the lowest depths of the sea, and this precious blue gold would serve only to glisten the sea floor. To these five representatives of Troy, a city not long ago destroyed by Egyptian raiders, we owe the celebration felt this day throughout Phoenicia."

As the king tepidly joined the clapping of hands in recognition of the Troyans, Avalcar watched the royal frown to deepen. The Phoenician captain had the thought that Barsuna would make Zoumar, and perhaps himself, to pay dearly for the attention given to Troyans that the king had not before met.

"Since how long past does the king wear clothing decorated in blue gold?" muttered Avalcar. "That precious metal was ever and only meant to be in the service of the military for armor and swords."

"We have long acknowledged that surrounded by enemies, the Kingdom of Phoenicia has no friends," spoke again the king. "That said, to these Troyans we give friendship. This night the finest food and wine will be served to our own heroes, and to our illustrious guests."

The formalities of the welcome ceremony ended.

"This day was supposed to be about me and *my triumph,*" fumed the king as he re-entered the palace, "not about Troyan pirates. I scarce before heard mention of the city of Troy, and I will do my utmost to never hear said anything more about that desolate place."

Following a banquet that had been that night hosted more by Zoumar than by the still resentful king, the Troyan royals paid the price for the admiral's commendation and his turnaround gift of a sword to Bashkeem, that was not so intended by the king. The Troyans were ordered into indefinite quarantine. For good measure the king included the two foreign horses in the quarantine, insisting that the equines be daily inspected for the outbreak of disease. Although technically not imprisoned, the Troyans were sequestered within the Old Garrison. The aging fortress that had long guarded the waterfront contained barracks, stables, and a plaza floored in dirt and grass.

"About issues of public health I do know something," remarked Admira to Bashkeem.

"She does at that," affirmed Ermal.

"So I ask you what good is a disease quarantine of us Troyans, when those Phoenicians with whom we lived aboard ship for twenty days roam freely throughout the city? And does the king not know that any contagion brought onto Troyan ships would have already manifested itself during our previous time of piracy?"

"You make good points, Admira," agreed Bashkeem. "But for now there is little that we can do to change our lodgings. Although we are deprived of free movement, the critical thing is that we are here closeted together." Following the lead of their commander, the Troyan princes and princesses refused to worry more about their sudden change of fortune.

Admiral Zoumar saw to it that the Troyan pirates suffered no want for anything. The words of friendship and loyalty, spoken by Zoumar on the terrace of the palace, were every day after felt deeply by the captains and crews of the Troyan pirate vessels.

Several things, including frequent visitations, transpired to make the relaxed days of quarantine to pass quickly. Admiral Zoumar, Captain Avalcar, and the rank and file of the Phoenician barge crews that had fought side by side with the Troyans, spent much time gathered in the garrison eating bread and goat cheese, and toasting each others' health. To a man Zoumar's sailors recognized that the Troyans had made possible the gift of the blue gold that would help to win future battles for Phoenicia, and that would ultimately serve to save the lives of many soldiers and sailors.

The two foreign horses provided another reason for the sentence of quarantine to not drag interminably for the Troyans and their crews. The horses needed, and wanted, daily exercise. Understanding the uniform animal language that Zoumar, Avalcar, and the Phoenician expeditionaries had across the sea been gifted by the touch of unicorn horns, the horses were appreciative and communicative for the attention they received.

Hammereins and Lucareins took much pleasure in equine feats of athleticism. Upon seeing two men box each other within a ring bounded by a rope, the horses decided to do the same. The sight of two horses boxing out front hooves gloved in cloth bindings, while circling each other jumped up on back legs, was so extraordinary that crowds of soldiers and sailors, followed soon enough by common people, came to perch on the walls and walkways of the old fortress to cheer and admire.

Upon observing barricades, hurdles, and Bashkeem's barrels positioned across the garrison's plaza to form twin obstacle courses for pairs of pirate sailors to race through, the horses became intrigued. Soon one stallion was racing his brother stallion through an obstacle course.

When Troyan pirates danced jigs around evening campfires in the fortress, the horses were called upon to be given their turn. The crowds that came to see the athletic daytime feats of the two equines lingered into the evening to marvel at the dancing form of the horses. As the fame of Hammereins and Lucareins spread wide, the fact that the names of the stallions corresponded to the now celebrated legacies of Sergeant Hammerclaw and his apprentice blacksmith Lucars... came to be everywhere known.

That the Troyans had prevented the Egyptian navy from commandeering the blue gold treasure, continued to be praised and honored. From that perspective the king's provision of indefinite quarantine came to be viewed as harsh recompense for the heroic service done for the kingdom of Phoenicia.

Zoumar, Avalcar, and the five Troyan leaders were summoned to elaborate on what the king found to be a curious alliance.

"How did Troyan pirates find out that Zoumar's fleet had re-entered their home sea?"

"A tremendous gale blew us far westward of where we aspired to continue our piracy," answered Bashkeem. "We had no idea that we were going to come upon either Phoenician, or Egyptian vessels."

"If not the Troyans," continued Barsuna, "then what spy leaked to the Egyptians the news of the return of the Phoenician expedition? For how else could the Egyptians have come to know when Admiral Zoumar would return? Not even I knew that my expedition to the unicorn hold had at last regained its home sea."

"My king," responded the admiral, "since we did not sight a single vessel from the day we left the new continent, until the day the Egyptian fleet found us, there is no way that anyone could have known that your expedition had returned. Our homeward passage had been long delayed by a horrendous gale that blew us far off course northward. More than that, had the Troyan vessels not been driven off course by the more recent storm just mentioned by Bashkeem, they would never have come upon us. For the rest of my days I will thank the heavens for the fortuitous happenstance of two storms, disconnected in time, that brought our two fleets together at precisely the needed moment."

"We entered the battle," added Ermal, "because after the destruction they brought to Troy, I and my brother and sisters hate the Egyptians that killed our father."

"We would not see Egypt strengthened at the expense of Phoenicia, or any other realm," seconded Admira.

Little by little the king's distrust of the Troyans abated. It finally became obvious to Barsuna that the Troyans were, indeed, who they said they were. The king's spies had verified that Egyptian war barges had some moons previous raided and destroyed the new city of Troy. One spy had even identified Ermir, Resi, Ermal, and Admira as precisely the offspring of the fallen king of Troy.

The day after the long interrogation the king and an entourage of military favorites entered the Old Garrison and witnessed for themselves the athleticism and intelligence of the two wondrous foreign horses. Barsuna surveyed fortress walls filled everywhere with spectators not come to celebrate their king, but to cheer two magic horses performing for Avalcar. At that moment the king coveted the two athletic horses that could talk to Avalcar, prance so well as to dance, and exhibit intelligence extraordinary. For one additional reason Barsuna coveted the two alien horses. With his own eyes he saw that Hammereins and Lucareins could race through an obstacle course as fast as any horse in the kingdom.

For the king, the issue at hand was that the faces of the common people perched above him were beaming... at the heroic sea captain. The people understood that the horses belonged to Avalcar. It was said that the captain had made great sacrifices to bring the two horses back with him to Phoenicia. Not a natural horseman, and further not coveting himself the two equines, Admiral Zoumar would have no difficulty supporting the ownership claim of his protégé, regarded as one of the best horsemen in the military. The matter of Hammereins and Lucareins merited further thought by Barsuna.

The day following Barsuna's visit the Troyan royalty, Bashkeem, Avalcar, and Zoumar found themselves before a king seated comfortably on his cushioned throne. With their master quietly stood Hammereins and Lucareins.

"While you remain in my kingdom you will to Phoenicia declare an oath of loyalty," announced Barsuna to the Troyans. "After your oath is given, you will be permitted to travel where you will in my dominion. Not in possession of my written permission for departure, you are forbidden to leave Phoenicia."

"So long as we here reside we pledge loyalty to Phoenicia," answered Ermir for his brother, two sisters, and Bashkeem.

"Good! Now, Admiral Zoumar, I am going to reappoint you as commander of my military forces. My soldiers and sailors honor your unfailing service to our country, *and* they respect you. Hmph! I will hear nothing more of you retiring... *to tend cows.* Year after year we are more threatened not just by the Egyptians, but also by the Hittites who have emerged to become a very powerful kingdom on our north. I trust, Admiral, that I make myself clear. The army *needs* you."

Zoumar bowed low. From his frown, and his pale demeanor, it was evident that the king's orders were not the ones the admiral wanted to hear.

"Thank you, Captain Avalcar, for honoring my request to bring your foreign horses to the palace. Is it true that the two talking horses obey only you?"

"Yes, my Lord. Although their loyalty is not easily bestowed, they have chosen me to be their master."

"Surely, Avalcar, there must be some way that these horses might be made to reside in my royal stable? I can provide them the richest rations of hay and grain that can be anywhere found."

From the king's gestures toward them, and as well from some of the king's words that they could understand, the horses knew that they were being discussed. Neither stallion liked the facial expressions or tone of voice of the king. Neighing, rearing up, and kicking out hind legs Hammereins and Lucareins began to demonstrate their displeasure.

"Errhmm..." the king cleared his throat, "Alright, so it is. Hmph, there is another matter, Avalcar. I will have you to pertain to my military council, and in that regard you are to lodge here at the palace. And I require one thing else. Your horses are to accept myself and my sons in their saddles. As the king I have the right to insist that your wondrous horses agree to be ridden, from time to time, by the royal household."

"While I shall remain your master," said Avalcar turning to the horses, "you will do me the favor of galloping on occasion with the king and one or the other of his two sons. Agreed?"

The horses shook sideways their heads, before relenting to nod heads up and down.

The king sent for his sons.

"Prince Maroun is a fine soldier and hunter," offered the king nodding his head toward his elder son. "My younger son Majit prefers painting birds... to killing them."

That evening, the last in the quarantine of the Troyans, Resi asked Avalcar what the two sons of the king were like.

"Both men of honor, the two are as different as night and day. On fields of battle the tall, slender, and dark-haired Prince Maroun has many times proven his courage. Absolutely fearless, the older prince has earned the respect of the army. He is not given to speaking unnecessary words."

"And the younger?" persisted Resi.

"The light-haired, clear-eyed, and solidly built Prince Majit is cut from different cloth than his older brother. Although I do not know him well, I am made to understand that Majit is not a friend of military discipline. He prefers to walk alone in the wilderness, where they say he can identify the call of every bird on wing. Because the athletic, smart, and well-spoken younger prince could quickly rise to prominent leadership, I will admit that his behavior is to me strange. However, as is often the case between an older and younger brother, Majit rejects the path taken by Maroun."

A Plea to the King

The four princes and princesses found time begin to weigh heavily on their hands, time that lent itself for fretting that no Egyptian vessels were presently being captured by their small pirate navy. Without command of more ships, the recapture of Troy remained distant and infeasible.

Walking in the plaza of the Old Garrison, that continued to be the Troyan place of lodging, Ermir complained to Bashkeem, "What is going on? I thought we would be given a warm welcome, receive a large reward, and then would be sent again on our way. Instead, I am not even permitted to board my own barge."

"Spies, whether Phoenician, Hittite, or Egyptian watch us," warned Bashkeem with a movement of his hand that signaled they should talk quietly.

"You are right, Bashkeem," answered Ermir. "The former Egyptian captain Olsi has noticed them. There is a certain artifice to their expression, or a certain accent that he can identify."

"Let me share my theory of what has happened."

"Please do, Bashkeem."

"The Egyptians and the Phoenicians had before established an uneasy peace that now after the naval battle for the blue gold, has come to be shattered. King Barsuna is ill-prepared to go to war with Egypt. And while still smarting from the defeat of the fleet they sent to commandeer the blue gold, the Egyptians are at this time more worried about Hittites than Phoenicians. It seems that you Troyans are a pawn in a bigger political game. It may be that the Egyptians are paying King Barsuna to keep your pirate barges from plying the sea. For the mighty Egyptian navy, we Troyan pirate captains have proven ourselves to be *more* than a mere nuisance."

The two men moved to the cooking fire to serve themselves a supper of savory vegetable stew.

"Ermir, I counsel patience," spoke on Bashkeem. "Let us find ways to flatter the king. If we poorly play Barsuna's game, it can consume years. Let us instead make the game come to us."

"I do not like to waste time, Bashkeem. There waits too much to do to re-establish Troy."

"This will not, Ermir, be a waste of time. We require allies at the royal court. We need to find a way to make ourselves useful to the king. Perhaps more than anything, we need to discover who our enemies are."

"Egypt did much damage to my country," reflected Ermir. "My heart will not rest until my eyes see Troy rebuilt. That said, Bashkeem, I count on you to one day understand well the board pieces we now play with the king."

"Events will turn in our favor. Our pieces will soon begin to advance."

Majit brought an invitation to the Troyan royals and Bashkeem to dine the next evening with the king.

"Very good, Prince Majit, we will be delighted to join you in the palace."

"And thank you, Prince Ermir, for accepting the invitation. My father has of late neglected you."

"Stay a little longer, Majit," said Resi. "Have a bowl of stew that I this afternoon prepared. I tell you that it is very tasty."

"Thank you, Resi. For the many in attendance tomorrow night, I will not then have much of a chance to converse with you and your siblings."

"So Prince Majit, I have heard that you love to spy on birds," continued Resi changing the direction of the conversation.

"I would rather study the habits of birds that I find to be both beautiful and graceful, and listen to their calls, than to hunt them," responded Majit with a slight smile. "I will allow that I draw them well."

"Perhaps you are the Phoenician that knows the most about birds?"

"Why no, Resi. There assuredly are many shepherds in this land that know far more about the habits of birds and animals than do I. Hmph! My father wishes that I knew less about birds, and more about warfare. But the shedding of blood repels me. Not me, but my brother is the natural born soldier."

Majit lowered momentarily his head, and then raised it to pursue more the conversation. "Young lady, what things do you like best? Do you draw?"

"I have come to love to sail. Bashkeem trained us to maneuver well a vessel on the sea, and all four of us found that for that we have talent. Can you imagine that Admiral Zoumar insists we four brothers and sisters are born sea captains."

"What else inspires you, Resi?"

"I love horses, and my sister and I both like to cook. The preparation of meat sauces requires a good sense of smell, and a delicate sense of taste regarding the best spices to use."

"These two young ladies are wonderful cooks," broke in Bashkeem. "During many nights both on land and sea, I have enjoyed their fish and lamb flavored to perfection."

"Something tells me that this stew will be the best I have ever tasted," responded Majit after elevating his bowl of stew to savor its aroma. "Again, thank you Resi for sharing it with me."

"Prince Majit," interjected Ermir, "please tell me how Phoenicia came to be so prosperous."

"Beset by a dry climate and thin soils, we became a nation of traders. Our blacksmiths that have remarkable skill in fashioning armor, weapons, and tools from the best mixes of metals, require many customers. Fortunately, our geography places us in a propitious place for trading goods all across the lands bordering our sea. Unfortunately, the place we inhabit is also very vulnerable to attack. In that regard the blue gold has helped to keep us safe from enemies found around us.

"Still, Ermir, the greatest treasure of Phoenicia is not its place by the sea, or the blue gold armor protecting the chests of its soldiers. Our true strength is the clever minds, strong hearts, and true tongues of our people."

"Zoumar and Avalcar are indeed honest men," affirmed Ermir.

"Because Admiral Zoumar has earned respect throughout our navy, young sailors fear and obey him. For his part, the forthright Captain Avalcar is known to ever speak the truth. Because he knows that neither would comply, my father the king dares not ask Zoumar or Avalcar to tell lies for him."

"You before mentioned briefly your brother," continued Resi.

"Proud of my brother, I place full trust in him to do his part to keep the land of Phoenicia well-guarded and prosperous. Nonetheless, we are but a small kingdom. The lands of our enemies extend twenty times greater than Phoenicia. Possessing talented warriors and a superb army, the Hittites have become a terrible threat to us. For his part, the pharaoh must be furious for the defeat of his fourteen war barges by Zoumar and you Troyans." Grown pensive, the young prince frowned.

"Majit, you in your own right are going to be an eminent prince," said Bashkeem with intent to cheer. "I value this conversation with you more than conversations I before had with governors in Egypt."

"I feel that in Majit I have found a new friend," said Ermir as he smiled at the Phoenician.

To each of the five with whom he had shared supper, Majit bowed. Thereupon into the descent of dusk he departed.

Having enjoyed several cups of wine before the arrival of his dinner guests, as he entered a hall full of prominent people the king was the next night in an expansive mood.

"I am entitled to be joyful! The success of the voyage of Admiral Zoumar has again made my kingdom safe. A thousand years ago our very first king, his name was Fahseed, sent the magic white herd across the ocean. With the unicorns, that king as well sent his grandson and granddaughter. Now I am the second Phoenician king to rescue the magic herd of unicorn horses. Even though my two sons absented from Zoumar's voyage, for this good deed surely the heavens will show favor upon my reign."

Applauding and cheering, military officers and merchants shouted for Zoumar to stand. The admiral motioned for Avalcar and Bashkeem to also stand and share in the accolades.

"Admiral, you are ever gracious to your officer colleagues," continued the king. "Tell our guests how you vanquished the colossus of the sea. Tell them how with the decks of your barges weighted by hundreds of unicorn horses, you defeated a thousand war canoes!"

Zoumar bowed to the king, pointed to his throat, coughed, and waved his hand in a gesture to indicate that he was in poor voice. For the obvious humility of the admiral the assembled guests clapped even louder.

"Is not the charm of these two young ladies unforgettable?" commented the king as he approached where his Troyan guests were seated. The large roomful of guests applauded politely in agreement. The cheeks of Resi and Admira colored pink.

"Should not these princesses stay in this land that has come to be crowned by their loveliness?" added the king.

"Your guests would know the excellence and strength of the blue gold sheets brought here by our venerable admiral," interjected Majit upon joining to where stood his father.

"Ahhh... yes, yes. Although it is hard to believe, I am told that the sheets of magic gold brought to our land by Admiral Zoumar are more pure than the original deposit that was once, so long ago, here found."

"Father," continued Majit, "how many soldiers have now been given swords and armor made from the newly gained treasure of blue gold?"

"Ermm... oh... well... many soldiers will come to wear new magic armor. Now fill my cup. For me this night has only begun!"

Majit walked his father back to his ornate chair where the king slumped down and began to nod off in drowsiness.

Flutes and stringed instruments played while food was served.

Well-wishers stopped by the table where Zoumar and Avalcar had newly seated themselves with Bashkeem and the four Troyans, and congratulated all for their seamanship and bravery. After the meal ended the reawakened king began to extol the virtues of his reign and the greatness of his rule.

Bashkeem squirmed uncomfortably in his chair. His conscience informed that in the presence of so many guests it would be less risky for him to raise a delicate subject, than for a member of the Troyan royal family to do so.

"Great King Barsuna, noble officers and merchants of this most prosperous coast... I raise this cup to toast the success of your merchant ships and navy!"

"Here, here!" answered delighted guests.

"Noble King, I thank you for the honor your invitation has this night bestowed upon us, and for the protection and hospitality you have all these past days afforded we poor representatives of Troy."

Again cries of approval were heard for the words of Bashkeem.

"That said, it is our humble petition that we may soon depart your most blessed kingdom to begin the hard work of rebuilding the suffering land of Troy."

These words were followed by silence in the great hall.

"I am not ready, Commander Bashkeem, that you should leave us," replied the king. "You must in our kingdom... stay long!"

For the benefit of the king's words polite applause was heard.

"My friends, in five days we once again celebrate the annual horse race around the walls of our beautiful capital Byblos," added the king changing the subject. "Our Troyan guests will surely want to witness this thrilling event."

"Avalcar," continued the king, "with your two foreign horses you must participate. Your entrance into the race will make the victory of my horses, errm the horses of the king's stables, the most impressive in our history. Come now, Captain Avalcar... we must have a wager!"

"Your majesty, it would not be right to wager these animals from a land so distant."

"Nonsense, Avalcar! If one of my stallions wins the race, your two equines become mine. If one of your two stallions emerges victorious, the two that from my stable race will become yours."

That was that. Bashkeem had raised the question that the Troyans had all wanted to be asked. The answer was not the one they wanted to hear. In the foreseeable future no permission to depart the land of Phoenicia would to the Troyans be given.

"The king took away the liberty of the princes and princesses of Troy," muttered Zoumar slumping down in his chair. "Now, the king will take for himself the horses so well-loved by Avalcar."

The admiral shifted his frame, rose to his feet, and cleared his throat. The hall became silent.

"Majesty, for more than one hundred days your incredible stallions have trained for this race. The two foreign horses brought here on my flagship have never even seen the course that is laid out."

The king waved off Zoumar's words.

"I *accept* the wager offered by my king!" exclaimed Avalcar found standing in the center of the great room. "Let the best horse win!"

CHAPTER 11

THE RACE OF THE WALLS

" Because the walls of long ago Byblos were poorly fortified," explained Avalcar the next morning in the Old Garrison, "in preparation for the approach of enemies fast horsemen were enlisted to ride the perimeter and sound the alert on all sides of the city.

"There was, however, no feasible land route on the east side of Byblos. So if raiders were found on the south or especially the southeast side of the city, the alert could be communicated faster to the north side by a horseman swimming the river that lies against the mountain beyond the east wall of our city, than by doubling back and traveling circuitously by land to the north side of the city. At least that is what was claimed. It may as well have been that the horse guards relished a good swim favored by a river current that flows northward. Competitive with each other, our horse guards came to view the sounding of the alert as a horse race around the four sides of the city. In that manner a race was born that came to each year be celebrated."

"How many horses participate?" inquired Resi.

"Four horses run in each of the four heats," answered Avalcar. "The winners of the four heats meet in the final. The horses race down the boulevard of the palace, out the west gate, and turn left. The horses continue south along the west half-wall, and then turn to follow eastward the southern wall of the city. The horses and riders enter the river that courses along the short-lengthed east wall of the city, swim northward until they emerge from the river, and continue the race along the city's north wall. The first horse to refind the gate in the middle of our western wall, re-enter the city, and break the thin woven cord hung before the palace wins the race."

"I would give *anything* to ride in that race!" exclaimed Resi.

Avalcar looked closely at Resi, "Hmmm, so you are... a horsewoman?"

"I was born to ride horses! Riding either saddle or bareback, I am as good as my brothers."

"Not true," corrected Ermal. "Resi rides better than me, and I ride better than Ermir."

"I tell you what, young lady," continued Avalcar, "later this afternoon I am going to take Hammereins and Lucareins on a ride around the walls of the city. Can you join me?"

Resi looked at Ermir. Her questioning look was by her older brother returned with a smile as he cautioned, "Just one thing sister. It would be better if you plug your hair under a turban and cover your mouth so that men do not stare at what the king said was your... *unforgettable charm.*"

"More than anything the king loves to win the Race of the Walls," continued Avalcar after taking another sip of spicy tea and another bite of flat bread. "Some say he loves winning that race more than he loves his own sons. Of course the king procures the best horses and riders in the land. So it is no surprise that one of his two horses invariably wins the race. His horses often place both first *and* second. Ha! The people say it is a good thing no one is allowed to enter more than two horses, otherwise Barsuna would own all sixteen horses entered in the race.

"Hah, harr! But not this time! The strength, speed, and intelligence of Hammereins and Lucareins will prove insurmountable for the king's fleet horses. This time it will be my two horses that place first and second."

"You, Sir," motioned Avalcar to Ermir, "your brother Ermal, Bashkeem, and Admira are invited to saddle up four of the garrison's horses and ride with myself and Resi mounted on Hammereins and Lucareins. We will together reconnoiter the route of the race."

"That works for me," returned Ermir. "Quite surprisingly, it just so happens that I have nothing better to do this afternoon."

Avalcar led the platoon of six horses and riders into Byblos. They stopped before the steps of the palace.

"To mark the start and finish line of the race, a thin cord is stretched from one to the other of these stakes," explained Avalcar. "The boulevard that stretches from here to the great gate of the city will be lined with thousands of cheering men, women, and children. The cheers and press of the great throng make it even more important for the horse and rider to concentrate on each other, and to communicate well. So, Resi, you and Lucareins will have to ignore the clamor."

Hammereins and Lucareins neighed that they understood the importance of the horse and rider becoming as one.

"Errr... wait! did you just say that I am to ride Lucareins?"

"This is not a favor to a princess," responded Avalcar. "I name Resi to be my rider... because I want to win."

"Here is Avalcar!" the captain had been recognized. "My money is on him to win the Race of the Walls!"

The famous captain tried to wave off the people that began to crowd around him; that effort brought him little success.

"Avalcar!" "Avalcar!" came one shout after another.

The noise brought the king to look out from the great terrace of the palace. If not genuine, his wave down to Avalcar looked to be at least friendly.

Avalcar and his companions pushed through the crowd and soon enough trotted out the gate of the city. They turned left and from the city gate followed the wall south to where it turned east.

"The southern wall is perhaps a half league long," observed Ermir.

"Yes, just like the northern wall," answered Avalcar. "The distance of the entire race is more than two leagues. That includes the half league round trip from the palace to the city gate and back again to the palace. The front and back walls of the city combine to be a little more than a half a league in length. The problem for the horses is that they have to run hard, swim hard, emerge from the river, and again run hard and long until they reach the finish line. Some very fleet horses arrive fast at the river. When their long swim is done they are exhausted, and have not the strength remaining to finish well the race. The river portion has the effect of making the race to be as much about endurance, as raw speed."

Six horses and riders approached the bridge spanning the river at the eastern terminus of the south wall.

"As you see," motioned Avalcar, "above this bridge, along the city wall there is no clean path down to the water. The horses must therefore cross the bridge, scramble down the river bank, and swim under the bridge. Entrance to the river is the most dangerous part of the race. Horses are sometimes injured negotiating too fast the steep bank down to the edge of the river."

Avalcar dismounted and walked Hammereins to the middle of the bridge where he spoke again, "I have always admired the placement of the great stones used to build this solid span. Look, Resi, the side walls of the bridge are as wide as one of my strides is long."

The captain quietly said something to Hammereins, who at that nodded excitedly up and down his head.

"What did you say, Captain, that so excited your horse?" inquired Resi.

"I asked Hammereins to run the race creatively; he likes that idea."

Watching the flow of water beneath the bridge Avalcar observed, "The current is today fast; I hope it flows equally fast on the day of the race."

"This horse moves strong in the water," noted Resi patting the neck of Lucareins. "I can feel his strength for swimming."

"Lucareins does indeed swim fast," affirmed Avalcar.

In acknowledgment of what was said, Lucareins kicked out rear hooves.

"In the distance you see the second bridge," pointed once more Avalcar. "The horse must swim under that bridge, reclimb the east bank, run across the bridge, and then race westward along the north wall. Because it is flat and proceeds on a straight roadway, the last part of the race promotes speed. I might add that people will be lined up and cheering along the entire route of the race."

"Even along the river?" asked Admira.

"Yes," answered Avalcar. "The custom is for boys and girls to sit wherever possible on the mountain side of the river. It is their job to encourage the swim of the horses with their riders."

On the evening before the race a new set of leggings and a new shirt were brought to Resi. Upon seeing the apparel she laughed and said, "So attired, no one will recognize my... *unforgettable charm.*"

"The treasure of your beauty will in the race be well-hidden."

"Why, Bashkeem, thank you for the compliment. What a kind thing to say. Your words relax me. Do you know that sometimes I feel that I am too athletic to be attractive to men?"

"Young lady, there is only one other woman in this city as attractive as you... and that is Admira."

Both princesses laughed as they patted the shoulders of the former slave of Egypt.

"Bashkeem, I am going to ask you something personal," said Admira. "Were you ever married?"

"No, Admira. As a valuable slave I was not permitted to enter the entanglements of matrimony. Of course about that I was not pleased. I must confess that as an alternative to enforced chastity, I married myself to science. Whatever I was called upon to build, I made up my mind to do it better than anyone. Hah! I will wager you never heard a confession like that before."

"So, Bashkeem," answered Admira, "that suggests that had you been permitted to marry, you would have also been a better husband than anyone."

"Sir, for my part I can only answer two things back to you," said Resi. "My heart sings because you are no longer a slave. I am as well truly thankful that you, a great engineer, are the commander of our small fleet. It is my opinion that you display the same class of seamanship as Admiral Zoumar. Oh... let me add a third thing. Admira and I both think that you would look even more handsome if you sported a beard."

"Huh! Then I am compelled to obey the wishes of two princesses. You will soon see Bashkeem to grow a beard."

Race

The day of the Race of the Walls shone in perfect sunshine. At the first light of morning people began to line the great boulevard and the walls of the city. Because most people could not remember the last time that the king did not win the race, Zoumar's horses were again heavily favored. Still, as a military horseman of notable fame, the underdog Avalcar had many admirers.

The novelty of the captain's two dancing horses heightened the interest in the race. Because the horses were named after the mysterious blacksmiths that mined the blue gold, about whose heroism many stories had spread, their entry into the race was made even more compelling. People anticipated a better race than usual, where the king's two horses often led the entire course of their heats, and also the final.

Hearing the many shouts of support for Avalcar, the king made sure to place the fleetest horses not his own in the two brackets where ran Avalcar's horses. The other entries in the first two brackets, where raced the king's horses, would be slower. Because the winners of all four brackets would in late afternoon run in the final, the extra rest provided to the winners of the first two heats constituted no small advantage.

Barsuna had contemplated paying riders to push Avalcar's foreign horses off the course of the race. The problem was that somehow, in some way, the wrong people always found out about his bribes. Against the war hero Avalcar, any cheating would have to be carried out with elaborate stealth.

Wearing a huge smile as he looked out from the terrace of the palace at the first group of four horses, the king nodded to each rider.

Drums rolled. A bugle sounded. The din of the crowd grew boisterous. With two horses placed at the ready on each side of him, a soldier swung his sword to cut the thin cord.

Four horses were off.

Flags along the walls of the city, one for each horse, would raise high to inform the crowd which horse led at that mark, which ran next, ran third, and which ran last.

At each marker position the flag of the palace raised first; the king's horse led the entire race. As his horse broke the cord stretched across the finish line, Barsuna reacquired his usual confidence.

"Take that, Avalcar!" exclaimed the king. "This day belongs... *to me!*"

The second heat of horses sped off. Once again at each course marker the first flag raised bore the colors of the royal crest. The king turned to his two sons seated with him, "My princes, this year the winner's cup will again to me belong. As will the second place finish!"

"While everything looks now for you promising," cautioned Maroun, "it is not the start of a day that counts; but the finish."

With a wine goblet gripped in his hand, Barsuna waved off his son's comment. Still, he could not help but shift and squirm in his chair. The observation of his older son did bother him.

The final two preliminary heats were to soon start. As they led their horses onto the boulevard, Avalcar and Resi were accompanied by Bashkeem. Suddenly, people everywhere in front of them began to surge onto the boulevard so that it became impassable.

"What is this commotion about?" inquired Resi.

"People are crowding around something that is moving on this grand avenue," answered Bashkeem.

"Look there! It is the king! But why on earth is he parading down the avenue in a chariot?"

To enhance her line of sight, Resi mounted Lucareins and observed, "The king's chariot is followed by one... no... two wagons. Young ladies perched on the wagons are giving something to the people pressing around."

Shouts rang out, "Wine!" "Free bread!"

"Can you believe that resplendent in a glorious gold gown the king commands wagons giving free food and drink to the crowd?" commented Resi to Avalcar and Bashkeem.

"King Barsuna has found a way to delay the last two preliminary races," answered Bashkeem with a sigh. "A long while will now pass before we race."

Avalcar was so displeased with this cheap trick that he wanted to swear an oath, but with a lady present he did not. Instead he forced a smile and said, "Hmph. Dwelling in the palace has permitted me to befriend the guards. Follow me, I know where there is plentiful grass and water for the horses. We will for awhile rest in the king's own garden."

Avalcar led the little company into an alleyway that ended at a back door of the palace. The captain inquired about the health of the children, whose names he fortuitously remembered, of the man guarding the entrance. The guard swung open a door that led to a well-watered green garden. The horses ate, drank from a fountain, and napped. While Bashkeem kept watch, Avalcar and Resi made themselves so comfortable that even they dozed off.

When the shouting and tumult outside the palace came no longer to be heard, Bashkeem awakened the little company. Two horses, two men, and one woman made their way back to the boulevard. It was not long before the king again appeared on the terrace of the palace.

Hammereins started the third preliminary race running easily. At each check point prior to the bridge the flag of Avalcar's military unit was the last to be raised. When the banners set at the halfway mark of the river swim raised, Avalcar's mount had moved into third place. For that the crowd gathered in the great plaza joined their voices to the distant cheering of children along the base of the mountain. Marker flags next informed that Hammereins was the second horse to emerge from the river. From the second bridge all the way to the entrance of the city, Hammereins ran a length behind the leader. Upon entering the long boulevard, Avalcar gave Hammereins free rein. The flag that raised at the finish line was emblazoned with the colors of Avalcar's army regiment.

Four horses and their riders readied for the last qualifying heat.

"Hammereins jumped directly from the bridge into the river," said Avalcar as he walked Resi toward the starting line. "That maneuver, which was much admired by the young spectators gathered on the mountain, bought us precious time and allowed Hammereins to close on the race leaders. Not happy about my doing that, the king will place files of soldiers against the walls of the bridge to force horses to run all the way across it.

Be careful, Resi. The other riders will surely try to push and impede your progress. Although your tall frame is slender, you are very strong. Do not let them bully you."

After some delay the four horses set to run in the last heat, stood ready.

The same as for Hammereins, the start of the race was for Lucareins slow. Resi was content to let the three horses ahead of her bunch together and run fast. At the first four markers, the banner of Avalcar's regiment was the last one to be raised. The other horses reached the first bridge with what appeared to be a ten length lead over Lucareins.

Resi found that Avalcar had been right about soldiers stationed at the sides of the bridge. But, like Avalcar the princess also had a trick up her sleeve. She pulled Lucareins to veer left and mount the wide stone rail of the span. Maintaining superb footing her horse ran along the siderail raised more than one pace above the bridge floor, until he jumped into the river.

When after swimming under the second bridge Lucareins emerged from the river, he had almost caught the other three horses. Resi was amazed that her mount was still not breathing hard. Along the northern wall Resi feinted to pass the leaders on the outside. Three horses moved to the outside of the roadway to block her. Before they realized what had happened, Resi had reined the very quick Lucareins to the inside. Her horse ran so close to the wall that Resi raised and stretched her legs behind her so that they would not be gashed by the rough finish of the city wall.

Once in the lead, Resi was not to be caught. Her problem was not her horse running too slow, but contrarily too fast. Try as she might she could not slow Lucareins down. Resi won her heat by twenty lengths. The crowd exploded in shouts and applause for a race they had never before seen run so fast.

The king immediately ordered that soldiers mount the stone guard rails of the first bridge so that no horse could jump over or off the railing into the river below. That done, Barsuna sank down in his chair. Resi's wide margin of victory was a terrible sign for his two horses. His hand was forced. Fortunately for him, the king had something up his sleeve for the final race that would crown the victor.

Bashkeem saw them first. The tails of the whips grasped in the hands of the king's two riders were embedded with little pieces of sharp metal. Those whips were not to slap the haunches of their mounts; they were rather intended to cut the hands, arms, and faces of Avalcar and Resi. The always observant Bashkeem called together the two riders and explained the danger of the whips carried by the king's horsemen.

"Resi, you and I will hang back for as long as we can," directed Avalcar. "If one of the king's riders brandishes his whip at you, let me handle it. I will not permit those metal points to cut your face. After all, unlike yours, my face is nothing special to look at."

Counting on Avalcar's horses to be spent from having run in the final two heats, the king did not long delay the beginning of the last and deciding race.

The crowd witnessed a slow start to the final run of the four winners of their heats around the capital city. Once in the lead, the initial strategy of the king's riders was to simply keep the following two foreign horses behind them. Three hundred horse paces before reaching the first bridge, one of the king's riders slowed and waved threateningly his whip.

Avalcar could not permit Hammerein's pace to be by one of the king's horses impeded, while the second of the king's horses raced fast away. Avalcar pulled behind the slowing horse. Hammereins feinted one way, the other, once more back, and then the fleet horse surged forward in a burst of speed that caught the whip in the wrong hand of the king's rider. Hammereins pushed his rear haunches into the belly of the opposing horse and forced it to stumble and loose footing. Only two lashes from the whip of the king's insolent rider achieved the purpose of cutting the arm of Avalcar. By the time the king's sacrificial horse had fully regained his footing, his rider's treacherous whip had become purposeless. Not only Avalcar, but Resi had sped ahead.

Just like the spectators, the numerous soldiers now arrayed on the bridge's sturdy sidewalls cheered for the captain and Resi as they passed over the foot stones of the span.

However, precious time had been lost in the confrontation with the whip. The king's fastest horse, a good swimmer, emerged first from the river and gained speed as his hooves clattered across the second bridge.

At every juncture along the northern wall the first marker banner raised high showed the king's horse, more rested and refreshed for having run in the first heat, protecting a notable lead. However, during passage of the western half-wall, the lead diminished. Upon entrance to the grand boulevard of the palace the king's horse held a lead of two lengths on Avalcar and three lengths on Resi.

Taking the race in her hands the Troyan princess commanded speed. Complying with the wish of his rider, Lucareins sped past Hammereins and caught the lead horse. The whip held in a hand of the king's rider came down on Resi's back. Resi slid to the side of her horse opposite the rider with the metal-flecked whip. She deftly pulled the reins to direct her horse to shift. As commanded, Lucareins banged hard into the king's horse. When Lucareins a second time shoved hard the king's horse, the sharp-edged whip fell to the ground.

With his head lodged under the neck of Lucareins, the king's steed galloped awkwardly. Two horses became locked together with their riders grasping at each other's reins. Avalcar immediately understood what Resi had done. She had made the race to be won by his horse Hammereins.

Avalcar thought fast. If he did not accept Resi's gift, her cuts and bruises would have come in vain, and perhaps neither Lucareins nor Hammereins would win. When Avalcar loosened the reins of Hammereins his horse flew past Resi and gained the finish by a length. At the last moment the head of Lucareins shoved past the nose of the king's horse to take second place in the race.

Made furious by the outcome of the Race of the Walls, Barsuna stomped about the royal terrace gesturing wildly with his hands. It seemed that no one in the crowd cared that the distraught king was protesting the result of the race. The multitude set before the palace began instead a tumultuous celebration for the victory of Avalcar.

The metal encrusted whip was retrieved. A youth mounted on the shoulders of a big man flecked it playfully against the back of another youth so mounted on another man's shoulders. The whip was thrown into the crowd and then tossed in return to the shouldered youths. The king's subterfuge had not worked. To make matters worse, he was now being publicly embarrassed by the sharp-edged whip he had ordered to be used as a covert weapon.

Avalcar was hoisted onto a spectator cart. The crowd simply could not get enough of the heroic military officer. Made to stand with Avalcar, Resi undid the wraps of her turban and let her long dark hair fall free. For that fortuitous surprise, the roar of the crowd became deafening. The very athletic woman that had disguised herself as a man, and that should have won the race, was also the very picture of beauty.

The four horses that had run the championship heat were made to stand side by side. The reins of the two horses that only a short time before had belonged to King Barsuna, were given to Avalcar.

The winner of the race was by exultant sailors and soldiers escorted to the steps of the palace. Midway up the palace steps, Avalcar stopped and motioned for Resi to join him. The king forced a smile as he embraced, albeit standoffishly, the captain and the princess. As he presented the winners to the cheering throng, and the trophy cup to Avalcar, the king made a show of waving and smiling. Upon the conclusion of the brief ceremony the king promptly disappeared into the palace. Admiral Zoumar, Maroun, and Majit came to stand beside not one, but what had clearly come to be two champions.

"You should have won the race, Resi," said Avalcar quietly.

"I returned the favor that you did me when before reaching the first bridge, you impeded the horse that tried to slow me down."

Those that had wagered on the king's horses could not help but smile as they paid their bets. After all, they had witnessed an exciting and entertaining final race with an exhilarating finale. Those that had won their wagers, among whom were many soldiers and sailors, spent their gains on food and drink for themselves and as well to entertain their suddenly numerous friends.

Long after the fall of night the plaza stayed loud.

While he that evening drank cup after cup of wine, the king vociferously complained about the insufferable noise outside. Barsuna finally found sleep mumbling that he would take revenge for the insults he had endured at the hands of Captain Avalcar, Resi, and the two foreign horses that did not belong in Phoenicia... at least if the equines were not to be owned by the king himself.

In order to walk off an aching headache, the next morning the king took exercise in his garden.

"Well, this time," muttered the king to himself, "the grass is nicely cut... what... no... it is freshly chewed.

What in blazes... hoof prints? Horses tracked up my garden and ate my grass!"

With his sandal the king pushed aside some freshly piled dirt meant for camouflage, bent down, and smelt horse dung. After expelling a big breath of air he exclaimed, "Whew! I must do something about these foreign horses... after all I *am* the king. No horse not my own will eat in my garden!"

"I guessed to find you here, Father," greeted Maroun.

"Son, today I find myself in a terrible mood. In the race I lost two prize horses, no doubt my best horses, not to mention the small fortune I bet on them. Now I find that horses, surely the two raced by Avalcar, messed in my garden. What am I to do? People are *laughing* at me."

"Father, when I suffer defeat I look ahead to the next battle. I have lost more than one battle and still won the campaign. You have to plan how you are going to win the final battle in this war of the foreign horses."

"But I can think of no plan that can get me Hammereins and Lucareins!" replied an exasperated Barsuna. "Consider that Captain Avalcar is protected by Admiral Zoumar. As much as they revere Zoumar, the people now love the heroic Avalcar. Princess Resi has become the talk of the city. Imagine that a woman, and at that she is strikingly beautiful, almost won our great race."

"Riding the fastest horse, Resi should have won the race. Now let us think on this. Father, there is no need for you to be discouraged. Avalcar finds himself in possession of two valuable horses. Because you have things that Avalcar wants, you hold a strong hand."

"What things... Maroun?"

"To begin with, Avalcar has developed a strong and intimate friendship with the Troyans. For their part the Troyans want desperately to depart Phoenicia and begin again their campaign of piracy against Egyptian ships, which by weakening your enemy would present to you a tactical advantage. The Troyans can, perhaps for years, keep the Egyptian navy occupied. Just thinking now... but perhaps you can find a way to make a bargain with Avalcar where you end up with his horses, and he is permitted to embark with the Troyans."

"Hmpf. My older son is onto something. I could have to be gone the Troyans, and as well be rid of Avalcar. But, this negotiation has to be done with subtlety. My first move will be to feign friendship with the Troyans. Do you have any ideas on how to do that? I do not want to host another embarrassing supper for them."

"If it were me, Father, I would start with something casual. How about planning a ride with them? You can use the excuse that you want to mount the horse that won the race. You ride one horse of Avalcar's, and I will ride the other. Anyway, for your future purposes the foreign horses will have to get used to the royal household."

"We will take a day ride to show them the mountain behind the capital," replied the king. "That would be viewed as a neighborly thing to do for my guests."

"Since Majit has of late spent a lot of time in the Old Garrison, he would be the perfect person to carry the invitation to Avalcar. In that fortress Avalcar's very fast horses are stabled."

"The excursion will happen tomorrow. Have your brother extend the invitation. Keep it small so that we can focus on Avalcar. He now possesses four fleet horses. His two and the two that used to be mine will serve perfectly for our excursion. It will be just you, me, the older Phoenician prince..."

"His name is Ermir," reminded Maroun.

"And Avalcar."

Two victories were now celebrated in the garrison that had become the temporary home of the Troyans, and for all practical purposes made to be as well the home of Captain Avalcar. The first was the return of Admiral Zoumar to Phoenicia, a homecoming made possible by Troyan pirate ships. The second was the victory of Avalcar in the Race of the Walls; a triumph that was aided and abetted by an athletic Troyan princess who happened to also possess stunning good looks.

On the morning after the running of the great race lavish gifts of food for the Troyans and their crews, and fresh feed for the horses, arrived at the garrison. That afternoon Avalcar and Resi lounged in the garrison doing... exactly nothing. The triumphant Hammereins and Lucareins rolled in the dust and also did absolutely nothing, except to wait for more oats and fresh-cut grass to be brought to them.

As Ermir walked alone about the confines of the Old Garrison, the older prince relished the *almost* victory of his little sister Resi. The four survivors of the royal family had escaped the burning city of Troy, won battles at sea, and now they were made to feel warmly welcomed by the people of Phoenicia. Still for all that had been accomplished, the older Troyan prince was not satisfied. Touching a hand to his chest, Ermir felt an ache in his heart that would not him depart.

Phoenicia was a prosperous land with a high-walled capital city. Even before it had been destroyed, Troy was nothing compared to Byblos. Although the Troyan princes were fortunate to be housed in the old Phoenician fortress, and as well fortunate to be now well-fed by the citizens of the land, Ermir did not want this peace and quiet to last. He set a goal for himself, "Within one moon I will be put back out to sea to continue attacks on Egyptian barges."

Accompanied by Avalcar, the king's younger son brought to the Old Garrison an invitation for an outing into the mountain that loomed high behind the capital. The king wanted exercise, hunting, and to show Ermir the beauty of his land.

"This is exactly what is needed to raise your cause with the king," said Avalcar to Ermir. "Of course I bring my four fleet horses to carry us on tomorrow's outing."

Although not terribly disappointed that she had not been invited to accompany the small entourage on the ride into the mountain, Resi pretended to be.

"Ermir, can you believe that the... almost winner of the Race of the Walls is not invited to go on tomorrow's outing? For that I should be... *deeply offended.*"

"Little sister you are tired, bruised, and in need of several days of rest. You will do well to eat, sleep, and relax tomorrow, precisely like you did today. Perhaps Majit will tomorrow look in to see how you are faring."

"I will tomorrow morning, and again in the afternoon make sure that you want for nothing," responded Majit tipping his head to Resi.

"Prince Majit, I thank you for looking as well tomorrow to my needs," interjected Admira. This was with slyness said, for Admira knew that Majit had grown fond of Resi.

Avalcar told Hammereins and Lucareins that the king and his older son wanted to ride in the company of Ermir and himself. The Phoenician royals would mount the magnificent stallions that finished first and second in the great race. The brother horses were to bite down a big supper and get a good rest, for on the morrow their legs would get twenty leagues of exercise. The two winners of the great race neighed that they welcomed a long jaunt away from the crowded city, and that as a personal favor to Avalcar they *would* permit the king and Maroun to mount upon their backs.

Like Resi, Majit was not upset that he had been excluded from the excursion. He did not feel jealous that his older brother would the next day be made to shine in the king's eyes. Majit preferred to spend the morrow with Resi.

That same evening found the king's mood much improved. He was ready to set in motion his plan to acquire two foreign horses that by unicorn magic... had assuredly been deeply touched.

CHAPTER 12

ESCAPE INTO MOUNTAIN

G alloping in the lead of the party of four horsemen, Maroun found that Lucareins was indeed fast. More than that, the prince had never ridden a horse that loved to run as much as did the younger foreign stallion. On the other hand King Barsuna found Hammereins to be headstrong, determined to run at his own pace instead of how directed his rider. Barsuna became annoyed that he had to repeatedly call for Maroun to slow down, and not move too far ahead.

Complimenting the king on his horsemanship, and lauding as well the horsemanship of his son Maroun riding ahead of them, Avalcar began an effort at diplomacy.

"Yes, me and my son are natural born cavalrymen. Only you, Avalcar, can command a chariot better than Maroun. Hmpf... but that reminds me of my other son. Majit is grown too old to still be a dreamer. You have no idea how much I worry about Majit. Perhaps it is my fault that my younger boy persists unserious about anything that matters.

"Maroun wants me to send his brother to serve in our army which, after all, is compulsory. Did you know that I wanted Majit to soldier with you, Avalcar? However, my younger son flat-out refuses to enter the military. Rather than practice his swordsmanship or compete in a wrestling match, he would draw a picture of a new bird he came upon in the woods."

With a hint of exasperation the king added, "The example set by the king's second son matters to our people. You know, Avalcar, my boy likes you. There must be some way you can help me to get through to Majit. I would heartily approve if you took him under your wing, and made a soldier out of him."

"At your request, I will seek to involve myself with Majit."

"Good! I commend you to do whatever you think best for my son. Everyone knows that when Avalcar says something, he means it."

"Sire, everything will come together for your talented second son. Some young men take longer than others to settle down. That is all it is."

"I surely hope you are right, Avalcar. It confuses me to have one son who is a strong warrior and brave of heart, while the other spends his time drawing pictures... of birds."

"Forgive me for saying so, but what you say is not true. My king, both your sons are brave... very brave. On a day of battle, to either one I would entrust my life."

"For saying that, Avalcar, I thank you."

Avalcar moved his horse ahead to where rode Ermir and begin to instruct the Troyan on the geography and significance of the place through which they were traveling.

"As the river on our left enters a more narrow part of the valley, where the cliffs on both sides climb high, it turns its course northward. The mountain we approach is the sacred sanctuary of our people. More than a thousand years ago, when our ancestors settled these parts, that place came to be their refuge. On top of the mountain there is a meadow with plentiful grass. Water flows down from the mountain into a waterfall that we shall soon come to glimpse. I have always loved to ride horses upon our sacred mountain."

"What makes it sacred, and not just a refuge?"

"That, Ermir, is a good question," replied Avalcar. "The mountain has no temples placed upon it. A general once told me that when encamped upon its heights there was a feel that could not anywhere else be matched; his heart there felt a sublime peacefulness."

"Is the sanctuary mountain fortified?"

"No, Ermir. We have relied on the shepherds that feed their goats and sheep in these valleys to repel thieves and intruders. So far the shepherds have not failed us. Now that I think about it, you do have a point. Strategically important to us, the historic mountain should be garrisoned. Upon seizing this mountain our enemies could look down on the capital and spy out the movements of our army. From the heights of this mountain an adversary could even count how many ships enter and leave our harbor."

A Gift Given

"I *cannot* accept the gift of such a finely made silk shawl."

"It is something special, something not before found in Phoenicia," offered Majit. "And I want to know what you think of it, Resi. Tell me... that you like it."

"The shawl is exquisite," responded Resi. "But you should not have done this."

"Since Ermir is today gone riding with the king," interjected Ermal, "it comes to me as the next older brother to say that it looks too expensive to be a proper gift for an unattached young lady."

"But Resi, you *can* accept the shawl," persisted Majit. "You will need it when you go to the palace... so that you there shine brighter than all the other young ladies."

"Does Bashkeem agree with Ermal, that it is not proper for me to accept such an expensive present?"

"It is delicately and extraordinarily made," answered Bashkeem as he ran his fingertips over the finely woven fabric. "Can I answer you in a personal way, Resi?"

"Of course you may."

"You know that as a child I was made to be alone. As the years of my servitude extended one upon another, I began to do the things that I was commanded better than anyone, whether slave or free. I saw that a number of slaves, with less talent than I, were awarded their freedom. Had I been more willing to negotiate for things, and to accept gifts, I would have advanced beyond my status. But lacking conceit, I remained a humble slave burdened by ever increasing responsibilities. What I am saying, Resi, is that as a young man I should have had the self-assurance to view myself worthy of receiving rewards and favors. So Resi, my counsel is that if you like this shawl, and think that it highlights the gift of your beauty, then with confidence inform your brother that you are going to accept it as a present given with open sincerity by Majit."

"I find... that I agree with the touching words of Bashkeem," said Resi to Ermal. "It is polite to be open to a present kindly given, even if the gift pushes slightly beyond the bounds of propriety."

"This shawl does indeed highlight my sister's prettiness. Perhaps in that regard it would be impolite of Resi to not accept it."

"What you just said about yourself is compelling," continued Ermal turning to Bashkeem. "I have seen many men, and women, with a high opinion of themselves do unkind things. I can believe that people devoid of conceits, like you were, suffer and are held back by others. In fact I think that a person possessing a modicum of conceit, pride in one's abilities and faculties, is better able to truly value the talents possessed by others.

"Now, my friend, just the same as you asked Resi to accept a gift genuinely given, and as well implied that my sister should highly value the beauty she was born with, I want you to no more undersell your many admirable accomplishments."

Resi took a step toward the kitchen area.

"Wait, Resi," interjected Majit. "Before you leave us, it becomes my turn to confess something to Bashkeem. Born high, I somehow came to think that I was better than others. For example, I told my father that unlike other young Phoenician men I should not be required to commit to military training. So in the future I am going to study you, and when I must make a decision affecting others, I will endeavor to do what I think Bashkeem would do."

"Does that mean you will rethink your decision to not serve in the army?" inquired Resi.

"Perhaps I shall at that." Majit smiled at Resi and added, "And, I am very pleased that the princess was prevailed upon to accept my well-intentioned gift."

Four Riders

Under the generous light of an abundant sun King Barsuna, Maroun, Avalcar, and Ermir pressed deep into a river valley where the adornment of yellow, pink, and blue petals crowned patches of wildflowers with prettiness. In exchange for the gift of water in a dry climate, trees lining the river banks returned abundant green foliage.

"How about you and me taking the lead for awhile?" suggested the king to Ermir. Maroun and Avalcar fell back.

"Your majesty, the grass in this luxuriant meadow reaches the knees of my horse," observed Ermir. "Is it not odd that we come upon no sheep grazing today the lush grass? It is as if they were by wolves chased away."

"Relax and enjoy the rich colors of this valley," replied the king. "Note, Ermir, how the somber cliff faces are delicately streaked with every kind of hue. This pretty valley has water, grass, and tall trees. What can be better than to be found on a pristine morning riding a superb horse along the course of a scenic river that with fish flows plentiful?"

"This river valley is indeed handsome. But why, Highness, do we not hear the songs of birds? I would expect many species of birds to inhabit this lush valley. Could something have scared them away?"

Hammereins halted and jumped front feet.

"This horse refuses to obey my reins!" remonstrated the king.

Hammereins turned back his head and neighed quietly to Avalcar, who quickly pulled beside the king.

"Majesty, your mount tells me that in the trees of the river bank, hide soldiers."

Hammereins neighed again.

"Ahead along the cliffs to our right lurk more soldiers."

Lucareins next neighed softly.

"My other magic horse tells me that fronting us more hidden soldiers block our progress. We are about to be ambushed."

Avalcar dismounted and made a show of looking at the hooves of his newly acquired mount, while at the same time he addressed his fellow riders.

"While Ermir and I create a blocking diversion to confuse and so stall the raiders, mounted on the fastest horses Maroun and the king are to break hard back to the capital. With a fast start your mounts Hammereins and Lucareins will quickly outrun this danger. When you reach the capital send Bashkeem and a Troyan barge crew here to rescue Ermir and myself. That is the only way this can work. And Prince Maroun, do not fail either your father or me."

"Now, keep up with me," said Avalcar to the older Troyan prince.

As he remounted his horse, Avalcar made a show of talking and laughing with Ermir. After subtly readying his bow he ordered, "Go... *now!*"

Hammereins and Lucareins wheeled about and reversed course.

The horses of Avalcar and Ermir charged ahead. As arrows flew at them, both men slid down in their saddles and veered their horses toward the cliffs positioned opposite the river. A second round of arrows was let to fly at the fleeing Barsuna and Maroun.

Outrunning flighted arrows, Hammereins and Lucareins gained such speed that all the king and Maroun could do was to hold tight to reins and horse manes. Before those waiting in ambush could mount in pursuit, it became apparent that the king and the crown prince would not by any horse be caught.

One arrow after another was quickly shot by Avalcar and Ermir into clumps of enemy warriors found at the base of the cliffs.

Ahead, Hittite soldiers moved into the open, raised shields, and brandished swords to block the forward movement of Avalcar and Ermir.

Avalcar yelled to Ermir to follow him; their horses broke in reverse course toward trees lining the river. Brandishing swords to fight through enemy soldiers, the two propelled their mounts to enter and swim across the current. Avalcar and Ermir wove their horses up a rocky hem of the protector mountain.

"Never before have Hittites struck an ambush so close to our capital!" exclaimed Avalcar. "Had the king and the crown prince here fallen, for Phoenicia it would have been an unthinkable disaster."

"These Hittites are sturdy soldiers," observed Ermir. "They will not quit, and we will not surrender."

"Thinking that they have us cornered on the mountain, they take the time to collect their horses and reform their battalion," answered Avalcar. Climbing more upward, the mounts of Avalcar and Ermir achieved full separation from their pursuers.

Upon crossing the stone bridge at the southeast corner of the city wall, the king and Maroun were made safe.

"Father, while you see to the defenses of the city, I will instruct Bashkeem and the Troyans to depart on a mission of rescue."

"Not so fast, Maroun. I need you here with me in the city. These two horses matter more to me than Avalcar and Ermir."

"I shall pretend that I did not hear my father to say such a heartless thing. You must remember that I gave my word to Avalcar. He saved our lives. Even if the captain were to perish, you cannot make these wondrous mounts to be your own. And our city does not depend on the Troyan pirates for its safety. To you I will soon return." Lucareins sped off toward the Old Garrison.

Upon reaching the southern gate the king alerted the guards to the danger. Riders sounding bugles and shouting, "Attack!" "Attack!" sped their mounts along the route only days before taken by the Race of the Walls.

Maroun gave the bad news to Ermal, two princesses, Bashkeem, and Majit found to be with the Troyans. Bashkeem and Ermal were immediately off to collect the ten or so horses stabled in the Old Garrison.

"Majit, come now with me to the city," ordered Maroun. "Our father awaits us."

"Brother, I today must follow the dutiful example of an illustrious Troyan ship commander, and do a rightful thing. Because I know exactly where the ambush took place, it falls to me to lead Troyans to rescue Avalcar and Ermir."

"By heavens brother, I gave you a command!" responded Maroun testily. "You do not even wear a sword, and you do not like to fight!"

"You are right, big brother. I seem to lack a sword." As he stepped to grab hold the shoulders of his brother, the smiling Majit added, "Can you spare me yours? I will always strike ahead, and not permit my own blade to cut myself."

The anger that had shown in the face of Maroun dissipated.

"In that case, I give my sword to a... *man of action.* Do it honor." Maroun could not help but smile back at his younger brother that had ever refused to engage in a fight with weapons, newly changed to be a willing combatant.

As Resi made ready to mount a horse, Majit restrained her arm and said, "Your country cannot permit to fall in one day four princely siblings now found in the far land of Phoenicia. You and Admira must not this day risk your lives."

Resi looked at Admira, and then both looked at Ermal. The two princesses reluctantly nodded their agreement to Majit's words.

"Just know, Majit, that we girls are not happy to stay behind," said Admira. Beset by worries for the safety of their brothers, the two sisters turned, clasped one arm to another, and together walked away.

On the Mountain

Passing a cascade of water measuring ten steps wide, that from far heights plummeted down, Avalcar led Ermir up a trail that wove into and around jutting cliffs. As before described, a lush meadow spread across the summit of the mountain. The escarpment at the far side of the plateau plunged a thousand paces downward to the river that boundaried the eastern wall of the Phoenician capital.

"Avalcar, to my eyes this view of Byblos is precious. From this height I can clearly see the palace. Over there is the Old Garrison where we are housed. Since from this high place one could certainly spy down on Byblos, placement of a garrison on this mountain would no doubt strengthen the defense of your capital city. In fact, the presence of a garrison in this place would to you and me right now prove very helpful."

"The question is, Ermir, with Hittite warriors in hot pursuit, and our backs against this impossible descent, where do we go from here."

"Avalcar, tell me what lies in that marshy area over there to the south."

"From that marsh big springs flow to the waterfall we passed climbing upward this mountain. The marsh is said to be most times cloaked in mists that have to do with why this place is special to us. It is written in our old saga that those marsh springs are the home of shadowy magical unicorns that watch over our city."

"Well then, we have nothing to lose by finding out if the saga is true," offered Ermir.

"Agreed. Right now you and I could use a magical unicorn as a friend."

Where began the marshes and springs, two riders dismounted.

"As children we were told to never approach this marsh... else the unicorns would desert our land," remarked Avalcar. "Hmph. Here are horse prints. Over there, trees grow thick on an island in the very center of the marsh."

The horses began to neigh and jump nervously.

"Perhaps our horses tell us there is something on the tree island that frightens them," cautioned Ermir.

"Let us rather hope that the presence of a unicorn on the island excites them. If we can make it to the island, we should at least have round us the protection of a shallow moat of water."

"But, Avalcar, on the island we would become trapped."

"Even with horses as fast as these, we are not going to outrun the battalion that pursues us. I would rather die on an island with lush trees, than have my life to end surrounded by enemy horses with nothing between them and me."

"This, Avalcar, is strange. If I am not mistaken, and I think that I am not, right here beneath the surface of the water a walkway of flat rocks leads to the island." Holding the reins of his horse, Ermir stepped gingerly onto the submerged path; his leggings became soaked.

"The rock plates do not teeter or give way. This is a fine path to follow, even if it be on the last day of our lives."

With no false steps, in the lead of their horses the two men reached the little island set amidst marshes and swirling springs. The men sat down on a fallen log; their horses began to graze.

"The enemy will soon be upon us," said Avalcar upon hearing the distant sounds of horse hooves. "As we defend the submerged rock walkway, our bows will buy us some time."

The two horses began to neigh and jump about.

"Our mounts will give us away. Go, Ermir, and quiet them. Better yet, take them to the middle of the island and tie them there."

Ermir grabbed two sets of reins and disappeared into clumps of trees. Avalcar crouched down behind a log providing a protective position of defense.

"Avalcar! You *must* see this!"

"Alright, but we have precious little time to prepare for attack." The tone of Avalcar's voice soon changed, "Great heavens! The old writings were true! Unicorns still live in Phoenicia!"

"I understand your speech," neighed the unicorn found to be resting on his belly. "I commend you for your mastery of the uniform animal language. That can only mean that by a unicorn you were previously blessed. My name is Mistral. I am going to give the same gift to your friend."

"Kneel before the unicorn," instructed Avalcar, "so that he can impart to you the uniform animal tongue."

After his horn bzzzd blue sparks against the side of Ermir's head, the unicorn neighed in satisfaction, "It has been a long time since my magic had a purpose. Still, I am certain that I have *not* lost my touch. Now I say again, my name is... Mistral."

"I understand perfectly the neighs of Mistral," answered Ermir. "You certainly have not lost your magical power."

At the edge of the marsh horse hooves were heard to splash.

"Your names are... ?"

"I am Captain Avalcar of Phoenicia."

"I am Prince Ermir of the vanquished city of Troy."

"Well Avalcar and Ermir, I cannot neigh that I am unhappy to have been found out. It has been too long a time since I have had any company. My life has become slow, and if I might say frightfully monotonous."

"Master Mistral, the Hittite horses that are now upon us promise to bring end to your monotony, and make us to be the last guests that you here entertain," replied Avalcar.

"*Yeerrrranghuh...* let us see how quickly I can summon the magic of my birthright to control the mists." Still set in a position of repose, Mistral began to weave his head back-and-forth. From time to time the unicorn grunted, "*Rhhrruuhhmm... rrrhhrrrgghhmm...*"

"Would you look at that!" exclaimed Ermir pointing. "A fog rises up... and extends outward." The little island became enveloped in a mist that soon spread over the surrounding springs and marshes.

As the splashing advance of Hittite horsemen stopped, the shouts of Hittite warriors were heard. Then followed what no doubt were oaths and curses.

"The Hittites have lost their bearings," observed the naval captain. "This mist is so thick that they cannot see their hands in front of their faces."

Frustrated for the obscurant mist, it was not long before the voices of Hittite soldiers were no more heard by Ermir and Avalcar. The sounds of enemy horse hooves grew faint.

"Where water bubbles and flows... my magic gift works perfectly," neighed Mistral as he smiled slyly at his two new friends. "Since my legs could use some stretching, it is convenient for us to now leave my island."

On no part of the mountain top were Hittite soldiers to be seen.

"This place well-enough suits me." In a spot of thick grass Mistral settled on his belly. "While my teeth pull at grass... I can listen. Why did you come to the top of my mountain?"

"Noble unicorn... " began Avalcar.

"Since the ability to conjure mist is the only magical gift I possess, just my name will do."

"Alright, Mistral. Prince Ermir and I accompanied King Barsuna and his son on a ride that began early this morning. At the base of the mountain we four were set upon in an ambush. Because the king and his son rode the two fastest horses in the kingdom of Phoenicia, horses that I brought back from across the seas where the white herd of unicorns now searches for a new hold, I trust that the king and the prince made it safely back to Byblos."

"Never once did I doubt that the white herd lived on," neighed in reply Mistral.

"After Avalcar sent the king and his son to safety," continued Ermir, "we rode through the Hittites who were in wait. Our only place of escape lay within the height of your mountain. We hoped to hold on to precious life until a search party made up of our sailors came to rescue us."

"*Nyhuuhhh…* your sailors would have arrived too late to save your skins," neighed the unicorn shaking his head at Ermir.

"Yes, Mistral, it is to you that we owe our lives," added Avalcar. "You must one day give us an opportunity to repay the kindness proffered by your protection."

The head of Mistral sank down; within moments the unicorn was dozing. When a sudden loud snore woke him from his short nap, the unicorn jerked up his head and continued the conversation from where it had left off.

"So, you want to repay my calling forth a mist. You just may be able to help me with one small problem. We will talk of that back in the capital city."

"That you are returning with us to Byblos is the best news I have had since my foreign horses won the Race of the Walls!" exclaimed Avalcar.

"If even one of the Hittites glimpsed me through the mists, I am no longer safe here. And since my sister unicorn and her colt departed, for me this mountain has become a lonely place. So, it is time I descend my mountain. For lack of exercise my muscles have grown soft. Still, I do not feel myself grown too old to serve as the guardian of the capital of Phoenicia. My friends, I will count on your protection. There is always some ne'er-do-well that covets the magic of a unicorn horn."

"Perhaps you will sleep better if you move in with us... into the Old Garrison outside the city," offered Ermir.

"You know, from up here the walls of the royal palace look to be too thick and cold for my tastes." That neighed, Mistral reclined his head and was again fast asleep.

Company of Searchers

Majit led the rescue party into the river valley where ambush had been sprung.

"At the far end of the valley we see the dust of horse hooves in retreat," observed Ermal.

"Notice how the ground here is disheveled," interjected Majit pulling his horse to a sudden stop. "The ambush happened in this place."

Majit dismounted and followed directionally the turned spots of dirt and sod.

"Here lie five unbreathing Hittites," said Majit pointing. After following more tracks toward the river he observed, "More dead soldiers are found over here."

"We need for our best scout to examine the other side of the river," directed Bashkeem.

"Will do, Sir."

After his horse crossed the river Majit's gaze shifted gradually upward. "Many horse tracks both climb and return from the mountain."

The company of sailors maneuvered their horses to the far side of the river.

"We cannot catch the remaining Hittites before dark," said Bashkeem. "And if we follow them, after the fall of darkness we risk ambush by a force several times larger than our own. We will instead follow the horse tracks up the mountain. One way or another, the two we look for will be found on top of this mountain."

"If Ermir and Avalcar fled up the mountain," said quietly Majit, "I fear we are too late to save them."

"I am thinking two things, Majit," answered Bashkeem. "My first thought is to be thankful that your father the king, and your older brother are safe."

"My next thought," continued Bashkeem turning to look at Ermal, "is to never bet against Avalcar. He is an intrepid fighter. I have the firm idea that with Avalcar at his side, your brother will somehow survive."

"Hear that?" neighed Mistral upon detecting the sound of horse hooves. "Soldiers come... this time to rescue you. We will join them, climb down the mountain, and with them go to your garrison." Mistral changed his mind, "No, the sky darkens. You will tonight rest with me on my mountain. It will be my last night watching guard over Byblos."

Avalcar and Ermir waved at the rescue party led by Majit, Ermal, and Bashkeem.

"They are still alive!" shouted Ermal. "With them is a... *unicorn!*"

Sensing the gravitas of Bashkeem's persona, Mistral imparted the gift of the uniform tongue to the former slave, and then introduced himself. The unicorn next sparked the heads of Majit and Ermal.

"I am Commander Bashkeem. I have the strong suspicion that you had much to do with the rescue of our two friends."

"Our lives were saved by the mist that Mistral conjured to hide us," interjected Ermir.

"Commander, for too long I have dwelled here. It is come time for a stubborn unicorn to depart his mountain. I will go with you to sojourn in your garrison."

"It will be our honor to have you come and stay with us," replied Bashkeem rubbing the mane of the unicorn.

The commander of the Troyan barges walked to the edge of the escarpment and looked out on Byblos and the nearby Phoenician coast. He lingered admiring the view of city, olive groves, parcels of wheat, and harbor. As twilight deepened Avalcar, Ermir, Ermal, and Majit joined with Bashkeem to admire the view.

"It is to me a great comfort to know that the dwellers of the beautiful city below us will tonight go to sleep in safety," offered Bashkeem.

"I can count the lamps that begin to shine in Byblos," observed Majit. Through a time with no more words shared, the lamps and fires of the capital city became too many to count.

"Let us mount up for the return," said Bashkeem to Avalcar and the three princes.

"No, no," objected Ermir. "Mistral insists on staying here the night. The descent of this high mountain will under tomorrow's light of day be easier for the unicorn, as well as for our horses."

"If Mistral was seen by the raiders he is no longer safe here," replied Bashkeem. "Under the cover of darkness, with as little notice as possible, we must get the unicorn inside the garrison undetected."

"Only if word of his presence does not leak out in the capital, do we keep Mistral safe," agreed Majit. "We can trust no one, not even my father the king, with the knowledge that a unicorn with you resides."

"In that regard, the Hittites knew that the king would here today be found," answered Bashkeem.

"Blast! Bashkeem is right!" exclaimed Majit. "The walls of the royal palace echo every word uttered inside them. Spies are everywhere."

"So, once again the thinking of my commander is not wrong," said Ermir placing his arm on Bashkeem's shoulder. "The only thing I ask is that it be you that convinces the unicorn to so far travel on this dark night."

"And what of the Hittite raiders?" interjected Majit. "They should be punished!"

"The Hittite ambush failed, and the enemy has fled," answered Ermir. "No Phoenician or Troyan life was lost in the raid. Patrols sent out tomorrow will find the raiders long gone."

"The king can send an emissary to complain to the Hittite King," spoke next Bashkeem, "or he can send out a Phoenician battalion to raid in turn the Hittites. However since the adversary grows ever more powerful with a huge army to someday be reckoned with, it may be that your father will put this attempt on his life behind him, and choose not to do anything that might provoke war."

"But Bashkeem, the audacity of the Hittites to attack the king and crown prince, and to do so right at the backdoor of the capital city, is a very bad sign," observed Ermir. "I fear that soon the Hittites will launch an all-out war against Phoenicia."

Turning to look at the dozing unicorn Bashkeem added, "It will not be easy to talk a big *stubborn* stallion into changing his mind. If it takes a small miracle to coax Mistral to climb down this mountain in the dark, then let us see if another miracle can be today procured."

The logic of Bashkeem's argument, and his skill in conversation, proved difficult even for a set in his ways unicorn to resist. Following a long night of travel the light of new dawn streaming through a window of a horse stall in the Old Garrison, found Mistral sound asleep.

CHAPTER 13

LIANVIL AND DANSEY TO THE RESCUE

"Why travel so many warriors northward? This unicorn is accustomed to see painted warriors moving the opposite direction."

"That, Naythorn, is a good question," groinked Hamilton in response.

"*Ahggrrmmnnkk!*" After clearing his throat and collecting his thoughts, Timidthy groinked, "Because springtime sun shines hot on the desert and grasslands that lie to the south of us, hunting grows better in the cooler climate of the north."

"Not only on our west side, but as well on our east side warriors travel northward," bleated Rambuncture. "And at that, they take their time. Some of them act like they are going to stay here until the next moon. For that, I worry that we are stranded."

"Just like my ram," added Ewelissas, "I would feel better if we were stopped on a real mountain, rather than on this high ridge set like a solitary island in the middle of this broad valley."

"The shame of it!" interjected Hamilton. "As just observed the ewe, I am trapped not upon a deserving mighty and majestic mountain, but on an undistinguished ridge. This boarling member of the magical band of Naythorn merits a better place to be stranded."

"Notwithstanding your satire," grunted Mama Pig as she snouted the broad neck of her biggest boarling, "this, Hamilton, is serious business." After resuming her position crouched behind a fallen log, the mama pig again peered out at hundreds of warriors slowly making their way northward on the floor of the valley.

"For safety's sake, we need to remain here for now," grunted the sow. "The canyon that shines with magic blue gold will patiently await our arrival."

"Once again the mama sow is right," agreed Naythorn standing well-hidden behind tree branches. "Until movement through the valley quiets down, we will up here continue. When we resume travel it will be only by night. That means that we will need to rely even more on the scouting reports brought to us each morning and evening by the duck and the goose. And since the eyes of Isabayas see well into the night, my winged filly will continue to spy out the darkness."

Hearing that, Isabayas began to prance with neck arched and tail waving. Naythorn's filly had become not only as fast in flight as Webstir and Featherspark, if anything she loved to fly even more than did the two waterfowl.

Lucars, Amaluna, Alexzana, Marsand, and Scarlet Point climbed higher the ridge to a place presenting views in every direction.

"Hmpf!" Lucars exclaimed slapping his thigh. "I do not like this at all. Just look at the great numbers of slow-moving warriors below us. Our band is in danger of discovery by warriors that we know nothing about."

"Observe the fire flares on the far western side of the valley," said Scarlet Point motioning with an arm. "My grandfather, a very experienced chief, told me that warriors on the march start fires for two reasons, to force game from cover and to destroy native camps."

"If I were burning habitat to flush out game," offered the Phoenician youth Marsand, "I would make the fires to spread long and continuous. That those fires are small in size, unconnected, and burn in no pattern makes me think that the lodges of enemies are being destroyed."

"That can explain, at least in part, the slow movement of the warriors; they pause their travel in order to make conquests," added Lucars.

"Can we know anything more about the warriors that travel below us?" inquired Amaluna.

"Close to us travel two separate tribes that do not intermix," replied Scarlet Point to his sister. "The two chiefs are surely allies that maintain separate authority over their peoples. I think that the alliance of the two tribes will not long prevail."

"Why, brother, will the alliance break apart?"

"Because the two groups are very different from each other, their alliance cannot be well-established. The tightly led and organized lead tribe fights more with war clubs and spears. The paint of the war-club tribe is bright in color, which bespeaks constant war. The warriors of the following tribe that favor the bow to hunt and fight, and that walk not behind their head chief but spread out in an unorganized fashion, are less cohesive and more individualistic. Not all of the second tribe's warriors wear war paint, but those that do are adorned with somber colors that do not glorify war."

"You need to share with Naythorn what you deciphered about the two tribes," said Lucars. "Who can say, one day your information may help us to turn one of the two tribes into an ally, just like we once did with your Eagle Feather tribe."

It was not long until Naythorn, Hammer, Lianvil, and Dansey were listening intently to what Scarlet Point had observed and interpreted about the two tribes.

"We members of the blackmane's band, including some being quite large, are too many to hide easily," observed Hammer. "Naythorn, if into this ridge hunters pursue deer, they will likely sight members of your band. We should prepare ourselves for the day that a party of warriors happens upon us. In that regard it would behoove us to learn more about the two tribes, each with many warriors, that slowly travel past us."

"Why not send a champion lion and a yellow wolf to investigate further?" barked Danseyelono. "To better observe, Lianvil and I will find a way to get close to the two tribal peoples."

"As I recall you are the best spy wolf ever to climb and descend mountains to gather intelligence," grrrd Lianvil as he shoved his head to topple over Dansey.

"On that I will agree with Lianvil," seconded Naythorn. "It was not so long ago, Dansey wolf, that your travel up and down three parallel ranges of mountains provided rescue to my band."

Into settling darkness Dansey and Lianvil slunk quietly away.

Two Chiefs Opposed

A big fire illuminated a place not far from where the wolf and lion positioned themselves to observe. On opposite sides of the flames two chiefs sat on conveniently situated rocks, each with a masked medicine man at his side.

"They have prisoners," yipped Dansey. "After burning their lodges and capturing them, it seems obvious that the two war chiefs are now arguing about what to do with the prisoners. I wish I could understand exactly what the chiefs are saying."

"Hmph," grrrd Lianvil. "The younger chief paces back-and-forth. He now motions with his hands that he wants to... kill someone."

"Yes... I think he wants to kill the fifty prisoners seated on the far side of the fire away from us."

"But since the prisoners are not armed and do not look dangerous... then why does he want to kill them?"

"Did you see that, Lianvil? The older chief that wears no war paint pointed to the prisoners, and then touched his hand to his chest. I think he is saying that these prisoners are his friends... or relatives. That means that the prisoners were taken by the younger chief."

"We crawl closer, Dansey. I want to better see the masks worn by the two medicine men."

Absorbed in the drama of the argument the warriors standing at the side of one chief, and as well at the side of the other, took no notice of the stealthy approach of two intruders.

"The medicine man beside the younger chief wears a mask made to look like a human skull," grrrd Lianvil.

"The totem of his tribe's brightly painted warriors calls for much death and devastation among the peoples they conquer. Dansey, you will not believe the mask of the other medicine man. Look carefully at both sides."

"I *see* it. The medicine man of the chief proffering friendship to the hostages wears a mask with a lion head on one side and a wolf head on the other side. That makes his people to be the... *Lionwolves!*"

"The same headdress hangs from the waist of the lionwolf chief," added Lianvil.

"The prisoners look resigned to their death," grrrd Dansey. "I feel badly for them. Wait! The belligerent chief just grabbed a hostage, and raised a war club above the prisoner's head."

"The argument between the two chiefs cannot last much longer," answered Lianvil. "And about that I am going to right now do something. If fortune this night smiles upon us, we will save the lives of those poor prisoners, and in so doing make new friends for our band. After all, I am a lion and you are a wolf, and there stands the chief of the lionwolves. Follow my lead, Dansey."

"Our entrance into the camp of heavily armed warriors is fraught with danger. If we are to pull this off, Lianvil, you and I will tonight have to shine as actors. Otherwise one, or both of us, may not live to tell this story. But if this subterfuge works, what we accomplish will when retold make a very good story. To make it interesting... I will not even have to exaggerate."

"You cannot tonight be an actor, Dansey. When we confront the death mask war chief, he must know that you and I are totally serious."

The lion stood on hind limbs and roared toward the campfire. When he nudged Dansey, the wolf also howled. The warriors by the campfire motioned knives, spears, and bows toward the murky darkness from where the sounds had issued.

While toward the fire Lianvil walked only on hind legs, Dansey came on all fours.

"Dansey, now we roar and howl to let them know we are getting closer." Two wolf howls, followed by two lion roars broke the silence of a night that had become newly still.

Still clutching his prisoner, the chief of the death mask warriors peered into the darkness. However, the chief of the lionwolf warriors began to move toward the sounds made by Lianvil and Dansey.

"Hanging from the neck of the chief that walks toward us are many claws, and he carries a bow. Show confidence, Dansey, as we walk toward the approaching chief."

When the lion and wolf became clearly visible to those around the fire, war cries split the night.

The lionwolf chief stopped, raised his bow, and pulled the bow string back. Still standing upright, Lianvil folded front paws over each other. The lion flicked aside an arrow flying at his chest.

"That was incredible," grrrd Dansey. "You batted away a flighted arrow."

"Done with the same magic that made me to walk upright," answered the confident Lianvil.

The bow was again raised and aimed.

Yelling loudly the lionwolf medicine man ran toward his chief, all the while pointing at one side and then the other of his headdress.

The lionwolf chief lowered his bow.

While with much emotion he argued, the medicine man grabbed the headdress hanging from the waist of his chief, and shook it at the stars. Become convinced by the words of his medicine man, the tall chief motioned to the two predators to follow him.

As he entered the gathering of warriors, the walk of the lion with anvil-hard sides was majestic. Dansey did his best to match the stately gait of his feline friend... but with notably less success. One on each side of the lionwolf chief, the two predators sat down. Slowly and carefully the chief lowered hands to pat the backs of Lianvil and Dansey.

No one spoke. From the astonished expressions worn on warrior faces all around the campfire, it was clear to both Lianvil and Dansey that no one knew what to say. That is, except for the medicine man wearing the mask of a lionwolf who began to speak slowly, and as well sign with hand gestures so that Lianvil and Dansey understood what he was saying, including the name of his chief.

"The Great Spirit that lives above us in the heavens sent this sign to our courageous Chief Bigclaws. Because tonight the lion and the wolf walk together, the long ago prophecy for our tribe is fulfilled."

Still clutching the hostage under one arm, the brightly painted chief lowered his stone hammer. The belligerent chief would listen concerning the fulfillment of prophecy.

"The Great Spirit wants all to know that it is wrong to kill these hostages," continued with both words and gestures the lionwolf medicine man. "Being a blood relative to these prisoners, that have not harmed anyone, my chief *demands* they be released!"

After touching again the lion and wolf resting beside him, the chief advocating leniency rose to stand. Bigclaws hit forearms to his chest to express strongly his conviction that the prisoners be freed.

"By standing we let everyone see that we agree with the words of the lionwolf medicine man, and the conviction of his chief," yipped Dansey. That said, at the sides of Chief Bigclaws the lion *and* the yellow wolf rose to stand on hind limbs.

"The chief that we stand with is not only tall, his hands are extra large," grrrd the lion.

"I just noticed the same thing," yipped Dansey as he wobbled to keep his balance. "They are even bigger than Hammer's hands."

Become affronted by the obstinacy of his ally, the richly painted chief shouted insults across the fire at the lionwolf chief. Having had enough of words, the belligerent chief again raised high his war club.

Not waiting for the war hammer to fall, Lianvil bounded so fast over the fire that not one hair of his belly fur was singed. He landed snarling in front of the chief holding the captive. The lion crouched to spring should the stone hammer drop to bash the head of the captive. With spears raised, several of the painted chief's warriors surrounded the great cat. Lianvil tensed limbs. Before dying from spear wounds, the mighty lion would in a painful and disfiguring attack destroy the throat of the death mask chief.

Bigclaws walked around the fire toward the richly painted chief, pushed down the arms of warriors encircling Lianvil, and faced off against his erstwhile ally. Moments passed slowly as the two chiefs glared at each other. When from the hand of the younger chief the war club was let to fall to the ground, Bigclaws pulled the hostage from the grasp of the painted chief.

Lianvil turned to walk behind the lionwolf chief and the freed hostage. Bigclaws once again sat down with Lianvil and Dansey resuming seated positions at his sides. The freed prisoner crouched in front of his rescuer.

To signal his disgust with the vehement opposition to killing the prisoners, the chief calling for blood tossed his cloak into the fire. With his medicine man and warriors in tow, the belligerent chief walked away from the campfire. Every warrior that had witnessed the tense resolution of the dispute recognized that the death mask and lionwolf tribes were no longer allies.

A chief now wearing his lionwolf headdress, a lion, and a wolf together rose to stand. The lion roared at the stars and the wolf howled at the darkness.

Wearing a lionwolf mask, the medicine man began to dance steps around the fire. As drums beat loud, warriors joined the medicine man in dance. Using his front paws to balance the awkwardness of stepping to drums like human persons do, Lianvil twirled about on hind paws. The yellow wolf did as best he could to move rhythmically while attempting to maintain balance on hind paws only. As the prisoners joined to joyously celebrate newfound freedom, shadows of many dancers twisted and leaped into the night.

"Enough drumbeat movement for me," grrrd Lianvil. Accompanied by a small wolf with a yellow-mottled hide, a big lion trotted off into the darkness.

On the new morning Dansey addressed Naythorn and the band members with him, "We last night took the initiative to do something all on our own."

"Go ahead and tell our story," growled the lion pawing lightly the head of Dansey.

"Alright, Lianvil. I leave it to you to correct me where I too much exaggerate." With all its details the story of the encounter with the two chiefs was told.

"In summary, Naythorn," concluded Dansey, "a yellow wolf and a great lion last night succeeded in making a new friend for our band."

"Can we place trust in the chief that wears the lionwolf headdress?" questioned Timidthy.

"I think that we can. Last night Lianvil and I earned the confidence of the chief that wears claws on his chest, his medicine man, and as well the prisoners that were freed."

In agreement with Dansey the big lion nodded his head.

"Sparksy and I once before saw the death mask totem," qvackked Webstir. "It was near the top end of the valley that lies before Prow Mountain, when the warriors making columns of smoke shot arrows into the sky at us."

"*Hronkk!* Webstir, you are right!" exclaimed Featherspark. "Those warriors that tried to shoot us out of the sky did so at the command of men who wore masks made to look like human skulls!"

Hamilton jumped himself up to stand on rear legs, but could not maintain his balance. At least the biggest boarling made it appear that he could not walk on only two feet.

"Dansey," grunkked Hamilton, "I do not believe the part of your story about you standing and walking on two paws, let alone that so situated you joined warriors to dance about the fire. Prove to me that you can dance on only two limbs."

"Nor do I believe it," concurred Hammer. "The yellow wolf needs to prove to us that he can hop and dance to the clap of my hands."

"But to do that," yipped Dansey, "I will need to follow the steps taken by the great lion that was given the magical ability to walk on just two limbs."

"Alright, Lianvil," encouraged Hammer, "show the yellow wolf how it is done."

Propping Dansey up from time to time with a huge paw, Lianvil helped the yellow wolf to demonstrate that he could indeed hop rhythmic steps while elevated on only hind limbs.

With the bison and the cattle on one side, late that afternoon Naythorn was standing lookout. On Naythorn's other side stood the half-horned Belfloralex.

"All over this valley move warriors," harrumphed Taurington. "I wish that our northern allies, the Eagle Feather warriors, were here to protect our return travel to the canyon of blue gold."

"Naythorn," brayed quietly the bison, "if you could give the gift of the uniform animal language to the chief of the lionwolf people, we could convince him to do us the favor of protecting our band from death mask warriors."

"The same thought had occurred to me," replied the blackmane. "Although, when to human persons our band is made known, we do face the risk that they will come to make war upon us. Still, Master Bison, if we do not obtain the friendship of those that are worthy, I am convinced that greater dangers will await us. I shall find a way to become known to the new friend of Lianvil and Dansey."

As darkness approached the duck and the goose stretched wings and fluttered upwards on a scouting mission.

"The darkening sky," grunted the mama sow, "will stop any reflections of sun bouncing downward from the golden breast armor worn by the waterfowl."

"And hereabouts," replied Practicia, "we have seen no wolves that would know to follow back to our camp the reflections emitted by a duck and a goose."

"Why cannot unicorn magic help me to sprout wings and with them fly?" groinked Roothyford. "Can you imagine the excitement I would feel soaring high above the desert floor!"

"Sister Practicia," grunted Hamilton, "just as happens when you walk, on wings you would wobble all about." Hamilton followed that remark with a display of how ungainly a pig could wobble and careen, while pretending to flap front paws like wings. He soon enough crashed himself into every other member of his wild boar family.

The bison walked over to where Hamilton was sprawled on his back with four legs sticking straight up in the air, and brayed, "What goes on here? Instead of funning, you should be trying to think of a way for us to get off this high ridge."

"Hamilton is once again hamming it up," observed Marsand as he sprawled down to grab the big boarling by the neck. "But do not worry yourself, Master Bison. I will scuffle the dickens completely out of him."

"I give up!" grumphed Hamilton as he permitted Marsand to pin him down. "Stop! You are hurting the fragile neck of a sensitive wild boar!"

Naythorn nosed Marsand off Hamilton and neighed, "I thank you both for providing a welcome break from the boredom that we have all come to feel for being stranded in this place with warriors all about."

"When I get bored I fall victim to my strange sense of humor," shrugged Hamilton.

The two scout birds flapped down into the middle of the camp.

"What news have you for us?" inquired the blackmane.

"In answer to your question..." hronkked Featherspark.

"There is a curious movement in the valley," interrupted Webstir.

"While the death mask warriors move north..." hronkked again the goose.

"From every other direction travel small groups of natives toward a place not far from where we stand," interrupted once more Webstir.

"They are going to congregate at the place where Lianvil and I intervened to save the prisoners," yipped Dansey.

CHAPTER 14

NO LONGER FORGOTTEN

The distraught Chief Bigclaws halted his northward march. It did not matter that the sun was still high in the sky. Standing stoic and motionless with a pained expression on his face, he over and over asked himself for what reason he had the previous night risked battle with the fierce death mask warriors. There was little to gain and much to lose in rescuing weak, disorganized, and decrepit prisoners simply because they were distant relatives of his mother. Besides, there was something odd about the look and customs of his pathetic relatives. They seemed, no, in the land where they found themselves they *were* lost and out of place.

Still, a small voice inside his head told him that he had made the right decision. Why else in the middle of an empty desert place would the two totems of his people, a lion and a wolf, come to sit beside him?

The lionwolf chief engaged his one surviving son in conversation. As they talked about the battle that was soon to come, a distracted Bigclaws again wished that wars had not been so costly to his own flesh and blood. He had buried three sons fallen in battles he had led. While the war chief was thankful his sons were brave warriors that died well, upon seeing features of fallen sons in the face of his one remaining son, his heart grew more heavy.

"Father," said the young man of about twenty-five years, "the prisoners you rescued from the death mask chief remain with us. As you lead us northward they are, whether closely or loosely, intent on following. From you the people we call the *Lost and Forgotten*, still seek protection."

At the words spoken by his son, the lionwolf leader grunted disapproval.

"Son, last night I was not firm in my conviction to save the prisoners. That is, until the lion and wolf came as a sign given. Although their animal eyes were unknowable, I knew what they were thinking, and what they wanted me to do. Since the lion and wolf desired what I wanted, it became necessary for me to oblige their wish. Even now I have the feeling that they are somewhere upon a ridge looking down at me."

About his suspicion of being watched, the lionwolf chief was not wrong.

"Lion," yipped Dansey, "does the blackmane worry that we again absent ourselves from his camp?"

"More than about us, Naythorn worries constantly for the difficulty and pain involved in binding together the two pieces of his horn. He has all but convinced himself that reattaching his half shard will actually lessen the magic that in him remains.

"Besides, other members of his band are for him the problem makers. Belfloralex pesters him to no end by kicking dust and dirt on him when he naps, tumbling all over him as if she had fallen when she really had not, and neighing giggles when he is saying something serious. And to her sire, Isabayas is just as mischievous as the half-horned filly."

"I wonder what he will now decide to do," yipped Dansey as he looked once more toward where stood the lionwolf chief. "Tolerating lots of camp followers is no way to prepare for future battle. Since the sun is about to set, I have the suspicion that we shall have to wait until tomorrow to see what next does the chief."

Side by side, a muscular lion and a yellow wolf soon stepped softly into delicately flowered hills meadowed in dreams.

The following morning Bigclaws would not by anyone be spoken to, not even by his son. When not standing aloof he was head down pacing back-and-forth. Refusing to give the order to march, the chief's will had become unknowable. His son had never before seen his father indecisive and made helpless to act.

In late afternoon Bigclaws called a council. Lesser chiefs sat cross-legged before the renowned warrior that had led them to more victories in battle than they could count.

"In the past I ever forbad my heart to lead me," began the lionwolf chief. "Upon deciding to once more obey my head, my heart this time rebelled. My chest tells me that if ahead of you I march forth, I will not with you return. For the first time in my life, I today suffered defeat. Over me gained victory my heart. Become resigned to my defeat, my struggles with my chest are ended."

"Without me, you will tomorrow go forth. In obedience to a heart reborn, I turn away from my former life. To a new home I shall lead the Forgotten People that follow after me."

Eyes grew big in amazement. Warriors could not believe the strange and unsettling words spoken by their chief.

"Days back the heavens gave me a sign," continued Bigclaws absent emotion in his voice. "At my side sat down a lion and a wolf. They insisted that I not permit the Forgotten People to be for no reason killed." The chief pointed, "Look over there. The same lion and the same wolf wait on me."

When the chief pointed, the big lion and the yellow wolf that had lain motionless on a rock outcrop overlooking the camp, sat upright.

"Come to me," said Bigclaws motioning to his son. From his neck the chief removed a leather cord with wolf teeth set between two lion teeth, placed it on the neck of his son, and pronounced, "This young man is today made chief of my people."

Inside his chest the son felt a surge of deep emotion that he was not supposed to show, and therefore could not.

"Follow him as if you were following me," continued Bigclaws. "He is as strong as I am. He is confident, but does not too much talk. He is not arrogant or greedy. He thinks and fights hard. He will lead you to many victories over our enemies."

Because the son of Bigclaws was both respected and well-liked, the whooping and yelling that broke forth from the lesser chiefs spread throughout the encampment. Drumbeats began to sound. Firelight soon authored the shadows of dancing warriors. Early the next morning the son of Chief Bigclaws would lead northward warriors no longer loyal to his father.

Walking into the dusk of evening, the old chief was observed to move rhythmically his feet. A wolf and a lion came to join the small circles stepped by the former chief of many lionwolf warriors. The place of the chief, the wolf, and the lion became vacant. To somewhere they had danced away.

New morning found the three returned to the now vacated campsite where two chiefs had disputed whether or not to condemn fifty prisoners to death.

"When I dance I twist, turn, and feel all the muscles and sinews in my body," grrrd Lianvil to Dansey. "You do not like me dance. At the same time that you move your paws and head, you keep your shoulders level. Where did you learn to dance like that?"

"It is what I feel to do. The rhythm beating inside my head is less bouncy than what you feel." Hearing that, the lion shrugged, pushed his head under Dansey's belly, and playfully tossed the diminutive wolf into the air.

"We go south!" exclaimed the chief at midday.

One by one, and in small groups, distant relatives of the mother of Bigclaws began to straggle along behind the chief and his two four-legged friends. Expecting only that the chief and his animal person friends would provide hope, where hope had before been unborn, the entourage of following men, women, and children came to slowly grow more and more in extension.

Wanting nothing to do with a renowned war chief that had seemingly lost his senses, groups of warriors traveling north through the valley steered clear of the path taken by Chief Bigclaws, a lion, a wolf, and his bad luck followers.

At camp the following evening Bigclaws would address those that came after. Standing on a boulder with Lianvil and Dansey at his sides, he motioned for his followers to draw close.

"When I look out at your despondent faces, the torn skins you wear, your skinny arms and legs, I see a people confused and lost. Now I declare that you are to no more know misery and hopelessness. When you are able to defend your homes and fields, you will rise to regain your dignity.

"From the faces I see about me I will select one hundred young men and women to anchor our defense in time of danger and attack. When the one hundred have trained both physically and mentally, when like the arms and legs of one body they know how to fight together in unison, when they know not only how to follow but how to lead, to them will be given authority to keep you safe.

"I now take you to a well-watered place with plenteous fruit and fish. There we shall halt our march. In that valley I will take one moon of time to train the hundred warriors. After my hundred are trained, we will travel southward and westward through lands that I have before seen. You are to reclaim your ancestral valley that lies before a mountain shaped like the prow of a great canoe. In that place you will grow maize and beans for nourishment, and build and protect homes for your families."

After pausing to study the passive faces looking back at him, Bigclaws exclaimed, "What is wrong with you? Do you not believe the words I speak? Why do you not smile and shout at this good news that I bring you?"

Irritated, the chief's mood turned angry. With Dansey and Lianvil at his heels he strode into the middle of his followers and brusquely motioned them to his left. With his spear Bigclaws scraped a line in the dirt.

"Only those men and women that vow to follow where I lead, and to obey my commands, will cross over to my right!"

Some few men and women crossed immediately to the chief's right hand side. More crossed. The movement grew. In spite of the anger the chief had displayed toward the stragglers, every single follower crossed to the right hand side of the line of demarcation.

"Hmpf! Before assenting with your feet, many of you hesitated!" scolded Bigclaws. "Did you cross over my line only because others did? You are a people *without pride!* You have no dignity! That must change! Since with the movement of your feet you have vowed to follow me, from this day onward I am your chief. I am become the one made responsible to keep you safe. Anyone that does not obey me will have to better me in a fight with axes. That is my way to..."

A commotion began as the chief was interrupted by the arrival of two strange creatures.

Belfloralex ran toward the chief. As she flew above, Isabayas brushed wingtips against her friend's back. In front of the chief, Lianvil, and Dansey the two unicorns braked hooves and wings.

"We were sent out to find you two," neighed Belfloralex stretching her nose toward the lion and wolf.

"This must be the Chief Bigclaws that rescued some of these same people a few suns ago," added Isabayas. "We were told that a man so noble needs to be given the gift of the uniform animal language. While I know that Belfloralex can by herself bestow the uniform tongue, I want to help. And since my horn is not yet fully grown, I require Belfloralex to assist me.

"*Nyeerrr!* I just had an idea!" whinnied excitedly Isabayas. "Belfloralex and I will at the same time touch our horns to the chief's head! That is bound to work!"

"But Isabayas, what if we have too much magic between us, and for that our sparks make his heart to quit beating... or by crossed magic our own hearts are overwhelmed?"

"Do not worry; the heart of Belfloralex is too strong to stop beating. And so is mine."

Isabayas put one ear to the chest of the stiffly standing chief, "This chief's heart is also very strong."

Two unicorns, one with a half horn and the other with a still growing horn, touched ivory to the chief's forehead. All about his head flew blue sparks. Bigclaws sank to his knees and began to fall back. The lion intervened so that the chief's back and shoulders came to rest against the big cat's side. Dansey licked not once, but many times the face of the unresponsive chief.

"He passed out," grrrd Lianvil to the unicorns. "Revive him with your magic horns."

The shorter horn of Belfloralex set on a line above the chief's right ear; the horn of Isabayas set along the other side of the chief's head. Two unicorn horns imparted this time a glow more red than blue, which caused curls of smoke to waft upward from the chief's thick black hair. Once, and again, moved the chief's head.

"I am made changed," mumbled Bigclaws. With some effort the disoriented chief regained his feet.

"Are you well?" neighed Belfloralex.

"Since your fingernails are not long, instead of Bigclaws you should be called Chief Bigpaws!" neighed Isabayas.

"I understand your horse talk," responded the chief pointing a big hand at the winged filly. "Yes, my hands *are* large."

Overhearing the yipping of Dansey, the chief bent to stroke back-and-forth the wolf's chest and added, "And you just muttered to the lion that you are relieved to see me recovered."

"Unicorn magic gifted you the uniform animal tongue," barked the wolf in reply.

"It certainly was not gifted by your licking my face," answered a smiling Bigclaws.

"From this day onward," responded Dansey, "the chief will not only be distinguished by his leadership, but also by lines burned above his ears by the horns of two unicorn fillies. By the way I am Dansey, and this big cat is called Lianvil."

"I was not only given power to talk your language," answered Bigclaws. "When I touched my hand to your chest I felt a heart that is true. What is more, Dansey, I sensed exactly how strong flows the bravery contained in your heart."

"Just imagine that!" yipped Dansey sporting a sly look. "The twice touching of two magic horns gave a double gift to Chief Bigclaws. As well as the ability to speak the uniform language, he now possesses magic to discern what is found in the depths of our hearts."

"Hmph," reflected Isabayas, "maybe the touch of only *my* horn would have been sufficient to give Bigclaws the uniform animal tongue."

"I am inspired to work," said the chief to the four animal persons about him. That stated, the chief turned to face his followers.

"Young people that want to be in my guards... approach now!" Extending both arms Bigclaws motioned for a line to form before him.

"You will do as a swordsman," said the chief upon pressing with his hand the chest of the first youth in line.

"You will do well as a scout," affirmed Bigclaws upon touching the shoulder of a lithe maiden.

"Your chest lacks resolve. You will not do," said the chief to a third.

"You will come to throw accurately and far a spear," offered the chief to the next in line.

"You will serve well as a sergeant."

So it went. Before long Chief Bigclaws had selected those that would become his soldiers. The one hundred were divided into ten platoons, with ten sergeants appointed in command.

After the two unicorn fillies departed the next morning, Bigclaws resumed march.

Lianvil and Dansey identified a southward trail that crossed several ridges before turning to the east. Following where led the wolf and lion, only a few days passed before the chief led his people into a valley made lush by mountain springs. There a military style camp was laid out with order and organization established for every family unit.

When some of the chief's followers complained, particularly those that made a habit of grousing about their neighbors, it took only a few of his judgments such as marching guard duty for three nights in a row, or chipping and sharpening arrow and spear points from morning to night, before every one of his followers decided that it was less difficult to cooperate with the chief's ideas, than to obstruct them.

One afternoon as he watched Lianvil and Dansey aggressively wrestle and play, the face of Bigclaws grew serious. He had had an idea.

The chief ordered that his soldiers watch Lianvil and Dansey demonstrate their fighting skills. The wolf and lion pawed and slashed at each other, jumped over, rolled about, and bit each other's tough hides.

Bigclaws next asked two exceptionally nimble young soldiers to fight each other, the bigger one pretending to be a lion and the smaller pretending to be a wolf. Using unsharpened sticks as crude weapons, the two soldiers at first fought tentatively and awkwardly. From time to time the chief stopped the fight to instruct the two on matters of martial arts. By the fifth round of their bout the two spry and sprightly soldiers were scratching, grasping, biting, jumping about, and tumbling almost like a real lion and wolf.

"Well done!" exclaimed the chief ending the match. "You each drew a little blood, but not enough to harm one another."

"There is a lesson here to be learned," instructed Bigclaws. "It was more than fun to watch two soldiers impersonate in combat a lion and a wolf. Their styles of fight were not only different, but the more they practiced the more they came to fight faster and more creatively.

"I issue a new order. Each platoon of ten soldiers will choose to fight one way or another, like wolves or like lions. I require you to observe and study the lions and wolves that roam around us. The members of each platoon must learn to cooperate one with another, the same way that fights a pack of wolves or a pride of lions. Train not only your bodies, but also your minds to pursue attack as does your totem predator. Our future enemies will not be accustomed to fighting warriors that are as quick and agile as lions and wolves.

"After each platoon has chosen, they will design and adorn themselves with a totem that symbolizes their lionhood or their wolfhood."

Whether fighting was practiced with hands, knives, swords, spears, or arrows it was done with movements of wolves and lions. Chief Bigclaws went so far as to adjust his gait so that at times he walked like a lion, and at other times he moved arms and legs compacted like a wolf.

On another evening the winged horse glided into camp and neighed to Bigclaws, "The blackmaned unicorn wants you to know that the valley before him at last empties of warriors interfering with his band's movement. He will soon depart his camp."

"I owe my new heart, and my new life, to the magic brought here by Naythorn," replied Bigclaws. "Since I now understand his quest for unicorn safety, I am duty bound to protect him. Where does he go?"

"He returns to the spired mountain that stands alone," neighed the winged filly.

"That mountain is only ten days travel from here."

"Through a cave Naythorn will enter the hidden canyon found within that mountain," continued the filly. "It will take more than forty suns to complete the fashioning of new armor for his band, and to bind Naythorn's shard to his half horn."

"I will ready my battalion of soldiers," replied the chief. "Look for me to make camp not far distant from the mountain of many spires."

Bigclaws called his sergeants, "While every big valley has a tribe and a chief, there is only one blackmaned unicorn. Lianvil and Dansey must return to protect Naythorn as he travels through a dangerous land."

As they departed the camp of Bigclaws the lion, the wolf, and the filly with wings walked between two files of fifty warriors with right hands clasped to their chests in salute, howling and growling in imitation of wolves and lions.

As the chief watched the departure of the lion and wolf that had transformed his life, he wondered in what future battle his battalion of one hundred wolf and lion warriors would come to the rescue of the blackmaned unicorn.

CHAPTER 15

THE CANYON OF BLUE GOLD

O n a night when the moon and stars chose to selfishly undecorate the sky, thick darkness camouflaged the descent of Naythorn's band from a high island-like ridge. Many days of travel followed.

Upon sighting the southernmost of the two pointer mountains capped by crumbling man-made triangular structures, the thoughts of the blackmane returned to a previous journey that followed one and then another pyramid-topped peak. On the morning that he and his band came to follow the trench of broken stones, Naythorn neighed for the younger blacksmith to join him.

"Lucars, I shall never forget how when I was overwhelmed by so many bloodthirsty wolves, you here came to my rescue. Ride on my back as we pass the places where I struggled nearly to my death. As I walk along this long trench of broken stones, it brings me comfort to feel the press of your legs against my sides."

"Thank the heavens that we cross this place today in safety. That signifies, Naythorn, that we will tomorrow begin a well-deserved respite in the canyon of blue gold."

The next afternoon found the swords of Hammer and Lucars prying open the stone door presenting into the magic canyon. Upon entering, those band members that had not before seen the canyon of blue gold lacked words to describe its beauty.

"This place of safety and calm is as special as I remember," whinnied Naythorn. "Water, grass, fish, fruits, berries, and nuts are in this canyon found. And I will never tire of seeing cliffs filigreed with dazzling blue gold."

As if oblivious to the grandeur of the place, the two blacksmiths went right to work at the forge. What most interested the senior smithy was not the repair of armor, but the novel challenge of binding together two pieces of unicorn horn. For that purpose Hammerclaw required that only the purest blue gold be used. Naythorn's horn needed to again become not only whole, but as well perfect. Be that as it may Naythorn decided, not unexpectedly, that the repair and making of new armor was the paramount priority.

Gold was mined, fuel was gathered, and soon the magic metal was made to flow hot and fine. Hammer and Lucars directed Scarlet Point, Marsand, and Alexzana to the work of pounding out the dents that had in the tumult and turmoil of battle been inflicted upon gold armor pieces whose edges overlapped. The three young people became apprentice blacksmiths learning each day new lessons in the art of the forge. In addition to the work of repair, pieces of armor required modification to adjust for bodily growth and muscular development. Of course the provision of armor for new members of Naythorn's company, was time consuming.

For the delicate work of fitting gold armor plates to bind into a tight pattern, threading feathers onto arrow shafts, and weaving strands of dried stringy plant fibers into rope, the slender fingers of Shawnee and Amaluna proved to be particularly skillful and clever.

Unwilling to assume that because Naythorn's band had safely reached the canyon of blue gold, that therefore everything would continue well, Naythorn's sire organized a guard unit. For all Cabalblade knew, wolves bent upon the annihilation of the blackmane's band were not far distant.

Because the stone door to Shining Canyon remained open to permit long runs and excursions, as well as the resupply of coal for the forge, Cabalblade set in shifts the two dogs and four wild boarlings to guard two-by-two the outside entrance to the cave passage. The bison, the longhorn cattle, the mama sow, and the two mountain sheep rotated guard at the inside entrance to the canyon. From the sky Isabayas, Webstir, and Featherspark performed daily scout missions.

In order to ensure that no band member dared to nap or become distracted while on duty, the ever serious Cabalblade adopted the habit of dropping in unannounced on the members of his guard details. When Hamilton complained that so much security was unnecessary, and that the entrance door to the canyon could just as well be closed shut, Cabalblade informed the wild boarling that marching guard duty also functioned as a character builder.

"But my mama sow tells me that I already possess *too much* character," objected Hamilton to that assertion.

Naythorn decided that with his sire supervising the band's security, and with Hammer in charge of the armor and weapons detail, the proper use of his time was to make sure that each member of the band stayed physically fit.

To that end sprints were every morning organized for unicorns, bovines, men, women, dogs, mountain sheep, wild boars, and even a goose and a duck. Wrestling matches were conducted by men, wild boars, sheep, dogs, and from time to time included the participation of Alexzana and Amaluna. As fast as might be accomplished, the lake before the waterfall was swum back-and-forth. In order to keep muscles toned and in shape stones of varying sizes were thrown, pushed, or with ropes dragged so far as strength allowed. Swords were brandished in practice, spears were thrown for accuracy and distance, and arrows were made to fly at grass-woven targets.

"I commend my big colt for keeping everyone active and alert," complimented Cabalblade. "Dwelling in this incomparable place, it would have been easy to relax discipline. Instead, for the training that you require your band becomes a more effective fighting force. Since we entered Shining Canyon I can see that muscles have grown, and physical endurance has bettered."

"It was you, Sire, that inspired me to work everyone hard," replied the blackmane pleased to receive from his sire a rare compliment. "When I saw with what discipline and preparedness you approached the work of the sentries, it made me realize that days can be wasted only at our peril."

Sweat and dirt from a day of hard work, guard duty, a session of military training, or a time of exuberant fun were most agreeably rinsed away in the cool flow of lake water fed by a waterfall. Of course more than any other band members, Webstir and Featherspark relished long and lazy swims.

The stay planned to last forty days, extended longer.

Aneilee, Elianor, and Rainsnow

"We are found out!"

"Yes, Rainsnow, that is so," replied calmly Aneilee. "The huge black wolf follows behind us. Behind the monster come more wolves."

"Why did the high escort of the unicorns not tell us before about the danger that she assuredly foresaw, the threat that now pursues us?" inquired Elianor. "You should have!"

"You know the answer to that," interjected the stallion. "Aneilee did not want to worry us... and she wanted to be absolutely sure before mentioning it."

"On both counts you are right. When something foresightful comes to me, I have discovered that it is best to not alert or alarm others by neighing about something that is not yet certain to occur. Add to that, discussing the future before it presents can change what is to come, and usually for the worse."

"So, Aneilee, now that we have returned from the seacoast," responded Rainsnow, "what exactly are we to do next? Do we continue travel toward the blackmane?"

The high escort lowered her head and did not right away answer. Upon finally raising her head she neighed, "Would you two be willing to embark on a truly big adventure, wherever it led?"

After looking at each other, the horse stallion and the guide matriarch both turned heads toward Aneilee, who waited patiently on their response.

"When I was young I wanted to see the lands that the sun follows westward," replied finally Rainsnow. "I had somehow formed the idea that mountains to the west climb very tall, and that luxuriant grasses cover their in-betweens."

"If we lead the black wolf and his followers far away, the white herd will not have to contend with at least one monster wolf," added Elianor. "But how long a delay can we afford before finding the blackmane?"

"I also miss Naythorn," affirmed the high escort, "and I very much want to see him again and offer the big fellow encouragement. After his ill-treatment by Hoovefort, I am certain Naythorn could right now use some heartening from all three of us. But a faint voice whispering in the wind tells me that Naythorn is not yet ready for us to find him. Perhaps the journey he is on will in three or four moons better prepare him to welcome us."

"But how can we delay so long our return to the white herd?" worried Elianor.

"Look again!" exclaimed Rainsnow. "With the big black beast come not only wolves, but also warriors! How did that wolf prevail upon unmagical warriors to join in pursuit of us?"

"It amazes me to see that uncomprehending the uniform animal language, warriors follow the orders of a wolf," neighed Elianor. "Let me see... hmph! Upon first contact with the huge black wolf, warriors saw that magic had made his size to be gigantic. And unfortunately, to the hearts of human persons the power of magic, dark magic at that, proves very persuasive."

"There is more to it than that," responded the high escort. "Desperate to increase the power of his small army, the black wolf leader discovered that with grrrs, head movements, and paw signs he could make himself by human persons to be at least partially understood."

"The huge black wolf has come to be very clever," neighed Rainsnow after expelling a big breath from his chest.

"Too clever!" exclaimed Elianor. "Now that he has learned to communicate with human persons, more warriors will come to follow him."

"In that case, Elianor," neighed the high escort, "it behooves us three to lead the dangerous black wolf on a wild goose chase far away from the white herd, and as well far away from Naythorn. Protected by our magic and Rainsnow's courage and strength, I have no doubt that we will come to very much enjoy a trek into high mountains."

"An army of wolves and warriors cannot travel as fast as the three of us," assured Rainsnow. *"Nyerrrhaharrgh!* This horse stallion is ready to chase after the sun!"

CHAPTER 16

AGAIN WOLVES

"Naythorn! Buckwhite! Taurington!" qvackked Webstir excitedly. "We saw lots of..."

"Wolves!" interrupted this time Featherspark.

"More than lots... *too many!*" exclaimed the duck. "They follow the trench of broken stones toward Spire Mountain! A giant gray one is in the lead!"

"How many?" inquired the blackmane. "Against fifty or sixty wolves my band can well-defend itself."

"At least two hundred wolves are headed for Spire..." hronkked the goose.

"But how can the wolves know that we are here found?" interrupted the duck.

"Spy wolves!" exclaimed the goose.

"Maybe the wolves approach not because they know we are here, but to hunt on this mountain." That said, the blackmane trotted away from the two waterfowl.

"Naythorn must know that two hundred wolves do not gather together to hunt rabbits and deer," qvackked Webstir.

"Our captain wants to be by himself," hronkked Featherspark.

"Come, Sir Cattle, let us go after him," brayed the bison disregarding the goose's directive. "For my part, I think that Naythorn requires some company."

The bovines refound the blackmane staring at the waterfall. They waited politely for Naythorn to acknowledge their presence at his side.

"I was sure that we would be safe here," neighed at last the band leader.

"From wolves we *are* here made safe," answered quietly Buckwhite.

"But Albarochk is gone away, so why do the wolves not stop their pursuit? I grow discouraged; I tire of battle that never ends. Why am I defending a herd of unicorns that have rejected my black coloring and my cleaved horn? Maybe it is all... for nothing."

After shaking his head and snorting to clear his lungs, the blackmane walked away.

"More than once Aneilee told you that the unique color of your mane is for a purpose," mrawed Taurington upon regaining the blackmane, "and that your destiny is to lead the white herd to a new hold. You cannot ignore wolves that are intent on destroying every unicorn. That would be... *giving up.*"

"But now a new huge gray wolf comes to attack me. I thought I was done with monster wolves."

"It may not happen for six, seven, or twelve moons, but you will soon vanquish the last monster wolf," encouraged Buckwhite. "Naythorn, you still have purpose to fulfill."

"Because of you, Naythorn," mrawed the cattle, "we two bovines were stopped from destroying each other. One way or another every member of your band owes their life to you. Because you give meaning and magic to our lives we need you to keep fighting, not just for the unicorns, but for each and every one of us that follows where you go."

"You Sir Cattle, and you Master Bison, also give meaning to my existence."

"Naythorn," continued Buckwhite, "I see no reason why you cannot for now disregard the wolves that come after you. Let them vent futile howls from outside these canyon walls. Let them angrily suffer the frustration that they can do nothing to make you depart this place. Here we are provided for. So long as it pleases you to remain, your band will continue safe in Shining Canyon."

"Even if the wolf general somehow convinced warriors to attempt to open the stone door that entrances this canyon, without the hardness of blue gold weapons their levering and pushing would fail," added Taurington.

"We must also recognize one critically important benefit regarding our uncomfortable situation," brayed again the bison. "While he waits impatiently outside our canyon walls, the monster wolf cannot attack the white herd. And because he gains no magic from attacking the one hundred warriors of Bigclaws, the giant wolf will not choose to skirmish against our friend the chief."

"Master Bison... on both counts you are right," replied the blackmane. "Since the white herd indirectly benefits from our presence here, I am going to take your advice and not worry about the gray monster. *Nyerrraarrghh!* More than anything, perverse wolves hate being ignored. When the day comes for us to leave, perhaps several moons from now, we will crash through the wall of wolves. If he remains not far removed from here, Chief Bigclaws can even be called upon to aid our departure from this place."

That decision made, Naythorn sprawled down and began to sun his side and neck as if he were a young colt.

After making sure that every member was accounted for, with their teeth gripping handles the bison and cattle helped Hammer and Lucars pull inward the stone door. As an added measure of security, Lucars jammed through the handle holds a sturdy branch to lodge against rock surfaces found on both sides of the stone door.

Wolves Made Angry

"Come out and fight!" howled Clak. "The cowardly blackmane needs to face the terrible gray-haired wolf!"

In support of that sentiment three fearsome sergeant wolves howled agreement.

"It took three moons for me to find where hid the blackmane," continued Clak. "Now my wolves have wasted two more moons scratching at the stone door leading into the canyon where the blackmane and his band are found."

"And the stubborn rock still does not dent!" exclaimed the smallest sergeant wolf whose jowls were deeply slashed.

"Our siege is lasting too long," snarled a second sergeant wolf with hide marked by torn patches of fur. "Not enough deer remain for us to hunt on the mountain of spires."

"In spite of their hunger, my wolf privates that cannot withstand the wrath of their monster wolf general, dare not desert me," snarled Clak.

"At least the lions that dwell on the mountain now fear us," growled the biggest sergeant wolf that moved with a damaged hind quarter. "We three sergeants have the scars to show that together we are more powerful than any lion."

"And my scarred face proves my undying loyalty to Clak," grrrd the smallest sergeant wolf.

"Hmpf! You three go and form up the ranks of privates for inspection," ordered the huge gray wolf leader. "A daily dose of discipline keeps the malcontents in their place."

Sinking his head down onto his paws, Clak grew reflective.

"If my black-haired brother finds, vanquishes, and drinks the blood of the two unicorn leader mares, he will become ruler of all the wolves. Then even I will have to obey him. I would hate for the slow-witted Trike to have authority over me. I need one thing only. Upon drinking the blood of Naythorn I will be the greatest wolf to ever live. Naythorn *has* to emerge from his canyon. Sooner or later... *he must.*"

That evening the big sergeant wolf limped back to report to his leader.

"Your spy wolf just returned. He barks that the two unicorn matriarchs and the horse stallion continue to elude Trike. The black monster wolf has not yet found a way to triumph over the leader mares, and perhaps he never will."

"Good!" growled Clak. "I want Trike to not defeat the guide matriarch and the high escort, at least not before I bring end to Naythorn. Then it will be me that reigns over all the wolves. *Rrarrrroooo!* I hate that from one sun to the next the cowardly blackmaned unicorn ignores me. There has to be some way to force him to emerge from behind rock walls."

"Our mighty wolf general will soon make the blackmane to come out," grrrd the big sergeant wolf. "When he does, Naythorn's doom will be sealed, and Clak will be greater than either of his two monster wolf brothers. You will be greater than was even... *Albarochk!*"

"Curse the blasted blackmane!" howled the enormous gray wolf.

CHAPTER 17

TWO LOST UNICORNS OF PHOENICIA

"It is almost evening," mumbled Prince Ermir awaking from long uninterrupted sleep. While his mind unraveled the invisible spider webs of deep slumber, a thought suddenly presented, "With us is a majestic unicorn. Does he still rest in his stall?"

Ermir found Olsi standing guard at a stable where on a thick bed of clean-smelling straw sprawled comfortably Mistral's legs, side, and neck. The unicorn unquietly snored.

"How came you to here stand guard?" inquired Ermir.

"It seemed to me that someone should watch over a beast so precious as this unicorn."

"I say *well done,* Olsi."

Ermir set off to make a round of inspections.

"Something is not the same here... what is it?" It hit him. "No Phoenician sentries today walk the walls of our garrison. All the guards are ours." That observation made, Ermir returned to the area of the cooking fire which for Troyan pirates served as both kitchen and dining room.

"Ermal, what happened to the Phoenician guards?"

"Brother, when King Barsuna was ambushed the city went on high alert; the guards from our garrison were recalled to defend the capital."

"Well, Ermal, I do prefer that our men guard the garrison. It affords us, and the unicorn more privacy."

"I hear what you say. We can trust very few people with the knowledge that Mistral rests here."

"I trust Avalcar, I trust Majit... and I trust one other Phoenician completely," responded Ermir. "Having fought side by side with him against Egyptian war barges, I know he would not betray nor Mistral nor us."

"You of course refer to Admiral Zoumar," reflected Ermal. "Bashkeem wants to speak to him. Hmpf. Majit can retrieve him to us. The younger prince will doubtless soon enter here to see how we are faring."

It was arranged so that the next day Majit brought Zoumar to supper. The admiral entered the Old Garrison hefting a bulky and tightly-bound rolled blanket. After looking in on the sound asleep Mistral, the admiral sat down with his friends and began to untie the blanket.

"When an officer friend of mine recently retired, this chest plate of blue gold came into my possession. Although perhaps not exactly according to protocols, it is right of me to give this piece of armor to Bashkeem. After all, had it not been for the incredible heroism of Commander Bashkeem I would not have survived the sea battle against the Egyptian flotilla, and the blue gold that was carried in my hold would not now pertain to Phoenicia. For four Troyan royalty I also bring blue gold swords."

"Just as I was once honored by your regifting of a magic sword, I am today deeply honored by the admiral's gift of blue gold armor."

That stated, after nodding his head at the younger princess Bashkeem added, "One can only approve of such a priceless gift so generously given." Recalling their earlier conversation about the present of a silk shawl, Resi returned Bashkeem's smile.

"The flat bread, and especially the bean soup, taste as good as can be found anywhere in Byblos," complimented the admiral wanting to change the subject from his extraordinary gifts.

"You, Sir, are too kind," answered Resi.

"And the Hittites?" inquired Bashkeem.

"Nothing more has been seen or heard of them," replied Zoumar.

"And the king?" continued Bashkeem turning to Majit.

"After losing the Race of the Walls, and then falling into an ambush that without the fleetness of Hammereins and Lucareins would have ended badly, my father lowered his profile. Since the day of the ambush he has not worn his robe of blue gold. And no more parties in the palace, at least for now."

"And what, Majit, of the king's thoughts?" inquired once more Bashkeem.

"No doubt my father looks to take some advantage from the bruises his pride has suffered. Because I know that I can trust you to not repeat my words, I speak freely to you as in the confidence of family."

"I will also speak frankly," replied Bashkeem. "For a long time I have searched for an answer to something."

The circle of friends tightened to listen closely to Bashkeem's next words.

"My mind, Admiral, has not reconciled with the arrival of an Egyptian fleet to position at the entrance to your home sea, and there attack you. How could the Egyptians know you would be where you were? When you were?"

"Bashkeem, since the Egyptian fleet fell upon my barges I have every day asked myself those same two questions. The Egyptians came to meet us knowing where we would be found, and that we carried a priceless cargo of blue gold. No one else but me and my crews had that information. For more than one year we had had no communication with Phoenicia. The odd thing, as you might recall, is that because of a horrendously damaging storm that broke masts and drove our barges far off course, our return was by more than three moons delayed. So, on every count the Egyptians could not have known what they clearly demonstrated that they knew."

"By any chance," continued Bashkeem nodding his head toward Ermir, "had there before been more unicorns with Mistral?"

"Mistral told Avalcar and me that his sister unicorn, and her offspring colt, dwelled formerly with him on the capital's mountain," replied Ermir.

"Then, Admiral," spoke on Bashkeem, "it is possible Ermir's information about two more unicorns will lead us to answer how the Egyptians knew where your fleet would be found, and when. After Mistral completes his rest we shall inquire more."

With Lucareins trailing behind, Avalcar rode into the garrison on Hammereins.

"Hah! I hope we arrived in time to share the evening meal," said the grinning Avalcar.

"It is about time that Captain Avalcar brought back his champion horses," greeted Admira with a big smile. "Hah! No doubt the palace would have kept them."

"A surprise waits in the stable for Hammereins and Lucareins," said Avalcar removing their bridles. "Go meet the unicorn stallion Mistral."

Two horses dashed away to greet the first unicorn they had come upon in the passage of many moons. Soon the two horses and the unicorn were rearing high together, kicking out hooves, and racing after each other in big circles. At last played out two horses and a unicorn trotted over to the cooking fire, sprawled themselves down, and whinnied their joy for new companionship.

"The long rest in the protection of the Old Garrison was exactly what I needed," neighed the unicorn. "I have more energy today than I have had in years. I feel to be half my age."

"Mistral," said Avalcar motioning with his hand, "I introduce you to Admiral Zoumar, Princess Admira, and Princess Resi. Kindly touch your horn to the heads of Admira, and Resi."

It was no sooner said than done. Possessing loving and generous hearts, the two princesses immediately understood perfectly the uniform animal tongue.

"Tell us, Mistral, what happened to your sister unicorn and her colt," inquired Ermir.

"I really do not know how I came to lose the two members of my family that had long kept me company.

You see, from our mountain I had gone away to search for signs of unicorns in lands to the east. That quest was fruitless. Upon return to my mountain, my sister mare and her colt had disappeared. All I found was a jumble of horse tracks that told me that there had been a struggle. My heart tells me that my sister mare and her colt still live. I hope that whoever captured my family treats them well."

"Who knew for certain of your existence in the marsh springs?" inquired Bashkeem.

"Until a few days ago no one... no... that is not true. Shortly before I left to journey east in search of unicorn survivors, we had a solitary visitor. It was King Barsuna. When he called to us I made the concealing mist to go away so that he saw us. After all... he *is* the king.

"I gathered that he had come to our mountain to bless us. With the touch of my horn I attempted to give him the uniform language. However, his mastery was so poor that he could hardly understand me. After raising high his hands, and speaking in a loud voice his blessing, he left."

"That, the blessing part, does not sound like something my father would do," observed Majit as he threw a stick onto the fire. "He does not go around venerating animals. Well, unless they are his champion race horses."

"So then while you traveled east, a short time after the king's visit, your unicorn family vanished?" inquired Bashkeem.

"To my great misfortune, yes," sighed Mistral.

"So, our king used the authority of his throne to verify that three unicorns existed, and where they could be found," said Avalcar. "Hmpf! I hate to say this, but in one way or another the king had something to do with the disappearance of Mistral's sister and her colt."

"Let me, Mistral, pose one more question," spoke again Bashkeem. "Would unicorn horses be able to sense the return of the Phoenician fleet from their mission to rescue the white herd?"

"I sensed a soon... *presentation* of blue gold magic," neighed Mistral quietly. "However, I did not know that ships carrying the magic gold were returning from across the sea. My sister unicorn, her name is Crimson, has the gift of knowing what bring the clouds. In her reading of the clouds she would have glimpsed that a cargo of the precious gold approached our sea. As ships bearing blue gold drew closer, Crimson would have become more animated. Without any concealment the joyful body language of Crimson would have acknowledged that new magic was coming to the land of Phoenicia. But more than that, the visions of Crimson often paint the sky. She likely colored the clouds with a vision, or a depiction, of the return of Admiral Zoumar's fleet."

"Would Crimson have told any human persons about the arrival of the blue gold?" inquired Avalcar.

"It would have been hard for my sister, who is open hearted and trusting, to not share the elation she would have felt for the renewed connection with the white herd... signified by the unalterable bond between unicorns and blue gold. If my two unicorn relatives *had* found friendship with human persons, and bestowed the uniform language upon them, the return of the happily anticipated magic gold would have been innocently neighed about."

"We can now," continued Bashkeem, "piece together the puzzle of how the Egyptians were alerted to the return of Zoumar's fleet. After capturing the two unicorns, King Barsuna found advantage in selling or dealing them to the Egyptians. From the imprisoned unicorns the Egyptians gained knowledge of Phoenician ships returning with sheets forged of blue gold.

"We can something more surmise. Somewhere in the land of Egypt are found the two missing unicorns. And, since the Egyptian navy depended on the intelligence provided by the unicorns, it stands to reason that Mistral's sister unicorn and her colt are housed at the great port of Egypt. Perhaps Olsi, who knows well that harbor, will concur with my deduction."

Upon being summoned, the crown of Olsi's head was by Mistral's horn sparked. The former Egyptian captain identified the sprawling citadel overlooking the port as the first place he would look for two valuable equine prisoners.

"By heavens!" exclaimed Avalcar slapping a hand to a thigh. "That is the only way to explain the ambush of our convoy! But I still cannot believe that my king, for anything in the world, would have risked the success of the return of our convoy."

"No Avalcar," answered Zoumar, "our king could not have known that the unicorn named Crimson would foresee our return. Barsuna himself told us that he did not know how, without the renewal of the army's blue gold armor, his kingdom would survive both raiding Hittites and encroaching Egyptians."

"But why did Barsuna give the two unicorns to the Egyptians?" inquired Avalcar.

"To answer that," responded Bashkeem, "one must ask the king."

"I am sorry, Mistral, for the nefarious thing that my king has done," said the admiral. "Thank the heavens that you were absent when your sister unicorn and her offspring stallion were captured."

"Had I been present my mist would have concealed my sister unicorn and her colt."

"Do not give up hope, Mistral," continued Zoumar. "We will find a way to rescue and return from Egyptian captivity your sister mare and her colt."

The admiral turned to Majit and Avalcar, "I require you both to accompany me back to the city. About this matter the three of us will talk further."

"The important thing for my father to ever keep in mind," said Majit before departing, "is that thanks to the courage and aid of the Troyan pirates, the cargo of blue gold made it safely to Phoenicia."

After Captain Avalcar, Admiral Zoumar, and Prince Majit had left the garrison, Bashkeem encouraged Mistral.

"Know, my unicorn friend, that Zoumar and Avalcar have accomplished deeds far greater than the rescue of two unicorns held captive by Egyptians. Your family will be brought back to you safe and sound."

"I believe you," replied Mistral nodding his head. "And for that I will again tonight sleep soundly."

"Here is what we now know with surety," began Avalcar as he walked back to the palace with Majit and Zoumar. "Two unicorns were taken from our mountain. Shortly before they were taken the king saw and spoke to them. The two taken unicorns now reside in the land of the pharaoh. Egyptians in authority believed the cloud signs that presented by way of Mistral's magic gift... that the blue gold was on its way to Phoenicia. Acting on the unicorn intelligence, the pharaoh sent a fleet to intercept and interdict our return to our home sea."

"I am surprised, more than that impressed, that based only on information gathered from two captured unicorns the Egyptians had the resolve to incur the expense of outfitting a fleet numbering fourteen large barges," reflected Zoumar.

"For a pharaoh desperate to acquire magical blue gold, the vision of returning barges in painted clouds, was definitive," responded Avalcar. "In fact, lending more credence to the issue, the unicorn mare's cloud presentation likely occurred many times. Besides, Egyptian spies had no doubt informed the pharaoh that a Phoenician fleet had previously sailed to rescue the white herd, and search for blue gold."

"No matter what was my father's involvement in this matter," joined in Majit, "Phoenicia would benefit if the unicorn horses now found in Egypt were brought back to this land, and here liberated."

"Majit," continued Avalcar, "as we just saw from the raid of the Hittites, the unicorns would not again be made safe on the mountain behind our capital city. A new and well-hidden home must for them be found."

"Majit's conclusion that Phoenicia would gain from the return of the captive unicorns intrigues me," offered Zoumar. "No matter what our king received for dealing horned horses to Egypt, he would benefit more if someone, let us say the Troyan pirates, stole back the two unicorns."

"Hmpf! Even if I, or better yet my older brother were to raise the issue, about this matter my father would be very touchy. Our king refuses to be questioned about policies and actions that to him prove embarrassing."

"On that point, Majit, you are not wrong," agreed Zoumar. "From long experience I can confirm that your father never takes well to any questioning of his decisions."

"If of a sudden I, Avalcar, disappeared from Phoenicia, what would happen to me? For leaving my military post without authorization, I would in absentia be condemned to death. Hah! But if I did not return to Phoenicia, that sentence could not be carried out. What would happen if without the king's authorization the Troyan pirates left our harbor? Their punishment in absentia would be less than mine. Not under oath to serve Phoenicia, they could not be condemned to death."

"If he could get his hands on them," responded Majit, "for their defiance my father would sentence the Troyans to prison. However, for having departed our shores the king would be powerless to enforce his sentence."

"If I interpret you correctly, Avalcar," said Admiral Zoumar, "although the risk for you is greater than for the Troyans, you would be willing to join a mission to recapture the two unicorn horses. Mistral would be required to also undertake the journey. Without the protection now afforded him by the Troyans, he would no longer be safe here. And as he drew close to his sister and nephew unicorns, Mistral would sense their location. There is no doubt that the presence of Mistral would increase the odds for the success of a raid to restore freedom to two unicorns."

"I do not like the risk you would be taking," offered Majit. "It would not be safe for you to return. And should you here return, Avalcar, perhaps my father *would* carry out a death sentence. He would not deign to remember how well, and for how long you served him."

Preparation

The next morning found Bashkeem leading a company of Troyan sailors to the harbor. Among other things, the sailors hefted buckets of hot tar. Only one soldier guarded the Troyan barges.

"Sir, no one is allowed to board the Troyan vessels," admonished the sentry.

"Does not Admiral Zoumar conduct maintenance on his ships while they are in port?" questioned Bashkeem.

"Of course, Sir."

"Well then, Corporal, my friend Admiral Zoumar told me that in that regard I have the same authority that he does to keep tight and clean the three barges under my command. Unless you are prepared to take this issue above the head of the admiral to the king, you best step aside and let us begin patching before the tar cools."

"I can right now go to request that Admiral Zoumar immediately attend here to this matter," volunteered Olsi.

The sentry looked at Olsi, at the sailors holding buckets of hot tar, and then back at Bashkeem. After heaving a deep breath the sentry consented, "That, Sir Bashkeem, will not be necessary. Do as you see fit to do."

The sentry moved aside for Bashkeem and his sailors to board the Troyan barges.

The crews began to apply tar to ship hulls and to tighten the riggings. Bashkeem ordered ship barrels replenished with fresh water. Upon finding that the seals of barrels with flour and dried fish remained impressively tight, Bashkeem gave Ermal a look of... *I told you so*. After a full day of tarring, washing, cleaning, tightening, and inspecting, Bashkeem and his crew deboarded.

"Corporal, I shall be back in two or three days. With more men I can in one day finish the work required."

"Aye, aye, Sir!"

Upon his return to the garrison Bashkeem found the king's younger son waiting to talk to him and the Troyan captains.

"I trust, Prince Majit, that this evening finds you faring well and in good spirits."

"That is so. And I perceive, Lord Bashkeem, that you are in especially fine spirits."

"We have just now returned from swabbing down our barges. I would say, Majit, that they are almost ready to set sail. Tightening our ships puts me in a fit mood."

"That is good to hear. The Troyan royalty and their sailors count it an honor to sail under your command. Every day or two Admira and Resi tell me that when on the high seas, your true genius is evident for all to see."

Resi brought cups of wine for Majit, Ermir, Ermal, Admira, and Bashkeem.

"Be so kind as to bring a cup for Olsi, and have him attend to me."

"Exactly right!" replied Resi. "I was told that with regard to the harbor sentry, Olsi today had his wits about him."

"Yes he did. The young Egyptian proved particularly timely with his suggestion that Admiral Zoumar be summoned to the harbor."

"Now, Majit, is there something on your mind?" inquired Bashkeem. "Are you thinking on the two unicorn prisoners?"

"Avalcar and I have formed the idea that on this matter nothing can be gained from consulting my father the king. On his authority you cannot, and will not leave our harbor for the purpose of unicorn rescue. It would appear that somehow the Troyan pirate ships have become a pawn for my father to play when, and only when he so chooses. If the matter of the unicorns that were made to be prisoners in Egypt was brought to his attention, he would become embarrassed and angry, or he would lie and deny it. Rather than permit your ships to sail in rescue of the unicorn horses, he would burn them, and so not complicate more his present tenuous relationship with the pharaoh."

After nodding his head in full comprehension of the words spoken by the prince, Bashkeem posed a question, "On the other hand, if we were to sail forth without the king's permission?"

"That is the point, Bashkeem. From my father's perspective he could not in any way be blamed if an *unauthorized* Troyan expedition set forth to rescue the two unicorns. If the unsanctioned expedition failed, my father would simply wash his hands of it by saying he had nothing to do with it. On the other hand if an unofficial attempt to rescue the two unicorns succeeded, then my father's great enemy Egypt would in an important aspect be weakened.

"Zoumar, Avalcar, and I have all concluded that it is better to do what is best for the unicorn prisoners, and forget about seeking the permission of my father."

"Prince Majit," offered Olsi, "it may be that your father will never willingly permit the Phoenician vessels to from here set sail. Because your father is presently fully occupied with the Hittites, and the aftermath of their attempt at ambush, few guards patrol the harbor. Now presents our best, and perhaps only, chance to escape Phoenicia. Added to that, the longer we wait the more likely that the presence of Mistral will be noticed." The weight of Olsi's words was felt by all.

The ensuing silence was by Bashkeem broken, "I am thinking that we will need the aid of Hammereins and Lucareins for our raid on Egypt to achieve success."

"Avalcar will speak for himself and his two fleet horses," replied Majit. "But, I know how he will answer."

"Will you also, Majit, help us to rescue two unicorns?" continued Bashkeem. "Hah! You know, your father asked Avalcar to involve himself with your nascent military career."

"Speaking for myself, the answer is yes," answered Majit smiling.

"Will our three ships attract too much attention as they sail along the coast of Egypt?" inquired Ermir of Bashkeem.

"I have been thinking that our two fastest ships will attract less attention," answered Bashkeem.

Ermir rose and began to pace before the fire. He paused, turned about, and said, "Allow us, Majit, some time to determine how and when our vessels might best slip away from the harbor."

The pieces of the plan of escape came together. It was decided that Resi, the much acclaimed *almost* winner of the Race of the Walls, would stay behind in Phoenicia to look after the safety of her crew. Her vessel, the Star Sheen, would not accompany the rescue mission. Along with notable beauty Resi possessed a keen intelligence, a knack for diplomacy, and a strong will that once set could not be dissuaded.

Without sharing details of the raid, Majit secured a promise from his brother Maroun that he would protect Resi from any intention of harm to come.

From the time that Avalcar had in the land of the white herd made the decision to release Hammer and Lucars from their oaths to the Phoenician army, the much decorated captain had found himself slowly but surely transformed. Avalcar now answered to a call greater than the army of his homeland. He had come to put the good of magical unicorns above the good of the Phoenician crown. As Majit had surmised, with Bashkeem would sail Avalcar and his two foreign horses.

The role laid out for Admiral Zoumar was simple. Other than invent excuses to delay any attempts to search out the two escaped Troyan barges, he was to do nothing. The admiral asked to be purposefully kept in the dark about details of the flight of the Troyan pirates. If Phoenician vessels were ultimately sent to find the escaped Troyan pirates, Zoumar would suggest that they sail not toward Egypt, but that they more fittingly direct northward toward Troy.

Majit stored a set of well-worn sailor's clothes in the garrison so that the entry onto the Jenelisa of King Barsuna's second son, the bird watcher, would go unnoticed. Admira prepared her own sailor disguise for boarding.

While Ermir captained the Flash, the well-seasoned Avalcar would command the even faster Jenelisa. Aboard Avalcar's barge, Bashkeem would fulfill his role as commander of the small fleet of two vessels.

The evening before their upcoming escape the Troyan pirates, as usual, gathered around the cooking fire.

"Admira, Majit, accompany me for awhile," coaxed Resi. "This fire has become too warm for the thick sailor cloaks that you both wear in preparation for the morrow." As the three walked away from the fire Admira fell a few steps behind, and then lingered apart.

"You and I are at last alone," said Majit softly. "I have tried in small ways to show how much your smile means to me. You must know, Resi, that I have many things to say to you."

"Majit, the same as you feel towards me, I feel towards you. I cannot tell you *how much* I am going to miss you while you are gone away from me. It would for me be an unbearably long separation if after the two unicorns are rescued you, Ermir, Ermal, Admira, Bashkeem, and Avalcar take them across the seas to join the white herd."

"It may come to be our duty to ferry the remnant of unicorns over the great water, so that with their horse kind they can be united and made fulfilled. If so, I dread being for so many moons from you absent."

"That dangerous voyage could take as long as a year to complete," responded the princess with a sigh.

Resi let down her hair; her chest heaved deeply and her eyes welled up in tears.

Majit impulsively clasped Resi in his arms as he reassured, "All will be well. Know that my heart loves you deeply."

"I really do not know... how much... I love you," answered Resi as she looked into Majit's brown eyes. "All I know is that I have never before felt this way about any man. Promise, Majit, that you will return to me."

"Dearest one, I promise."

Admira, Resi, and Majit returned to the fire and beside each other sat down.

"Your eyes are red," remarked Ermir looking closely at his sister Resi. "It does not seem that the exercise with Majit and Admira did you well."

With her hands the blushing Resi covered her face.

CHAPTER 18

BREAKOUT FROM PHOENICIA

The day dawned for Troyan barges to break out of the Phoenician harbor.

Bashkeem led two full crews clad in worn pants and frayed shirts to the vessels. Tote sacks were carried over shoulders; buckets and sailors' swabs made of strands of thin cords were hand-carried.

"Corporal, we will today finish shining up our ships," said Bashkeem saluting in return the sentry on duty.

"Aye, of course Sir!" came the reply.

The sailors fitted themselves onto the smallest Troyan vessel, the Star Sheen, and went to work. It was not long before the two crews boarded the two larger vessels tied one on each side of the same dock, and again put to work.

In mid-afternoon a noisy commotion began over the sails. Become irate, Bashkeem shouted at the crews that now that they had made the error of raising one sail, they would have to raise and check the cloth of every sail.

When Bashkeem saw that all was made ready, he ordered the mooring lines tied to wharves to be cleaned. Knots were retied and anchors were cleaned of barnacles. The Jenelisa and the Flash came to be each held to the dock by one mooring line.

"What is it, Corporal? Cannot you see that I am today *very busy?*"

"Yes, but... Commander Bashkeem. It is just that with sails raised, you must not lift anchors or untie shore lines. See how the sails whip about in this wind? One of your ships could haphazardly push away from the dock."

"Right you are, Corporal. Say there young man, do you hear the maidenheads to sound?"

"Yes sir, Bashkeem. I have heard them many times. Because the wind is picking up, their fluting now strengthens."

The sentry soon again approached Bashkeem, "Sir, I say again that you must retie the shore lines, drop the anchors, and drop the sails. If you do not at once comply, I shall have to report this activity to my superior."

"Hmpf," pointed Bashkeem. "Over there, a strange mist rolls onto the docks. What can that be?"

"That... is the darndest thing I have ever seen," answered the sentry. "And it is especially strange at this late time of day, when fogs almost never form. How can a thick mist direct toward one, and only one of our docks? About this I will go see!"

Bashkeem motioned to a group of sailors to follow the corporal. Within moments the sentry was gagged, bound, and deposited behind wheat sacks lining the dock.

Although not seen because of enveloping mist, the clatter of horse hooves was heard. Avalcar guided his mount Hammereins, along with Lucareins and Mistral onto the Jenelisa.

When Bashkeem waved back-and-forth his arms, rowers powered the Jenelisa and the Flash into the harbor.

From adjacent docks came shouts of military alert.

By the time Phoenician naval officers gathered crews and launched barges to apprehend the pirates, the fast under sail Troyan vessels were more than a league out to sea. When in the fading light of evening the pursuing ships became no longer visible, pirate sailors cheered. Found on seas alone, two Troyan barges changed course to southward sail.

"Now, Mistral, it is up to you," said Avalcar that night. "You must open yourself to the beckoning hearts of your family, and direct us toward where they are in captivity held. Would that I were found at your side the moment your family is again made to be free."

"Never doubt that my heart will find them." That neighed, Mistral moved to a spot that looked comfortable, sprawled down, and reclined his side against a barge rail. With head propped between forelegs, he was quickly asleep.

"There is nowhere I would rather be than riding into the Egyptian desert on the back of a horse stallion touched by unicorn magic," said Avalcar to Hammereins and Lucareins. "But, Bashkeem is right. My true and best talent is at the helm of a sea craft. After you are deboarded, I am needed to keep safe the Jenelisa."

"The platoon of rescue will in Egypt be guided by an Egyptian," neighed Hammereins.

"Knowing very well his country, Bashkeem will lead you admirably," responded Avalcar.

Watching stars begin to shine and multiply one on top of each other Bashkeem, Majit, and Avalcar sat later that evening together.

"For escorting Admiral Zoumar back to Phoenician shores, I had hoped that King Barsuna would have showered us with gifts of gratitude," offered Bashkeem. "I wonder if the king is now concluding that had he shown us more generosity, we would still be lounging tranquilly in his garrison."

"To my father that thought would never occur. I can visualize him right now dressing down the company of guards that today patrolled the docks. He will throw the sentry and the sergeant of the guards in prison, at least until my father once more needs them. I would give anything to be hidden in a corner when my father summons Resi, Admiral Zoumar, and my brother. The admiral and Maroun will protect Resi. Riding the fastest horse she could have, and should have won the Race of the Walls. For the nobility of her deference in the race to Avalcar, the people love her. Perhaps she will for now be told to cool her heels in the Old Garrison."

"Zoumar will invent some story, and the king will swallow it," offered Avalcar. "Within three days the admiral will have convinced King Barsuna that the escape served to uncomplicate his affairs of state. And since our king has difficulty maintaining for more than a few days the same thought, his mind will soon find other things to think about, including the dangers presented by Hittite ambushes."

"Before this ship reaches Egyptian shores Resi will be dining at the palace with the king, my brother, and the admiral," added Majit.

"Speaking of the king," said Bashkeem, "why have we not observed soldiers wearing new blue gold armor? Had it been me in charge, I would by now have had every blue gold sheet pounded into armor and swords for the army."

"I have wondered the same thing," replied Avalcar. "We will someday know the answer to that question."

"I am confused!" exclaimed Majit upon finding Bashkeem in the new light of morning. "When I closed my eyes to sleep we were sailing southward toward Egypt. This morning I find we sail in the opposite direction. I thought we were to land in Egypt as quickly as possible to there rescue unicorns from an Egyptian prison."

Without answering, Bashkeem motioned to the boat bringing Ermir, Ermal, and Admira, the three royal siblings, to board the Jenelisa commanded by Avalcar.

"For worry, I could not last night sleep," began Bashkeem as he studied the faces of his captains and ranking officers. "My mind saw fast horses carrying Egyptian spies southward from Phoenicia. At each succeeding garrison post of the Egyptian army, fresh mounts would be waiting for them. Those messengers would travel fast to the port where the unicorns are held. If that were to happen, before we arrive to free the unicorns the Egyptian navy would intercept us."

"You devised another *plan,*" offered Admira.

"Ha! It is time to once again become two pirate crews in search of adventure," responded Bashkeem. "Too many days in garrison quarters have one upon another accumulated. Besides, I had the thought that our flotilla could make good use of one more pirate vessel... to replace the one lost battling the Egyptian fleet."

"Good! Then I shall have a chance to redeem my naval career," interjected Ermal.

"Do tell us more, Captain."

"Of course, Resi. I have little doubt that it did not take long for Egyptian spies to put the pieces of the puzzle together," answered Bashkeem. "Specifically the rumors of a unicorn, the strange mist that enveloped the dock as we cast off, the fact that only two of our three vessels weighed anchor, the disappearance of Prince Majit, and as well the absence of Avalcar and his two fleet horses. Yes, the Egyptian military will be awaiting us. Our counter response will be to delay our arrival, to camouflage our ships, and to increase their number from two to three."

"Since it is believed that our three pirate ships remain stranded in the Phoenician port," interjected Admira, "Egyptian trading vessels have relaxed their guard."

"And upon being told that we are to take another prize, the crews will take heart," added Ermal. "With the plunder taken from an Egyptian trader, our sailors can replenish their empty pockets."

"The Egyptian flags and colors previously found on our two barges remain stored below," added Ermir. "Of them we will make good use."

"Along with replacing our colors, we will adapt the cut of our sails to make them all appear similar," agreed Bashkeem. "Egyptian military uniforms will be worn by the men that come to form the unicorn rescue party. The important thing for us to keep in mind is that it is better to take the time to do a job well, rather than to initially fail and have to repeat our hard and dangerous work a second time over."

"Hahah, Bashkeem!" exclaimed Majit pumping his right arm upward in a fist. "I am often a restless and impatient person. Still, I know that you are right... and for that I very much like this plan. But, where are we now headed?"

"We sail toward the heel of the big boot that comes down from the north to intersect our sea," replied Bashkeem. "From the great port of Egypt, where Olsi believes the two unicorns are held, traders will toward our new destination be sailing with cargos of wheat to trade for olive oil and barrels of wine. Once we have captured an Egyptian trader, we will return to the river port where we last conducted boat repairs. There our three barges will be refit to the colors and patterns of Egyptian..."

"Then after the initial alarm in Egypt has proven false," interrupted Admira, "we will finally send a rescue party ashore for the unicorns."

"That is right," replied Bashkeem nodding his head. "Upon concluding that it was a false alert, the Egyptians will let down their guard.

"Now we will only once be able to enter the Egyptian port. Since we do not know the exact location of the two unicorn prisoners, or how difficult will be their extraction, our vessels cannot tarry in the port. After disembarking the rescuers, our two barges will immediately leave the port, and as a ruse sail west. Since the Star Sheen remained behind in Phoenicia, based on their previous intelligence the Egyptians will assume we command only two barges. Giving chase westward they will not suspect that our third ship sails the opposite direction to carry out the rescue of the unicorns.

"The two rescued unicorns, running alongside Mistral, Hammereins, and Lucareins, will flee eastward through the desert. When after five or six days the escaped unicorns reach the shore, our surprise barge will be there waiting. After exiting the port and outrunning the pursuing Egyptian vessels, our two decoy barges will circle back and rendezvous with our third vessel carrying the rescued unicorns."

Bashkeem turned to Olsi standing nearby, "Was it not you that brought the captains over in the small boat?"

"Aye, Sir."

"I need you to relay a message to the crew of Prince Ermir."

"Be glad to, Sir."

"Tell the crew to look sharp and be prepared to fight. Also tell them that within the passage of fifteen days they will again find gold coins to jingle in their trousers."

When the message carried by Olsi was relayed, not just from one, but from the crews of both barges resounded cheers and shouts of approval.

As was his custom before retiring, Avalcar went to spend time with his fleet horses that as usual were found with Mistral. The Phoenician captain talked to Hammereins and Lucareins the way he would converse with a brother or sister. In the same way as respect and confidence was accorded to them, the horses responded in like fashion.

After sharing with the two horses and the unicorn the new plan of rescue, Avalcar smiled and added, "I would never have thought through, as has done Bashkeem, such an ingenious plan. I have to say that our commander is a very astute Egyptian."

At the information brought by Avalcar, Mistral walked away to be alone with his thoughts.

"Mistral is disappointed for the delay of the rescue," neighed Lucareins. "Still, we shall soon enough run fast through the storied Egyptian desert."

"The postponement of our mission concerns me little," answered Hammereins. "But I do worry about the army units found all around the Egyptian port. When the rescue happens we horses will be called upon to not only show speed afoot, but also keen thinking."

"Just as I was before certain that you both would win the Race of the Walls," interjected Avalcar, "I am equally confident that you two will win the race across the desert."

That night under a curtain of a thousand bits of starlight, and the diamond sparkles of their reflection in a sea made mirror-like, as cleanly as newborn foals slept two horse stallions and their unicorn friend.

CHAPTER 19

SULAY THE AFRICAN-EGYPTIAN

Inspecting closely each sail that loomed on the horizon, Bashkeem led westward two pirate barges.

Although during the passage of several days none of the sighted barges met his needs, Bashkeem refused to worry. Each night before falling to sleep he muttered, "I say that tomorrow we will capture the Egyptian trader that I require."

What Bashkeem wanted was on the eight day found. Flying the colors of the port city where the unicorns were likely held, a large Egyptian barge with sleek lines came into view. Its sails looked to be finely woven and newly made. Golden wheat mounded high the hold of the barge. Two Troyan pirate ships came to block the sea lane of the trading vessel.

"Halloo barge captain! I am Commander Bashkeem! Beside me stands the most blessed animal of creation!"

"I am Captain Sulay!" came the immediate response. "Remove yourselves from where I sail! The invincible navy of Egypt protects this vessel!"

The three vessels drifted closer together.

"Captain Sulay my force, that twice outnumbers your sailors, is committed to a mission more important than any military matter. While not wanting to cause needless suffering to your crew, we require your help to rescue the family of this unicorn that stands next to me.

I think that Captain Sulay has never before seen a magical unicorn."

"No, Bashkeem, never."

"When this unicorn touches his horn to your head you will understand the words that he neighs, and he will understand the words you utter. Come and converse with a unicorn. I give you the word of a proud Egyptian that no harm will come to Captain Sulay."

"Commander Bashkeem, my sword is held in a true hand. I *always* do my duty."

"In a true hand is also held my sword. I promise that on my barge no harm will come to you. Are not you curious? Come and meet the only free unicorn in all the lands that touch upon this wide sea."

"Ha! I *will* trust the word of Bashkeem," responded Sulay with his face breaking into a wide smile. "Some benefit must accord to the meeting of a magical unicorn."

Sulay became jubilant. A horse that bore a horn on its forehead was actually neighing words to him. It was not long before Mistral had told his story to Sulay. In turn Sulay reciprocated with his own story.

"Across the vast deserts of Egypt travel my people. Born into a prominent family, upon reaching my fourteenth birthday as a prince in waiting, it became my duty to learn the ways of other lands. Serving many years the military of Egypt in that pursuit, every day I have found something new to comprehend. I before led soldiers into battle; I now command sailors on board a ship. Harr! And this day I have learned to talk to a sacred horned horse!"

"Captain Sulay," Bashkeem's eyes were grave as he spoke, "we require your barge to rescue Mistral's sister unicorn and her colt that find themselves imprisoned in the great port of the Nile. Join us, and no harm will come to you and your men."

"Even if my heart would approve to so do," replied Sulay, "I cannot break the vow I made to defend the ship placed under my command."

"Myself a military commander, I understand that you cannot break your oath."

Olsi, who stood nearby overhearing the conversation involving his Egyptian countrymen, motioned to speak.

"Ahem, Sir, Bashkeem, one might inquire if Sulay would follow the conventional rules for defense of his barge. When I captained a barge, at the approach of danger I was instructed to line the deck rail with sailors bearing swords."

After nodding his head approvingly at Olsi, Bashkeem inquired of Sulay, "Let me ask you this. Would you defend your ship from attack in the conventional way by positioning a line of swordsmen along the deck rail?"

"I would defend my barge the way I have been taught to defend it," answered Sulay.

"You would not prepare to defend your ship from an attack by horses?" inquired in a quiet tone Bashkeem.

"Diay! Whoever heard of a cavalry attack in the middle of the sea! That is something we are not taught to defend against."

The meeting finished, Sulay returned to resume command of his vessel.

Bashkeem set a plan in motion.

"Thank you for bearing today the burden of battle," said Avalcar as he hugged Hammereins with one arm and Lucareins with the other. "I as well thank you, Mistral, for shouldering the brunt of this fight. Your heroism will today save the life of Sulay, and the lives of his crew. Now, I will have a unicorn and two horses to fight fast while protecting each other."

It was not long before the two Troyan ships bottled between them the Egyptian vessel. When the Sun Flash bumped the starboard side of Sulay's barge, the sailors commanded by Ermir shouted threats and waved swords. Sulay's sailors rushed to the deck rail closest to the Sun Flash, and readied to repel a conventional boarding of swordsmen. In this they were disappointed. While they made as much noise and commotion as possible, Ermir's threatening crewmen did not fling themselves onto Sulay's barge.

When the hull of the Jenelisa touched gently against the port side of Sulay's ship, there was no shouting of pirate battle cries. However, this time the attack was not a feint. Three big equine bodies launched over the rail of the Jenelisa to land on the deck of Sulay's ship. With unmatchable balance in their hips and legs, Hammereins, Lucareins, and Mistral jumped and whirled about as they collided into the onrushing swordsmen defending Sulay's ship. The combination of surprise at, and fear of large riderless equine bodies wheeling about in such close quarters, made the thrusts and jabs of swords to no avail.

Egyptian sailors were by horse heads, horse sides, and horse shoulders bounced back. Some sailors were kicked so hard by the hind hooves of Mistral, Hammereins, and Lucareins that they were propelled to splash into the sea. When the back hooves of Hammereins launched Sulay into a group of startled Egyptian sailors, so toppling them, swords dropped to the deck. Yet standing Egyptian soldiers fell to their knees in surrender. Ropes flung from the two Troyan ships fished from the sea Egyptian sailors gasping for breath.

Admira splashed wine to disinfect the bleeding wounds of an African-Egyptian rendered unconscious. Thanks to the gentle care of the Troyan princess, it was not long before Sulay's wounds were closed. He began to turn slowly back-and-forth his head.

"Why, Captain Sulay, I am very pleased that you decided to come back and join us," encouraged Admira.

"Finding myself now well-bandaged, soon I will be well-mended. Your hands, young lady, possess a strong power to heal."

As his thoughts cleared, Sulay remembered exactly what had happened.

"That, young lady, was the most devious trick I have ever seen in a battle upon the open sea."

"Yes, Captain Sulay, we used a unicorn and two horses touched by unicorn magic to not only create havoc, but to as well spare lives. Not one of your men was cut or wounded by a Troyan pirate sword. And, I expect every one of your men to recover from blows dealt by horse hooves."

"I now know how tastes defeat," sighed Sulay. "Hereafter I shall wear my head a little less high."

"Nonsense!" returned Admira. "If one day asked, you will tell your superiors that the only way you could be beaten was by... unicorn magic. Upon learning that, no one will condemn your defeat this day. Carrying not the magic of blue gold in their swords, Egyptian soldiers could not triumph over magical equines that talk and think like men."

"Young lady... you are right," replied Sulay. "Until I am by men defeated, I will not before men lower my head."

"This ship will do just fine. It is perfect!" commented Bashkeem upon inspection of the captured barge.

Walking at the side of Bashkeem, Sulay took the time to talk about every part of his ship. "These boards are the surest on the deck; they never make a sound when my feet pass over them. Over there! That one section of rail is less sturdy than any other." Rubbing with his hands the sail cloth, Sulay observed, "This is the design of the newest sails now made in the big port of Egypt. Notice, Commander Bashkeem, how fine is the knotting of the threads."

"Perhaps you will one day, under my orders, captain again this ship," said Bashkeem turning to the vanquished barge captain. "If you accept my charge and never more return to your post in the Egyptian army your life will ever after be linked to mine, the lives of my officers, and to the magic of unicorns. Captain Sulay, I would be honored to have a young man like yourself to join my little flotilla."

"To Bashkeem I say... *yes,*" answered Sulay. "With you become my teacher, both me and my men will be made to be better sailors than before. My future actions in peace and war will return honor to you, and to the sacred unicorn. Besides... the time approaches for me to rejoin my tribe."

The new name of the captured ship reflected the heroism of Mistral, Hammereins, and Lucareins in their fight to overwhelm Sulay and his crew. The ships under the command of Bashkeem had grown to number three: the Jenelisa captained by Avalcar, the Sun Flash now captained by Ermal, and the newly named Sea Stallion captained by Ermir.

Fair winds brought the convoy to the part of a peninsular land mass where a heel formed in the shape of a boot. When the cargo of captured wheat was unloaded and sold in a commercial center located on the under arch of the landed boot, sailors including those manning Sulay's vessel, came to again relish the jangle of coins in their pockets.

Shore leave for the sailors was that afternoon done in groups, with leaders enforcing a code of conduct. When asked where they were from and where they were going, sailors replied that by sea winds they had there been brought, and would seek adventure wherever the winds next carried them.

On the following day Commander Bashkeem navigated his vessels back out to sea. Soon the three Troyan pirate ships gained entry to the river where they had before found dry dock for rebuilding the hull of a barge. With no delicate questions asked of them,

Bashkeem's sailors were in this port welcomed as old friends.

Sulay's vessel was refitted with a third mast, tight woven extensions to the sails, and a long and sharp battering ram. The sails of the other two pirate vessels were freshly dyed to match the color of the cloth flying above the deck of Sulay's barge. Hulls and decks were tarred tight and barrels were restocked. Ermir and Admira trained the former crew of Sulay on the fighting tactics of the Troyans.

All had been made ready for passage to the great port of Egypt. And, after fifteen days of hard toil the crews were anxious to be underway. When sails were raised, three ships sporting the same Egyptian colors threaded the river to its mouth, and thereupon embraced the waves of the open sea.

As soft edges of twilight caressed the horizon, Bashkeem looked about to see that all was well. Soon, beneath a starlit sky he settled into sleep. This time it was Bashkeem who awoke to find that in the passage of one night all had changed.

"Avalcar!" shouted Bashkeem. "I went to sleep sailing south! I awake to find that we sail in the opposite direction!"

Avalcar motioned for Admira to join him. Before either one could speak, Bashkeem stopped them short by saying, "You take me... *home.*"

"Yes, Commander Bashkeem," answered a smiling Admira, "it is time that you see again the land of your childhood. Since we found ourselves not so far distant from Illyria, the officers serving under you decided to see for themselves if the mountains of your homeland are as tall as you make them out to be." Not answering, Bashkeem turned away to be alone with remembrances of childhood, and thoughts of family long lost to him.

When the Troyan fleet dropped anchor in a narrow bay, the now trusted Olsi remained behind in command. As he climbed upward a mountain valley that swept inland, Bashkeem walked alone. Mounted on his favorite horse Hammereins, Avalcar followed. With equine backs unburdened by the weight of a rider, Lucareins and Mistral walked behind the Phoenician naval captain. Close after followed Sulay, Admira, Ermal, Ermir, and Majit.

"Houses sit where I remember them," muttered Bashkeem upon entering the place of his birth. "My village has scarcely grown at all."

Come to be gathered in small groups, villagers stared at the strange procession of two horses, a unicorn, and sailors that looked to not all hail from the same country.

"Is it Bashkeem?" exclaimed a tall man with long unkempt dark hair and a thin beard. "Can my brother Bashkeem really be returned to me?"

"It is Bashkeem!" yelled a villager. "In spite of his wearing the dress of the Egyptians that stole him from us, I recognize him!"

With arms opened wide Bashkeem and his brother ran toward each other.

"You really are... Cholo! Praise the heavens I refound my little baby brother!" The two men long embraced.

A jubilant crowd formed, enveloped the brothers, and pushed them along the path that led to the house that once was the home of two small boys now grown to manhood. Outside an open house door, and beneath the accustomed brilliance of clear sky, was seated a man with hair unwhitened by the addition of many years lived.

"It is Bashkeem!" declared an exultant Cholo as he helped his father to stand. "He resembles me, and I look like him!"

In welcome the old man held out his arms. But before embracing his long lost son, Bashkeem's father shifted hands upward and gave thanks for the arrival of a day long awaited, and long dreamt.

Mistral sparked the heads of Cholo and his father.

"You remember, Bashkeem, that when your baby brother was born he came along too early. He was so small he fit into the space of my two hands. Look how he has grown! Cholo is now *taller* than you."

"My brother carries himself well. His belly is as tight as are his arms." With one hand touching a shoulder of his reseated father, and his other hand resting on a shoulder of his younger brother, Bashkeem continued, "Father, you and I were the very same day captured and taken away. I was certain that you had perished in Egypt."

"Son Bashkeem, since seven years past I am returned home. I would not permit my life to end without seeing again my village. Fulfilling well the role of a slave, I eventually earned the friendship of my master. Knowing that I had formulated my plan of escape, my master did not bother to interdict my departure from Egypt, but instead chose to let me live out my days in peace. Ha! Or perhaps my master did not want the expense of feeding a slave whose years numbered many, and whose legs and back were giving out on him."

"And mother?"

"Your mother died of heartbreak. Within a year of my and your departure, her spirit departed into our mountain to dwell with our ancestors. I went a few times to the mountain where she is buried, and talked to her. While she never answered me, my heart told me that she heard my voice."

"I am Avalcar from Phoenicia. Standing with me are Princess Admira, Prince Ermir, Prince Ermal, Prince Majit, and Sulay who is destined to someday become a prince of his people. Hmph! Cholo's grip presses tight; he has strong hands."

"I am *not* the weakest man in this village. Milking forty goats strengthens a man's fingers and wrists. Ha! I confess that I prefer the company of my goats... to the company of my pesky neighbors."

At that comment Cholo's neighbors that had gathered about to closely listen, erupted in good humored laughter.

Cholo turned to the bystanders and explained, "You witness the powerful magic of a unicorn. From the touch of his horn my father and I were made to understand words spoken in another tongue."

"Tell them, Cholo, that I hear your words as though they were spoken in the language of my native country of Troy," added Admira. That was no sooner said, than done.

"I can see that Cholo carries himself well," offered Avalcar.

"During my absence from the land of my birth, Cholo's grandfather taught my younger son to be a great athlete. When my father rode up the mountain to visit the graves of his wife and daughter in law, he made my little boy run beside his horse. That is why the only part of Cholo that is not thin, is his thighs."

"My arms are not that thin. And if my beard would bush-out like the beard of my brother, my face would not look so thin."

"The angular set of your face bespeaks strength of character," complimented Avalcar. "So... running up mountains grew your leg muscles?"

"I cried a few times when I fell," offered Cholo. "But, I soon learned to jump over, glide around, and slip through rocks and boulders. The day finally came when I beat my grandfather's horse and arrived first at the gravesites."

"Because of his big leg muscles, no one has ever beaten Cholo in a race."

"That, Papa, is not true. Do not exaggerate."

"Then tell me the name of someone that won you in a race?"

"Hmpf! I lost races in places where the names are too hard for me to pronounce."

"This man," declared Majit pointing to Sulay, "runs faster than any man I have ever seen... and I run faster than Sulay."

"On both counts Majit exaggerates!" exclaimed Sulay. "I found myself many times beaten in races. But just like Cholo, because my memory is bad I cannot remember the names of the men who ran faster."

At the insistence of villagers that had followed the gist of the conversation, a one thousand pace race course was quickly laid out.

Running neck and neck, Sulay, Majit, and Cholo turned at the halfway mark and accelerated their feet as they approached the finish line. With fifty paces to go in the race, Sulay was leading. Somehow Cholo pulled ahead and beat Sulay, who fell to third place behind Majit.

"Harr! I told you my son was very fast!"

"You were today faster than I," said Sulay gasping for breath. "You run strong!"

"Sulay, my new friend," answered Cholo, "one day I will teach you to win our races."

"I must say that it was accommodating of both Sulay and I to let Cholo win in front of his family and friends," said Majit winking at Sulay. "I trust that when we one day race in my home country of Phoenicia, that you two will let me to win."

Noticing that the commander of the Troyan ships had barely touched the lamb that was served for the afternoon meal, the Phoenician prince said quietly, "I have been thinking about your father, Bashkeem."

"I also, Majit, am thinking on him."

"It must be hard for you to see your father grown old, and to recognize all the years not together shared with him."

Tears came to moisten the eyes of Bashkeem.

"Your head begins to drop, Father," said Cholo with tenderness sounding in his voice. "After a day filled with much thanksgiving, it is time for you to rest. You will once more tomorrow relish the return of your son Bashkeem."

Gathering the frail frame in his arms, Cholo carried his father inside to his bed.

"During the twenty-five years that I dwelled in Egypt, I everyday remembered my father as a man that was tough and strong," said Bashkeem to Majit. "Today I find that he has come to be only skin and bones."

"His mind, Bashkeem, is still very sharp."

"How came I to forfeit so many years of my father's life?"

"I will tell you how," answered Majit. "Your father does not look like an Egyptian. Asking questions about your whereabouts he would have been found out, caught, made to be again a slave, or worse yet executed as a runaway. He knew that. You know that."

"What you say, Majit, is true enough. My father could not risk traveling around Egypt to find me. I did not risk leaving Egypt to return to Ilyria. Instead, I turned away from loneliness to embrace science. And, paradoxically, as a slave in the advanced culture of Egypt, I could do that."

"Bashkeem, you know that you can remain here. The Troyan royals gave you your liberty. If you do decide to stay behind, I will be ever thankful for your exceptional service to my country of Phoenicia."

When Bashkeem did not answer, Majit redirected his conversation, "Cholo, do come and sit beside your older brother. You two have many years to catch up on, and many memories to share."

"I would have given much to have watched my younger brother grow from boyhood to manhood. I would give all I have to turn back the clock, and spend with you your formative years. I should have found a way to do what Father did, and escape back to you." Upon hearing that said by his brother, Cholo lowered his gaze.

"Little brother, over the passage of many years life turns hard. The four Troyan princes and princesses that made me to be their commander, lost in a raid their father, their friends, their home... everything. That is why I stay with them. The Troyans and I know only too well the sorrow brought by marauders." With lowered gaze Cholo continued to listen.

"I am compelled to complete the mission of rescue that I began with the Troyans, Majit, and Avalcar. Two imprisoned unicorn horses are to be brought out of Egypt and set free."

"I would, my brother, give much to accompany you on the rescue of pure and innocent unicorns. But if I with you went away, who would look after Father?"

Joining the reunited brothers Admira inquired, "Cholo, your brother named his barge after a pretty girl that he remembered from this village. What became of Jenelisa?"

"Ah yes. She was a very pretty girl that still today remains striking in her looks and joy of life. Jenelisa hid well herself from the raiders that ravaged this place. Left with no parents, she was taken in by relatives from a far village. Very talented, she became a singer and actress. People especially love her performance in a play about a greedy king that wanted his beautiful granddaughter Maryeta, the part played by Jenelisa, to marry not the brave Lieutenant Abel but to wed instead a rich and obnoxious prince from a distant land."

"That classic work of drama is also known in my land!" exclaimed Admira. "If I am not mistaken, the two unicorns in the play were named Briarburr and Peli, and the brother was named Lyons."

"The curious thing is that for such a vivacious lady, she did not marry. Jenelisa has always said that except for a certain boy that got away," Cholo poked his brother with an elbow, "no man was good enough for her."

"I cannot now delay afford," responded Bashkeem. "But one day I shall refind Jenelisa."

"Surely you must do so, Sir Bashkeem," encouraged Admira.

A new day awoke with warmth golden and skies empty of clouds. Forming in midafternoon, the procession that began to move toward the three barges found at the shore grew to include almost all the men, women, and children from the village of Bashkeem's birth.

A while longer lingered Bashkeem with Cholo and their father.

"Go, my son, and do your duty. Because an important commander, a man who is my son, returned to me my thoughts are now forever free. I am proud of the things you have done. I am very proud for the honorable way you have lived. You were a slave whose heart ever remained free."

Tears came to Bashkeem's eyes. It meant everything for him to know that his father did not fault the tardiness of his return to the village of his birth, and to his family.

"Bashkeem, for the last twenty-five years I have despised myself for not protecting a defenseless ten-year-old boy from Egyptian ravagers. I will no more detest myself. I will only rejoice that my older son lived on. And I will smile when I think of you traveling the sea with magical horses. If I were young again, I would also travel with you and the unicorns."

After hugging long his father, Bashkeem embraced his brother Cholo. Wiping away tears Bashkeem smiled the most open smile that in many years had come to frame his face. Seeing that the eyes of the commander of Troyan pirate ships shone with the warmth and tenderness felt deeply in his heart, his father and brother knew that Bashkeem truly loved them.

A long lost son bid his family farewell.

The meticulous Bashkeem would not sail away from his native coast without making sure that every sailor was stationed in place, and that he had done every little thing right to prepare to cast off. When the three barges finally weighed anchor, the people waiting patiently on the shore shouted goodbyes and waved farewells to their native son.

Hearing renewed shouting on the shore, Bashkeem and Majit turned to see a man swimming toward the Jenelisa.

"What... the blazes! exclaimed Bashkeem. "Who is that? Drop the sails!"

"The man who swims after our ship is a very strong swimmer!" shouted the lookout.

"Aahaa! Cholo does indeed swim fast, but I swim faster," offered Majit.

Majit was soon helping Cholo onto the deck.

"Brother, it is under orders that I come here. Father insisted that I made sure to take good care of you on your voyage."

"Then who... will take care of father?"

"He said not to worry about him. He promised me that he would not starve to death. Besides, you left too many gold pieces on his bed. Now he can live like a rich man and not spend a fortune buying food for a grown son that milks goats and has a huge appetite!"

"Hurrah Cholo! Hurrah Bashkeem!" came enthusiastic shouts from the crew.

Because it was impossible to not immediately like the tall, long-haired, and athletic Cholo whose chiseled face seemed always to wear a smile, he was promptly hefted onto the shoulders of two stout seamen. Bashkeem was hoisted onto the shoulders of two more sailors. The former Egyptian slave told himself that because his brother was with him, he actually relished being paraded before his crew.

"My brother with me sails!" exclaimed Bashkeem stretching out his arms. "This day brings nothing but good news! That is except for one thing. I am now going to be very overworked. Before me is the difficult task of teaching my younger brother... to be a sailor."

"Do not for that worry!" exclaimed Cholo. "Just like the older brother, the younger is a fast learner."

As he that night watched the deep and tranquil sleep of Cholo, Bashkeem could not for happiness find rest. The more he thought about how much his father had that day sacrificed to release Cholo into his protection, the lighter became the heart of the Troyan commander. Again and again Bashkeem whispered to himself, "I now truly know that my father loves me."

As he tried to sleep, Bashkeem's mind struggled to resolve one question... was it more important for him to know love *for* his father, or more important for him to feel the love *of* a father. Bashkeem finally decided that it was precious to feel oneself loved.

CHAPTER 20

RESCUE OF UNICORNS

With a plan of rescue emphasizing execution and speed, three Troyan pirateers sailed south toward Egypt.

In middle night two pirate vessels were to enter the great port of the Nile. Under the command of Avalcar the fastest ship, the Jenelisa, was to race ahead to quickly land Mistral, the two horses, and ten men armed with swords. Commanded by Ermal, the Flash would trail the Jenelisa into the port. The deboarding completed, both vessels would exit the port and race westward as decoys. Avalcar was confident that he and Prince Ermal could outrun any number of following Egyptian ships. Having finally shaken off pursuit, the two Troyan vessels would circle back to the east.

After previously separating his vessel from the other two pirateers Ermir, the most experienced captain among his siblings, was to bring the Sea Stallion to rendezvous somewhere along the desert coast with Bashkeem, Majit, Sulay, Cholo, and the rest of their platoon of sailors, horses, and unicorns. Some few days after the two captive unicorns were set free, the barges captained by Avalcar and Ermal would be on the lookout for Ermir and the Sea Stallion.

On a night when recalcitrant clouds forbad the stars and moon to shine down on the Egyptian port, escorted by Mistral's mist the Jenelisa and the Flash entered the estuary of the Nile.

With Bashkeem's arm resting on Mistral's back, the unicorn stallion felt himself drawing closer and closer to his family. Barely able to contain his excitement, Mistral shook his head and mane, lifted hooves in little jumps, and restrained the impulse to neigh loudly to his two lost unicorn relatives.

"As you no doubt recall, Bashkeem, over there on the highest hill sits the citadel," said Olsi pointing. "No better place can in this city be found to hide unicorn horses."

"Olsi, how well do you know this port city?" inquired Bashkeem.

"Because I was here born and raised, I know no place in Egypt better than this city."

"Then Avalcar's first mate Olsi is the one that needs to steer this vessel to the dock where we disembark."

"This is the place," neighed Mistral. "Not far distant are the unicorns I search for."

"In that case, Olsi was right," answered Bashkeem. "They will surely be found in the citadel that looms above us. Can Mistral's mist envelop us as we move along narrow streets?"

"*Yeerrhrrunhrrunh...* stay close and my mist shall well-hide you."

A vacant dock presented and the rescue party disembarked. Avalcar gave the order for his sailors to row their barge back into river current. Soon the Jenelisa and the Flash sped out of the port, this time trailed by several Egyptian war barges.

With Bashkeem at his side, Mistral followed winding streets that inclined upward. Hammereins and Lucareins formed the second file. Nine men walking three abreast followed after.

Oblivious to the mist that rolled past them, at that late time of night most street guards slumped in corners half asleep. Sulay and Cholo used the butts of their swords to convince a few dedicated sentries to take a break from the tedious work of night watch. Guards awoke later wondering exactly what from out of a strange and inexplicable mist had hit them so hard as to make their heads to ache badly.

"On the other side of this wall is found my family."

"As befits the noble Mistral, he will through the front door enter," answered Bashkeem. "Thank goodness for the mists you this night weave."

With swords unpracticed at slicing apart thick fog, Egyptian soldiers found themselves thrown back by horse hooves that they did not see coming. By the flat of sword blades, guards were slapped so hard that they became disarmed. The front gate to the citadel was made to swing open.

The neighing of unicorns was heard. In soon answer, the powerful hind hooves of Mistral kicked apart the door to the fortress stable. Toppling guards, Mistral pushed through brokenness. When Bashkeem brought down hard his sword forged of blue gold, a thick chain strapping shut an equine prison cell was severed. "Two unicorns are unbound!" exclaimed Bashkeem.

Hammereins and Lucareins pushed and shoved with conviction, so that several Egyptian guards came to be restrained in the stabled partition where shortly before two unicorns had been held captive.

"Follow me! I know a way out of here!" neighed the younger of the two released unicorns. The platoon of liberation clambered along corridors stretching higher and higher, where no sentries were posted, until they reached a courtyard fed by a fountained spring.

"Drink deeply," said the young unicorn, "on the other side of these walls begins desert where little water can be found. I will be back shortly." Quickly returned, the young unicorn whinnied, "The door that formerly passaged through the back wall of the garrison, has been bricked-up. No door presents to leave out this place."

"Where there once was a door," neighed Hammereins, "another can be made." The combined force of the rear hooves of Hammereins and Lucareins pounded until a newly broken space in the wall was kicked large enough for a horse to pass through.

"We five horses and unicorns will each carry two men," neighed Mistral. "We must travel fast, or we will come to be surrounded."

The weight of the two biggest men mattered little to the strong back of Hammereins. A big man and a smaller man were mounted on the backs of each of the other four equines. The five unicorns and horses galloped fast through streets that soon enough ended in unkempt places where mud brick houses became more and more sparse. The shouts of Egyptian soldiers in pursuit came no more to be heard.

Three unicorns and two horses drove hooves into hills of desert sand that through the passage of new morning grew taller. No one in the company led by Bashkeem doubted that Egyptian cavalrymen still advanced somewhere to the rear of raiders that had displayed the unbelievable gall to steal from an imposing citadel two prized unicorns possessed of strong magic.

Mounted with his brother Cholo on Mistral, Bashkeem called a rest. In a spot of shade the platoon of men, unicorns, and horses collected themselves.

"Would not you say, Mistral, that it is time to introduce your family to us," suggested Bashkeem.

"That, Commander, will be my pleasure. This great dame, my older sister unicorn, is called Crimson. Her colt, this strapping young unicorn stallion, goes by the name of Seahorse."

"Crimson, Seahorse, please tell us for what stand your names," requested Majit.

"When long ago my mare first saw me color the clouds above my head in reds, oranges, blues, and purples, she decided the name Crimson suited me. But I am afraid that my artistic talent has little use on this earth."

"By no means is that so, Dame Crimson," answered the artistically minded Majit. "You possess a talent most wonderful."

"When we were imprisoned," continued the unicorn mare, "the part I missed most about the loss of my freedom was that I could not see how I had before prettied the sky at sunrise. Because our prison window opened only to the sea and the setting sun, my coloration was limited to that part of the sky."

"I wish that I could do something that added so much beauty to evening skies," rejoined Majit.

"My sister mare one thing forgets," neighed Mistral. "In exchange for her artwork, the clouds return something back to her."

"Yes, that is so. The clouds show me what passes beneath them. That is how I sensed that Phoenician barges carrying the magic gold were found in return to our sea."

"As for me," neighed the young unicorn stallion, "I am told that I swim like a dog... but far better than a dog. Still, I am glad that for a unicorn the name Seahorse sounds more dignified than the name Seadog. Finding myself in deep water, I feel complete freedom of movement. I can swim all day and all night, and still not tire. As my name suggests, swimming is my humble gift and talent."

"So, Seahorse," answered Cholo, "that makes two of us that love to swim. One day, you and I shall in the ocean swim side-by-side."

CHAPTER 21

TREE HORSES

"Soldiers walk the clouds!" neighed excitedly Mistral the next morning. Traveling a line parallel to and only some leagues distant from the seashore, the eastward movement of the platoon of rescue halted.

"That is so," confirmed Crimson. "In my vision celestial many soldiers are found along the coast."

"So Crimson's amazing cloud painting shows that soldiers block our outlet to the sea," observed Bashkeem. "That means that we cannot proceed directly to where our ships are to meet us. Nor can we turn back. The only alternative that remains is to circle away from the coast into the vast desert. Hmpf! But, that many soldiers could not have been so quickly mobilized to chase after us."

"While I do not know how that large army came to be gathered, I do know a way through the desert," offered Sulay.

"Then it shall be Sulay that guides us onward," replied Bashkeem. "And please bring us to a well of water."

"I will run as do the youths in my village!" Sulay set out in a long-legged lope. With men mounted on their backs, as they followed after Sulay five horses and unicorns alternatively trotted and cantered.

Riding now double with Majit, the leader of the platoon of rescue made an observation, "Young prince, because you are polite and very well spoken, I can usually count on you to offer comments that encourage us. How is it that you have nothing to say?"

"I am at that a talker, Bashkeem. It is just that I have been captivated by the panorama presented by the sand dunes that we travel through. Even as we watch, desert winds sculpt the dunes to make each one unique."

"Contemplation of a vast desert landscape brings me peace."

"The same for me, Bashkeem. It is as if the heavens gifted us this wondrous desert to remind us of our limitations as men. No matter what or how I should in some way attempt to alter this vastness, the power of desert winds would make all my efforts come to naught. Hoof prints made today by magic unicorns, will on the morrow by delicate winds be made to vanish. Hmph. I think, Sir, that this day's elusive breeze is more powerful than a thousand Egyptian war barges."

"I hope that a future painting of yours will highlight the shimmering caress of a desert breeze."

"For that purpose I will commit to my memory the grandeur of sand, dunes, and wind that you and I right now behold."

"Very good, Majit. May I suggest that the inclusion of a unicorn, and his fading tracks in the sand, would heighten the magical quality of that work of art."

The seemingly tireless legs of the African-Egyptian did not stop until dusk, when Bashkeem's company came to a low line of hills that through the hot afternoon had beckoned to them.

"Now I rest," said Sulay who immediately sprawled tired limbs on the sand and began to snore.

"Look there, Cholo," Bashkeem motioned toward the repose of the exhausted Sulay. "Just like you, when he sleeps his arms and legs do not move."

"Well then, brother, just like me Sulay enjoys the sleep of... *the innocent.*"

"Try as I might, Cholo, my body requires itself to move about while I sleep."

"Hah! My brother has too much on his mind. He is burdened by so much responsibility that while he dreams his mind still moves at work. But speaking of movement, I am going to climb this hill to see what on the other side awaits us."

"Do not linger long away from us."

As darkness descended Bashkeem reflected upon where he found himself. During his many years in Egypt he had come to love the sense of solitude and vastness encountered in an immense desert. Settling to rest, he remembered that as a youth he had searched for a formula permitting computations and numbers large enough to count the seemingly uncountable grains of desert sand. He fell to sleep wondering how many years would have to pass before shifting winds should come to again repeat with exactness this day's pattern of sand dunes.

"Wake up, Brother," interrupted the returned Cholo. "There is a campfire."

Not long after, lying prone on the crest of a ridge Bashkeem and Cholo stared intently down on a desert wash where grew palms and stunted trees, and where burned a large fire. Around the flames were gathered tribesmen.

"Their long spears could at fifty paces kill a lion, or for that matter a man or horse," affirmed Cholo.

"Brother, about that you are not wrong. More than one hundred well-armed warriors block our route forward."

"Bashkeem, do you see the girl drawing water at the well?"

"Now I do, Cholo. You just reminded me how thirsty I am. Let us with Sulay talk about what we next do."

Upon return to camp the brothers found Sulay sitting quietly on his haunches. He rose to salute Bashkeem, "Commander I can guess that at the well you found a tribe."

"Behind a girl drawing water, were warriors armed with long spears. Their numbers are many more than ours."

"Are the faces of the adult men marked, as is mine, with three scarred lines on each cheek?"

"We did not get close enough to see if their faces are marked," replied Bashkeem.

"Commander, because some tribes are less friendly than others, we need to know who they are. Do you give me permission to crawl close enough to identify them?"

"Good idea, Sulay. But since I do not this night want to lose the noble African-Egyptian, I order you to be extra cautious."

Making nary a sound, Sulay vanished into the night.

"Cholo, Majit... follow after Sulay," directed Bashkeem. "Report back to me what is happening with the tribe. If Sulay comes to find himself in trouble, we must act quickly to rescue him."

Majit soon found himself leaning his side against a comfortably contoured rock. He whispered, "Do you see Sulay? I cannot."

"Neither do I see him," replied Cholo. "Surely Sulay will want to quietly observe the tribesmen for some time to... wait! Against the flames I see his outline. He walks openly toward the fire."

"Sulay must know that the camp is peaceful," offered the younger Phoenician prince, "or he would not so dangerously expose himself."

"I go closer to the fire," said Cholo. "I want to see what next happens to my friend Sulay."

"While you move quietly into the draw below us," replied Majit, "I will report back to Bashkeem, and ask to bring Lucareins here with me. If the tribesmen come too close to the draw where you are hid, our fastest horse will retrieve you. Cholo, be careful. If we are discovered all may be for us, and the unicorns, lost."

Returned with Lucareins, Majit and the horse focused their eyes on the place in the draw where they detected the hidden Cholo. Sulay was nowhere to be seen.

"Prince Majit," neighed Lucareins softly, "I go where waits Cholo. I will more closely see what is happening with the natives. Come you with me?"

"I had better stay up here on the hill," answered Majit shaking his head sideways, "so that I can relay any new intelligence back to Bashkeem. Move stealthily, Lucareins. The tribe may have posted sentries."

"I see you," whispered Cholo to Lucareins. "Join me. If we are found out I will grab hold your mane and kick myself up onto your back."

"What is happening in the camp?" neighed the stallion, "I do not see Sulay."

"Not long ago our friend disappeared into the big tent where tribesmen are gathered outside," answered Cholo. "Look! The tent empties. They have given Sulay... *a spear.*"

"A man with a spear separates from the other warriors," neighed Lucareins.

"He is to face off against Sulay," replied Cholo. "Unfortunately, he is taller and looks to be even more muscled than is Sulay."

"A fight with sharp spears is a battle to the death," neighed Lucareins. "Cholo, what can we do to stop this from happening? We cannot risk the death of our guide, now become friend."

"I just noticed that Majit left his position to report what is happening to Bashkeem," replied Cholo.

"I do not like standing by while Sulay is threatened with death," neighed Lucareins.

Sulay and the opposing warrior began warily circling each other. The newfound enemy of Sulay feinted to launch his spear, and in reaction Sulay swerved quickly his legs. In this way the match continued; the two warriors were not in a hurry to kill each other.

The men and women of the camp began jumping feet to the sound of drums; night air came to be filled with high-pitched cries.

Scrambling out of the ravine he shared with Cholo, Lucareins charged ahead. Approaching the fire, Lucareins began to weave back-and-forth.

Spears were raised and aimed menacingly at the horse. Shouting loud, Sulay waved about his arms to dissuade a menacing flight of spears. Drumbeats stopped. The men and women of the tribe waited in silence for what next would happen.

Upon observing Lucareins begin to prance, once again drumbeats began to sound. The rhythm of the beats came to follow perfectly the hooves of the stallion.

Slipping through the line of tribesmen with spears still raised, a young woman began to imitate the steps taken by Lucareins. Another young woman joined the first, then another and another. Sporting buoyant smiles, a line of women came to dance opposite the steadily approaching stallion.

Drawing closer to the gathering, Lucarein's paces became mixed with head movements and jumps that were in turn matched by the rhythmic movements of the native women. For their part, the file of young women edged dancing feet closer to a stallion weaving back-and-forth upon hooves that maintained the tempo of beating drums.

The sound of more hooves was heard. A horse and three unicorn reinforcements arrived. Bashkeem, Cholo, and Majit slid off equine backs.

Hammereins joined the dance of Lucareins. Once Hammereins matched the rhythm of the drumbeats, the unicorns joined the equine line. Five horses and unicorns were soon in unison prancing.

Spear in hand, Sulay moved to join the equine dance. Holding high their spears, a line of warriors began to dance behind the line of women. Slowly, but surely, two lines of men and women dancers came from opposite directions to encircle the horses and unicorns. Still moving hooves and feet to the beat of drums, the five equines and Sulay began to move in their own circle.

Drumbeats stopped. Sulay walked forward, planted his spear in the ground, and straightened himself to stand with much dignity. After planting his spear into dirt, Sulay's opponent joined to the side of his erstwhile adversary. The dance of the horses and unicorns had changed the outcome of the kill, or be killed, fight.

An elder tribesman joined to Sulay; the two men clasped each others' shoulders. A chair woven of reeds was brought for the older man to sit upon. Members of the tribe, as well as those present from Bashkeem's platoon, collected themselves before the seated chieftain.

Sulay leaned over to whisper something, and at that a big smile spread over the headman's face. The man in authority motioned to Mistral, the biggest of the unicorns, to approach. Desiring Mistral to anoint him with the uniform animal speech, the old chief pointed to his mouth, and then motioned for Mistral to tap his head with his horn.

Against the older man's forehead Mistral's horn sparked blue. That accomplished, the headman would talk.

"What is your name?"

"Mistral."

"My name is Fadil. This night I am again made to be *chief*."

The headman laughed, smiled big, and added, "My rival had from me taken my power. Upon my cousin's return, knowing that Sulay would defend me, my rival made his son Enos to fight Sulay to the death. Enos is our strongest warrior. One of the two would not live to see the new morning. But Sulay had done nothing... *wrong*. Enos had done nothing... *wrong*. Sulay is not only my relative, he is my friend. It is not right to take, for no good reason, a man's life.

"These horses and unicorns saved the life of either Enos or Sulay, or perhaps both their lives. The smiles of the prancing horses showed us that it is better to not carry a heart filled with jealousy and bitterness."

The men and the women of the tribe shouted approval for the words spoken by the elder man that had that night been restored to leadership.

"The selfish usurper should be thankful that I do not throw him to be trampled by the horned horses," admonished Fadil turning toward the one that had before taken his title and position. "However, for the unjust fight with spears that a bad man made this night to happen, a price *must be paid*. For the next twelve moons the usurper's son Enos will be known as... the servant of Sulay. Enos will obey every command that Sulay gives him."

"I have no need for Enos," objected Sulay.

"Not only must Enos obey his chief, Sulay must also to me be obedient. If with these magic horses Sulay tomorrow departs, then Enos goes with Sulay. If you do not together come back, neither one can return to look upon my face."

The dignified chief proclaimed with authority, "Sulay commands! Enos obeys! Like brothers you two will take care of each other!"

"Until the day comes that I once more command myself, at Sulay's side a proud warrior shall come to be an even greater warrior," responded Enos after being head-touched by a unicorn horn.

"You who wears comfortably the dress of Egypt," directed Chief Fadil to the oldest man among the intruders, "tell me where in the company of five magic horses Sulay takes his servant Enos."

"Before a slave of Egypt, I am Bashkeem. Here stands beside me Majit, a son of the king of Phoenicia. On my other side stands my brother Cholo. I am proud that Majit, Sulay, and my brother helped to set free two of these unicorn horses that were held captive in the port of Egypt. In a few suns our ship will come to the seacoast to find us."

Bashkeem politely paused. When no one spoke, he continued, "For having freed the two unicorns, the Egyptian army is with us angry. Even now as we talk, Egyptian soldiers come after us. Somehow we must escape to the coast and find our ships."

"Will soldiers of Egypt come to this place in search of you?" asked the stately headman.

"Our tracks in the sand will bring them here," replied Bashkeem.

"Hmpf!" responded the chief. "I must learn more about the great magic of the unicorns." Fadil motioned for Sulay to walk with him.

Food and drink were brought to the visitors.

Native men and women gathered around the five equines. More than anything the women wanted to touch the ivoried horns and caress the white manes of the unicorns. As the night traced a cooling breeze over desert sand, children ran about slapping hands playfully at the foreign men, unicorns, and horses. The children laughed at the mere idea of being to the strange visitors bothersome.

When the left-behind sailors in the platoon came to join the tribal camp, Bashkeem instructed, "For now we will not trouble ourselves about the Egyptian soldiers that follow after us. Tomorrow will bring time enough to worry, and perhaps to fight."

"The sun is up," muttered Bashkeem rubbing sleep from his eyes. "How is that I slept so long through the night?"

The commander and his men were soon breakfasting fried bread, goat cheese, and pomegranates.

"For my tribe pomegranates symbolize the blessings of life," informed Chief Fadil after he and Sulay joined Bashkeem and Majit. "In that regard it is for me a *big* blessing to count you as my friends. Ha! Sulay has something to show you! After breakfast Bashkeem and Majit will go with Sulay to see the tracks of horses that in the night passed by our camp."

"How is it, Sulay, that horses last night came here?" inquired Majit as the three men began to walk into the desert. "Hammereins and Lucareins should have alerted us to the sounds and scents of passing horses."

"Look carefully at those tracks, Majit."

"Yes, Sulay, they are the tracks of horses. But I still do not understand how they came to be here."

"Then I will show you."

Upon climbing to the top of a high desert dune, Sulay motioned an arm, "Look there, Majit. See in the distance the five horses that made these tracks."

Neither Majit nor Bashkeem could believe their eyes. Men were walking high off the ground with legs bound to the trunks of sapling trees, and feet gripping niches made into sawed off branches. Three men followed mixing their footprints into the marks made by the tree sticks.

"Hahah!" exclaimed Sulay. "What do you think of Chief Fadil's idea to camouflage your tracks with those of tree horses?"

"Those tracks look real," commented Bashkeem. "This, Sulay, is an ingenious invention."

"The hooves carved on the bottom of those saplings must have been by artists made," declared Majit.

"The tree horses will walk all morning into the desert, and after disappear into a trackless rocky ravine," commented Sulay. "In the meantime, the men of our tribe will sweep into smooth sand the real horse tracks you leave behind. Now, Captain, we must go. We can lose no time. Egyptian soldiers come soon."

"Chief Fadil," said Bashkeem in farewell, "I can never repay the kindness that you have shown to me, and to those with me."

"You will do so, Bashkeem, by relishing the *blessings of life.*"

"After today, every pomegranate that I eat will remind me of a very wise desert chieftain... and the sweetness of life."

Thanks to the generosity of a tribe of African-Egyptians camped by a desert well, skins filled with water were given to Bashkeem and his men.

With hugs and affectionate words whispered, Sulay extended farewells to his family and friends. As they neighed goodbyes to the men, women, and children of the desert tribe gathered about them, five unicorns and horses reared high. In salute to a chief once again seated on a chair of woven reeds, the equines a second time flashed front hooves. Standing apart, the eyes of Enos watered with emotion.

Following after the long running strides of Enos and Sulay, Bashkeem led his mounted troop eastward into desert. As Sulay had said would happen, tribesmen with reed brooms made the tracks of flesh and bone unicorns and horses to be swept away into sand.

That same morning the desert nomads departed from the well. No Egyptian army captain would think to follow Chief Fadil and his tribe in order to inquire about unicorns. How desert nomads rode horse hooves carved into sapling tree trunks became a story recounted by one generation to another.

Many Egyptian Soldiers

"The African-Egyptians run as good as a horse!" neighed Hammereins to Bashkeem.

"It is very impressive to observe the endurance of Sulay and Enos running in front of the horses," responded Bashkeem.

Upon overhearing the comments of Hammereins and Bashkeem, Majit decided that he could also match the strides of the two runners. The younger prince of Phoenicia dismounted to join the race of Sulay and Enos. When he saw that Majit did not tire, Sulay pointed to the horse from which Majit had dismounted. When Majit nodded his head yes, Sulay joined the riders. Shortly thereafter Cholo jumped off his mount, and motioned for Enos to ride.

The terrain changed from desert sand to rocky ledges fingered with dry washes. After carrying heavy loads of two men on their backs, the horses and unicorns required rest. Bashkeem called for his troop to encamp for the night.

"We traveled far today," offered Majit. "If the Egyptian army still follows us, from these rocks and ledges they remain distant."

"The Egyptian army cannot run all day as did Cholo, Majit, Enos, and I," agreed Sulay nodding his head.

In an indent into the base of a cliff a small fire was built and flat bread was roasted crisp. By kindred hearts the humble supper was savored as if it were a feast in the palace of a king.

Bashkeem gathered Majit, Cholo, Sulay, and Enos to sit close by where rested together three unicorns and two horses.

"Commander Bashkeem, Enos knows these lands better than I," informed Sulay.

"In not too many days," responded Enos, "we will be at the point where the curve of the sea shifts from east and west, to north and south."

"That being the case," interjected Bashkeem, "it is better to find our way northward than to continue eastward into more desert. I am not sure where we shall encounter the Egyptian army, but we have to be prepared for them finding us."

"I wonder what Chief Fadil would do if he found himself in our present situation," inquired Majit.

"As to what my chief would do, I think I know," responded Sulay. "He would like a leopard stalk the enemy soldiers. He would make sure the enemy did not see him move through the hills and rocks. He would follow the soldiers along the coast until he found an opportunity to over them gain victory."

"Hmpf! The stalking part makes sense to me," responded Bashkeem. "Enos, can you from here find a fast way to reach a part of the coast boundaried close by hills, ravines, and boulders?"

"Because I have many times traveled these lands, I know where is found each place of water between here and the seashore setting you described," replied Enos.

"How many days will it take to travel from this place to there?"

"If we run all the way, Commander, it will take three days."

"Then Enos will guide us... to the sea."

"In view of the long day tomorrow," neighed Mistral, "we equines need to get to sleep. *Nyerrrr!* It is time for you men to quit talking."

Relishing his new status as guide, Enos the next day kept his senses acute both to the men he led, and to the terrain he led them through. Something about the way Cholo carried himself, wearing always a ready smile, made him a favorite of Enos.

"Cholo, you act all the time natural," remarked Enos that evening. "I see that you do not worry about anything. You are a man that loves to laugh. In that way you are very different from your brother Bashkeem."

"Because my grandfather who raised me felt guilty that from our village my older brother had been stolen, he held the memory of Bashkeem high over me. He often reminded me that Bashkeem was more serious than I, herded goats better than did I, and fixed corrals better than me. I suppose it was because of that, Enos, that I grew tired of trying to imitate a grave and solemn brother, at that unknown to me. I decided to *not* be serious, but to instead enjoy life. Whether it was running races, jumping, wrestling, or throwing stones for distance I came to excel at sports. I discovered that I liked to eat well. I came to love to laugh. Ha! Who knows, Enos? Perhaps over-reacting to the earnest nature of my lost brother, I did not myself work hard enough on becoming a man serious about life."

Enos extended an arm; two hands clasped in friendship.

"Now my friend," said Cholo after exhaling a big yawn, "let us rest so that we can run hard tomorrow... and the next day."

After two more days the company of men and equines found themselves overlooking a shoreline that framed the sails of several Egyptian barges. But it was what they saw on the wide beach below that dissuaded hope; company by company was encamped a large Egyptian army.

"To have so many Egyptians guard the coast against their escape, the unicorns must be very important," remarked Enos to Cholo lying prone beside him.

"My brother Bashkeem told me that no earthly magic is stronger than that borne of unicorn horns."

"Not one of the healers or miracle workers in our tribe can make a horse to speak words that warriors understand," responded Enos. "Not one of our magicians can make a horse to dance to the beat of a drum."

Since the sea coast was that night dotted with too many soldier camp fires to count, the prevailing mood in the huddled company of Bashkeem was one of discouragement.

"Perhaps, Bashkeem, we can find a way to sneak past the fires and without being seen swim out to our barge when it here presents," offered Majit.

"The problem," replied the commander, "is that if Prince Ermir sails the Sea Stallion from due north toward this coast, he may not come to see Egyptian patrol vessels before they see him. And upon sighting the approach of Ermir's vessel, Egyptian warships will encircle and trap our barge of rescue against this shore."

"I can admit that troubling thought also occurred to me," answered Majit.

"Our situation here could hardly be worse," continued Bashkeem. "Egyptian soldiers and barges block our way to the Troyan vessels. We and our ships are perilously isolated from each other. Our supplies of food and water are minimal. And, if somehow we found a land route back to Phoenicia, our ship captains would not know that is to where we had disappeared."

"Commander," offered Majit, "farther along the coast the Egyptian army cannot be as heavily reinforced as it is here. If we could get a message to our ships to meet us beyond where the coast turns north, we would have a better chance of success."

"Agreed," responded Bashkeem. "How do you propose we penetrate the line of soldiers below us, and then somehow find our ship of rescue, wherever in this great sea it now sails?"

"Here is a thought," replied Majit. "Maybe we can find a strong swimmer with stamina to paddle for two days on ocean waves. Hah! That is me! I can out-swim anyone."

"This idea of yours, Majit, is not... half bad," assented Bashkeem. "If I knew that you could swim for two or three days in salty water, without sinking to the bottom, I would be tempted to approve your plan."

"The name Seahorse signifies that I am the champion swimmer. I will find your ship and deliver the message to locate Bashkeem above the curve of the coast."

"Because that was my idea," answered Majit, "if anyone swims out into the deep water, it is me."

"Seahorse possesses a name that proves he is a great swimmer," answered Bashkeem calmly. "We have also seen Cholo swim fast, and heard him speak of being proud of the way he swims."

"I am pretty sure that I can swim faster than Majit," offered Cholo. "But I dare not tackle a swim that could last several days. I am not *that* strong a swimmer. In my humble opinion, no one is."

"About that, Master Cholo, you are wrong," averred Seahorse. "My body floats on water. Although I would become hungry and thirsty, I could travel the sea for a whole week without losing my bodily strength and my ability to swim. The magic of my horn would also guide me toward Ermir's barge."

"Who among us has a better idea than Majit's?" inquired Bashkeem. No man, horse, or unicorn could come up with a plan more likely to succeed.

"Lacking alternative ideas on how to proceed, I will accept the plan offered by Majit... albeit with one change," consented Bashkeem. "Since Majit came up with the idea, and insists on being the one sent out into the ocean, why then he will go. But, since Seahorse is to my mind the best swimmer found among us, he will accompany Majit.

"Seahorse and Majit will together swim to find our ship, or ships, and direct them to meet us somewhere after the coast curves north. In late night you two will leave our camp and pass through the Egyptian lines. Once we are certain that you are set safely upon the sea, the remainder of our company will advance eastward. Now... everyone get some rest."

"Majit... a word."

"Yes, Commander Bashkeem."

"Why are you so intent to swim forth? Your mission will be fraught with danger, and I will wager that my brother Cholo can actually out-swim you."

"Sir, the other night with spear in hand Sulay demonstrated his courage for all to see. Rather than dishonor his heart, Sulay would have accepted death. You, Sir, had the courage to live more than twenty years as a slave that kept his honor intact. Growing up with no advantage, your brother Cholo made himself to be a superb athlete. Unlike Cholo, Sulay, and yourself, I was born into privilege, and I have done nothing to show that I merit *the blessings of life* that I have received. It is come my turn to make a sacrifice, to risk everything by doing something brave. It is now for me to defend the lives of your platoon of men and magic horses. That is all, Sir."

"For the honesty of your answer, I thank you Majit. In return for today honoring your request to undertake an act that is fraught with peril, I tell you that you must not tire. Unless I bring you back from this voyage, I cannot face your father the king or your brother Maroun."

"Commander Bashkeem, this very strong swimmer will obey your command. When I tire I will cling to the mane of Seahorse. While they are still far away and beyond our sight, Seahorse will sense the blue gold swords carried on your Troyan barges. Do not worry for me or for Seahorse; we *will* find you somewhere after the turn of the coast. And, Sir, for your part you must safely arrive at our new place of rendezvous, wherever that turns out to be."

"Majit, as I lead our friends to the place where we shall after meet, I will petition the heavens to protect all of us."

"Fire!" "Fire!" shouted Egyptians.

Soldiers on foot and on horse were sent westward toward the large night fire that burned upon the crest of a hill fronting the sand beach. For the frantic rush toward the blaze no one noticed that a league away from the fire the beach was left unguarded. It was in that place that Majit ran beside Seahorse into the waves.

"Seahorse, I cannot keep up with your swimming strokes."

"It does not do for you so early on to be left behind. Climb upon my back and crouch low. We will soon be out of sight of the shore. Because the Egyptian barges also move toward the decoy fire, they do not spot our night swim." Grabbing a handful of mane Majit pulled himself onto the unicorn's back.

"I am in your debt, Seahorse. It is a good thing that these waters are warm, or my body would by morning be chilled through."

"Enjoy the freshness while it lasts. The coming afternoon will bring a hot sun to burn down upon us."

Into the sparkling bower of a star filled night swam Seahorse with his rider.

CHAPTER 22

Two Armies and Cloud Magic

"With no notice of their departure, Seahorse and Majit swam into the waves," commented Enos to Cholo as they loped beside each other. "And not until new daylight will the Egyptians find our tracks."

"Ahhuh," agreed Cholo. "It was such a simple plan. Light a deceptive fire, sneak two of us into sea waves, and in the created confusion the remainder of our platoon breaks away."

"Master Cholo and Enos had best preserve their breath," cautioned the also afoot Sulay. "The pace of this fast run will by midday leave us exhausted."

As darkness gave way to pale shades of dawn, Enos led Bashkeem to fresh water. "This is the last well located anywhere close to us," warned the African-Egyptian.

"Did everyone hear Enos?" inquired Bashkeem. "Before this travel is over we will come to know thirst. Fill every water bag to the brim, and I want every man, horse, and unicorn to drink their bellies full."

Perched on the back of Hammereins, Bashkeem was the first to notice the dust in the distance. Motioning an arm he exclaimed, "Far behind us is the dust of an Egyptian cavalry. If they are presently not aware that we preceed them, they soon will be."

Bashkeem's heart sank at the thought that the Egyptians would be well-supplied with water. For a new thought, Bashkeem's heart sank even more. The Egyptians would conclude that not knowing where water was to be found amidst limitless sand, Bashkeem's platoon could not venture into the interior. Nonetheless the former slave of Egypt promised himself that for the sake of the nine men, two horses, and now two unicorns that with him traveled, he would remain positive.

"Thank goodness for these great steeds that we ride!" encouraged Bashkeem. "The Egyptians will not prevail over the valiant hearts of Hammereins, Lucareins, Crimson, and Mistral!"

After reaching the bend in the coast, Bashkeem had turned the travel of his platoon.

"What do you think of our chances?" directed Bashkeem to Sulay. "Traveling the last two days north we managed to skirt enemy outposts and keep Egyptian pursuers behind us."

"True enough, Commander. However, the detachment of Egyptian cavalry that trails us takes a more direct route along the coast, than we do in these hills that front the shore. And a growing force of foot soldiers accompanies them."

"I still do not understand how they are able to keep up with us; we have the best mounts."

"But, Bashkeem," replied Sulay, "our exhausted horses and unicorns have slowed to a walk; we are all thirsty and hungry. Each time they come to a new army outpost fixed to the coast, the Egyptian cavalry and foot soldiers restock water and food. If we are not soon safely boarded onto our barge, the following Egyptian force, that every day seems to number more, will prevent our further travel."

"Finding here no Egyptian soldiers, we will move our path closer to the shore where level land is more conducive to speed," responded Bashkeem.

Two By Sea

"We have swum far, Majit," neighed Seahorse.

"It has been three nights at sea. But at least the nightly squalls served to quench our thirst."

"Should I continue to paddle my legs northward? Or do we change course to the west?"

"Regarding whether to swim one way or another, Seahorse, we can surmise that our vessels are not yet to be found east of us. Given that confidence, let us compromise and for now swim in a northwest direction. By the way, I am again today impressed to see that your swimming stroke wastes neither motion nor energy."

The next morning the sea rolled solitary with only a unicorn and his rider specking a vista unbounded.

"Should we pick a strategic location where we can best intercept Ermir, and there wait for him to cross paths with us?" inquired Majit.

"That makes sense to me. In fact, now that I think about it, the water right here feels comfortable. You would not mind too much if this unicorn takes a little nap? I promise to stay afloat."

With his nose bobbing on gentle sea swells, Seahorse slept; his rider marveled at the buoyancy of the unicorn's body. Majit thought about taking a small nap himself. But with the unicorn asleep, it was his duty to keep a lookout for billowing sails.

"Wake up, Seahorse!" exclaimed Majit kicking at the sides of the unicorn. "Ship sails! Heh, heh! And I recognize those sails! It is the Sea Stallion! It is Ermir!"

Seahorse churned faster his legs so as to intercept the ship.

"Prince Ermir!" shouted the lookout. "Far out on our starboard side something moves in the water. It appears to be... a man... waving at us."

"There is something more there," answered the captain. "What exactly is the man seated on?"

"He sits on... the back of a horse..."

"*That* can only be one of Bashkeem's men," answered the captain.

As the rudder turned to propel the Sea Stallion in a southerly direction, the maidenhead lady adorning the prow came to whistle a melody toned joyous.

"The captain of the Sea Stallion welcomes aboard... a unicorn stallion! Majit, how did you come to find us out here in open water?"

"Ermir, because Seahorse is a grand swimmer his legs gave us the chance to locate you far away from the soldiers that swarm the coast."

"So how does our commander navigate a course through enemy soldiers?"

"Bashkeem races along the seashore. He will await you and the Sea Stallion somewhere after the Egyptian coast turns northward."

"Then that is where we will find him."

"Ermir, have you any sighting of the other two Troyan vessels?"

"No, none... unfortunately. That tells me that after they left behind the great Egyptian port, Avalcar and Ermal were hotly pursued."

As the sun commenced another late afternoon journey to its place of rejuvenation, the new course set by Prince Ermir directed straight east. Leaning relaxed against a sound asleep unicorn, Majit finally took his turn to nap.

A supper of hard bread and a soup of round white beans was brought to Majit. As his stomach warmed with the hot soup, Majit began to notice the eastern sky color differently. It did not take long before hues of red, orange, purple, and pink were made bright.

"I have never before seen the heavens to show such prettiness," muttered Majit. "I wish that someone could paint for me a picture of the sky's beauty this evening. But, since the sun is on the other side of the sky, from where comes such brilliance? Wait... *I have it!*"

Jumping to his feet Majit ran to where stood Ermir.

"Admire you right now the gleam of the heavens?" inquired Majit.

"Why yes, that is so. I have never before seen clouds glow so warmly. There is something absolutely hopeful about that formation of richly colored clouds. It is almost as if... ship sails billow in the clouds... but of course their look is strange. Hmpf. The cloud sails even appear to expand and... contract."

"Ermir, does not the cloud image seem too real? Could it be..."

The two men turned heads to study the sails of the Sea Stallion.

"This is amazing, Majit. The cloud image depicts our vessel sailing eastward."

"You recall that the magical gift of the sister unicorn of Mistral, Crimson is her name, is to glimpse what a far sky finds beneath it, and then to color the clouds with what she sees. As we sail toward the painted clouds, Crimson senses our presence. Noting the same clouds, Bashkeem and his troop of soldiers and equines will know that our barge approaches."

"That is fantastic!" exclaimed Ermir. "My hope is that the barges of Avalcar and Ermal are close enough to also see the painted clouds, and are as well able to interpret the meaning of the brilliant colors. Now that we know where to find him, the location of Bashkeem becomes our destination."

Bashkeem Surrounded

Having the eyes and ears of a hunter ever searching for movement of predators that could do him harm, Enos saw them first, "To the northeast, Commander Bashkeem. A second army comes toward us."

Hammereins, Lucareins, Mistral, and Crimson scaled a height offering the vantage of sight into far distance.

"From twenty chariots the Hittites can in a matter of moments make to fly a thousand arrows," added Sulay. "Blocked by Hittites on our front and Egyptians at our rear, what are we to do?"

"Having two armies advance so close to the land of Phoenicia cannot in any way be good," responded Bashkeem. "If a battle is in the offing, I hope they face off against each other, and that neither army has the intention of invading the realm of King Barsuna.

"We have no food to eat, precious little water to drink, and the horses and unicorns are exhausted. Our only advantage, if you want to call it that, is that the Egyptians and the Hittites despise each other. Should battle erupt, we cannot let ourselves become caught in the middle of that fight. We go onward to search for a place along the shoreline that we can defend. Until Ermir and the Sea Stallion arrive, we may there have to hold two enemies at bay."

"Have you noticed the coloration of the clouds this evening?" inquired Cholo of his brother.

"They color intensely. It is as if they portray billowing ship sails. Hmph! Bring Crimson to me."

"Dame unicorn," said Bashkeem, "are the clouds above us of your making?"

"Why... yes... Bashkeem," neighed Crimson lifting her gaze upward. "I have been so worried about the soldiers found all about us that I did not notice what my magic had presented. I abhor the bloodshed and destruction brought by war. This is perhaps the first time that my gift of magic made to color clouds above me, and I was unaware that I had done so. Bashkeem, my instinctive painting of the clouds shows that your ship comes to us. It will be here in middle night."

"That, Crimson, is the best news anyone could bring me. We know now our task. We must hold our ground until under the cover of darkness we can swim out to our ship. However, given that we are caught between two hostile armies, holding our ground may not be that easy to do."

Along the beach big boulders came to array in a disorderly fashion.

"We make for the rocky place ahead!" exclaimed Bashkeem. Upon gaining the boulders, the company dismounted and gathered together.

"What protection we can find is amongst these rocks," observed Bashkeem. "Do not interfere with any soldier intent on attacking either Hittites or Egyptians. If they want to fight each other, let them. But, let us keep both armies apart from us."

From opposite ends of a long beach the Egyptian and Hittite armies advanced toward each other. The two armies halted less than a league apart, with the platoon of rescue caught in between.

"Can Mistral's mist this night protect us?" inquired Cholo.

"Knowing that our small company is here stranded, both the Egyptians and the Hittites have more than enough soldiers to penetrate through unicorn mist."

"Commander Bashkeem," offered Sulay, "the Egyptians want to capture alive the unicorns. The Hittites may not have the same goal." Shifting his gaze from Bashkeem to Mistral and Crimson, he added, "Sir, common soldiers assuredly do not fathom the great magic of our unicorn friends. To clarify the nature of unicorns, and to as well gain delay, it may be helpful to demonstrate their magic to the soldiers of both armies."

"That... is clever thinking, Sulay," responded Bashkeem.

The commander solicited, "Mistral, Crimson, it would be helpful if you could make your magic known to both the Hittites and Egyptians. Two unicorn horses may save for us this day."

"That being the case, I have need of your chest armor," responded Mistral. "It is my idea that the magic gold will provide a way for Crimson and I to combine our separate gifts of cloud color and mist."

Bashkeem removed his breastplate.

"Go to the high point of this place and hold up the blue gold armor."

"I do as you instruct, Mistral."

Stretching necks above the breast plate, the two unicorns touched together the tips of their horns. A mist came to envelop the camp. The mist began to color delicate horizontal shades of purple, pink, red, scarlet, and yellow. As the dusk deepened, layers of color floated skyward.

Feeling the weight of the armor plate become unsustainable, Bashkeem dropped to his knees. Two African-Egyptians were immediately at his side. Together Sulay, Enos, and Bashkeem raised the piece of blue gold armor up to their waists, but could lift no higher the breastplate.

"The gold flakes of my armor rush into the cloud!"

"Yes, Bashkeem," affirmed Sulay. "The mist colors are surely of magic gold made."

"A unicorn runs the sky!" exclaimed Enos.

Spell-bound, the three men watched a galloping unicorn ascend brightly colored layers of mist. Climbing hooves upward the unicorn reached a cloud meadow where she paused to rear high and long on back legs.

The ascendant sparkles began to make bizzing sounds. The piece of blue gold armor held by the men was eaten through. When the shield's magic metal came no more to be, the mist of many colors swirled upward and the magic light vanished into nothingness.

The entire company of Bashkeem was absolutely astonished at what they had been privileged to witness. Hammereins and Lucareins jumped front hooves and neighed excitedly. The men in Bashkeem's company burst out in cheers. Enos and Cholo began to jig arm in arm.

From the ranks of both Egyptian and Hittite soldiers came cheers for the display of incredible unicorn magic.

When Mistral nuzzled his sister unicorn's eyes, he felt tears to run down her long horse face. From his sister mare the stallion separated himself.

"What is wrong, Mistral?" asked Bashkeem drawing next to the big unicorn. "Are not you proud of the incredible display of magic you and Crimson just made to happen? I am convinced that no one has ever before seen the image of a unicorn to run the clouds."

"The unicorn that climbed upward the clouds flashed hooves at me," answered Mistral lowering his head.

"Then you were privileged that the cloud unicorn saluted you."

"Cloud visions are meant to remain separate from those gazing upward. But although set apart, with Crimson at my side I was part of the vision." That neighed, Mistral turned and walked away.

"What is wrong with Mistral?" inquired Cholo upon the return of Bashkeem.

"Whatever the concern, brother, it will not by Mistral be shared."

Sulay and Enos marched guard around the now confident platoon of Bashkeem. Everyone else, including the exhausted horses and unicorns, nestled into slumber.

"Sir, a faint form moves in the water," reported Sulay as he roused Bashkeem in middle night. "We think it is Seahorse swimming toward us." Bashkeem accompanied Sulay to the beach where waited Enos.

"Nothing matches the vigor of an ocean swim at night," neighed the unicorn shaking water off his hide. "And nothing renews the spirit like water reflecting starlight."

"Seahorse, you find us here fronted and backed by two armies," replied Bashkeem. "What good news do you bring?"

"Prince Ermir awaits your boarding of the Sea Stallion. From far out at sea we saw colored light and cloud sails emblazon the sky above your camp. We next saw a unicorn climb upward the sky. I did not know that my mare and my uncle unicorn had inside them such great magic."

"I am delighted that colored skies and cloud images drew the noble Seahorse to us," responded Bashkeem.

"If Ermir sails too close to where we are standing, his barge will be seen," neighed Seahorse. "For that, you must leave right away. Swim straight west and you will find the Sea Stallion,"

"It will be Seahorse that leads us to the barge."

"No, Commander, I stay behind to create a distraction that delays the discovery of your departure. The last thing that you need, Bashkeem, is for archers to shoot sharp arrows at defenseless swimmers. Besides I really, really need to graze; I dropped too much weight swimming several days in the ocean."

"I sincerely wish that you did not remain behind. I may never see you again."

"Bashkeem, Sulay, Enos, do not tell Mistral or my mare that I am here or that I stay behind," instructed Seahorse. "I cannot bear teary farewells. Oh, and make sure that my uncle unicorn casts a mist over the barge that awaits you. If he does not, in the light of new day Ermir's vessel will be found out."

On silent hooves Seahorse trotted away.

"Sulay, Enos, go rouse the camp," ordered Bashkeem. "I require everyone here... now." It was not long before Cholo led ten men, two horses, and two unicorns into the waves.

Finding himself in the open space between the two armies, Seahorse reared up and made his horn to glow a brilliant blue. Upon seeing the lighted horn, no Egyptian or Hittite sentry paid any more attention to the spot where Bashkeem's platoon had been ensconced; no sentry bothered to notice the shadowy forms of men and equines entering a quiet sea.

Seahorse began to prance in a circle that with each circuit grew smaller. Aware that his rounded paths came within the range of archers, he felt confident that soldiers from the two armies would respect his magic.

The unicorn's performance ended, to one army and then to the other, he bowed.

With his horn still aglow Seahorse began to trot toward open country. Approaching the end of the lines of the opposing armies, Seahorse broke into a fast gallop. Amidst the unsettled dust raised by his hooves, the unicorn stallion heard the whoosh and thud of arrows fall to earth.

The unicorn smiled to himself as he muttered, "Come tomorrow, Egyptian and Hittite soldiers will conclude that Bashkeem's platoon was caught up in the magical display of colored light, and so was made to disappear into the heavens."

Seahorse turned his gallop toward the Phoenician capital. Looking back from mountain passes the next day, and the next, he followed the course of the two armies marching one after another northward. After three days of fast travel interrupted by much grazing, the walls of the city came into view.

"I will seek out the Old Garrison where I was told dwell Troyan sailors," neighed to himself the unicorn. "Surely the renowned Admiral Zoumar will be looking in on the one crew of Troyans that stayed behind. Knowing that the admiral speaks the uniform language and holds unicorns in high regard, I will acquaint him with our adventures in Egypt, and tell him of the threat posed by the Hittite and Egyptian armies."

Two guards standing at the gate of the garrison waved spears at the unicorn. Seahorse was taken aback by the unfriendly sound of the words yelled by the sentries. When a spear was thrown at his hooves, it became obvious that he was not there wanted. The friends of unicorns were no longer in control of the fortress.

Seahorse felt himself to be very much alone. He began to worry that the Troyan pirates would not bring his mare and uncle unicorn back to Phoenicia, but would instead take them across the sea to be there united with the white herd.

The idea of return to Mistral's mountain, where absent his uncle unicorn's power over mist he would live each day in fear of discovery and recapture, held little appeal.

"Since I love the sea, perhaps I can swim out from here and let the currents carry me to a new land. Maybe I shall swim all the way to Troy, and there make a new life with Prince Ermir and the royal Troyan pirates... once they return to rebuild their city." The unicorn stallion next wondered where exactly was to be found the land of Troy.

Seahorse decided that about that he was only dreaming; for the present all he could do was wait for an opportunity to find Admiral Zoumar. Someone needed to be told that two hostile armies were marching toward Byblos.

From inside the walled city came sounds of revelry.

"Human persons love to celebrate with strong spirits a festive occasion," neighed the unicorn stallion. "Still, it must be far more fun to swim in the sea, than to imbibe spirits accompanied by loud shouts and too much commotion."

The unicorn decided to walk not toward the city, but toward the quiet harbor. He was surprised how few soldiers guarded the port.

"Two ships approach," neighed Seahorse to himself. "At least that will add some excitement to this dull day."

As he walked above the harbor pulling at grass and savoring the flavor of each mouthful, the gaze of Seahorse was drawn back to the sails in the distance. Of a sudden the unicorn recognized what he was looking at.

"Because the cut and color of those sails are remindful of the ship that rescued Majit and I, those vessels can only be the Jenelisa and the Flash. *Nyeerrrhaha!* It was silly of me to worry that the Troyan pirate ships had departed for the far land of the white herd. They could not travel so far... *without me!* When they dock, I will be waiting for them."

The first to deboard was Avalcar, who was immediately set upon by soldiers. "You, Captain Avalcar, are under arrest for desertion of duty!"

"I have no time for this, Sergeant. Conduct me at once to the palace."

"Sir, you know full well that orders are orders. But, charged with desertion, you are on your way to a dungeon beneath the palace."

"The king does not know that Phoenicia is today threatened... *by war!*"

"War... Sir... today?"

"About military engagements, Sergeant, I never lie."

"Right, Sir."

The sergeant motioned for two of his men to accompany them. Ermal, Admira, and Olsi followed. Sighting the unicorn, Avalcar waved for Seahorse to join him.

"Two Hittite and Egyptian armies approach from the south," neighed the unicorn stallion upon reaching Avalcar. "They surely intend to invade Phoenicia."

"Captain Avalcar!" exclaimed Prince Ermal. "The sails of my brother's barge the Sea Stallion are in the distance seen!"

"Praise the heavens!" shouted Avalcar. "The third Troyan pirate ship approaches our harbor!"

The procession that was headed for the palace would wait for Prince Ermir, Bashkeem, Majit, Sulay, and Cholo to join them.

Ermir enfolded at the same time his brother Ermal and his sister Admira in a large hug. Cholo presented Crimson and Seahorse to Avalcar, Ermal, Admira, and Olsi. Bashkeem introduced Enos all around.

"Bashkeem did it!" exclaimed Ermir slapping the shoulders of Avalcar. "He rescued the two unicorn prisoners! Is not it wonderful to see Crimson and Seahorse standing here reunited with..."

"Captain Avalcar," interrupted the guard sergeant. "I expect that this is the first time you have disrupted a royal wedding."

"Whose wedding?"

"Why Sir, it is the wedding of Prince Maroun. He is to this day marry the Troyan Princess."

"That cannot be!" exclaimed Majit. "Resi loves me!"

"Majit, at this unwelcome news I feel badly for you," consoled Avalcar. "Still, we have no time to lose. Seahorse told me of the two armies intent on invasion. And of course you as well glimpsed the many Egyptian warships that chased our three barges into this harbor."

With tear-moistened eyes and his heart aching, Majit nodded his head.

The procession reformed. Equine heads raised high, the backs of pirateers straightened, and the steps of three barge crews fell into cadence. Moving forward with military discipline, no one was afraid to face the wrath of King Barsuna.

CHAPTER 23

CLOUDS OF WAR

"Avalcar is a traitor!"

A quick-acting Cholo shoved Avalcar, so removing him from the trajectory of a thrown spear. Three unicorns encircled the captain to protect him. Having seen the man responsible, Lucareins broke through the soldiers lining the boulevard and with his head shoved down the spear thrower.

"Lucareins, release that wretch of a man!" ordered Avalcar. "The cowardly countryman that throws a spear at the back of an officer in the king's army is not worth your worry!" As the offender fled toward the main gate of the city, the procession led by Avalcar resumed march toward the palace.

Noticing the commotion, Maroun and Resi descended the palace steps.

"Brother Majit, Captain Avalcar, Princes and Princess of Troy, Bashkeem!" saluted Maroun. "I am delighted to have you returned to celebrate our wedding. When you were so long departed, Resi and I became convinced that you sailed for the far land of the magic white herd."

"Little sister, you look more beautiful today than I have ever before seen you," complimented Ermir upon receiving Resi.

"Especially beautiful in your wedding dress," muttered Majit with his complexion turned ashen.

"But, Sister... you told me you were in love with Majit!" exclaimed Admira.

"It was too much!" sobbed Resi. "Majit left me! My family left me and stayed too long away! I was too many times told that I would never again see Majit, my two brothers, or my sister."

"I had no idea that my brother was in love with Resi," interjected Maroun. "I knew Majit cared for her... but I thought as a dear friend."

"For all his fine qualities as a man," continued Resi leaning into Maroun's chest, "I came to love the older prince. In the face of Maroun I could also love the memory of Majit's brown eyes."

"My future queen," said Majit as he kissed the hand of Resi. He wanted to say more to the princess he still loved, but words failed him.

"Prince Maroun," interjected Avalcar, "there is a pressing military issue that you must right now consider with your father the king."

"Surely so, Captain Avalcar. But I require the remainder of this day to be officially wed."

"Unfortunately, Maroun, the issue is too urgent to brook *any* delay," persisted Avalcar.

After studying briefly the eyes of Avalcar, Maroun nodded his head.

Led by Prince Maroun walking hand in hand with his bride to be, Avalcar, Majit, Ermir, Ermal, Bashkeem, and the five equines entered the palace and proceeded to the throne room, where was found not only the king, but Admiral Zoumar as well. Everyone could immediately see that regarding the interruption of the wedding ceremony, King Barsuna was irate.

"Arrest Avalcar, Bashkeem, *and* Majit!" ordered the king barely containing his anger. "Throw them into the deepest dungeon below the palace!"

Guards stepped toward Avalcar.

"You will *not* lay a hand on me!" threatened Avalcar drawing his sword. "Not... until I have had my say!"

"Arrest them, now!" shouted Barsuna stepping down from his throne.

For the second time that day unicorns rushed to protect Avalcar.

"Father, you will listen to Avalcar," insisted Maroun as he approached the throne.

"My king, on this sacred day do not stain with blood the ceremonial floor," solicited the admiral.

"Avalcar! Avalcar!" came shouts from the plaza. "Avalcar the champion!"

Although it was common knowledge that the king viewed Avalcar as treasonous, the news he had brought that war was soon to be upon Phoenicia, had spread like a wildfire.

"I suppose that Avalcar cannot be harmed in front of the bride-to-be." That said, King Barsuna returned to his seat, motioned toward Avalcar, and then motioned for Ermir, Ermal, and Majit to join him and Maroun.

"Make it quick, Avalcar. Know that I hold you responsible for taking my son Majit away from me. That treachery is unpardonable. So what have you to say for yourself?"

"Byblos is to be blockaded by Egyptian barges," began the sea captain.

"That is preposterous!" muttered the king. "We have never been blockaded!"

"A long line of Egyptian vessels filled with heavily armed men forced my barge, and Prince Ermal's barge back to this harbor," continued Avalcar. "Of course I could not challenge so many warcraft,"

"For the same reason my barge was also forced to seek protection in the Phoenician harbor," added Ermir.

"Egyptian barges that here present themselves will be defeated!" responded gruffly the king. "This corner of the sea belongs to my navy, not to one led by officers that know to plow wheat in the valley of the Nile, and build pointless monuments in desert sand. Now, off to the dungeon with you!"

Not liking either the words or the tone of the king's rejoinder to Avalcar, Seahorse and Bashkeem joined to the side of the men standing before the throne.

"How dare the king address in such a manner Captain Avalcar, a man known to be an honorable and courageous soldier!" neighed Seahorse. "Is not this the same monarch that sold me and my mother mare into bondage? King Barsuna had better calm himself and listen, for we have more war intelligence to share."

"What? How could a horned horse know anything about this supposed war that is upon me?"

"So this time the king understood the neigh of a unicorn," rejoined Seahorse. "I came upon this knowledge on my return from a prison in Egypt, the place where you sent me to suffer."

"Arrrghh... just give me the information you possess," harrumphed the king not denying the accusation. "Then be gone with you!"

"After the rescue of my mother mare and myself," neighed Seahorse, "we fled across the desert. Bashkeem led his platoon of liberation beyond the curve where the line of the sea turns north toward Phoenicia. He was there cornered against the coast with a large Egyptian army below him, and a large Hittite army blocking the coast above him."

"King Barsuna," interjected Bashkeem, "my platoon did not engage in any military action, nor did the Egyptian army provoke the Hittite army. Not one arrow was launched by Egyptians against Hittites, or by Hittites against Egyptians."

"Early yesterday as I galloped toward Byblos, I glimpsed far to the south the two armies marching toward this city," continued Seahorse.

"They timed their assault to coincide with the wedding of the Crown Prince," offered Majit. "Our enemies know that for the next seven days Phoenicia will be focused on celebration, and not defense."

"King Barsuna, Egyptian sails begin to crowd the horizon!" interrupted a newly arrived military officer. "The number of the ships in the line facing us grows quickly." Hearing the new information, the haughty mood of the king changed to one of perplexity.

"I can think of no reason why many of the soldiers lining the streets do not wear blue gold armor," observed Avalcar. "Certainly by now everyone in the army should have been issued the magic swords and armor."

"You, Captain, have better things to think about right now... like how you are going to adjust to imprisonment."

"I too want the same question answered by my king," seconded Admiral Zoumar. "Where are the blue gold sheets that I delivered to become the armor needed by our army. For the hard battle, that is now to take place, your soldiers will require the protection afforded by the magic gold."

"I also want to know the whereabouts of the magic sheets," added the voice of Crown Prince Maroun to the chorus. "You used blue gold to prepare a most elaborate royal gown for yourself. You know where the magic sheets can be found. We need them, and we need them right now."

"The blue gold is *my* concern," muttered the king slumping lower into his throne.

"Enough of this," said Prince Maroun. "Come with me, Admiral. I can guess where will be found the magic gold sheets."

"Who do you think you are? I will disinherit you!"

"Father," cautioned Majit, "if you abandon Maroun you will then be left with no son to inherit your throne."

Maroun and Zoumar pushed past the throne toward the chambers of the king.

"Stop them!" yelled the king.

No guards moved to interdict Maroun and Zoumar.

When the king pounded the armrests of his throne Majit moved to restrain his father.

"Why, you have me in your grip," observed Barsuna frowning. "I never knew my second son was so strong."

"Swimming the ocean strengthens a man's arms," answered Majit.

Waiting outside for the formal presentation of the bride and groom, the crowd began to stir.

"The people are to be disappointed," said Admira to her sister. "I am sorry to say that this is not the day for a royal wedding." Upon hearing that, Resi bit her lip and forced herself not to cry.

Each carrying a sheet of blue gold, Maroun and Zoumar returned. Even lower into his throne slumped the king.

"Father, how *could* you do this?" scolded Maroun. "The people trusted you to turn the blue gold sheets into the salvation of our army."

"Blacksmiths found in this city will immediately be put to work forging magic gold swords and chest plates," said Admiral Zoumar with an authoritative tone to his voice.

"But, before they start to work," added Prince Maroun, "I require that my father *does* something. Because in the upcoming days we are to be set upon in battle, the absence of magic armor will become a great hindrance to our winning the war to come. Soldiers not equipped with the magic armor can, and will, die.

"Your subjects will question why the magic gold was not already molded into swords and armor. You must tell the people gathered outside the palace that this negligence was not the fault of Admiral Zoumar, or Captain Avalcar. Accept, Father, the fault that is yours...

only you can be blamed for your greed. And convince your subjects of the present danger faced by the kingdom. We are at one and the same time to do battle with two empires, each one many times larger and stronger than we are. There is no time to lose."

Finding himself outnumbered by his sons, illustrious military heroes, and magic unicorns Barsuna rose and with head lowered said softly, "My sons... and daughter Resi... come with me to the terrace of the palace, and there stand beside me. The time has come for me to make a needful, and painful, confession."

After lifting his arms for silence, the king addressed the crowded plaza, "I present to you the Crown Prince, his bride-to-be, and Prince Majit!" A second time the king lifted his arms for silence.

"Hear this! I *wronged* the army. I told myself that in this time of peace our military would not need the blue gold sheets, and that I could with the magic gold instead adorn the palace. War is now upon us, and because of my fascination with the wondrous gold our army has lost precious time needed to forge the magic metal into swords and armor. I humbly ask you to forgive your king."

"Aherm... the unicorns," insisted Majit looking sternly at his father.

"I will confess one thing more," said the king nodding to his younger son. "It was I that sold two unicorns to Egypt. In order to seek the favor of our enemy, I traded two pure and innocent unicorns not mine to possess."

The crowd began to boo and jeer; the people were unready to forgive their king.

Barsuna dropped down on his knees, bowed his head, and waited for the verdict of his people.

The arms of Majit and Maroun made their father to stand. The three embraced. No son would seek to displace his father from the throne of Phoenicia. Resi also embraced the king.

"I stand with King Barsuna!" proclaimed the admiral stepping forward and raising his sword.

"I stand with King Barsuna!" joined in Avalcar.

Positioning themselves directly behind the king, the three unicorns began to rear in unison, and Hammereins and Lucareins began to prance one on each side of the horned horses.

Feeling the balm of forgiveness to lighten his heart, King Barsuna stepped back to one by one embrace the resettled Seahorse, Crimson, and Mistral.

Avalcar and Resi rejoined the king, raised high his arms, and with him paraded the length of the palace terrace. Upon seeing the confidence in their king held by the heroes of the great race, the crowd before the royal terrace took up the chant, "We stand with King Barsuna! We stand with King Barsuna! We stand..."

"Crimson, can you color the clouds to show the people in the plaza the ships coming to blockade the harbor?" inquired Bashkeem.

"Yes, I can... with the help of Mistral, Seahorse, and a piece of magic armor."

Seahorse and the uncle unicorn joined to the sides of Crimson. Avalcar handed his breast plate to Bashkeem.

Once again joined by Sulay and Enos, three men held waist high the blue gold armor.

Facing the western wall of the city, Crimson opened her heart. Seahorse thought about the feeling of oneness with the sea he had swum. Mistral willed for the cool balm of swirling mist to permeate his being. When the three touched their horns above the blue gold shield, wondrous unicorn magic revealed.

People pointed to the cloud of mist that horizontally colored in bands of orange, red, yellow, azure, and purple. Rising higher, the colors dissolved into swirling mist.

"I see barges!" Across the plaza the shout was repeated.

"These are Egyptian war barges sent to blockade our harbor!" shouted the king. "Their approaching line stretches wide across the sea! We must at once prepare for their assault!"

Crimson repositioned herself to look southward.

Into the mist a new pattern emerged; this time it was of men marching. The mist cloud showed an army on the move clad in Hittite uniforms.

When the perspective presented by cloud mist moved past the Hittites, another army was seen to follow the first. As the focus of Crimson narrowed and descended down, the people in the plaza could identify the distinctive uniforms worn by marching Egyptian soldiers.

Crimson's eyes showed panic for the battle to come. Her knees began to shake and her breaths came hard. Slumping down, her vision ended. When two unicorn horns touched a third, the mare that could paint the clouds was soothed by great love felt for her.

"Father, with your own eyes you have now seen the approach of war barges and two enemy armies," offered Majit. "Attack is nigh. You must quickly mobilize the blacksmiths of Phoenicia to forge blue gold armor."

Barsuna motioned for Hammereins. The impressively built horse came to the king, understood what was asked, and bent knees for the king to mount upon his back. The horse reared high once, twice, three times. Seated on the back of the big stallion the king had the attention of everyone standing in the great plaza.

"Having glimpsed the terrible dangers we face, we must defend our homes, families, and this capital city! United together we will prevail over the ships and armies of two great empires! Join our army at the harbor! Join our army on the wall of Byblos! Fight shoulder to shoulder with my two sons!"

Zoumar caught the king's eye and pointed to the piece of armor covering his chest.

"Every blacksmith must now forge magic armor!" continued the king. "Every piece of magic armor is destined to save the life of a Phoenician soldier!"

"We stand with King Barsuna!" echoed through the plaza.

"While the wedding ceremony is postponed, the battle cannot be! Go now and join to the coming fight!"

The crowd in the plaza began to disperse. Companies of soldiers marched double time as they positioned to fortify the walls of the city. It was not long before shepherds from the surrounding hills and valleys entered the gates of the city, herding before them their precious goats, sheep, cattle, and donkeys. The great plaza changed its character with tents poling up, children running about, and animals mrawing, braying, bahing, and bleating.

War Council

"I pose two questions," began King Barsuna as he addressed military advisers, his sons, and Bashkeem. "How will the Hittite commander attack? And will the Egyptian commander in the same way attack?"

"Distrusting each other, the two enemy armies will battle separately, and not reinforce each other," answered Admiral Zoumar. "After Egyptian barges blockade our harbor, Egyptian soldiers will march against our port and harbor fortifications. We can surmise that the Hittites will separately push against the south wall of our city.

"The Egyptian blockade is the most critical element for the success of our enemies. Stopping our sea commerce strangles us and destroys our ability to rearm and resupply. If Egypt's barges can stop our shipping, they do not have to actually seize our harbor.

"From the Old Garrison our infantry will take on the Egyptian army. We defeat the Egyptians first, and the Hittites second. The gift of Mistral's magic mist can help our soldiers and sailors to stealthily attack places of weakness found in opposing lines. In that regard, I would not want to be enemy infantryman facing charging equines emerging from out of magical mists."

"So then, how do we break the blockade?" inquired the king turning to address Avalcar.

"As just suggested by the admiral, the extraordinary mist is key. Accompanied by Mistral's cloud of magic, the four Troyan vessels can attack one side of the Egyptian fleet. At the same time a separate formation of Phoenician vessels can break through the other flank of the Egyptian barges."

The king next asked his sons for their views on the battle plan.

"Admiral Zoumar can exercise command from the forward position offered by the Old Garrison," responded Maroun. "We need his insights and experience to lead our sailors and marines against the double threat of the Egyptian army and navy. Under Zoumar's leadership, Captain Avalcar is the ideal officer to spearhead our naval thrust to break the Egyptian blockade. Led by the stalwart Bashkeem, the Troyan princes and their four crews will support Avalcar. If it so please your highness, against the Hittites I will lead the defense of the capital's south wall. My brother can serve as my adjutant. I trust Majit completely."

"While I have little standing in this meeting of military minds," offered Bashkeem, "I request the king entertain an idea that comes from my own slight experience in matters of war."

"I am told that with respect to fleetness," replied Barsuna, "the design of your vessels is superior to the design of Phoenician barges. Sir Bashkeem, we are listening."

"Considering that our Troyan ships are designed for speed, a naval attack after the fall of darkness tonight would cause enemy soldiers to lose confidence, and as well slow their advance. Even a one day delay of the attack will benefit Admiral Zoumar, Prince Maroun, and the blacksmiths forging blue gold armor."

"I like your thinking," affirmed Barsuna. "The discovery of our enemy's plans improves the odds for the success of an ambush. What do you suggest?"

"Five warriors mounted on Hammereins, Lucareins, and the three unicorns will violently pass through the middle of a column of soldiers. After striking down many enemies, our raiders will swim out in return to my barge. Since the Egyptian fleet will not seek to enforce their blockade until tomorrow morning, tonight the Jenelisa sails free."

"That is... *brilliant!*" exclaimed Avalcar clapping his hands. "In the ambush I will ride on the back of Hammereins!"

CHAPTER 24

ASSAULT ON PHOENICIA

When under the cover of darkness the Jenelisa departed the Phoenician harbor it was hard to tell whether Hammereins, Lucareins, Mistral, or Seahorse was the most excited about the raid. As could be expected, Crimson saw the raid not so much as adventure, but as duty.

"For a thousand years Phoenicia was home to our unicorn clan," neighed Mistral. "We unicorns that do not fight unless it is to save ourselves and our homeland, are destined to not quit this land until it is once again well-protected by the magic of blue gold armor."

"Mounted on the back of the speedy Lucareins, the quick Sulay will lead our platoon," instructed Avalcar standing beside his mount Hammereins. "The heart of the athletic Cholo matches well the young stallion, Seahorse. The quiet voice of Enos is to command Crimson. Can you, big and powerful Mistral, handle two riders?"

"*Nyeerrrhhyess!*" exclaimed Mistral.

"Very good!" declared Avalcar. "Then Admira and Ermal will together mount Mistral. Ha! And in that regard, I am sure that the prince will make sure to not cut his sister with his sword."

"Actually, I am far more concerned that I will get in the way of Admira's sword."

Saddles were cinched onto horse and unicorn bellies.

Upon sighting in the distance the advancing torches of Hittite soldiers, the Jenelisa left off its southward sail and turned hard to shore. After splashing through shallow waves five equines and their riders took to the cover of trees lining a low ridge. As the enemy army marched past his position, Sulay twice over counted slowly to one hundred.

At the Hittite column charged five equines carrying six riders.

With little opportunity to defend themselves, infantryman in the outer marching files were knocked down by hard-muscled horse and unicorn bodies. Swords fell upon Hittite infantrymen found to the right and left of trampling hooves. Trumpets sounded alarm. Confusion reigned in the night. The five equines turned about and a second time broke across the Hittite column.

Sulay reined about Lucareins to lead the third foray into and through the enemy column. That accomplished, the fleet Lucareins led the horses and unicorns into the sea. Out of the darkness the Jenelisa arrived to reclaim five steeds and their riders.

"You did it!" exclaimed Avalcar as he hugged first Hammereins and then Lucareins. "The raid was a total success. I congratulate both of you! And you three unicorns fought superbly!" Jerking upward his head in surprise, the captain said quietly, "But, Crimson bleeds..."

"Come Seahorse," neighed Mistral, "let us put to work the healing power of unicorn horns." Soon Crimson bled no more.

"While it was big work for all five equines," offered Sulay, "these magic horses and unicorns maintained admirably their footing and balance."

"It was next to impossible for Hittite soldiers to defend themselves against the hooves of Seahorse, pounding out of darkness," added Cholo.

"Night enough remains to hit the following army of Egyptians," suggested Bashkeem.

"Can these great steeds have strength remaining to undertake a second raid?" asked Avalcar. "Because the following army may have been alerted to the presence of raiding parties, a second foray can be even more dangerous."

"No matter!" exclaimed Mistral. "I want the Egyptians that stole my family to feel the wrath of my hooves. Turn south the barge, and this war unicorn will this night earn an extra ration of oats."

This time the shoreline offered concealment. Horse hooves battered shields and helmets, and unicorn horns and legs tumbled and trampled bodies. No way was found to stop the onslaught of five swift horses and unicorns moving in line one with another. After Sulay led the platoon of raiders to dissect the column of soldiers, he immediately turned in reverse direction. For a second time two horses, three unicorns, and six riders brought devastation to Egyptian infantrymen. Soon after the five equines mounted planks leading onto the deck of the Jenelisa.

Her breath giving out, Crimson collapsed onto the deck. Mistral and Seahorse bent knees and sparked two horns against Crimson's forehead.

"At least this time she does not bleed," affirmed her rider Enos. "She is totally exhausted."

"My mother mare will quickly recover," comforted Seahorse.

With sails extended full, and oars pulling hard, the Jenelisa sped in return toward the Phoenician harbor. Soldiers at the wharves of the harbor welcomed the returning raiders as heroes.

"Into the hearts of enemy soldiers we tonight sowed fear and uncertainty," reported Avalcar to the admiral seated in his command post inside the Old Garrison. "For his idea to raid the armies of the enemies, we Phoenicians are in debt to Bashkeem. What Hammereins, Lucareins, Mistral, Crimson, Seahorse, and their mounts this night accomplished will inspire us to win coming battles against a powerful navy."

In order to prevent more raids, the advance of the two infantry columns was halted. Enemy scouting parties were sent out to the north, south, and east. Because the Hittites and Egyptians were made newly wary, the onset of war was by two days delayed.

A new morning found Hittite soldiers set before the southern wall of Byblos, and Egyptian soldiers positioned on the southern side of the harbor.

In defense of the harbor, Zoumar had claimed the high ground for the placement of his soldiers. The admiral counted sailors sufficient in number to row forth forty war barges. With five hundred horsemen, Majit prepared to charge out from either the large western gate of the city, or the smaller southern gate.

For his part, Crown Prince Maroun hardened defensive positions along the southern wall of Byblos.

King Barsuna called for the five magic horses and unicorns to attend him at the royal palace. The horses found that instead of new orders, something was to be by them received.

"Do you recall how out of finely woven blue gold filaments I had to be made a beautiful flowing robe?" began Barsuna. "That was an unwise thing to do. Upon realizing that I no longer need to wear finery fashioned of blue gold, I had expert tailors convert, strengthen, and augment my robe to become magic shirts to be worn by three unicorns and two horses. Harder than iron, the delicate mesh will wear lightly on your necks and haunches. My hope is that in the battles to come, these magic blankets of most precious gold will well-protect you." That said the king bowed individually to each horse and unicorn, that bowed regally in return gesture.

"Wearing the magic gold makes even more beautiful my dear sister mare," neighed Mistral to Crimson. Bystanders in the plaza soon found five horses and unicorns prancing about as they delighted in their new armor mesh.

Egyptian and Hittite generals requested parlay.

Bereft of hope that any good thing could come from talks with enemies so powerful, Prince Maroun nonetheless rode out on Hammereins. In his hand was held a small leafy branch easily interpreted as a symbol of peace. When ordered by two generals to surrender Byblos to the combined Egyptian and Hittite armies, which numbered three times the armed might of the Phoenician military, Maroun plucked one by one the leaves from the stick, broke it, and let the pieces fall to the ground.

"Like leaves your soldiers will fall, and like this branch your armies will be broken." With no more words spoken by the crown prince, Hammereins galloped back to the protection of the city's south wall.

Bugles sounded attack. Fast moving chariots carrying Hittite archers made volley after volley of arrows to fly at the defenders on the wall. As well as they might, enemy foot soldiers scrambled up ladders. Few of the enemy made climbs high enough to fight sword to sword with the defenders on the walls.

"Brother, it will take far more to defeat us than pelting us with arrows and throwing up ladders against our wall," allowed Majit.

"In the distance the Hittites are constructing something big. I fear that they will soon enough deploy a tower and battering ram," responded Maroun. "That said, you are now to put our cavalry to work."

The Hittites were front-on warriors whose customary strategy was to overwhelm the enemy with wave after wave of onrushing swordsmen and archers. Execution of that aggressive tactic, however, presented the prospect that the flanks of the Hittite army should become vulnerable.

Led by Majit mounted on Lucareins, the Phoenician cavalry rode through the uncontested west gate of the city to attack a flank of the Hittite army set before the south wall.

As with amazing speed Majit's mount Lucareins wove through enemy lines, it was next to impossible with sword or spear to bring down the war horse protected by blue gold armor mesh. The cavalry charge decimated the ranks of enemy soldiers, and moreover caused a new element of prudence to be inserted into Hittite tactics.

Upon the Sea

"Sirs, if we do not soon disrupt the Egyptian blockade," fretted Zoumar to Avalcar and Bashkeem, "the barges returning to us with ores for our smelters and wheat for our hearths will be every one captured or sunk. If the blockade seals shut our harbor, the inhabitants of Byblos will surely come to face starvation. Add to that, we require that returning sailors provide needed reinforcements, and that their vessels replenish our losses of barges."

"Sir, do you command that we launch an attack today?" asked Avalcar.

"I want to hear first your ideas."

"Lord Admiral," responded Bashkeem, "I would strike the north edge of the blockade. I would fight with everything I had to open a sea lane along your north coast to accommodate returning Phoenician commerce."

"Bashkeem is right," agreed Avalcar. "The priority of the Egyptian navy is to block the sea on our south, so that we are not able to convoy troops and raiders to assault the rear of the Egyptian army. Given that, our best prospect is to open a sea lane to the north."

"What else, Avalcar?"

After pacing the floor deep in thought, Avalcar halted his steps.

"Perhaps we can improve upon Bashkeem's idea. Stage one, as a subterfuge we send the fast Troyan vessels, accompanied by the mists of Mistral, to attack the southern arm of the blockade. Egyptian barges are there so numerous that they will pile up on each other, permitting the Troyans to break through. Stage two, we send thirty war barges to penetrate through the naval cordon along the northern coast above our harbor. Upon the removal of enemy vessels, we immediately dispatch freighters to sail out through the cleared sea lane. Stage three, once our freighters gain the high seas they announce to encountered Phoenician vessels that the northern coast still permits open passage to our port. Of course it would behoove our barges to form convoys before returning to our harbor."

"I like this three-part plan," responded Zoumar heaving a sigh of relief. "Bashkeem and Avalcar, ready your ships and crews to sail in late afternoon."

Compared to the forty Egyptian barges defending the southern flank of the blockade, the four vessels sailing under the command of Bashkeem were very few. However their speed and maneuverability, along with the magic mist of Mistral, kept the Troyan barges afloat and in the fray.

The five magic horses and unicorns launched themselves to land on Egyptian decks, where they sowed havoc. Lucareins whirled and kicked out with such speed and vehemence that he was by Egyptian swords unstoppable. Crimson and Seahorse instinctively knew how to stop blows aimed at the other. Working in tandem, the powerful chests and shoulders of the big Hammereins and Mistral together splintered masts. Frightened and bewildered enemy sailors knew not how to stop the devastation brought by magical equines with necks, shoulders, and hips protected by chain mesh forged of blue gold.

The Troyan vessels broke through the blockade, which managed to quickly reform. However, the Troyan barge captains were not done. They circled out to sea and returned to approach the coast from the north.

While the attack to the north of Avalcar's thirty barges was met by the converged might of the enemy navy, Egyptian captains had not anticipated being back-sided by fast and highly maneuverable Troyan vessels. A northern sea lane opened to resupply Byblos.

Siege Machine

Onto the field of battle the Hittites brought a siege machine with roof slanted from close to ground level on one end, to ten paces high on the other, and placed it against the city's southern gate. The diagonally slanted roof protected soldiers swinging an iron-tipped ram to batter the lower part of the gate.

Heavy rocks thrown from the high wall bounced down the slanted timbers that ceilinged the battering ram, and thereafter rolled harmlessly on the ground. Burning coals cascaded downward from the wall. Unfortunately for the defenders, the thick slanted timbers topping the siege machine had beforehand been charred so as not to burn anew.

Hammereins, Lucareins, and the three unicorns jumped onto the top of the siege machine and slid hooves downward to plant themselves unhurt on the ground.

Grasping containers filled with hot coals, from on top the wall Cholo, Sulay, Enos, Ermal, and Admira slid down ropes. Afforded protection by the equines, they lit afire the base of the siege machine. The tender belly of the battering ram burned hot.

Penetrating into Hittite infantry units, Majit's cavalry joined to the riders of five magic horses and unicorns. When stalled the advance of the Phoenician cavalry, fierce and brutal resistance met Majit's retreat toward the western gate. Blood swathing her flanks, Crimson fell back. The unicorn mare, and her big colt Seahorse, were the last equines to re-enter the city.

Crimson

Through day after day of battle Crimson's coloring had paled, and sheened more delicate. By the sight of very much bloodshed her innocence had been desecrated. The magic of Mistral and Seahorse could not this time close Crimson's wounds. Of a heart despairing the bloodshed and death found to be all around her, the unicorn mare that could paint the sky... was dying.

"Great unicorn dame, this strife will soon end," neighed Lucareins as he nuzzled the cheeks of Crimson. "Do *not* give up."

"Crimson's gentility and goodness are uncompliant to the shedding of so much blood," neighed Hammereins.

347

"I wrongly permitted Crimson to become a war unicorn," neighed Mistral shaking his head.

Lying on her side, the unicorn mare turned her head toward Mistral. "Do not, brother unicorn, mourn for me. In this battle you needed my help. Had I died in captivity, my colt Seahorse would have been left all alone in the world. When you liberated my colt and me from a prison stable in Egypt, you fulfilled my destiny."

Crimson turned eyes toward her colt, "Seahorse, receive my blessing."

Shaking his head in disbelief and despair, Seahorse looked for reassurance from his uncle stallion. But Mistral could only lower his eyes. The horns of the colt and mare touched.

"My colt Seahorse... will come to know... a hold graced by many unicorns... and there find peace." The sensitive unicorn mare would no more paint the clouds in brilliant colors of unsurpassable beauty. In a last farewell to heavenly artistry, the clouds on the western horizon lit themselves in myriad tones of scarlet, as if on fire.

From Crimson's unmoving body, flecks of blue crystalline light took on the form of the unicorn mare, and swirled upward. The spirit of the unicorn mare was seen to gallop across cerulean clouds she had once painted. The shimmering form of Crimson halted, reared high upon a cloud top, and one final time waved her hooves in farewell. Into billowed mists rimming a setting sun galloped forever away the heavenly painter.

"When we were before positioned between two armies, the cloud unicorn waved hooves at me," neighed

Mistral. "I knew then that I was watching Crimson bid me farewell, but I did not want to believe what my heart told me was to happen."

"Although every drop of Crimson's blood was opposed to war," neighed Hammereins, "she put her sensitivity and emotions aside to help us to survive this fight. Surely for us she gave herself, sacrificed herself."

"I before hated warfare," said Majit quietly, "and I despised weapons of death. Now for the loss of Crimson, I find myself charged with anger. Even as my sword has dulled with much cutting in battle, so my heart now dulls to the feeling of hope."

Crimson's body was laid gently upon the deck of a captured Egyptian barge. Sailors covered her mane and torso with flowers portraying every color that Crimson had before appointed to paint delicate and wondrous sky tapestries. With its sails filled by a sudden gust of wind, the vessel became inflamed. The Egyptian blockade parted to let the burning funeral barge pass into open seas, where soon enough it became only ashes.

The wind that carried Crimson seaward reversed direction; dark clouds sped back from the path taken by the funeral barge. Waves began to crash hard against the shore.

"Nature laments for the loss of the noble unicorn mare," declared Avalcar standing at the harbor.

"Crimson's funerary gale has the making of a tremendous westerly," observed Bashkeem placing a hand on the shoulders of Avalcar. "This is our chance, and we must take it. The only thing is that to enhance the maneuverability of our vessels we need the winds to shift slightly to the north or south. If we destroy the Egyptian blockade, we cut off the resupply of the pharaoh's army. I have confidence that Phoenician pilots can better sail this storm than their counterpart Egyptian navigators. A great gale, plus forty barges sailing for Admiral Zoumar, will defeat eighty Egyptian barges."

"The admiral is a decisive commander that time and again has proven himself willing to take noteworthy risks in battle," responded Avalcar. "When we relay your strategy to Zoumar, he will surely with you agree and wager everything on the storm. We must ready our crews to set sail at first light."

CHAPTER 25

STORM AND TURMOIL

"This is the *nastiest* gale I have ever seen!"

"What was that?" yelled Cholo straining with Ermir at the rudder to keep their barge perpendicular to crashing waves.

"The force of these winds is incredible!" yelled again Prince Ermir.

"This weather is beyond nasty!" answered Cholo. "Facing the strength of this mighty northwest wind, on this morning both our sails and our rowers have their work cut out for them!"

With more manageable sails and a sleeker trim to the prow, the Troyan barges had been placed at the front of the line of barges sailing out from the Phoenician port. Ermir, Ermal, Admira, and Bashkeem gave each other wide leeway in which to maneuver their vessels. For the turbulence of the towering waves, Hammereins, Lucareins, Mistral, and Seahorse did not this time accompany the Phoenician barges.

Provoked by gale force winds, Egyptian vessels lost the tight formation maintained on previous days; all hands aboard the Egyptian vessels struggled to keep their blockading barges in position and under control.

Giving the Jenelisa more sail, Bashkeem sped toward a large Egyptian barge. Timing perfectly the descent of a great wave, Bashkeem smashed his vessel's ram into the stern of the enemy vessel, wrecking the hindmost section and incapacitating the rudder. The captain of the listing vessel waved colors signifying surrender.

"You made disabling the Egyptian craft look easy!" exclaimed the first mate Olsi slapping his captain on the back. "In spite of the storm, you with your mind won victory!" Bashkeem signaled for the Egyptians to let their vessel blow toward the shore.

Still smarting for having lost the Wave Rider in the conflict against fourteen Egyptian war barges, Ermal was particularly proud that his new vessel, the Sea Stallion, quickly sank an enemy barge. It was not long before the Jenelisa, Sun Flash, Star Sheen, and Sea Stallion had incapacitated seven Egyptian barges.

The loss of the barges disabled by the Troyans opened a large hole into the middle of the blockade. Before the morning was ended, Phoenician and Troyan vessels made to collapse the remainder of the line of blockade.

Zoumar and Bashkeem brought the good news to the king.

"The blockade of our harbor is ended," reported the admiral. "On the Egyptian front we have made outstanding progress."

"Unfortunately for us," responded Barsuna, "the Hittite army continues to receive supplies and reinforcements come by land from the east."

Upon noting the face of Bashkeem relaxed into a sly grin, the admiral offered, "I believe that the worthy commander of the Troyan barges has something to share."

"I do, at that. The storm authored by the demise of Crimson continues into the evening. Upon considering her horror at bloodshed, it occurs to me that shortening this war is the most appropriate way for us to honor her legacy. And I may have come upon a strategy that can accomplish that end."

"Shedding less Phoenician blood in victory would be most welcome," replied the king.

"Your highness, while I have not before met him, the reputation of the general that commands the Egyptian forces is one of astuteness. Because he is governed by reason rather than blind ambition, there occurs to me a way to prevail upon the Egyptian commander, and so change to our advantage the odds that still favor the combined might of our enemies."

"That strategy, Bashkeem, is exactly what this day my ears need to hear," replied the king. "I hesitate to admit this, but until now I have continued unconvinced that Phoenicia could triumph over the imposing armies of two great empires." That said, the king stepped down from his throne and motioned for Bashkeem to there sit in his stead.

"More slave than royal, I cannot accept the offer of King Barsuna to sit upon his throne. Fleeting as it is, for such an honor I am unprepared."

"Nonsense, Bashkeem. Because of your leadership the magic sheets brought by Zoumar did not fall into the hands of Egyptian sailors. Under your command the Troyans, the magic horses, and the unicorns mightily contributed to breaking the Egyptian blockade. And now your genius will provide the key to winning the war. Would not the admiral agree that Bashkeem merits a rest seated in the comfort of a richly cushioned throne? Hah! Observe also, Zoumar, how well I today practice my... *newfound humility.*"

The king motioned once more for Bashkeem to sit.

"Well at that, I did recently promise someone that I would be more open to future praise," rejoined Bashkeem.

"Actually my king, I find that with his frame settled upon your throne, Bashkeem's beard looks quite regal," observed a smiling Zoumar.

Bashkeem proceeded to detail a strategy that, as a precondition for negotiation, was intended to soften the resolve of the Egyptian general.

"So tell me, Admiral, what make you of Bashkeem's bold idea?" inquired the king.

"It is audacious, plucky, and if I do say so myself... *brilliant.* It will truly honor the legacy of the now departed Crimson."

"I did not before think that a lavishly appointed throne could to a former slave be made to feel comfortable," commented Bashkeem upon stepping down from the high seat. "About that, King Barsuna, I seem to have been mistaken."

An Egyptian Change of Course

In the aftermath of the storm the next day dawned gray, soaked, and sullen.

Unfortunately for the Egyptian soldiers that awoke irritable and hungry, every canvas cover tenting the army's food supplies had somehow become untethered. Oddly enough, the damage had transpired at the same time that a strange mist encompassed the exact place where were stored the inventories of grain. The mist swirled so thickly that guards found themselves powerless to halt the rampage of several equines bent on destruction. Egyptian stores of bread and flour had consequently been drenched and muddied in the gale.

The leader of the Egyptian forces received a message requesting a meeting to take place within the confines of the Old Garrison. Although to his subordinate officers it was apparent that the Egyptian general commanded the most sour mood of anyone in his camp, the request was agreed to.

"General, I am going to suggest something that you will initially view with disfavor, but upon closer examination you will find merits your careful consideration," began Zoumar.

After furrowing eyebrows and grimacing, the Egyptian commander answered, "It costs me... nothing to hear what you say."

"Sir, my barges yesterday ended your naval blockade. Most of your one hundred Egyptian ships are now sunk, damaged, or captured. Barges now limping back to Egypt will carry to your pharaoh the news of the defeat of his navy.

"The daily resupply of wheat and troop replacements for the Egyptian army is now ended. To compound the issue, it was just reported to me that last night your remaining supplies of food somehow became wetted, muddied, and spoiled.

"Your navy has been beaten, your stores of bread and flour have been spoiled, and your chain of resupply has been severed. Your soldiers will not long fight on empty stomachs. Neither does a hungry army march well. If you today set out in retreat back to Egypt, many of your men will come to perish in the desert. Under a hot sun, with only meager supplies of food, that journey would be torturous.

"You have no doubt requested wheat from your Hittite allies. We both know that they will refuse your request. More than he fears Phoenicia, the Hittite ruler distrusts Egypt. Even if the Hittites should in this war prevail against Phoenicia, it would now be entirely a Hittite victory. As the Hittites do not share their food with your soldiers, neither will they with Egypt share victory over Phoenicia."

After pausing to let the force of his words sink in, Admiral Zoumar resumed, "Sir, I offer you a chance to recast a humiliating defeat, one that would disgrace and destroy your military reputation, into a great victory for Egypt."

"Continue, Admiral Zoumar," answered the Egyptian commander slumping shoulders in his chair.

"Ally with me, General! Ally your army with Phoenicia! If you do so you will be the first general in your country's history to achieve a devastating defeat over Egypt's great rival the Hittite Empire."

"You propose something... *preposterous,*" answered quietly the Egyptian shaking his head.

The general rose and with his back turned to Zoumar, added, "Hmpf. Having said that, is it fair for me to inquire what battle plan can defeat the Hittites?"

"In order to show the sincerity of my offer," continued Zoumar, "I will be frank and open with you. My plan is four-pronged. First, since the harbor has been cleared I will tonight barge Phoenician marines south to land below the Hittite lines. Tomorrow morning those marines will attack the rear of the Hittite army. Second, a Phoenician cavalry and following army will at dawn pour out of the south gate of our walled city to attack straight-on the Hittites. Third, from the west your army will attack the exposed side of the Hittite forces. The Hittite commander cannot be prepared for an attack from the south, north, and west. He will be caught in a vice with his only escape to the east. And fourthly, I will place reserves of infantry and cavalry to pounce upon the remnant of the Hittite army, as it retreats to the east." Zoumar allowed several moments for his words to sink in.

"There remains one other matter to settle. Showing good faith in our alliance, my king can afford to be generous. You will receive all of the wheat, and olive oil we capture from the Hittites. I will even make sure that you obtain undamaged Hittite chariots and bows to disassemble and study, for they are the most advanced anywhere made. Egypt will as well receive half of the gold, silver, armor, and swords that we capture. One thing more I will do for you. Following your victory over the Hittites, you and your troops will be transported in barges, both mine and yours, to land in empty desert a few days march from the great port of Egypt."

"Sharing equally the plunder would help convince the pharaoh that my treason to his orders... was in his best interest. The captured armor and weapons could be recast to outfit an entirely new army. And my ruler never has enough gold and silver to suit his pressing needs."

"And after the devastating loss suffered by his navy, would not your ruler despair the starvation and destruction of this his mighty army?"

"All Egypt would lament the loss of my army."

"Join me in victory!" exclaimed Zoumar clapping his hands for emphasis. "Return a hero whose praises will long be sung in Egypt! If on the other hand you choose to not accept my offer, with no mercy shown I will slowly but surely grind apart your hungry army."

Try as the Egyptian commander might, the logic of Admiral Zoumar proved not possible to resist. The Egyptian general exhaled deeply.

Zoumar reached out to shake on the agreement.

"The magic of blue gold armor and unicorn horns, has undone me. I consent to your plan, Admiral Zoumar. After all, any win is better than a defeat." As he grasped the proffered hand the Egyptian commander added, "Following one last hard day of fighting, Admiral Zoumar and I will together know victory. Before me I now have the difficult work of convincing my officers to switch horses in the middle of a stream. However, given yesterday's shattering of our naval blockade, and last night's loss of our food supplies, my officers will come to see that this is the best outcome that to us remains... not only for me but also for them. My officers have their own careers and reputations to salvage. Hmpf. If I am to be blamed for this action, I can say it was the fault of our naval commander. His defeat left me no alternative but to join with you against the Hittites."

"So then, General, we are agreed," spoke on Zoumar. "At middle night my Captain Avalcar departs to barge marines to land south of the Hittite army. I count on you to attack tomorrow at first light. I go now to relay your acceptance of my terms to my king. Tomorrow shall bring victory to Phoenicia... and to Egypt."

At the first hint of new day Prince Maroun mounted on Hammereins, and Prince Majit mounted on Lucareins, led out the combined cavalry and infantry of the Army of the Wall.

"Where are the Egyptians?" Majit asked his brother. "It is first light. They should from the west be advancing."

"No matter," answered Maroun, "our attack is set to begin."

Pausing a few moments longer to listen, Majit motioned with a forefinger and said, "Brother, if my ears do not deceive me, to the south the attack of Avalcar commenced on time."

"You and I can *always* count on Avalcar."

Hearing their men begin to cheer, the two princes looked to the west to see a file of Egyptian soldiers mount a rise. Another long file of Egyptian infantrymen came into view, and then another.

"With Avalcar's sailors attacking from the south, and our newly made Egyptian allies now advancing from the west, our troops are confident," observed Majit. "Let us, Brother, accomplish this thing."

"Stay close by me," answered the older Phoenician prince. "You and I will protect each other's backs."

Keen for the war to end, Avalcar's brigade of marines found strength and stamina in their arms and legs that they did not know they possessed. The sea captain told himself that he had never before commanded battalions of sailors that fought so well with firm land under their feet. To their south the Hittites found no outlet of escape.

The ferocity of the Egyptian fight demonstrated that it must not have been so difficult for their commander to convince his officers and men to turn against their former Hittite allies. Both Maroun's foot soldiers and Majit's cavalry determined to fight with more zeal and success than their new Egyptian collaborators. Neither the army defending the wall of Byblos, nor the Egyptian army, could be stopped. Rather faster than could have been anticipated, Hittite soldiers broke in escape to the east.

The swordplay of two companies of cavalry led by Admira and Ermal mounted double on Mistral, and Sulay and Enos mounted on Seahorse, stymied enemy flight. In return for each errant spear launched at Mistral and Seahorse, unicorn hooves and horns did surprising damage to Hittite foot soldiers and horsemen scattering this way and that in disarray.

Trespassing the camp of the Hittites, through post-battle devastation walked slowly Avalcar's marines. Wounded Phoenicians were given care. For some, their last breaths on earth would take place bouncing about in the ill-comfort of an ox-drawn ambulance cart.

In the middle of a field of battle made desolate Zoumar, Avalcar, Maroun, Majit, Ermir, Ermal, Bashkeem, Cholo, Sulay, Enos, and Olsi found one another. Few words needed to be spoken. The unlikely company of friends, become battlefield comrades, walked together with Hammereins and Lucareins back to the palace of the king. Remaining on the battlefield, Admira busied herself cleansing and bandaging the wounds of Hittite soldiers.

"I do this for Crimson," muttered Admira to herself. "Once ended the war, rather than to ignore the suffering of enemy combatants the gentle unicorn mare would have wanted me to help." Assisting in matters of healing two, no longer three magic unicorns, stayed behind with Admira.

"No more trouble yourself this night with Egyptians and Hittites," said Avalcar patting an arm of his seated king. "There is time enough tomorrow for the division of spoils with the Egyptian general."

"Avalcar can always tell what I am thinking," responded Barsuna. "And you are right; I have for this day worried enough."

Majit looked at Cholo, who looked at Sulay, who looked at Enos. Then all four men turned to smile at Prince Maroun, who himself turned to the admiral and said, "I thought you had taught me everything you knew. I still cannot believe that our Admiral Zoumar convinced the Egyptian commander to ally his army to ours."

"Is the... big wedding on again for tomorrow?" responded slyly the admiral.

At that comment everyone smiled at the predicament of Maroun and Resi. Their wedding day had by the outbreak of war been postponed. By any comparison a new wedding day would be anticlimactic.

"No, not tomorrow," answered Prince Maroun. "My second wedding day will be from tomorrow one week. I need eight days to put behind me the battle just waged, and our soldiers need time for the healing of battlefield wounds to begin."

"Each and every one of you fought with all your strength," pronounced King Barsuna extending wide his arms. "For that, I am... *indebted.* Without your courage this palace, like the former palace of Troy, would now be nothing more than a smoldering ruin."

As his eyes began to moisten the king motioned for Maroun and Majit to come so that he could grasp their hands.

"My sons, I was on the verge of losing everything. My pride cost me the love of Majit who did not fit the iron mold I had fashioned for him. So that he did not have to spend time with his father, Maroun distracted himself with the army. It pains me to admit that among some of my most talented officers, thankfully not to include Zoumar and Avalcar, I had become a standing joke. To hide from my eyes my unhappiness and failure, I compounded errors by losing myself to greed."

The king turned from his sons to once more address all those gathered before him.

"When the awful conflict with the Hittites and Egyptians broke upon me, it was not from any valor or strategy of mine that we won the war. You who stand before me brought the victory. Your loyalty not only saved the kingdom, your loyalty saved me. Because of your good will and faithfulness toward the crown, I have regained not only my sons, but also myself.

"From this terrible war a blessing is strangely born. I begin a new stage in my life. I am remade to be an honest king, an honest man, and a fortunate father soon to welcome a courageous and talented daughter into my family."

Silence prevailed. Since no one knew what to answer the king, those gathered together in the palace thought on the gifts of love received from their own families and friends.

The king looked toward Hammereins and Lucareins. Within hearing of all he said, "It would have broken my heart to have lost you two valiant horses in battle."

"Sir, mount upon my brother stallion," answered Lucareins. "As we walk through the city, on my back I will carry Prince Maroun. Many are this night needful of a kind word from their king and their prince."

For the first time ever, Barsuna had understood perfectly what was neighed to him by a horse touched by the magic of a unicorn horn. Two stallions and their riders departed the palace and entered the plaza of the capital city.

"The king will only reluctantly part with Captain Avalcar's horses," observed Bashkeem. "I wonder if a suitable trade can be made for Hammereins and Lucareins. If Avalcar were given a leave of absence from the Phoenician army, say for two or three years, the trade might be worth it."

Those within earshot of Bashkeem understood that he hoped for Avalcar to lead a Troyan expedition to carry two unicorns to the far land of the magic white herd.

CHAPTER 26

AFTERMATH, CELEBRATION, AND A HORSE TRADE

"Admiral Zoumar, it is not that I would not *like* to dine with your king, but so doing would be for me disadvantageous. If I were to enter the palace grounds my enemies back in Egypt, that will be exceedingly jealous of my victory over the Hittites, should accuse me of becoming an agent of Phoenicia and so a traitor to my own country."

"Understood, General," answered Zoumar. "What else can I do to accommodate your last day in Phoenicia?"

"There is something that would for me be exceedingly helpful. If a missive were to be prepared on behalf of King Barsuna that to the Egyptian officers was complimentary, and that in particular praised my leadership, that letter might just salvage my military career."

"What does it need to say?"

"Something to the effect that... without my leadership the Hittites would have from this battle emerged more powerful than ever. In addition, the impact of the sea storm might be overplayed to make it appear that the storm destroyed my blockade, and not the valiant seamanship of your naval captains."

"Yes, yes, that can be written."

"Hmph. There *is* one thing more, Admiral Zoumar. If it were hinted that our alliance against the Hittites was more my idea, than yours, that would for me be helpful. If the pharaoh and his high council were to think that the idea for my army to shift sides came from an Egyptian general, they would see in a more favorable light my treason against the Egyptian alliance with the Hittites."

"My king will be amenable to your suggestions. It will be done as you say."

The letter was prepared, sealed with the royal ring, and along with a copy of the letter's contents given that same day to the Egyptian commander.

Upon reading his copy of the royal missive the Egyptian commander said to Zoumar, "All that will matter to the people of Egypt... is what our pharaoh tells them took place in the *Battle of Byblos*. The pharaoh will find that the contents of this letter suit his interests. With this letter my disobedience to my king's orders will be forgiven... and soon forgotten."

"You do not object to the last codicil, the request made by King Barsuna to free the Troyan slaves?"

"I shall see that it is done. After carrying my army to Egypt, the Phoenician barges that return to this harbor will have on board liberated Troyan slaves. It will be up to them to find their own way from this port north and west to Troy. By the way, Admiral Zoumar, I am impressed with the quality of the paper used in this letter."

"Some very talented people in Byblos know how to manufacture a better quality paper."

"I foresee that Byblos shall become famous for its superior making of paper," responded the Egyptian commander.

"As a matter of fact, this new kind of paper has been so well received, that it is no longer referred to as papyrus, but as... *Byblos*.

With the trusted Captain Avalcar at his side, Admiral Zoumar watched barges loaded to capacity with Egyptian soldiers, treasure seized from the Hittite army, and unblemished Hittite chariots depart for Egypt.

"Admiral, since that not so long ago day when you and I sailed out of this harbor to rescue the magical white herd, we have together come far," offered Avalcar. "Our soldiers and sailors are now well-protected by magic armor. Troyan royals have been made to become a valuable ally for our king, and a Troyan princess is to be the noble wife of Prince Maroun. And, against all odds you and I helped our military to gain a glorious victory over a combined Hittite and Egyptian force that threatened to overwhelm and destroy Phoenicia."

"One thing more, Avalcar," replied Zoumar. "You and I helped our king learn something important. Publicly exposed and taught a lesson, he will no more succumb to personal greed."

"I might also mention, Admiral, that I am very proud of your behind the scenes support for the expedition to rescue two unicorn horses imprisoned in Egypt."

"Without the aid in battle brought by Mistral's mists, Crimson's sky painting, and the intelligence gained by Seahorse about two fast approaching armies, we would not have won the war."

"Add to that, Admiral, the storm authored by Crimson's demise, and the unicorn mists that made it possible to destroy Egyptian food supplies, led directly to the destruction of the blockade and Egypt changing from enemy to friend. Seen in that light, the expedition to free two unicorns was indeed... a very important achievement."

"While the gentle unicorn mare that could paint the clouds is now from her colt and brother stallion departed, I fervently hope that Mistral and Seahorse can one day join the unicorn herd across the sea."

"When that comes to pass, both you and I will be ever thankful," responded Avalcar.

Prince Maroun and Princess Resi

Upon losing the privilege she had been born with, Princess Resi engaged in piracy to seize ships and treasure from the country that had despoiled the reign of her father. She had captained the Star Sheen in the battle that rescued the Phoenician blue gold treasure. In addition to all that she had taken as a pirate, Resi had stolen the heart of a future king.

On this day there would be no tumultuous and unsettling disruption by Troyan pirates, no dread news of a naval blockade, and no casting gazes to the south to glimpse not one, but two powerful enemy armies advancing toward the capital city.

For the seafaring nation it was symbolically important that the marriage procession enter the capital through the wide western gate that opened to the harbor, thus bringing to the land of Phoenicia the blessings of the sea.

Trumpeters led the marriage procession onto the boulevard stretching to the palace. Following behind the horn blowers, King Barsuna and Prince Maroun sat astride the backs of Hammereins and Lucareins. As the two stallions pranced so smoothly that the king and crown prince rode without the slightest bounce to their backs, bright afternoon sunrays made to dazzle the magical mesh vestments worn by the equines.

Walking together Admiral Zoumar, Prince Majit, and Captain Avalcar next approached the palace. Knowing that these three had together done much to rescue the kingdom, the people crowding the plaza applauded their heroic deeds.

"So far so good," muttered Avalcar. "Not one spear has today been flung at my back."

Drums pattered.

When at the western gate lifted a shimmering mist Princess Resi was revealed mounted upon Mistral. The unicorn stallion's neck was garlanded with strings of flowers that swept with colorful petals the cobblestone boulevard. Head held high, the elegant and dignified unicorn walked majestically.

By sparkling rubies Resi's long dark hair had been made to glisten. Bordered in wide seams of royal purple, her yellow satin gown swept back over the magical mesh covering the hind quarters of Mistral. Newly added blue gold lace decorating the sleeves and bodice made her dress unique to this, and not the previously appointed day for her wedding.

Mounted upon Seahorse, Admira followed next. For the sake of propriety, Majit's one of a kind silk shawl had been regifted to the older sister of the bride. Caressing the exquisite fabric, the red hair of the older Troyan princess curled soft and fresh.

Behind Admira walked Ermir and Ermal. At the insistence of the bride Cholo, Olsi, Sulay, and Enos closed out the procession.

"Your eyes, my princess, shine today more beautifully than on your first wedding day," complimented Bashkeem waiting at the bottom of the palace steps to help Resi dismount. "And I like this wedding dress even more. I am glad that King Barsuna undid blue gold from a cloak, to make your dress to sparkle."

"Because my brothers, my sister, and you are today here with me, you find a bride made happier than when I was to first exchange vows. I am today, Bashkeem, at peace with all... and even more in love."

"Including at peace with Majit?"

"Including particularly Majit, and especially with King Barsuna who I find changed to be a better man."

After climbing the stairs to the wide terrace of the palace, Bashkeem presented the bride to the waiting groom. The young couple knelt upon purple cushions set before King Barsuna. Resi's sister and two brothers came to stand at the side of the bride. Majit, Avalcar, and Admiral Zoumar joined to the side of the groom. Compared to the previous ill-fated wedding day, on this occasion all would proceed flawlessly.

Maroun vowed to uphold the laws and throne of Phoenicia, pledged loyalty to the Phoenician army, and promised everlasting love, protection, and devotion to his bride. Resi pledged fealty to the king. With heart, mind, and body she committed to love her husband.

Wine drunk from the other's cup signified that the marriage vows were made law. The brief ceremony completed, King Barsuna motioned his sons and Resi to his side, put his arms around them, and called on the heavens to protect his family.

The wedding ceremony of Prince Maroun and Princess Resi inspired, and more than that made hopeful the hearts of those many watching in the royal plaza. Women, and men as well, recalled that in addition to her demonstrated mastery of horsemanship it had been widely repeated that Princess Resi knew how to delicately and deliciously season her stews.

Boisterous well-wishing erupted from the throng set before the palace. Men began to dance together in circles. Inside and outside the circles of men danced circles of women. The best wines were drunk, and the best cheeses and sausages eaten.

Sitting later at the banquet table inside the palace, Majit reflected that he had never before seen his father's eyes moisten, and tears to fall because of a heart over-brimming with joy and good will. After glancing at his brother, Majit raised his glass and said in a loud voice, "I am gladdened to see our king completely communicant with the great blessings brought this day to his first born son, my brother Maroun."

"My turn to toast Prince Maroun!" exclaimed Admira coming to her feet. "Because he gained the love of my sister, I gained the captaincy of a fast barge!"

Preparation

For the first time ever the king gave to Admiral Zoumar his full trust in matters of the army and navy. For his part, the admiral was confident that he knew what needed to be done. The soon departure of four Troyan vessels from Phoenicia was by Zoumar quickly approved.

As his crews readied Troyan barges for the long voyage to ferry two unicorns across the immense western sea, Bashkeem devised a way to connect the rudder to a helm wheel, thereby giving the pilot more control and precision in guiding the direction of the vessel, especially in inclement weather.

Taking for granted that neither the king nor Zoumar would stop him, Avalcar made up his mind to depart with Bashkeem, Mistral, and Seahorse. When the captain requested Hammereins and Lucareins to with him sail, in spite of the dangers that Troyan vessels could capsize in a storm or be attacked by sea monsters or warring natives, the two stallions readily assented.

As difficult as would be the sea passage to a very distant land, the captain knew that absent the presence of unicorn magic on board, the return voyage to Phoenicia would be even more arduous. For that reason Avalcar made sure that his personal affairs were in good order.

Mistral and Seahorse felt their hearts to be divided. While they were excited at the prospect of gaining the white herd, they would forever after miss the mountains of the land of their birth.

No longer a rebellious prince that insisted on drawing pictures of birds to the exclusion of service to his country, and with a sheathed sword now worn comfortably at his waist, Majit also chose to embark on the voyage across a vast sea. While just like the unicorns he would miss the land where he was born, the younger prince was consoled by the new realization that even if the love of Resi had to him been denied, his father *truly* loved him. It was not lost on Majit that he was following in the tradition of a long ago Prince Lyons, that had also set forth across the immense sea on a voyage of unicorns.

The day for departure came.

Mounted for what they imagined would be their final time on Hammereins and Lucareins, King Barsuna and Crown Prince Maroun led the way from the palace. One by one the soldiers and sailors lining the boulevard saluted the progress of their king and the hereditary prince.

On the backs of Mistral and Seahorse followed Bashkeem and Prince Majit. Prince Ermir, Prince Ermal, and Princess Admira walked at the sides of the two unicorns. On this day the people cheered louder for those riding and accompanying two unicorn horses, than they did for the king and Prince Maroun.

Princess Resi, Avalcar, and Zoumar followed riding horses that matched the white coloration of the two unicorns.

The four Troyan barge crews led by Cholo, Sulay, Enos, and Olsi proceeded as relaxed companies, not everyone in step with each other.

Upon admiring the Jenelisa's large green banner emblazoned with a white unicorn, the crowded onlookers doubted they would ever again have the opportunity to see magic unicorns board a barge in departure from Phoenicia.

Three Gifts

The king called for Avalcar, Majit, and Bashkeem to present before him; Barsuna proclaimed the three men Lord Protectors of Phoenicia.

Barsuna was handed a shield.

"On this far voyage sail not one, but two sons of mine. I now look upon Avalcar, the commander of this expedition, as my own son made to be a distinguished military leader. When I asked you to take Majit under your wings, your tutelage made my son to become a renowned warrior. As much artist as blacksmith, the man that crafted this shield assured me that it is the finest ever made in Phoenicia. Fabricated with not only blue gold, but also with unicorn magic, Mistral named this shield *Stomp.*"

Holding the shield up to flash blue and gold in sunlight, the king added, "Made magical by the touch of a unicorn horn, this shield will make the arms of Avalcar to stop the blows of enemy swords and spears. Hah! This shield will even dissuade a spear thrown at Avalcar's back!"

"Thank you, my king, for this great gift. Since I have many times seen the hooves of Mistral to mightily stomp the enemy, the name chosen for this magic shield is very fitting. But if I might inquire something, how does my king explain the paradox that Mistral's magical goodness is constituted into a golden shield used on a battlefield not only for defense, but also to maim and kill? Now I know that if should ask him, Mistral will again tell me that because all things in life are touched by love, that love has everything to do with those that fight to protect friends and family in a cause that is just."

"You see, Avalcar, when Mistral furnished great magic to your shield his mind was seized upon your image. For that, the magic he invested in this shield will come to serve you alone. Mistral also knows that any cause you fight for... will be a just one. By the way, I did ask Mistral why in possession of magic so powerful he could not save his sister Crimson from the perils of war. He answered that no earthly magic is... *unbounded.* So be reminded, Avalcar, that while the magic of this shield will well-protect you, it does not in battle make you invincible."

A spear was handed to the king.

"Take Majit, my son, this spear. Its point and the inlaid filament running the length of the shaft are of magical gold forged. The lightness of the heft of the spear will make it to fly far. The provisioning of much magic makes the flight of this spear follow to where your eyes direct. This spear, named *Horn* by Mistral, is the only one that can do this. Now go forth and to Phoenicia bring glory."

A sword was next handed to the king.

"Receive, Bashkeem, this doubled-edged sword forged with the finest workmanship by the most renowned blacksmith in our land. Swung in any direction, the light and balanced blade will cleave marrow from bone. The touch of Mistral's horn made this blue gold sword, named *Gallop*, magically responsive to your heart. Instead of your arm moving about the sword, this sword will move fast your hand and arm to defend a heart that is true."

After thanking the king, Bashkeem unfastened from his waist the sword he wore. "Would the king do me the courtesy of returning this sword to its rightful owner?"

"Hah! I loved this sword!" exclaimed Barsuna. "It is kind of you, Bashkeem, to remember that I before gifted this very same sword to another. It offended me when without asking my permission, Zoumar regifted this beautiful sword to you. I know now that he was right to have done so. That said, I shall place a second time this sword in the hands of our illustrious admiral."

Zoumar received the sword that he had once before been given.

Majit, Bashkeem, and Avalcar bowed to the king.

"What vessel approaches?" inquired Barsuna.

"It is one of the Phoenician barges that returned the Egyptian army back to its home," replied Zoumar.

"Then why is it crowded to overflow with people? It should be returning... empty."

"I shall find out." That said, Zoumar walked to where the barge was docking.

The admiral soon returned with a man in tattered clothes walking at his side.

"Since you speak our tongue, inform the king who you are," instructed Zoumar.

"I am a slave of Egypt... no... because I no longer wear shackles, that is not longer true. Marching through my village, the commander of an Egyptian army told me I was to return to Troy a free man."

"I am become absent-minded," replied Barsuna nodding his head. "I had forgotten something put in the letter given to the Egyptian general. By the way since this is not Troy, this free man still has a long way to travel."

Ermal embraced the Phoenician ex-slave.

"Prince Ermal, *it is you!*" The young man, made to be no longer a slave, slumped down clutching the waist of his prince.

"If my people that were by the Egyptians captured," said Ermal turning to Avalcar, "that are now made to be freed, do not receive help they will not find their way from Phoenicia back to Troy."

"Yes, you have a point Ermal." That spoken, Avalcar approached again the monarch.

"I think, King Barsuna, that the time has come for you to own the two best race horses in Phoenicia, those being my Hammereins and Lucareins. Let us come to terms and make a fair trade. In exchange for transport of the former Troyan slaves that gain this harbor, back to their homeland, I offer you my two wondrous horses. I am taken with the idea that you will treat them well."

The king pulled at his beard. As he answered his eyes turned from serious to merry.

"So long as the fleet horses are agreed, Captain Avalcar... *has a deal!* Because Hammereins and Lucareins are the greatest gifts I have ever received, they will be treated like equine princes. Better than anyone you know what the two touched by magic stallions mean to me.

"Ha! More absent-mindedness! I just remembered a possession I found in the palace and had brought with me." A servant stepped forward and handed the king a small bundle wrapped in a soft woolen skin.

"In my hands is a wooden box engraved with the images of a blackmaned unicorn and a winged horse... that can only have to do with the two unicorns that safe-guarded the founding of Phoenicia. To this day our children are taught that in their long ago quest for freedom, the people that settled this land were by unicorn horns pushed together. Be careful when you open the lid. Beset by the detritus of a thousand years, the fragile box is ready to crumble."

"I will treasure this priceless box that will ever remind me of my king."

"You know what, Avalcar? If in the land of Troy there was again to be found a king, I would feel better about the prospects of the liberated slaves that return from Egypt in quest of their homeland." That said, the king turned to direct his gaze at the older of the two Troyan princes.

When all eyes fell on Ermir, the prince lowered his head.

"The time has come for my older brother to become obedient to his destiny," said Ermal touching gently his brother's arm.

"Hmpf!" Ermir drew in a deep breath, raised his head, and finally answered, "My brother, you know that I have anticipated the great adventure that awaits our barges, the new seas we shall sail through, the new lands we shall sail by, and the magnificence of the white herd that in a faraway land searches for a hold. However, given your support and that of our sisters, I am compelled to do my duty. Rather than come to know the distant land, I shall remain behind to serve our people."

"I think," interjected Ermal turning to Bashkeem, "that my brother is partial to one of the Troyan vessels."

"About that, Ermal, you just might be right," answered Bashkeem. "However, since I myself am partial to the Jenelisa, I hope your brother selects one of our other three barges." The Flash would sail not across far seas but instead return Ermir, accompanied by newly freed slaves, to the city of Troy.

"My king," interjected Avalcar. "As a codicil to our agreement regarding Hammereins and Lucareins would you have Admiral Zoumar adopt the policy that no more marauders, whether Egyptian or pirate, will invade Troy until we return from this voyage of the two unicorns?"

"Agreed," responded King Barsuna. "And I will do even more. So that he does not return home to an empty treasury, I shall also provide a generous gift of gold to the new Troyan King. Of course... I had always intended to provide a reward to the Troyan royalty for their rescue of Admiral Zoumar in the *Battle of Fourteen Egyptian War Barges.*"

Disheartened by the likelihood that they would never again set their eyes on their oldest brother and youngest sister, Admira and Ermal embraced one last time Resi and Ermir. Tears ran down the faces of four Troyan princes and princesses that had together learned the art of sailing the sea, survived many battles, and gained stunning victories.

Under the command of Avalcar three Troyan ships captained by Bashkeem, Ermal, and Admira set forth from Byblos.

New Voyage Begun

"It is hard for me to accept that I have left forever behind the mountains where I kicked up my hooves as a foal," neighed Seahorse.

"Although it is difficult for me to comprehend," responded Mistral, "it seems that of the one clan of unicorns that long ago stayed behind in Phoenicia, we two are the only ones that live on. How can it be that neither you, nor I, nor any other horned horse shall again graze in the land that was ever the heritage of our unicorn clan?"

"Come now big fellows," encouraged Ermal, "you two are off on a great voyage of discovery. Just imagine all the new friends you will make when you join to the white herd."

"As our barges sail a distance immense across dangerous seas," offered Majit, "the valiant hearts of Mistral and Seahorse are needed to embolden all of us. The magic of your unicorn horns will be our safe protection."

"Ermal, Majit, you are right to stay positive," answered Mistral. "Following your lead I am going to right now enjoy the fair winds that on this pleasant evening propel westward this sturdy barge named appropriately... the Sea Stallion."

"Our three barges travel fast, and at exactly the same speed," observed Majit.

"For three fast-moving prows to maintain an even line, the sails of each vessel have to be trimmed to perfection," responded Ermal.

"It is a very impressive thing to see," agreed Mistral. "I cannot believe the excellence of our three sea captains."

"I see that Ermal waves at his sister," noticed Olsi standing on the prow of the Star Sheen.

Turning her head, Admira waved in return.

"Set beside Ermal and Majit, the two unicorns now flash hooves at us," added Olsi.

"What a delight that is to see," answered Admira. "Their greeting makes this evening special to me. As a girl I was fascinated with unicorn figurines. Now I am toying with the idea of staying on in the far land to make certain that our two unicorn friends gain the white herd. Perhaps I will even accompany the white herd in their quest to find a new hold, the new place of refuge where from monstrous wolves they shall evermore be protected."

"I admire your adventuress spirit, Admira," replied Olsi. "But, what if instead of you, your brother Prince Ermal continues on in the new land? You know that he has talked about doing that."

"But, Olsi, that cannot happen. It is the obligation of my brother to return to Troy and support the throne of our family. It is the custom for men to rule. Fortunately for me, I am not a man."

"Admira, it would be a comfort for the two stalwart unicorns to know that you are pledged to help them gain the white herd *and* the new hold of the unicorns."

"Avalcar and Bashkeem are looking our way. Wave at them, Olsi!"

In return greeting the commander and his senior captain waved and yelled "Halloo!"

"It does appear," remarked Bashkeem, "that Admira and Olsi enjoy good conversation this evening, just as do you and I this night on the Jenelisa."

"So tell me," responded Avalcar, "how is it that I find myself again traveling across a seemingly endless sea toward the far land of the white herd and the storied blackmaned unicorn? Better than anyone, I know that the risks we take on this voyage... *are enormous.*"

"You are not second guessing your decision to a second time commit to travel across boundless seas?"

"The risks we face, Bashkeem, are indeed very many. I hope to never again confront a storm like the one that disrupted Admiral Zoumar's fleet in return to Phoenicia. At least we do not voyage over the shortest days of the year... that is when the storm crippled our vessels."

"That is a remarkable coincidence. It was precisely on the longest night of the year that the fleeing Troyan royalty seized control of my barge, and in so doing transformed my life."

"Hmph. It seems that our lives were interwoven by destiny," responded Avalcar.

"Although our foremost purpose is to unite Mistral and Seahorse with the white herd," continued Bashkeem, "you and I both hope that a way will be found to locate again the canyon that sparkles of magic. Wearing armor and wielding swords forged of blue gold would mean *everything* to the future army of Troy. The magic gold would serve to inspire a people before taken captive, to again believe in themselves."

Avalcar later sat alone as he unwrapped the gift that had been given him.

"The king was right. This box is ready to crumble."

Avalcar found five objects inside the box. He first inspected a finely wrought blue gold diadem. On the left side of the diadem was engraved the image of a grand columnar pavilion. The image on the right side of the diadem appeared to be that of a peculiar looking mountain shaped like the prow of a ship. Also contained in the box were two wrist braces forged of magic gold and embellished with images of lions, and two extraordinary halters woven of fine blue gold.

"So the stories of my youth were true," allowed Avalcar. "These precious objects were gifted a thousand years ago to the legendary Maryeta, Lyons, Briarburr... and what was the name of the unicorn with wings? Ahh yes, I remember now. She was called Peli."

CHAPTER 27

INSPIRED

"Look! The mists of the waterfall have formed into an extraordinarily colored rainbow!" groinked Timidthy.

"And the top of the rainbow is strangely pointed!" exclaimed Hamilton joining the run of Timidthy toward the lake at one end of Shining Canyon. "*Grunk! Grunk!* Its shape is half rainbow and half pyramid!"

As they watched the small rainbow grow taller, the two wild boarlings raised a ruckus, which of course brought the rest of the band to the edge of the lake.

"I think that the rainbow is remindful of a doorway," groinked Timidthy.

"Since rainbows that are remindful of pointed arches are so rare that they are almost never seen, the presence of this one must be for a purpose," declared Practicia.

"Naythorn, do you remember that after the two mountain sheep joined us, and guided us down the deep gorge, how Rayalas thought to fan the pooled water?" inquired Roothyford. "Her magic made it possible to see *mist-wolves.*"

"We were astonished at her magic," answered the blackmane. "Let me guess. You and Practicia think it would be worth a try for our winged filly to augment the mists creating the rainbow that we see. Well then... if Isabayas inherited from her mother mare the same winged power, it would be helpful for us to learn what these mists formed with magic can show us."

"My precious foal," neighed the blackmane to Isabayas found at his side, "your mother mare once made visible the forms of wolves in pursuit of us. Can your wings make to happen under the rainbow, another mist vision?"

"There is no reason, Sire, that my wings cannot do so."

"Naythorn," grunted Timidthy, "it just occurred to me that the blue gold armor of Master Bison and Sir Cattle could introduce greater magic into the vision, making clearer the images inspired by the wings of Isabayas."

"Why, that is an *excellent* idea," answered the stallion. "Buckwhite and Taurington will be glad to stand in the water, while our filly's wings make to blow windy mists over their blue gold armor."

Taken to the air above the backs of two bovines, Isabayas began to beat her wings faster and faster. From troubled water was made to swirl a very thick mist.

"Waves roll in the picture-mist!" squealed Practicia.

"It is... the sea!" gasped Roothyford.

"Oh my! A barge carries two unicorns!" grunted Mama Pig.

"It also carries our friend Avalcar," observed Lucars. "He was the captain that gave leave for Hammer and me to leave the Phoenician army, and return to Naythorn."

"The young man standing beside Avalcar wears exquisite armor," observed Hammer. "His breastplate portends an important personage."

"There is a second barge!" exclaimed Amaluna. "On this one a beautiful red-haired young lady holds onto the arm of a broad-shouldered man whose face bears resemblance to her features. Their armor is also beautifully made."

"They must be a brother and sister prince and princess!" said Alexzana with her clear voice toned in excitement.

"And look, there is a third barge!" exclaimed again Amaluna.

"So the officer friend of Hammer and Lucars returns with three vessels, important personages, and two unicorns destined to join the white herd," observed matter-of-factly Rambuncture. "Hmph! I have no doubt that Captain Avalcar will in return require sheets of the magic gold to take back across the wide water to his king... and that will sadly complicate things for us."

"If that is the case," offered Hammerclaw, "Captain Avalcar will remember my description of the whereabouts of Shining Canyon. I expect that the vessels shown in the mist now sail for the coast before Spire Mountain."

"Master Hammer is right," neighed Naythorn shaking around his head. "Since we are to have visitors, we surely must prepare ourselves for their arrival."

"But because wolves block entrance to this canyon," bleated Rambuncture, "we now have a big problem to solve."

"Let us not forget that the presentation of the unique rainbow augurs hope," responded the ram's mate Ewelissas. "Since the three barges are still at sea, there remains time to do something about the wolves found outside our canyon."

"I agree with Ewelissas," groinked Practicia. "Something good will come from the presentation of the magic rainbow and Isabaya's mists. In fact, I think the purpose of the deeply colored rainbow's pointed door was to entrance into our hearts... *heavenly hope.*"

"Sire," neighed Isabayas, "since wings are my only magic gift, I did not call here the magic rainbow."

"My filly, if it was not you then it must have been the magic of Belfloralex, or your grandsire, that called forth the rainbow."

A Secret Revealed

The next morning found the family of wild boars bathing together. Just as on many before occasions, Mama Pig was feeling exceptionally proud of the intelligence of her offspring. Since she felt that way, she found it proper to offer a compliment.

"Timidthy and Hamilton were smart to notice yesterday the pointed rainbow, and Roothy and Practicia was smart to suggest that Isabayas fan her wings to produce a mist vision."

"And I will affirm," responded Hamilton, "that most of the good ideas credited to Timidthy and myself, happened to be mine alone. Was it not me that first saw the mists?"

"Wrong, Hamilton," corrected Practicia, "Timidthy saw them first."

"Roothy," continued the girl wild boar turning to her sister, "thinking on the *doorway* rainbow, a thought just occurred to me. Did the human persons who built the hidden pavilion know of this place?"

"Who else but the master engineers that raised high the beautiful pavilion, could have built the stone door that opens into this vale? That door fits so tightly that it can only be pried open by the hardness of blue gold swords."

"But sister, if that is so," continued Practicia, "why is there not found here a second doorway, like the one we discovered and then used to make our escape from the canyon of the pavilion?"

"You are exactly *right!*" squealed Roothy. "If an enemy were to seize control of the entrance cave, those within this magic canyon would become trapped."

"Just like we are now," answered Practicia.

"So sister that must mean... that somewhere can be found... a second way to depart this place."

"See! This is what makes me extra proud of all four of my offspring. Dwelling on the issue of our now being found trapped in this canyon, and having seen the curious doorway rainbow, Practicia and Roothyford put two and two together and concluded that there must here exist a second way of departure."

"Hah! And that shows that my sister pigs are almost as smart as I am," groinked Hamilton.

Mrs. Razorthwacker called together the entire band to present the issue raised by the girl boarlings. The conclusion was unanimous; a second way must logically exist to enter and exit Shining Canyon. The meeting done, everyone set out to search for the still unfound second entrance.

Lucars headed for the little lake. Because the hidden doorway in the hollow canyon of Prow Mountain was set behind a cascade of water, his idea was that the second passage was to be found underwater. With Lucars swam Featherspark and Webstir. The three resurfaced and dived a second time... a third time... then a fifth time. However, no underwater passage was there to be found.

Buckwhite and Taurington decided that scratching sharp horn tips against rock would reveal the seam where a stone door was placed. Following close behind the bovines, with finger swishes and big expelled breaths Alexzana and Amaluna dusted the scratch marks made by two sets of big horns. To their frustration, and that of the bovines, no door seam was by horn scratches identified.

Because the canyon's north wall descended abruptly to a level plain, where everything close or far was visible to an observer, Isabayas decided that side of Shining Canyon offered little advantage for the placement of an emergency breakout door. Besides, too many wolves were presently there found to make viable an escape through a second north entrance. On the other hoof, the south wall of the canyon stood within the mountain itself. If one could penetrate through the south wall, there might well exist a pathway into the heights of Spire Mountain.

Up and over the south canyon wall wafted the wings of the fast growing filly.

All she saw at first were rock spires needling skyward. But it was not long before her wings hovered over what hinted to be a narrow pathway. The filly decided that there really was the faint outline of a trail overgrown with evergreen trees, where one might walk between the spires. On each side of the path the rocky outcrops vaulted high, thin, and jagged. She alighted, and stepped her way slowly ahead. Each step walked by the hooves of Isabayas brought her closer to the south wall of Shining Canyon.

Her path ended at a rock overhang that underneath extended inward like a big tight-sided barrel placed lengthwise on its side. The indentation was large enough to comfortably accommodate at one time the bodies of Taurington, Buckwhite, Belfloralex, and Naythorn. After blowing hard through her nostrils to clear the dust, by the glow of her horn a seam could be dimly seen that separated surrounding rock from what appeared to be an entrance portal into the canyon of blue gold. Neighing and rearing up excitedly for the joy of discovery, Isabayas banged her head and horn against rock. Still smarting from the bruising, the winged filly picked her way back along the path she had before taken.

Isabayas took to flight, but not to rejoin her sire. With eyes peeled she followed on wing the outline of a ragged and unkempt trail, that as it rose higher and higher, passed through grassy spots and clumped trees. It appeared that lines of distant tree tops continued to demark the trail.

"I think that trail cuts all the way to the top of Spire Mountain," muttered the filly. Proud of what she had discovered, back to Shining Canyon flew Isabayas as quickly as her wings could carry her.

"Sire, at the end of an obscure trail, on the other side of the canyon's south wall, I found a rock indentation with a seam. I think that is where a stone doorway was long ago made."

This time it was Naythorn that jumped hooves and neighed excitedly. Soon band members were arrayed all about the filly. As she explained a second time her conclusion, the eyes of Hammer and Lucars fixated on the face of the south wall of Shining Canyon.

"Oh, Sire, there is one thing more; the stone seam was rounded."

"I have it!"

"What have you, Master Hammer?" inquired Lucars placing a hand on a shoulder of his former sergeant. "I remind that when we before thoroughly checked the south wall, no exit was there found."

"It is not a simple doorway, Lucars. A stone rolls back to give entrance to the portal. We must identify a boulder that has curve to it, and can be rolled one direction or another."

Only one boulder set against the south wall had a rounded shape. Above the stone was a curious marking, the only engraving to be found along that wall of Shining Canyon.

"You know Hammer, I before wondered what those horizontal lines surmounted by squiggly lines, and then a jagged saw tooth line were meant to signify," commented Lucars.

"About their meaning I remain befuddled," responded Hammer.

With leverage gained from bovine horns and poles hefted by strong arms, the boulder was made to move in a gradual upward incline, whereupon a second entrance to Shining Canyon was revealed. A handy stone was lodged at the base of the rounded blocking door to prevent it from rolling back to again shut the entranceway.

Since good news was invariably by band members celebrated, the discovery of a second doorway was marked with bucking, jumping, body bumping, and a medley of loud animal noises and yells.

Buckwhite went first into the rounded opening. Soon he was returned, "Just as Isabayas told us, on the other side traces a forgotten path. When our stay in Shining Canyon is over, we can on that path depart unnoticed."

"Master Cabalblade," neighed Naythorn to his sire, "in order to reconnoiter the route of our future departure from here, over the next few days I want you to scout out a pathway into and across Spire Mountain. Take with you Isabayas, Lianvil, and Dansey, the same three companions that accompanied you on previous travel into a big mountain. If you come upon some of our wolf enemies, keep each other safe. I cannot afford to lose my filly, my sire, or either one of my two former enemies now become my trusted lieutenants."

Into the rounded passageway trotted a unicorn stallion, a unicorn filly with wings, a big tawny lion, and a mostly yellow wolf.

"I can guess what crosses your mind," muttered the bison as he nodded knowingly to Mrs. Pig, "and I agree with what you are inclined to think. You presume that

Naythorn does not want either his sire or his filly to observe what he is now to endure, the welding of his horn shard to his half horn."

"With the soon arrival of the three barges, Naythorn can no longer delay fusing together the two halves of his horn," answered Mrs. Pig. "Having suffered much when his horn was severed, the blackmane fears that reattaching his shard will be equally painful. I only hope that by the time our four friends return from their scouting mission, Naythorn will again find himself made as good as new."

Torches were fashioned and sparked to burn. Holding each a torch, the two blacksmiths began a close inspection of the newly discovered second passageway.

"Look here, Lucars." Hammer pointed to a place in the ceiling of the tunnel, "By the looks of it, this might be the purest vein of gold that we have yet found. What say you?"

Lucars squinted, changed his position, and then from another angle of observation squinted once more upward.

"The master smith is not mistaken. The large vein of blue gold that passages this rock surface displays not one trace of impurity. The blue sheen is here deeper than elsewhere, and it actually seems to glow. This vein of magic gold will do perfectly for Naythorn's horn bindings."

Lucars moved to stand on the mountain side of the doorway tunnel. "Did you notice these markings over here, Hammer? We see the same straight, wavy, and sawtooth lines found on the valley side of this tunnel.

Next to them is an etching of what I take to be a unicorn with wings."

"Well, it is said that a very long time past it was a flighted unicorn that discovered this canyon. It may be, Lucars, that the layered horizontal lines represent rising elevation from ground level, the squiggly lines represent clouds or winds that blow strong into mountain heights, and the sawtooth etchings represent the mountains themselves. Interestingly enough, the number of the sawtooth triangle markings is the same as the number of pyramid-crested peaks in the formation that points to Shining Canyon, when approached via the trench of broken stones. If so, this outside etching that also depicts height, wind, and mountain peaks identifies the presence of this entrance into Shining Canyon."

The two meticulous blacksmiths continued their investigation of the rock ceiling behind the round door.

"Over here, Hammer. I think this third carving, threaded by small veins of blue gold, represents a crown... made of the magic ore. On one side of the crown is the outline of a unicorn head and horn, the wing of a unicorn is on the other."

"Hmpf. Could it be that this engraving represents a prophecy pertaining to a future king?" After reflecting further the senior blacksmith added, "Do not for now say anything about this. Let me first try my hand at fashioning a crown faithful to this image. Having never made something so precious, I cannot guarantee how adequate my attempt will be."

"My lips, Hammer, are sealed. Just like the placement of the pyramid crests on mountaintops, the image of this crown was surely put here for a reason. Why else would it depict a winged unicorn? Isabayas brings to life the prophecy presented in this carving of a crown."

"If we are indeed fortunate," responded Hammer, "you and I will find out who is someday to wear the blue gold crown that I am about to make. Do not forget, Lucars, that this is our secret. On some future day I want to surprise a new monarch that just might happen to find himself, or herself, lacking a royal crown."

Better than New

By the afternoon of the next day more than enough of the vein of, most pure gold, had been extracted for not one but two purposes. In addition to the fashioning of golden reinforcements to bind together the two halves of a unicorn horn, a royal crown was to be later made.

"Lucars, here is how we will rebind Naythorn's horn," instructed Hammer. "You will create two ribbons of gold twice as wide as my thumb, which shall come to be wrapped criss-cross around the two halves of unicorn horn. Use the shard to pattern the spiraling of the ribbons. I will lengthwise chip a small channel down the center of the broken-off shard. When the time comes for the rebinding to take place, I shall also chip a small channel down the severed length of Naythorn's still attached half horn. When filled with gold, the two halves of that channel will lock permanently the shard into its rightful position.

"I will also chip five little cross channels into the shard where the liquid gold will force out to the horn's surface. The gold ribbons must align to weld firm to the cross channels of gold. At the top of the unicorn shard I will make a counter sink with a diameter as big as the tip of my little finger. At the point of the horn, gold within the ivory core will seal with the spiral ribbons that wind upwardly about the horn, and so create a golden cap for the reborn horn of Naythorn."

"That... sounds... perfect," agreed the younger blacksmith. "Now, Hammer, it is become time for me to create the finest and purest gold ribbons that have ever been made." The next evening found the horn shard cored, the ribbons molded as per the dimensions of the shard, and a quantity of gold set aside to be reheated and then poured into the core. On the following morning the blackmane was by the burly blacksmith summoned. With him came the half-horned filly.

"For what I am about to do, I require that your horn be maintained in a vertical position."

"I will do my best, Master Hammer."

"Cushion your head upon my mantle so that it holds steady while Lucars and I work. Should a splatter of hot metal singe your hide, in spite of the hurt please do not jerk your head."

"And, Naythorn will also place his head against my neck," neighed Belfloralex. "I will make sure that his head not only holds steady, but that Naythorn remains as comfortable as he can."

"Very good, Belfloralex. That will do nicely."

"Now, Naythorn," continued Hammer, "your markings will soon include not just the color black, but also the glow of exquisite blue gold. While the pain of burning and scaring your horn cannot be dispensed with, bear in mind that you have more than once suffered worse."

"To sustain me through the pain I will concentrate on the warm feel of the neck of this brave unicorn filly," replied Naythorn as with little success he attempted to smile.

Two blacksmiths set to work. Hammer began by carefully grooving a channel into the half horn protruding from the forehead of the blackmane. That channel would align perfectly with the channel already cut down the length of the horn shard. While that was taking place, Lucars heated the set-aside blue gold hot enough to make it flow liquid; he also warmed the gold ribboning to make it more pliable. That work accomplished, the blacksmiths were ready to proceed with the delicate task of permanently reuniting two halves of unicorn horn.

Hammer held the horn shard tight to Naythorn's half horn. With fine tongs Lucars wound the first heated gold ribbon from the base of the horn, to its tip. Then the second ribbon was wound in a crisscross pattern up the length of Naythorn's horn. Lucars made sure that the gold strips were placed to cover each crosscut hole in the horn shard. In order to manage the pain introduced by hot gold ribbons as they hardened, with eyes closed tight Naythorn continued to tensely press his head against the neck of Belfloralex.

Ever so carefully Hammer dripped gold into the hollowed countersink. A fine straw of hot liquid ran down to fill the channel running the length of

Naythorn's horn. Feeling with his fingers the heat to penetrate the ribboning, Lucars verified that the liquid gold coursed into each of the five crosscut holes.

After the two ribbon ends were smoothed together, the horn's golden tip extended beyond the ivory by two lengths of Hammer's index finger. Until the magic gold set hard as rock, Belfloralex cradled the neck of the blackmaned unicorn so that his horn remained in an upright position. By the time the sun entered the western half of the sky, the long awaited restoration of Naythorn's horn was accomplished. An exhausted blackmaned unicorn fell asleep.

"I can hardly believe what today took place," neighed Naythorn in midafternoon as he stared at his reflection in the water of the canyon's lake. "My horn is brand new. It is even better than before." Gathered round the blackmane, band members nodded their heads in agreement.

"Captain Naythorn, you need to tell Belfloralex that she was of much help to you today," said Hammer. "Without her steadying your neck and head, Lucars and I would have been hard-pressed to finish the work required."

"My friend is right," answered the stallion nodding his head at Belfloralex. "You made this day's hard work to progress indeed well. Thank you, pure heart."

Lucars tugged at the master smithy's sleeve and whispered something.

"You tell me that to be on the safe side, you made extra blue gold ribboning?" The face of Hammer opened into a small smile as he next moved his hands to touch the mane of Naythorn. When the blacksmith whispered a few words, the effect on the unicorn was dramatic. Naythorn stiffened his frame, looked at Belfloralex, at Lucars, and back at Hammer. Then Naythorn reared high and did so again.

"Belfloralex, come with me!"

"But Naythorn, where do we go?"

"We go with Hammer and Lucars back to the forge. You see, dear one, now it is my turn to cradle your head while the remaining blue gold ribboning is woven onto your horn. You are to once again wear a horn fitting to your beauty."

The surgery on the horn of Belfloralex was far less difficult than that performed on Naythorn. Up the short length of her half horn two strips of the precious gold ribbon were tightly wound. After soldering each intersection of the two strands, the two ends of the spiral bands were twisted together. The broken tip of the horn of Belfloralex was, with blue gold, made to be smoothed and grown longer.

Belfloralex raised her head from off the neck of Naythorn. Rolling upward her eyes she was able to glimpse a long tapered point of blue gold, that now extended by half the previous length of her broken horn.

"My dear filly, your lovely horn now matches perfectly the new horn of Naythorn!" exclaimed Mrs. Pig. "Among the white herd you will be widely admired for being the only lady unicorn with a golden horn!"

"Roothy, Practicia," grunted Mama Pig, "do you not wish that you had such a pretty ivory and gold horn as now possesses our dear friend Belfloralex?"

Wearing big smiles two girl wild boars groinked agreement.

A unicorn stallion reunited with a horn shard that was once buried in the heart of a monster wolf, and a unicorn filly whose half horn vanquished a sea colossus, came to enjoy high-spirited gallop and play.

"Dear filly, the magic of this new horn feels different," observed Naythorn as he settled to trot back-and-forth with Belfloralex matching his step. "It will take some time for me to get used to."

Belfloralex placed the side of her horn against Naythorn's chest, dug in her hooves, and brought the big stallion to a halt.

"Did you see that, Naythorn? My horn is not only pretty; it is stronger than it looks."

The remainder of the day became a holiday where everyone celebrated the restoration of two unicorn horns back to their old measurements, or in the case of Belfloralex almost to its former length.

The next morning Cabalblade, Isabayas, Lianvil, and Dansey returned to Shining Canyon to find Naythorn and Belfloralex with horns made splendid to see.

"While I love my sire's new horn," neighed happily Isabayas, "the long golden tip that extends the horn of Belfloralex will be the envy of every filly in the white herd, including me!"

"The horns of Naythorn and Belfloralex now possess the magic of unicorns *and* blue gold," grrrd Lianvil to his best friend Dansey. "I can hardly wait to see the great things that shall next be done by these two most courageous unicorns."

The four scouts had verified that a discernible path, well-supplied with water and grass, led upward from the rounded door to cross the heights of Spire Mountain.

That afternoon there was more than enough good news to quench the austere appetites of a serious-minded bison and a dour bighorn sheep. Accordingly, Rambuncture cavorted with his mate Ewelissas as if he were half his age, and Buckwhite ambled across the meadow sporting the biggest smile he could possibly manage.

Feeling under their armor the freshness of lake water, four wild boarlings took to lounging on muddied bellies.

"If only life could stay just like this, Roothy, would not that be perfect?"

"Yes, Practicia, this afternoon we are given over to rest and thoughts of happiness for the good that was done to the horns of two unicorns."

"And more thoughts of happiness for the confirmation of a trail that leads from the rounded door all the way across Spire Mountain," added Hamilton. "However, it pains me to admit that I had nothing to do with that discovery."

"But brother and sister boarlings," interjected Timidthy, "you do know that this cannot last. Something always comes along to spoil the leisure of our rest and relaxation. It is as though there can be no perfection, no promise or length of happiness complete."

Isabayas took to the air. In her eye was a mischievous glint. Soon her wings were splashing water on four boarlings with the intent to upset their restful relax.

Joining in the fun, Belfloralex bounded about in the water as she chased the winged filly that always managed to fan her wings slightly beyond the reach of the gold-horned filly's clicking gums and teeth.

"See that, Hamilton?" groinked Timidthy. "I just told you that something *always* happens to spoil our relaxation."

Then it really happened.

A new image began to form in the mists where batted the playful wings of Isabayas and cavorted Belfloralex. Gaining definition and clarity, the vision came to show Avalcar and two unicorns walking in front of a platoon of sailors. The previously revealed princess rode one of the two unicorns.

"The barges landed!" squealed simultaneously Roothy and Practicia.

"But, where can they be?" brayed Buckwhite arriving quickly to the edge of the lake.

"Since my magic gift is to command the wind, I will show you!" neighed Belfloralex. Repositioned to stand on the shore, the half-horned unicorn began to twirl her body. When the swirling mist became anchored to the horn of Belfloralex, she began to walk away from the lake. The mist followed after.

"You were right, Lianvil!" barked Dansey. "Golden bindings have made the horn of Belfloralex to become even more magical!"

With each step taken by the filly, the vision moved to show what was next to be found in the direction the landed barge party walked. The members of Naythorn's band followed after Belfloralex and the swirling mists that she now controlled.

"I know the hills found in front of the land party," grrrd the lion. "The travelers now find themselves three days distant from us, directly to our east."

"So, Lianvil, we shall see them soon," responded Naythorn.

"Look, Naythorn," continued the lion, "Isabayas moves the vision toward Spire Mountain. Our eyes travel far in this vision."

"Seeing the mountain from above, I say that it is truly majestic," answered Naythorn.

"My spired mountain is the most beautiful of all mountains," grrrd the lion. Lianvil's neck and shoulders stiffened, and his joy for the aerial view of his mountain ended. Then they all saw what the lion had glimpsed.

"Beyond the sunset side of Spire Mountain travel many warriors!" exclaimed mama pig.

"Look, Dansey," grrrd Lianvil, "there is the chief of the death mask warriors that we before stopped from murdering defenseless hostages. He and his warriors have changed direction to now travel southward."

When Isabayas veered leftward her hooves, the mist vision followed.

"*Grarr!* In front of the chief that Dansey and I despise," growled Lianvil, "a warrior who would have sacrificed the weak for no reason, travel many wolves!"

"Move the mist more southward," neighed the blackmane.

"Oh no!" groinked Roothyford. "At the front of the long column of wolves and warriors trots a giant black wolf, that is almost as big as was Albarochk!"

"But... what are they chasing? Who are they going to fight?" grunted Timidthy.

As Isabayas walked more southward, the mist vision climbed high and traveled over a mountain set at the western side of the entrance to the great basin containing Prow Mountain.

"Look! There! There is movement!" barked Trackler.

"On the side of the mountain walk Aneilee, Elianor, and Rainsnow!" yelped Blackler.

"Below and ahead of them walk forlorn looking natives with torn clothing," brayed the bison. "It must be that the great wolf and the death mask people are intent on destroying the guide matriarch and the high escort of the white herd, and as well the helpless people that proceed before them."

"Death mask warriors loathe the refugees that were saved by Chief Bigclaws," barked Dansey.

"How is it that the matriarchs are gone down below us?" mrawed the cattle bull. "In the lead of hundreds of unicorns they should be traveling toward the fixed star. Would not you agree, Master Bison, that something is very wrong?"

"Sir Cattle is right," brayed Buckwhite. "Without the leadership of Aneilee and Elianor things with the white herd cannot, and will not go well. But surely the two mares did not voluntarily depart the unicorns that for so long they selflessly served. They must have been compelled to leave behind the white herd."

"If Elianor and Aneilee know that they and the refugees are being pursued," groinked Timidthy, "and they would surely sense that to be so, they are intent on finding a place of protection. In the great basin they are entering, there is only one place where safety can for them be gained. The canyon of the lost pavilion is entered through a tight passageway that can be defended by a mere handful of strong warriors, perhaps even come to be defended by two unicorn mares and a horse stallion. If before being overtaken by death mask warriors the two matriarchs and Rainsnow gain the hollow canyon of the lost pavilion, they at least have a chance to survive."

"But even if they reach the lost pavilion in time to save themselves, the three of them cannot day and night stand guard at the entrance," brayed the bison stomping his hooves. "If not from teeth and knives, they will drop from exhaustion."

"And, if the two mares succumb to the teeth of the great black wolf," grrrd Lianvil, "the evil contained inside the monster will greatly increase."

"Just like my horn was cleaved in two," neighed the blackmane, "the death of matriarchal leadership will break apart the white herd. We have no choice. We must go to the rescue of Aneilee and Elianor."

"But Naythorn, what of Captain Avalcar and his company?" inquired Rambuncture. "You cannot forget that even now they proceed toward us."

"A winged scout will alert Captain Avalcar, who himself speaks the uniform tongue, that we departed for the fight that far to the south awaits us," answered the yellow wolf for Naythorn. "We can through the rounded door exit Shining Canyon. Since no one else knows of the existence of the second way to leave here, the door that we take can remain open for Avalcar to enter this canyon and procure blue gold."

"The two unicorns that accompany Avalcar will surely join to our fight," groinked Timidthy. "They cannot stand by while the leader mares are endangered."

Dansey began to turn nervously in circles; he stopped to face Naythorn.

"There is one thing more, Captain. Since our friend Chief Bigclaws bears animosity toward the death mask chief, we must ask him to help us in the battle that is to come. Although inexperienced, his army of one hundred warriors is by a great general led. Knowing this land better than anyone, the chief will move fast toward Prow Mountain."

So it was decided. Because she knew him, Isabayas was sent to request Chief Bigclaws to join forces with Naythorn.

Featherspark took to wing to inform Avalcar of all that was about to happen. The goose had been instructed to not directly ask the captain to join with them in the upcoming battle against death mask warriors and the huge black wolf. That would be left entirely for the Phoenician captain to decide. But, if Avalcar required Featherspark to guide him to Prow

Mountain, the goose would identify shortcuts promoting rapid southward movement.

Because wolf scouts would spy out any force that traveled down the open plain, both Avalcar and Chief Bigclaws were to be told that Naythorn's company would advance southward inside the gorge of the Pavilion River.

In the lead of his band, through the rounded door Naythorn departed the canyon of blue gold.

CHAPTER 28

STRAGGLERS RESCUED

"The bedraggled people that walk before us on the plain appear to have little idea where they are going," neighed Elianor standing with a horse stallion and the high escort on a fold of a mountain. "Their path angles one way, and then goes another."

"Clinging to meager hope they move without spirit," responded Aneilee. "It heavies my heart to see human persons in despair of the world."

"The plight of those refugees is remindful of my horse herd after it was riven apart by wolves and warriors," reflected Rainsnow. The three equines continued to watch as the disparate file of forlorn looking natives led lethargically southward.

"Two members of the column fall back," observed Aneilee. "One looks to be an old man, and the other a maiden. They... will be left behind."

"They *have* been left behind," affirmed Elianor. "I wish that we could offer them protection."

"In order to elude wolves intent on our destruction we were four moons ago forced to detour far to the west," observed Aneilee. "And now, even though Naythorn is to be found not so far away, we ourselves *remain* in danger."

"Only a few suns past you sensed the presence of the monster gray wolf at the entrance to the mountain of spires," added Elianor. "Of course we were not absolutely certain that Naythorn and his company were inside the mountain."

"Not so, Elianor. I am convinced that the only reason the huge gray wolf, and many other wolves with him, are at the canyon of blue gold is because Naythorn is indeed inside," responded Aneilee. "Besides, we could never have opened the stone door that through a cave gives entrance to the shining canyon."

"It is fortunate that we were careful to stay hidden very far distant from the big gray wolf," neighed the guide matriarch. "We certainly do not need two monster wolves pursuing us at the same time."

"Recall, Elianor, that I do know how to entrance the hollow canyon inside Prow Mountain," neighed Rainsnow. "For that to happen there is no door to shoulder open. Hmpf! A thought just occurred to me. Perhaps the two that have fallen back from their column might travel with us toward Prow Mountain."

"You, Rainsnow, are right," responded Aneilee. "I grow tired of worrying about myself. This journey in search of the blackmane has become too long and hard. I was certain that in the mountains to the west we would lose the big black wolf."

"We managed to stay well-ahead of the monster," responded the horse stallion, "but unfortunately his scouts were too many, and his army of wolves and warriors continued to grow in numbers."

"The important thing," asserted Elianor, "is that for several moons we kept the huge black wolf distant from the white herd. And, Aneilee, you and I will continue to believe that our long journey was for a purpose, and not a waste of our time."

"*Nyeerrrarrrgh!* Nor, Elianor, would it be a waste of our time to do a good turn to two defenseless stragglers, that if not soon rescued, will surely not survive." That neighed, Aneilee began to descend the mountain toward where an old man and a young maiden wilted under a hot sun. It was not long before the heads of two natives were by the touch of magic horns given the gift of the uniform animal tongue.

"Grandfather Calichay! The old stories are true! The white bison with a long neck and one horn really does exist! Is not that wonderful?"

"We two are not bison, but unicorn horse mares," corrected Elianor.

"While my eyes tell me that my granddaughter is right, my mind cannot comprehend so marvelous a thing as to actually behold the horned bison... err, horned horses that my own ancestors told stories about."

"I am Rainsnow. This is Aneilee, and this is Elianor. They are the two matriarchal leaders of the white herd of unicorns. How is it that..."

"My grandfather hobbles," interrupted the maiden. "For his injury he cannot keep up with our people who go to the south. When he fell back I decided to stay with..."

"My headstrong Swiftdeer is too loyal for her own good," interrupted Calichay. "While my legs give out, she runs and jumps like a deer. She should have kept going onward with our people."

"But other than you, grandfather, I have no one."

"Hmpf. My granddaughter wants to stroke the hides of the beautiful horned horses. Can she?"

"While with her hands Swiftdeer strokes my hide," responded Aneilee, "Calichay can tell us more about his people."

"Long ago... very long ago... my tribe was the master of the great basin before the mountain shaped like the prow of a massive rock canoe. During the passage of many many years..."

"Hundreds and hundreds of years!" exclaimed Swiftdeer.

"We for a long time lived in peace," continued Calichay. "We had found a strong ally in the newcomer people that built with stones inside Prow Mountain. My ancestors, and the strangers, came to speak a common language."

"What is the name of your tribe?" neighed Rainsnow.

"Because our ancestors long ago placed pointed tips on the tops of mountains," continued Calichay, "we before were called the Pyramid People. Since we have fallen so far from what we once were, we are now known as the Forgotten People. The passage of so many years was unkind.

"Plagued by one famine after another my ancestors left Prow Mountain and sought refuge in the hills and ravines to the west. When to our dismay the dry conditions followed us westward, we were made to become wanderers. Upon learning of our distress the death mask people took advantage, and determined to destroy us. Because a chief by the name of Bigclaws will one day lead many of our people back to Prow Mountain, to once again make us safe, our sad caravan directs toward that place."

"That great chief teaches our young people how to fight!" exclaimed Swiftdeer.

"Death mask warriors have sworn to destroy Bigclaws and those of my people who with him travel," continued Calichay. "As for me... I am old, broken, and hungry. It is become my time to die. As I leave off this earth, my stubborn granddaughter decided to partake with me my journey."

"That will not do," ncighed Rainsnow. "You and Swiftdeer are going to mount my back. Accompanied by Aneilee and Elianor, I will take you to rejoin your relatives. Since some time ago I myself visited a blackmaned unicorn that had inside Prow Mountain rescued my niece filly from evil wolves, I know the place to where Bigclaws leads. If we are to die, we will together do so defending the hollow mountain."

"But, I might fall off..."

"I will not let my grandfather fall off the back of Rainsnow," encouraged Swiftdeer.

With an old man and a young maiden mounted on his back, Rainsnow led two unicorn mares toward the column of Forgotten People. It was not long before Rainsnow and his two riders were in the lead of more than one hundred slow-walking native refugees.

CHAPTER 29

Before the Pavilion River

Into tight clusters of tall rock spires two bovines led upward. The next morning found the company of Naythorn traversing a last watered meadow greening the summit of Spire Mountain. Given the difficulty of the high climb, Mrs. Razorthwacker appreciated that the conditioning program conducted by Naythorn in Shining Canyon had served to keep her thighs taut, and her belly firm.

Upon leaving behind Spire Mountain, Naythorn's band directed toward a far rim of peaks. Traveling fast, that night the bovines brought the band to the crest of the mountain chain. Descent the next morning entranced into the broad basin anchored by Prow Mountain. The remainder of their southward trek would proceed within the deep gorge of the Pavilion River.

After a long and fast march, Prow Mountain loomed close. At the very place where the newly grown wings of Rayalas had first come to fly, Naythorn called for rest. Whereupon the bison and the bull began to recount vivid memories about the day when under attack from wolves, they had made incredible leaps off the notched landing. The acrobatic flight of Rayalas had leveraged the jumps of Buckwhite and Taurington to land with great splashes into the current that now ran beside them.

The returned Featherspark reported that Avalcar and his platoon, which included two unicorn stallions, would soon join themselves to the upcoming battle. For their part, Lianvil and Dansey were sure that Chief Bigclaws and his battalion of one hundred young warriors would also join the looming fight against wolves and death mask warriors.

Upon climbing out of the river gorge, the band entered the great plain that spread before Prow Mountain.

Rainsnow's Column Met

"It is a miracle!" exclaimed Rainsnow.

"I too see the wings of the flying horned filly!" neighed the guide matriarch. "This can only mean that we will soon be reinforced by the band of Naythorn!" Upon seeing the grace of Isabayas as she wheeled about in flight, the hearts of the forlorn refugees following behind Rainsnow beat fast, but this time not in fear.

In midafternoon the unicorn matriarchs found Naythorn galloping toward them.

"You have little time," neighed the blackmane. "An army of wolves and warriors closes on you. Rainsnow, do you remember the river's elbow-shaped indentation right to the west of Prow Mountain?"

"I do remember that place."

"Lead quickly there Aneilee, Elianor, and your column." That instruction given, Naythorn galloped fast away.

At middle night Rainsnow, Aneilee, Elianor, and the company of refugees arrived at the place where the banks of the Pavilion River crooked inward. With the advantage of only one front to defend, the company of Naythorn had formed a defensive line. Although not mentioned, everyone recognized the strategic disadvantage of Naythorn's position. Bounded on three sides by imposing cliffs, with only one narrow path winding down to the river, in that place would be offered no chance for Naythorn's forces to retreat. At the bend in the river would unfold the destiny of Aneilee, Elianor, and the column of stragglers.

The next morning the duck and gander flitted down to update the two leader mares. With neck arched up, and breast feathers fluffed out, Webstir began, "Dame Unicorns, from the sky we today saw a lot of movement coming..."

"Coming down the plain toward us," interrupted this time Featherspark, "the Phoenician captain and his platoon, including two unicorns, draw near."

"A chief by the name of Bigclaws also comes here to help," qvackked Webstir,

"Worst of all," insisted the gander, "a ferocious black wolf..."

"He is almost as big and ugly as was the monster grayback Albarochk!" qvackked excitedly the duck.

"*Hronkk!* As I was saying before being so rudely interrupted," continued the goose.

"You interrupted me first!"

"Worst of all... an enormous black wolf leads too many wolves and painted warriors to count!"

"The giant wolf, the Phoenician captain, and the chief are almost here!" exclaimed Webstir.

"In spite of the approach of the monster black wolf," responded Elianor, "your report of welcome reinforcements grows our hope that we will survive to see tomorrow."

"But Elianor," neighed Rainsnow, "Naythorn and his two allies will have all they can do to defend themselves. The many enemies that come will surely find ways to break through the line of the blackmane and bring destruction to the defenseless people found behind us. To protect the people we led here, you and Aneilee must raise the unicorn shield."

"We are but two unicorn mares," replied Elianor. "Our magic is not strong enough."

"Within me is a heart that knows no fear," answered the big stallion. "Lean your sides against mine. My neighs will whisper strength to calm you and give you confidence. With my help the hearts of Aneilee and Elianor will do the needful thing, and raise skyward the magic shield of the unicorns."

Slowly but surely the sparks of two unicorn horns gave life to a protective shield that, unfortunately, was far less impressive than when raised by the entire council of unicorn elder stallions in the final battle against Albarochk.

"The shield wall stands only half as tall as I want," neighed Elianor, "and it is not as long as I want."

"Somehow we must make sure that no warrior or wolf is permitted to break through, launch over, or go around the magic shield to attack the refugees that we protect," answered Aneilee.

"Think on the strength of my heart, and do not fear," encouraged Rainsnow. "While we three persist in hope, all will be well."

Avalcar

In the distance to his right, the Phoenician captain glimpsed a gigantic black wolf surmount a rise. A long column of wolves and painted warriors were soon seen to follow him.

"The enemy intervenes!" exclaimed Avalcar. "Before we attain the company of the blackmaned unicorn, wolves and warriors will front us; we shall be required to fight for our lives. Being eleven in number, our only chance for survival is to rapidly and tightly channel through a narrow part of the enemy column.

"Once more mounted double on Mistral, our right side will be defended by Princess Admira and her brother Prince Ermal. Riding again Seahorse, Sulay and Enos will maintain the integrity of our left side. I and the magic shield gifted to me by King Barsuna, Bashkeem and his incomparable two-edged sword, and Majit wielding the great magic of his spear will defend the center of our formation. Positioned between Bashkeem, Majit, and myself will advance Cholo and Olsi."

"Hmph! I *knew* it was a mistake to leave Hammereins behind in Phoenicia!" exclaimed Olsi. "Cholo and I would right now be most happy to ride double-back on the incomparable war horse."

The company of Avalcar charged into the fast advancing column of wolves and warriors led by the monster black wolf.

Confident that his overwhelming numbers would crush the small platoon of Avalcar, the monster black wolf absented himself from the fight. That self-assurance proved to be rash. Before the enemy had a chance to organize a defensive line, Avalcar's eleven forcefully broke through the wolves and warriors set against blue gold armor, unicorn horns and hooves, and a magical spear, shield, and sword. Gaining free passage, Avalcar led his force to position itself on the right side of the blackmane's company.

The merged line of Naythorn and Avalcar charged westward toward the approach of Chief Bigclaws, his one hundred warriors, and a long column of native refugees. Unprepared for the outbreak, in an irregular and haphazard fashion the giant black wolf shifted back the line of his forces.

Gaining the advancing chief and his followers, the foray of Naythorn and Avalcar achieved its purpose of rescue. The thousand refugees following Bigclaws merged with the hundred refugees previously led by Rainsnow. The war chief positioned his battalion of warriors on the left side of Naythorn's company.

The rapid movement of the lines of battle created a fortuitous opportunity. Seemingly out of nowhere a massive black bear, twice as large as a normal adult bear, came crashing through the poorly defended eastern flank of the monster wolf's disorganized army. Behind Tristanbear galloped a dozen ferocious bears.

"Old friend Tristy!" saluted Naythorn. "Your frame is grown even *more* long! While my line moved west to connect with Chief Bigclaws, and so kept the big wolf occupied, it was smart of you to circle the enemy force and from the east join to me. But that presents a question. How came you to us in my time of great need?"

"I was lonely to see the blackmane. Ever since you first presented to rescue a young bear, that being me, from Albarochk and his pack of five wolves I have been able to sense what direction to take to find you.

"Wanting some time alone, a few moons past I said farewell to the bears that accompanied me up north. I then set out upon a southward route. Since I am prone to have adventures, one and then another restless bear that I came upon decided to with me travel and experience something exciting. So in spite of my preference for solitude, one after another bear joined to me.

"Three days ago we came upon the trail of a very large war party that with purpose led southward. I decided that if you were once more in trouble, that war party had to be the reason. Following the progress of the war party, or war army, led us here to you."

"Thirteen bear soldiers are here most welcome."

"You miscounted, Naythorn. When I stand erect on two legs the tip of your horn barely reaches to my waist. So, because of my double size I count as... *two bears.* That makes my platoon to number not thirteen, but fourteen."

"About that you are exactly right, Tristan. I most welcome the reinforcement of... *fourteen* bears. Our needed requirement is to prevent enemy wolves and warriors from penetrating through the magic shield raised by Aneilee and Elianor. Raised not so thick, long, or high as wanted, their shield is vulnerable. Since against the river there is no room for retreat, do not let the wolves and warriors in the army of the monster wolf slip around your bears and so breach our line."

"Understood, Captain Naythorn. Positioned at both ends of your defensive line, we bears will not permit the enemy to outflank you. By the way, I like that when there is a lull in the battle I can quench my thirst with river water."

It was not long before Tristanbear refound the blackmane.

"By the way, Naythorn, when I went down to the river to satisfy my thirst, I found there a big unicorn stallion that goes by the name of Mistral. He had never before spoken to a bear. He said he had no idea that a bear could grow so large. When I explained that my size was gifted by the touch of your horn, he mentioned his gift. Can you believe that when water is found nearby, Mistral can raise a magical mist?"

"Like you, Tristy, I find that to be very interesting." Naythorn went to look for Mistral.

"I was just told, Mistral, that you exercise power over mist."

"Many times I have done so."

"Can you call forth a fog to enshroud the ground that we behind us own? Such a mist would disorient enemy wolves and warriors; they would not know whether or not we be continually reinforced. It would also give comfort and confidence to the unicorn matriarchs, that though their magic shield should weaken, a thick mist will compound both their safety and that of the refugees they protect."

"Captain Naythorn, I will do as you say. But in spite of the close river, because the air in this high climate feels dry to me, I do not know how long I can sustain the covering shroud."

At Mistral's feet Naythorn saw mist begin to swirl.

Battle Begun

The giant wolf launched himself at the blackmane. Dashing hooves to meet the charge, at the last moment Naythorn swerved his body and jabbed his newly rejoined horn into the side of the huge wolf. An enormous rear wolf paw batted back and bloodied the unicorn stallion. The hard fall left the chest of Naythorn gasping for breath.

After banging hard against the forehead of the monster wolf, the thrown magic shield named Stomp bounced back to land at the feet of Avalcar. Majit threw his spear. For the sharp-pointed and deep penetration a geyser of blood, that gleamed bluish, spurted out of the black wolf's huge neck. The force of the monster wolf's jetted blood dislodged the magic spear named Horn, shoving it back toward the feet of Majit.

Howling pain and rage, the giant black wolf jumped at Bashkeem come to be set before Naythorn. A flash of Bashkeem's magic sword Gallop broke one of the giant wolf's enormous front teeth. No matter, the wolf grabbed in his jaws the head and shoulders of the Egyptian.

The point of Bashkeem's sword sliced into and through the monster wolf's snout. Feeling pain unbearable, the giant wolf spewed from out his jaws Bashkeem still grasping Gallop in his hands. The Egyptian dashed to the side of the still prostrate Naythorn. Rather than pursue more the blackmane, the monster wolf snarled at Bashkeem and retreated to lick his wounds.

"What you did was incredible!" exclaimed Avalcar upon gaining Bashkeem. "How did you manage to puncture the snout of the monster... while clamped in his teeth?"

"It was as if my sword directed itself upward. Held firmly in the hands of a man chested and helmeted in durable blue gold armor, Gallop is indeed made to be a powerful weapon."

"I had thought that with the magic of blue gold now forged into my horn, I myself could have stopped the monster," said Naythorn upon retaking his hooves. "Instead, my newly bound horn proved to be only a thorn in the side of the monster wolf. I needed you three to save me from the huge wolf's depredation."

"Do not be discouraged, Naythorn," reassured Bashkeem. "Once you become accustomed to the blue gold bindings, your horn will ultimately prevail."

"Now that you say that, Bashkeem, the new magic of my horn does feel strange; it will take some getting used to."

The well-fitting and accommodative armor fired and hammered in Shining Canyon by two Phoenician smithies, prevented much shedding of blood among Naythorn's company. However the peril did not lessen, for when an enemy fell, another wolf or warrior quickly took the place of the fallen.

"This place against the river is made too bloody too fast," brayed Buckwhite.

"I keep expecting that the wolves and warriors will lose heart," answered the cattle. "They do not."

After punching his horns at several more of the enemy, Taurington mrawed again, "Master Bison, your armor no longer looks to be new. For all the hard work Hammer invested in refitting your metal suit, you should take better care."

"Sir Cattle, if we both do not take better care, the armor fitted to two big bovines will again need to be remolded by Hammer and Lucars."

"I have never before seen Naythorn to fight so valiantly," observed Taurington. "The wrath of wolves and painted warriors is at him most directed."

"He has come to fully command his newly remade horn spiraled in blue gold," observed Buckwhite. "Despite the seeming invincibility of the giant black wolf, this is Naythorn's finest display of courage."

CHAPTER 30

DANSEYELONO CENTER STAGE

Twilight brought pause to battle.

Enormous paws crunched aside wolves and painted warriors that did not fast enough clear from the black monster's path. Twenty paces before Naythorn the massive wolf sat down. With weapons forged of extraordinary magic Avalcar, Bashkeem, and Majit came to stand together on one side of the blackmane.

"The black wolf general and the infamous blackmaned unicorn will be met. I, Trike, am the strongest of three wolf brothers grown large on meals of unicorn flesh. Upon my drinking the blood of Hoovefort, I was made to be almost as big as was Albarochk on the day that the pierce of your horn... *killed him.*"

At the news of Hoovefort's demise Naythorn shook his mane, lowered his head, and neighed, "Would not any ordinary wolf so sated with magical unicorn blood, grow to be as unsightly as you?"

"The dark insolence of your heart matches the offensiveness of your freakish mane!"

Naythorn lifted slightly his head and shrugged his shoulders.

"So the blackmane thinks he is clever to raise a protective shield, and blow up a mist. For doing that... you are only a little clever. The magical mist intended to camouflage your strength requires rain to sustain. No drops of rain fall tonight from the sky."

Naythorn again shrugged his shoulders.

"You are a rogue unicorn exiled by his own kind. Rather than represent goodness, the blackmane embodies deceit. From your wretched dealings with Lianvil, the traitorous captain of the mountain lions, I know that you can be counted on to weave only lies. I cannot tell you how much I, the biggest and fiercest wolf anywhere, anticipate devouring your blood, your flesh, and even your bones."

"You gloat and howl nonsense because in your heart you are afraid of the ruin my powerful allies will bring upon you. Have not the pricks and bruises of a magic shield named Stomp, a magic spear named Horn, and a magic sword named Gallop lessened your resolve?"

"Those weapons can cut my hide, but they will never vanquish me." Through narrowed eye openings the gargantuan wolf's hatred fired more harsh.

"The golden spirals pretty your horn," snarled Trike stretching his neck to inspect more closely his adversary. "But now that the halves are fused together by bands of metal ribbon, you face a problem insoluble. On a field of battle there is no way for you to break off a horn shard, and plant it in my heart. *Raaarrooorrooo!* For you, Naythorn, that is a portentous thing. Since unlike Albarochk I cannot by your unicorn horn be killed, I am beyond the power of the blackmane. I am... *invincible!*"

"I came to know well the first fearsome wolf general, and he was twice the leader you are," neighed Naythorn as he began to pace back-and-forth. "You brought uncountable wolves and painted warriors to do what Albarochk could have done with only a few hundred. In fact, with only one hundred fifty wolves the first monster wolf defeated me at the *Battle of Tall Trees*. That you require thousands to fight my few soldiers is a sign of weak leadership. Your only strategy is to hurl mobs of wolves and warriors at your enemies. Because your commands provoke confusion, your troops fall over each other. When this night you lose the battle against me you will be... *nothing.*"

Raising with their hooves a cloud of dust Buckwhite and Taurington ran to Naythorn. Instead of a show of belligerence, their purpose was to prevent Trike from noticing the trail of blood that Naythorn left wherever he walked.

"My captain loses blood," brayed quietly the bison as he and the longhorn cattle moved to stand between Naythorn and Trike.

Belfloralex trotted to attend Naythorn; Isabayas joined her. Magical horns touched the neck of the Blackmane to provide the sooth of healing. Because of his heartfelt love for his winged foal, and because every day grew more his love for Belfloralex, the touch of the two unicorn horns meant everything to the blackmane.

"We stopped your bleeding," neighed softly Belfloralex, "but there is not time enough right now to properly deal with two arrow points buried deep in your flesh. They must be removed."

With a plop Lianvil deposited Danseyelono before where stood the bison and cattle. Deciding to insert the wit and intelligence of the wily wolf into the drama of the standoff, by the nape of his scrawny wolf neck the lion had carried Dansey to the battlefield's center stage.

In answer to the insulting way the great feline had mishandled him, and with no thought for the presence of the monster wolf, Dansey shook himself and yelped, "How dare you treat in this uncourteous way your mild-mannered wolf friend!"

"What exactly made *Dansey* to become a good wolf soldier?" growled Lianvil loud enough for Trike to hear.

"Hmph! You know perfectly well that the taste of Naythorn's blood colored more yellow my hide, and made more nimble my paws."

"Well then," responded the lion, "you must show Trike how fast move the paws of the yellow wolf."

"So you are the infamous traitor wolf," growled Trike. "I was before informed that your name was Danseyelono."

"The long version of my name refers to me as the dancing-yellow-lone wolf. I prefer the short version that bespeaks the rhythmic grace of my dancer limbs."

"Because the magic blood of the unicorn made you to shrink with scurvy, your nimbleness counts for nothing," growled Trike. "Although you may be smarter than the average wolf, you are certainly the ugliest wolf alive."

As Dansey raised his head, and looked from left to right, the look that smeared over every part of his face had never before by the yellow wolf been worn. Dansey's lower jaw thrust out with teeth bared, his eyebrows arched high, and his raised upper lip initiated an unseemly forced smile. The image presented was exactly the opposite of an... intelligent wolf.

When a paw of Lianvil batted Dansey towards Trike, the yellow wolf tumbled and rolled back up on all fours.

"Something tells me that this is going to be a grand performance," muttered the cattle nudging a shoulder against the bison.

Walking upright, Tristanbear joined the bison and cattle. His great bulk made Buckwhite and Taurington feel more secure as they fronted the monster wolf.

"You really... *are huge,*" continued Dansey.

"This night you will pay the price for being the abject yellow traitor that you are. *Raaarrrooo!* Savor, if you can, your final moments of dwarf wolf existence."

"Big monster wolf, do I not from somewhere know you?"

"Had we ever before met, I would have right then and there made end to your cowardly existence. A dirty yellow hide would by blood have been drenched red."

With his upper and lower teeth still incongruously thrust out from his lips, Dansey ambled unsteadily closer and closer to Trike. Dansey elevated his head to identify the smell of the huge wolf face.

"I swear, General Trickster, that we have before met. Once I smell up close your face, I will tell you when and where we were first introduced to each other."

"My name is Trike... *not* Trickster!"

A huge paw swiped at Dansey, who appeared to have been hit hard by the blow, although he had not been. From the feigned impact of Trike's missed blow Dansey rolled three times head over heels before landing upright.

"That was... *unkind*. Because I am small, and matter nothing, the mighty Trickster can be more generous than that. I only ask for a whiff or two, up close, of your scent. On the eve of your great victory what does that cost you? Well, that is if tonight you come to enjoy great victory... and not embarrassing defeat."

Trike shifted shoulders, leaned his head forward to almost touch the ground, and once more swung an enormous paw at the yellow wolf. The dust cleared to show that Dansey had to somewhere vanished. Instead of surprise, the features of Trike showed annoyance. With ears set back he turned right and left his huge head. No yellow wolf was to be seen.

"Look behind your leg," clued the lion.

When Trike raised his left front leg, Dansey was revealed quietly seated behind where had been positioned the big wolf's limb. Before Trike could swipe again, Dansey scrambled up the back of Trike's other front leg. The big wolf turned circles snapping at the yellow wolf whose teeth came to be latched into the fleshy part found between Trike's shoulder blades.

Letting go his teeth hold, Dansey bounced off the back of Trike. In the very spot from where he had first addressed the great wolf, again landed the yellow wolf once more sporting an absurd smile with teeth thrust out and eyebrows arched goofy.

"You came in the litter born next after Albarochk!" exclaimed the yellow wolf. "When you were but a few suns old, I came to know your scent. When you wanted milk from your mother, with the wee voice of a little wolf pup you yipped *Trike... Trike....* In fact, I was the first wolf to call you by that name. There were three cubs in that litter. That means that the other two giant wolves are your brothers, and that to all three I am your wolf cousin."

"You are wrong! I claim my name from a very cunning wolf that stole rabbits from other wolves!"

"Trike and I are... *cousins,*" barked Dansey. "When Albarochk and I left the pack of our birth you were only the size of the head I now wear. Your mother, my dear auntie wolf, would not approve your killing a small and weak relative... namely me!"

"I will kill you now, and to all our cousins I will brag that I did so!"

"But to kill me you have to first catch me. I will have you know that Albarochk did his best to chase me down the night that I and the anvil-hard lion betrayed him. So to pin me down, you will have to move your great limbs faster than did your older brother."

The yellow wolf scampered under Trike's huge belly, scurried between his back legs, and grabbed in his teeth the tail of the big wolf. For that, the monster wolf shot back his head and bit hard.

In the nick of time Dansey's teeth let go their grip. The yellow wolf tumbled back to land on his rump, with his ludicrous smile renewed. Caught in an ungainly mash of giant wolf teeth grasping a huge tail, the momentum of the wolf general made him lean so far that he lost his balance, and fell over.

Hammer and Lucars could not help but burst out in laughter. The mirth spread wide through Naythorn's band and beyond, so that Avalcar's platoon and Chief Bigclaws's battalion joined the laughter. Finding they could not themselves restrain, some of Trike's wolf soldiers and painted warriors joined to the merriment. But, when Trike scowled at his fighters they immediately resumed a serious demeanor.

As if to jump against Naythorn, the huge wolf jerked his body up. The monster wolf reconsidered the obstruction presented by two bovines, a lion, and an enormous bear. Braking himself in midleap, the monster wolf crumpled upon himself in an ungainly heap.

Trike raised his head to see Tristan boxing long bear arms at a point before the position of the great wolf's nose. At this moment of humiliation, when all eyes were upon him and no one else, Trike decided it would not do to play the part of an enraged and foolish wolf general. The giant wolf retreated ten paces.

Trike began to walk parallel to Naythorn's line. Mimicking the motion of the great wolf's ponderous steps, Dansey followed after. The monster wolf ignored his diminutive yellow-hided wolf cousin.

"I do an inspection of my enemy's line!" howled Trike. "Do not think to stop me, or with one snap of my jaws I will break the back of a bison, cattle, bear, or traitor lion!"

"General Trickster," responded Dansey, "a practitioner of honest battle, Captain Naythorn has nothing to hide."

"I keep telling you that I am *not* General Trickster."

Returned to face once more the clutch of animal persons about Naythorn, the monster wolf snarled, "This is what I see. Having lost much blood Naythorn cannot long sustain his strength. The weakening magic mist recedes enough for me to see that you have no reinforcements to take the place of fallen soldiers. Behind the paltry magic shield stand only the cowardly Forgotten People. I count far fewer than two hundred soldiers in Naythorn's army.

"With your backs against a deep river chasm you have nowhere to retreat. While Naythorn's men and beasts are hard-spent by the fight, the many wolves and warriors in my reserve are fresh. *Now...* is my time of great advantage. When I crush Naythorn fear will fill the hearts of Aneilee and Elianor, their protective shield will fall, and my painted warriors will know revenge on the pathetic tribe that offended them."

General Trike set down his rump and proceeded to relax the look of his face.

"I find, yellow wolf, that at least a little I like you." The great wolf dipped ever so slightly his head to Dansey. "Although you are surely to me a traitor, you present a character true to yourself. I think that Albarochk kept you alive because there is no other wolf as clownish as you."

His grin removed, Dansey nodded his head in return gesture. "That is nice to hear. Still it is an awful thing to know that my wolf cousins are intent on tearing apart my measly yellow hide."

"So you neigh that I lack original tactics," growled Trike turning to Naythorn. "For that I will change the advance of my wolves and warriors."

Upon pivoting to face his army the great wolf howled new orders.

Trike's wolf sergeants immediately began to snout and paw wolves and warriors to form into columns. In the corridors between combatant columns the sergeants moved to enforce discipline, so that Trike's fighters were required to maintain their positions in file.

"Advance at the sound of the drums, and do not for anything stop!" commanded Trike. "If you are cut down, I order you to fall forward!"

The wolves and death mask warriors fronting each enemy column were to chop down, cut through, and so destroy Naythorn and his army. Wolves and warriors in the second and third ranks were to step upon and over the bodies of their fallen comrades. If the blackmane did not perish by the cuts of wolf teeth, knives, or spears he was to be pushed into the river.

Naythorn's forces readied for new attack.

"A message, Captain, from Aneilee," whinnied Rainsnow sliding his hooves to stop before Naythorn. "She requires one thing only. You are to hold strong past middle night."

"But why, Rainsnow, does she say past middle night only? What if the battle continues into tomorrow?"

"I gather that holding through half night, something will occur in your favor."

"But, Rainsnow, what can on this gloomy night happen? I have no more allies to reinforce me that are not already here."

"I saw a look of hope to enter Aneilee's eyes. She knows something."

"Then Rainsnow, inform Aneilee that one way or another, I shall hold into the night."

CHAPTER 31

INTO THE NIGHT

The one hundred fifty soldiers in Naythorn's army were to be shoved into the river.

Elegant in its simplicity, the tactic employed by the compacted columns of enemy wolves and warriors was akin to stampeding bison into a river, where finding themselves bogged down in water and mud they could neither escape, nor with their horns defend themselves. With wetted hide, and movement made heavy by the weight of water, a bison could with one spear-throw be brought down. Naythorn and his band, Avalcar and his company, Tristan and his bears, and the animal totem warriors of Chief Bigclaws were to be *the bison* in the hunt.

"The battle compresses," neighed Elianor grimly. "The position of the blackmane is at risk of being overrun. What can we do to help Naythorn?"

"Our leader's position is grave," replied Rainsnow pawing nervously the ground. "He will not survive the long passage of this night."

"My heart knows that something aberrant and violent, that oppositionally returns life, is to this night happen," neighed Aneilee. "I do not know what it is, but even if I had an idea of what shall turn the outcome of this battle, it would not do for me to neigh about it."

"Still, there must be some way that we can help Naythorn," responded Elianor.

"With Naythorn and those standing with him bearing the brunt of the assault, the wolves and painted warriors completely ignore us," observed Rainsnow. "It is as though we do not exist. Even if the raised shield were to fall, Trike would not propel toward us his attack."

"How many warriors defend the women and children with us?" inquired Aneilee of Rainsnow.

"Fifty men bear arms in defense. Some of the women hold spears, and others brandish knives."

"I am heartened that the women show courage," answered the high escort. "Because this battle has come to be more about them, than about we unicorn leaders, the Forgotten People must also this night show courage and make sacrifices.

"Elianor, do you agree that our fifty warriors go to fight with Chief Bigclaws? We can ask valiant women to take the positions of the men defending our raised shield. Although the weapons held by the refugee women will be few, what matters is that the monster wolf thinks the shield is defended. You, Rainsnow, and I could have slipped unnoticed into the pavilion, but more than a thousand men, women, and children cannot into thin air disappear. It is right that in this terrible battle the refugees protected by the line of Naythorn, do their part."

"Calichay and Swiftdeer speak the uniform tongue," replied Elianor. "Find them, Rainsnow, and tell them to order men in possession of knives and spears to join Bigclaws in the fight. Inexperienced though they are in the ways of war, the chief will use well his new refugee soldiers. Have Calichay and Swiftdeer instruct able-bodied women to tie their hair in the manner of men, and one by one take the place of a man along our front line."

The thoughts of the high escort began to drift. Where on this night was to be found her beloved white herd? How many of her unicorn friends had by packs of wolves been assailed, and as a consequence no more walked hooves on solid ground? How had so much evil come to be borne against her kind, and what was to become of the innocence of horned horses?

Her thoughts were interrupted by the movement of women taking up defensive positions that men had relinquished. Hoods and pieces of masks disguised feminine features. Blankets enshrouding thin shoulders were fluffed out to add bulk to the wearer's appearance. Boys as tall as their mothers had also disguised themselves as grown-up warriors. Aneilee was comforted to see that a weak and frightened people were inspired to directly address the dangers brought on this night of battle.

Stylized Defense

With their feet cadenced by the beat of drums, Trike's wolves and warriors moved relentlessly forward. If a painted warrior could not step ahead, he was forbad to step backward. Foot soldiers that grew faint or afraid, and in every army there are hesitant privates, were set upon by huge wolf sentries bounding about the corridors that separated one column of Trike's combatants from another. The dead and maimed piled high.

One pace at a time defensive formations were slowly, but surely, forced to give way. If Naythorn's line of defense did not fall back, enemy wolves and death mask warriors climbing upon and over their fallen confederates would gain the attack advantage of height. Still, surprising strength came from the different ways members of Naythorn's allied forces defended themselves.

As dictated by their totems, the young warriors under the command of Chief Bigclaws fought with the stylized martial arts of springing lions and clawing wolves.

At one side of the blackmane Buckwhite, Taurington, Belfloralex, and Cabalblade coordinated movements of slashing horns and pounding hooves. Positioned on the blackmane's other side, Hammer and Lucars flashed swords in defense of each others' backs. Joined to them, the wearing of new blue gold armor elevated the fighting prowess of Marsand, Scarlet Point, Amaluna, Alexzana, and Shawnee.

Flying to where she was most needed, the quick movements of the wings of the newly armored Isabayas permitted her horn and hooves to bring hurt to warriors unaccustomed to being assaulted from above.

Plugging holes in the defense Lianvil, Dansey, Blackler, and Trackler combined to fight in a way that no enemy warrior had before encountered. Balanced on hind legs, the lion slashed two swords and gnashed sharp teeth at the enemy. Wolves and painted warriors were startled, and then terrified, to find the teeth and claws of two dogs and a yellow wolf thrusting out from under, over, and between huge lion limbs.

Tristan and his friends clawed as bears and bears only. Through what seemed to be a never ending night of tumult and upheaval, Treestandbear stood steady and tall like a great tree trunk. His thick hide deadened the points of many arrows.

While Ermal, Admira, Cholo, Sulay, Enos, and Olsi, fought in the highly trained manner they had learned across the great sea, Mistral and Seahorse fought with synchronized whirling motions.

Whether due to the magic of the wondrous weapons Horn, Stomp, and Gallop or the communion of kindred hearts united in a struggle against pure evil, Avalcar, Majit, and Bashkeem did not by the teeth of enemy wolves or the weapons of death mask warriors have shed one drop of their blood.

With the interminable slowness of battle time, the long night slipped on. Casualties mounted in Naythorn's line of defense, especially among the warriors led by Bigclaws that wore no magical armor.

Healing

"Three of my warriors and two unicorns are hereby commissioned to provide a battlefield hospital."

"But, Captain Naythorn," protested Shawnee, "I have never before nursed in the middle of a battlefield."

"Just follow the lead of Admira and Marsand. I was told that the Troyan Princess and the Phoenician youth have the gift of healing, and I am to be your first patient."

While Isabayas and Belfloralex sparked their horns to cast light on Naythorn's bloody wounds, Marsand and Admira quickly unhooked Naythorn's breast plate.

"Two arrow shafts entered at the base of his neck," observed Marsand.

"I see them," answered Admira. "Penetrating deep into his flesh, the glow of magic horns provides the needed light to perform surgery. Both arrowheads are buried five finger-widths deep into Naythorn's flesh."

"Grasp with both hands the end of the broken arrow shaft," instructed Marsand holding steady the unicorn's head, "turn slowly, and maintain pressure as you pull."

"Notice, Shawnee," observed Admira, "that when I jiggle the shaft while I turn it leftward, I do not too much tear the flesh."

From the chest of Naythorn two arrowheads were dislodged.

"I know that hurt," consoled Marsand. "Thank you, Naythorn, for not neighing in pain while we did our work. One thing remains. Belfloralex, Isabayas, place your horns against Naythorn's chest and close his wounds." The magic of two unicorn horns worked double fast; from two arrow wounds Naythorn's chest closed perfectly.

"Admira, Shawnee, and Marsand are naturals at the work of healing," neighed Naythorn shaking his head to clear his mind. "Many more wounded patients will this night come to you. By the way, if Lianvil or Tristanbear should require healing, tell them I will be very cross if during the pain of surgery... *they bite you.*"

A wedge of very fierce wolves separated Cholo, Sulay, Enos, and Olsi from Avalcar and the protection of his magic shield. The four became an island surrounded by bloodthirsty wolves.

"Go! Break away! I do this for Egypt!" That said, Olsi launched himself upon and into a snarling wolfly mass, all the while slashing back-and-forth his sword.

Enraged wolves swarmed the valiant warrior that had sacrificed himself for his friends. In the confusion of the heroic moment Cholo, Sulay, and Enos fought through the remaining wolves that separated them from the place where fought Avalcar.

Inspired by the heroism of Olsi's self-sacrifice, the company of Avalcar found new strength to stop any wolf or painted warrior that penetrated their line of defense. Nonetheless against an army so overwhelming, the Phoenician captain could not help but to also slowly give way.

Each costly step forward taken by Trike's columns of fighters caused Naythorn's line of defense to bend inward. For Naythorn, Avalcar, Chief Bigclaws, and Tristanbear the raised unicorn shield loomed closer and closer.

When the beat of the drums quickened, a new tactic presented. Instead of shoving straight ahead, the most forward painted warriors and wolves suddenly stepped aside to permit wolves and warriors rushing ahead at full speed to recklessly throw their bodies at Naythorn's defenders. With each charge several of the wolf general's fighters penetrated through the blackmane's defense and raised havoc.

The battlefield hospital was forced to reposition to the edge of a high and precipitous cliff overhanging the river. While healing with her horn a wounded animal totem soldier fighting with Bigclaws, Isabayas heard Lucars yell. Pushed backwards over the bodies of fallen foes he tripped, lost his footing, and tumbled over a cliff. Isabayas hurled herself downward and lunged to grasp in her teeth an arm of Lucars. As she curved her flight upward, the hooves of the winged horse scraped against river bank rocks.

Lucars landed on his feet beside an astonished Hammer who exclaimed wide-eyed, "Well I have *never...*"

The Spirit of Aneilee

"How is it that I am so much changed?"

Preoccupied with the declining fortunes of battle, Elianor answered with a tone of bewilderment, "What... what is that you neigh?"

"Long accustomed to dwell on things pure, on things beautiful, I find myself diminished."

"That... cannot be."

"Yes, Elianor, the blood and loss of this battle have undone my heart."

The head of Aneilee dropped crestfallen. Almost immediately she raised again her head and arched high her neck.

"Elianor it... *it happens.*"

Mistral suddenly felt his body made limp and helpless to command. He felt an odd sensation, as if his shoulders were lovingly grasped and held tightly in the front limbs of his deceased sister Crimson. Waves of raw and unquenchable emotion washed through his neck and chest. Like clouds caught in a gale wind, a thick mist that he no longer controlled swirled out from his hooves.

"Look, Elianor!" whinnied Aneilee. "Mistral's mist billows!"

"And his mist colors brightly in shades of scarlet!" exclaimed the guide matriarch.

Unable to move his limbs, Mistral saw the mist he authored roll into the enemy; the faces of wolf and warrior adversaries disappeared into a thick cloud clung strangely tight to the ground.

Death mask warriors screamed fearfully. Wolves abjectly howled. As the cries progressed closer and closer, Mistral comprehended that a force very powerful had co-opted his magical gift. Step by step an obscurant phantom undid and laid waste the army of the wolf general.

Hearing the cries of pain and surrender, but not seeing enemy wolves and warriors to fall, the line of fighters anchored by Naythorn, Chief Bigclaws, Captain Avalcar, and Tristanbear came to stand motionless in shocked silence. The fight had moved beyond the strength and valor of attacker and defender.

"The unicorn shield melts into the ground!" exclaimed Rainsnow. "No longer needed, our magic shield ungripped its hold. The battle is surely... *ended.*"

The faces of those set in defensive positions behind where moments before had stood the magic shield, broke into broad smiles. Mothers, sisters, brothers, and friends shared heartfelt embraces.

443

Aneilee moved toward the sound of an enemy warrior groaning in pain. His arms clutching at bloody wounds, the fallen soldier was a mere youth. Kneeling, against a gashed belly she placed her horn. The healing process would take time, but she would have the horribly wounded young warrior to again be made whole.

An enormous bulk shifted upward; out of the mist emerged the huge body of the wolf general. Before him was the high escort made defenseless.

"No wolf has before killed a unicorn high escort. I will right now destroy you!" howled Trike gnashing teeth at Aneilee.

"No, Trike, you cannot," neighed Aneilee still on bended knees. "Do you not see how I have changed? Look at my hide. It is so much by blood stained red, that it even colors the mist. No longer pure, I am of no importance to my herd of white unicorn horses. Drinking my diseased blood... will poison you."

"I before saw Naythorn's black markings," grrrd Trike. "Now I see a unicorn hide marked red." Looking quizzically at Aneilee, the monster wolf inquired, "But how did your tainted magic sustain the protective unicorn shield?"

"Had your wolves and warriors attacked my shield, they would have found that it was only a mirage. Thank you, General Trike, for not testing the shield."

"What befell me?" whimpered the monster wolf with his reddened eyes flashing in fear. "Where are my wolves with teeth sharp as knives? Where are the long spears of my painted warriors? Does the one that laid waste my army, here remain?"

Together Trike and Aneilee turned heads to look into the surrounding mist. The shoulders of Trike shook with fear as he lamented, "Something is... there. What is... *there?*"

"Trike had better beware. Whatever lurks below the fog of this place will not for long stay hidden," answered Aneilee.

"Having this night lost my army, I flee behind them. But how can my two great brother wolves ever understand the ruination that this night, in this place, befell me? They cannot and will not comprehend, for they were not here."

Become a shadow of night, the form of Trike melted away.

Aneilee walked purposeful steps to a place where the ground ahead of her rose up and took form.

"You... waited for me," neighed the high escort.

Like coals of black fire, two eyes burned their gaze into the heart of the high escort.

"Both the night and my might are spent," growled a voice unearthly. "I care not in the first light of day to be revealed, even to your eyes."

"You saved Naythorn, his band, and those allied to him," neighed Aneilee. "From desolation and destruction you preserved native refugees. Had you not on this night come, great evil would have obliged terrible defeat."

"When I am near to you, Dame Aneilee, I do not feel myself in the grasp of unrelenting agony. Better than anyone, you know that evil haunts my very being. Tell me when shall I... of myself be free?"

Swirling mists came to enwrap eyes that fired unearthly.

Battle Won

Crimson boundaries of mist rose up to augment the descending blues, silvers, and purples of the Rayalas Borealis. Shafts of velvety light, with a feel merciful and gracious, shone above a field no more in either battle or mist contested.

Along Naythorn's line of defense exhausted men and beasts slumped backs against each other, leaned against rocks, reposed on patches of grass, wherever and however so that needed rest could be encountered.

"When with my own eyes I saw you tumble over the river cliff," said Hammer quietly, "convinced that I had lost forever my best friend, I turned to slash my despair at the enemy. Now you sit here with me, unhurt. Lucars, this is a day of..." Hammer was interrupted by Isabayas, Alexzana, and Amaluna embracing Lucars in two wings and four arms.

"I thought I lost you!" exclaimed Amaluna jumping up and down for joy. The girl grasped the young man's hand still gripping the handle of his blue gold sword, "Lucars, when you fell towards the river, you did not unhand your sword."

"Amaluna, can you believe the speed of Isabayas in flight? Faster than I fell, flew her wings. Her teeth grasped hold my arm, and as her wings thrust upward from the depths of the gorge, her neck bore my weight entire."

With his free hand Lucars reached for the free hand of Amaluna. Staring intently at the maiden he added, "Because I do not lose something that is mine, when I fell I held close my sword. I embrace and stay loyal to a thing of great value that to me was generously given."

Alexzana and Isabayas together looked at Amaluna staring back at Lucars.

"Your cheeks color!" exclaimed Alexzana as she touched her friend's arm. "You are blushing!"

"No, no, it is nothing," came rather too quickly Amaluna's answer. She shook slightly her head and added, "Actually, Alexzana, that is not so. My cheeks reflect the happiness of my heart to see Lucars rescued and from danger made safe." That said, separating from her friends Amaluna walked away.

Bigclaws, Avalcar, and Tristanbear reported.

"Naythorn's strategy worked!" exclaimed Avalcar. "Our lines held through the night. Of course it did nothing hurt to receive miraculous assistance at the last."

"I should have fought better," said Chief Bigclaws with a tone to his voice that was matter of fact. "For the first time ever, I was in battle forced to step away from the charge of my enemy."

"No, Chief Bigclaws," answered Naythorn. "Facing the most fierce of the death mask warriors, your young lion and wolf totem soldiers would not and did not submit."

"Without your arrival, Master Tristy," neighed Naythorn turning to the huge bear, "all would have been lost to wolves and painted warriors. Above the cliffs of the river your bears well-secured each end of my line."

"Your battles, Captain, keep me fit and trim," wuffed Tristan as he beat paws against his chest. "But that said, my muscles every one and everywhere, ache. Can you for two moons postpone your next fight? Doing that will give me time to eat great quantities of fish and berries, and so recover my strength."

CHAPTER 32

MUD BATHS

" *Grumph, grumph,* I... am... exhausted," grunted Mrs. Sow.

"Because I fought harder than my three siblings," responded Hamilton, "I am the wild boar that most deserves to sprawl his belly in this refreshing river mud."

"There goes Hammy exercising once more his proclivity to exaggerate," chided Practicia.

"No, sister, this time I really mean it; my tusks did an awful lot of damage to enemy wolves and warriors."

"Be that as it may, relaxing here together with our friends, we wild boars need to be polite and steer the conversation away from ourselves," grunted the sow. "Blackler, Trackler, I hope that this delicious mud bath slowly but surely heals your cuts and gashes."

"I do appreciate the concern of the mama wild boar," barked Trackler. "The fight totally drained me. But, I can report that as compared to last night after the hard battle was won, I am feeling three or four times better. And, how fares my brother hound?"

"*Rrrarrff.* I yet hurt from the teeth and claws of fifty vicious wolves... *at least fifty!* It was all I could do to quick enough jump one way or the other so that my unprotected parts were only nipped and scratched. Had it not been for Lianvil's timely biting and clawing, I would have been done for."

"As for me," bleated Rambuncture to the matron pig, "I am proud to report that in this battle Ewelissas saved my hide more times than I saved hers. My mate made many wolves and painted warriors regret their introduction to a very fierce and quick moving big-horned mountain ewe."

"Rouse yourself, Sir Taurington!" brayed the bison to the cattle. "Mrs. Pig inquires how we all are doing."

"I am... *worn out,*" snorted the cattle. "I have barely the energy to notice that you resumed your former color. Your muddy coat shades once again black, just as should a bison hide."

"I will require a long bath in river current before I once more assume my role as a... *sacred white bison.*"

Dansey stood and vigorously shook himself, which muddied the head of Lianvil. The yellow wolf proceeded to arch his back, stretch, and look askance at his muscular friend. The mountain lion shook mud from his face, reached out a great paw, and shoved Dansey down. Upon extracting himself from murky water, Dansey performed a bounding dive.

"Why, Lianvil, I do thank you for necessitating my dive," barked the diminutive wolf stepping again close to his lion friend. "Nothing revives one's spirits like an afternoon swim." That barked, the yellow wolf shook himself and so drenched the head of the lion.

After looking lazily about, Tristan opened wide his jaws... as if to address the razorback sow. The mere fact that the usually unsocial bear would initiate conversation with a pig, or for that matter with anyone, was enough to catch the attention of all gathered about the mud hole.

"Madam Wild Boar," wuffed finally the big bear, "remind me of what all is happening with our band and our allies, even now while I contentedly deposit my frame into mud."

"Master Tristy, this is what I know. Chief Bigclaws and his soldiers were sent this morning through the basin northward, then into the hills and mountains beyond to ensure that no wolf and death mask enemies remain to bother or spy upon us.

"With members of his company, and the addition of refugee natives, Captain Avalcar now travels into the hills and mountains to the southwest. Long dwelling in those lands, the Forgotten People know where to search for whatever supplies of maize, beans, edible roots, nuts, and fruits that can there be found.

"Accompanied by more refugees, Naythorn and the rest of our band went to harvest any food stuffs that can be obtained in more northwesterly valleys.

"Isabayas, Webstir, and Featherspark do winged scout duty for Chief Bigclaws, Avalcar, and Naythorn. Six or seven days from now Naythorn, Avalcar, and the chief will have returned. We will then be made not only safe in the hollow canyon of Prow Mountain, but well-supplied with food. Oh... one thing else. Along with the Egyptian engineer Bashkeem and his brother Cholo, Hammerclaw and Lucars have begun to draw up plans to rebuild the hidden canyon where stand the ruins of the pavilion. When Naythorn's band and Captain Avalcar go to mine blue gold for the Troyans, and afterwards go their separate ways, Chief Bigclaws will remain behind in command of Prow Mountain."

"You are very smart, Mrs. Pig, to remember all of those details," complimented Tristy nodding his head.

"Naythorn knows that if trouble hereabout arises," added Timidthy, "you and your platoon of powerful bears will keep the rest of us secure."

"That we bears can, and will do."

"You know, Tristy, it should give all of us great satisfaction to know that a worthy thing was here accomplished," groinked Timidthy. "More than Naythorn, Aneilee, and Elianor, the ultimate beneficiaries of the hard-fought battle are the many refugees led here by Chief Bigclaws and Rainsnow, that in this place will now settle. Because Naythorn won the *Battle of the Pavilion River,* the Forgotten People regained a hold in Prow Mountain."

CHAPTER 33

A BROTHER DISTRAUGHT

"This cannot... *be!* Tell me the rumor that you are to stay behind in Prow Mountain with Chief Bigclaws, is not true! My last words to father were that I would bring you back to him."

"But, Cholo, the work here is... *needful,*" answered quietly Bashkeem. "More than a thousand natives must now be made safe, and many more refugees will make their way to Prow Mountain. To those made desperate, I can provide hope."

"Because our father needs us... we need to be with him," responded Cholo. "Someone else can remain here in your stead."

Overhearing the passion of Cholo, the two brothers were joined by Chief Bigclaws, Captain Avalcar, Prince Ermal, Princess Admira, and Prince Majit.

"My friends," said Bashkeem, "you find me torn between the duty of a son compelled to return to his father, and the duty of an engineer needed by the natives that now take refuge in Prow Mountain. Perhaps without my ability to build things that last long, the second colonization of Prow Mountain will also come to fail."

"The duty of a soldier is most times at odds with his personal life," offered Avalcar. "I wish I could, but on this trying matter I cannot give advice."

"If only there were some way that the father of Bashkeem and Cholo could be made to understand how much his older son is here needed," reflected the chief.

"Hmph. Actually, Chief, now that I think about it, there just may be a way," responded Avalcar. "Did you not tell me that you can sense what in a man's heart is found?"

"The scarred lines above my ears offer proof that I was twice touched by not one, but two magic horns," answered the chief. "When I received two gifts my lips learned to speak the uniform tongue, and my heart learned to divine trueness in others."

"Then, Chief," responded Avalcar, "place your hand on Bashkeem's chest. Perhaps his heart will tell you what Bashkeem needs to do."

"Relax, Bashkeem," said the chief as he pressed both hands to the chest of the former Egyptian slave. "Ahh now. Yes, yes that is so. Your heart tells me that to be content you must engineer unique and wondrous things, and that if you were to depart Prow Mountain a precious part of your spirit would here remain. The plight of the abandoned refugees brings back memories of how to your own family you were once lost."

"Your father needs to be as proud of your accomplishments as I am," said Admira with her eyes taking on a serious look. "Without Bashkeem's astute, principled, and courageous leadership the magic gold once carried in Admiral Zoumar's flagship would not have found its way to Phoenicia, that country would not have been made safe from warring Hittites and Egyptians, my sister Resi would not now be happily married to Majit's brother Prince Maroun, and my brother Ermir would not now be returned to reign over Troy.

"The day after we escaped a burning Troy, you told us that in your hands things are made better. Bashkeem, you have made me to be a better person than I was."

"Not just Admira, you made *four* orphaned princes and princesses to be better," said Ermal.

"And Admira is right. Because of you, two princes of Phoenicia survived a terrible war," added Majit.

"Perhaps on one future day," continued Ermal, "your father will come to understand that his older son did not return to him because he was by *sacred duty* made to guide the vulnerable refugees now found inside Prow Mountain. What father would not be overjoyed to learn that his once enslaved son had been placed in a position of high leadership?"

Lost in thought, Bigclaws stepped away. Upon returning, the chief had a question, "Ermal, how came you and your sister to be princely?"

"It happened this way," answered Ermal. "When the clans of people dwelling in the place that came to be called Troy would not stop their endless conflicts, gifted with a keen military mind our father stepped in and to the land brought peace. Upon observing not only his brilliance in battle, but also the fairness of his decisions regarding civil disputes, the people petitioned that our father be made king."

"Like the father of Admira and Ermal, my valor in battle led to my being made a chieftain," said Bigclaws.

"Through his valor, my son also earned the right to lead my tribe."

"Bigclaws is *getting* at something," observed Avalcar.

"I am at that. I say that mightily wielding his magical two-edged sword, Bashkeem has in battle earned the right to lead Prow Mountain. Finding that his son was proclaimed the ruler of a nation of refugees, the father of Bashkeem will come to understand that it was not the fault of his older son that he was here detained."

"But you are the rightful ruler of Prow Mountain," responded Bashkeem. "It was you that to this place led the Forgotten People. They owe their very survival to your leadership."

"It is true that I led here. But in one year you accomplished more for six princes and princesses of Troy and Phoenicia, than what I in my entire life did for my tribe. Still, I am about one thing curious. How is it that a slave in a foreign land came to excel as a great engineer?"

"When made a captive and a slave, I became angry. I could not accept that I had become less than I had formerly been. One day everything for me changed. My master, a man that would one day rise to be a governor of Egypt, took me into his house and sat me at his table. We two ate in silence. After I had finished the best meal of my life I was asked if the food I had eaten made any difference as to whom and what was Bashkeem. I answered *of course not*.

"I was next asked if servitude had changed my heart, what I was on the inside. Again I answered *of course not*. My master said *very good,* and left the table. The next morning I awoke to my duties with a heart that had grown. The insightful questions of my master made me understand that what counted is not what people did to me, but what I did with and for myself.

"Newly motivated, I engaged my hands and mind in learning. As my abilities and talents were recognized, I was given greater authority. I came to make the lines of pyramids to be straighter, and the lines of ships to be faster. When four princes and princesses of Troy made me once more to be free, my life did not change. Whether slave or free, I am a proud Egyptian that thinks for himself."

"As we saw when Olsi sacrificed himself to save the lives of Cholo, Sulay, and Enos, the pride of an Egyptian is a very powerful thing," concluded Majit.

"Hmpf!" grunted the chief. "Four Troyan princes and princesses made Bashkeem to be free. I now declare Bashkeem to be *Governor* of Prow Mountain, for whom I am privileged to serve as his lesser chieftain."

Smiles broke out all around, even to spread wide over the face of Cholo who offered, "My father will be proud of the prominent new status of his son... the governor."

"There is one thing left to do," added Bigclaws smiling wide. "I will make a feathered headdress for Bashkeem to wear."

"I do not think I ever saw an Egyptian governor... to wear hair feathers," responded Bashkeem.

CHAPTER 34

THE PAVILION REGAINED

"This marvelous pavilion was surely by my Egyptian forebears built!" exclaimed Bashkeem gesturing wide with his arms.

"But Governor Bashkeem, I before pointed out that unlike Olsi, you were not born an Egyptian," needled Hammer. "For that you cannot have Egyptian forbears."

"Not so born, Master Smith, I became so."

"I agree with the governor," interjected Lucars. "Egyptians have always been the most advanced builders. This pavilion palace simply had to have been built by engineers hailing from the Valley of the Nile. And even after the passage of a thousand years, it is plain to see that they made a brilliant job of it."

From a shoulder bag Bashkeem dug out a piece of parchment and a quill, and said, "The most critical things must always be done first. I begin my list with dry and well-ventilated storehouses for food supplies. Over there against the eastern cliffs one can still see the broken foundations of sheds built long ago to store food. Where storehouses once stood, they will again stand bigger and better.

"Next on my list is to dig cisterns and encase water lines. The conduits will direct from the fountain pool by the pavilion to the southern wall, where several large cisterns to store water will be chiseled into rock.

"Third on my list is to mount a stairwell into one of the rock walls that surround us. In order to detect movements of war parties into the basin that outside spreads wide, Chief Bigclaws will need to station lookouts on the top of Prow Mountain. Just imagine the grandeur of the vistas from up there.

"The fourth and last construction project on my list, to rebuild the crumbled floors and columns of the pavilion, will require much effort. When finally finished, the pavilion will again be made... magnificent."

Bashkeem looked to Hammer for approval.

"Is it alright for me to call the governor by his given name?"

"The name I have long carried needs no embellishment."

"Then Bashkeem," continued Hammer, "I say you are exactly right. Food, water, lookouts on the walls, and a rebuilt pavilion comprise the priorities. But permit me, Sir, to include on your list of construction projects one thing more. You require a forge."

"That will be my fifth construction project. Where would Hammer place the forge?"

"Close by the cisterns, but not too close by. That way the forge can possess all the water needed to clean and cool metal, without risking contamination of the water supply."

"We will build your forge at the southern wall, to the west of the cisterns," answered Bashkeem. "Into the base of the wall will be cleft indents to store the charcoal, mineral rocks, and sands that you and Lucars require to smelt metal."

Hammer glanced at Lucars, who nodded knowingly his head.

"Err, Bashkeem, with these five projects Lucars and I would much like to help you. As for myself I would like nothing better than to every day work, and someday retire in the shadow of the imposing pavilion. The issue is that our destiny lies with the blackmane."

"I was thinking that I had more use for the very talented and skilled Hammer and Lucars, than did Naythorn," replied Bashkeem. "I am very sorry that in a few days I shall be required to bid you farewell." As nothing more was needed to be said, Bashkeem turned away to by himself begin the inspection of crumbling pavilion columns.

"Had to be said," commented Lucars to his friend. "I know that our smithing skills are here needed by Bashkeem. But, Naythorn and the white herd need even more our strong arms. Hmph. I was just wondering if among the refugees there are undiscovered blacksmiths that can someday become almost as good as Master Hammer? After all, these descendants of Egyptian pyramid builders carry in their bloodlines a reminder, or maybe we can call it a forgotten recollection, of the engineers that long ago made a hidden pavilion to be majestic."

It did not take long for the natives to make the reconstruction of pavilion floors and columns their favorite project. Stones were made to fit perfectly back in original places. As soon as a part of a floor or column was rebuilt, the cleaning and scrubbing began. The pavilion began to gleam.

"Just imagine that our very own ancestors raised high this wondrous temple," was heard to be said over and again.

"Today my stonecutters accomplished something that not even their ancestors could do," proclaimed one afternoon Bashkeem. "They made it possible for lookouts to monitor movement all across this great basin. Although the steps cut into the north wall are not as wide or prominent as I would have liked, they present a back-and-forth spiral staircase that is pleasing to the eye.

"From this day forward sentries will quickly spot any war party that enters our territory. A day will come when we follow high trails leading to the far sides of these mountains. The ability to safely transport supplies over many leagues will strengthen and protect us against future enemies."

To Bashkeem was given the honor of cutting a ceremonial cord placed at the bottom of the newly chiseled staircase.

"Captain Naythorn, Dame Elianor, Governor Bashkeem, and Chief Bigclaws," addressed Avalcar, "now that Prow Mountain is made safe and secure, I am compelled to soon depart for Shining Canyon to forge the sheets of magic gold wanted by the Troyan King."

"It is also become time," neighed the guide matriarch, "for Aneilee and me to again lead the white herd. The news we carry of the great victory against General Trike will provide reassurance, and unicorns will again welcome our leadership."

461

"As for me," spoke next Chief Bigclaws, "since I now have many more warriors than before the battle against Trike, my people, for they are become my people, should now unify."

"My construction projects have progressed faster than I had anticipated," offered Bashkeem. "I cannot tell you how pleased I am to see former refugees become master rock cutters. That being the case, I have decided to build a great pyramid, a structure never before seen in this new land. With the help of Chief Bigclaws and his people, I will display the true greatness of Egyptian architecture."

"Upon raising high a great stone monument to touch the sky, the refugees I led here will reclaim their former name as the Pyramid People," affirmed the chief.

"So you are all made ready," neighed Naythorn nodding his head to Avalcar, Elianor, Bigclaws, and Bashkeem. "As for me, I had not yet thought to depart Prow Mountain."

Aneilee Despondent

As Avalcar's preparations for departure proceeded the next morning, Aneilee sequestered herself in a cluttered corner of the pavilion with head cradled on front legs, and with thoughts apart and alone. Naythorn, Elianor, Rainsnow, Mistral, Dansey, Timidthy, Cabalblade, Hammer, and Shawnee came to attend Aneilee. However, their attempts to cheer the high escort were to no avail.

Aneilee finally raised her head. With eyes brimming in tears she neighed, "Naythorn... do you not see... the red blotching of my coat?"

The blackmane jerked his head upward in surprise. Instead of answering, the bewildered stallion guarded his silence.

"My new coloration shows that I am no longer worthy to be the spiritual leader of the white herd. Naythorn, when you were a colt with black markings I looked down on you. Now, I am the one marked differently from other unicorns. The battle against the monster wolf Trike confirmed the paucity of my goodness, and the inadequacy of my character. Had I led well, the white herd would not now be turmoiled and divided. If permitted by Governor Bashkeem, I shall here remain where I can still be of some small service." That neighed Aneilee again reclined her head.

"You are the very heart and center of our white herd," comforted Elianor. "The glow of your horn has ever been my guiding light, and I need you now more than ever. Consider, Aneilee, that while the white herd wanders leaderless in search of a future hold, the Forgotten People have already gained protection in Prow Mountain."

"When Naythorn was but a suckling colt," replied the high escort raising again her head, "I thought I had a clear view of my world. I trusted no animal person not a unicorn. I could not have imagined myself having any close association with human persons. I never envisaged that deep within the heart of a unicorn can grow the seeds of jealousy and hatred.

"I now know, I have learned, that behind all things there is a foreordained plan of consequence. It became my destiny to involve myself with the plight of desperate natives and lead them toward the mountain that within holds a hollow canyon. I have been taught that the high escort must care and feel for others unpossessed of a magic horn.

"Elianor, I can here find a way to redeem myself. I will listen to the wisdom of Governor Bashkeem. I will learn from the knowledge gained by Chief Bigclaws during a lifetime of command. And then on some future day, I will find myself again renewed in spirit."

"Is there nothing that I can do, Dame Aneilee, to change your mind?" responded Elianor. "If not you, then who shall guide me back to our white herd?"

"With you, I shall go," neighed Rainsnow who had until then stood by silently.

"When the time comes to regather the white herd," added Cabalblade, "both Rainsnow and I will be there to assist Elianor."

"Seahorse and I will also protect Elianor as she returns to lead the white herd," neighed Mistral. "After all, the purpose for our departure from Phoenicia was to gain the white herd."

"I learned the hard way, Dame Elianor, that some paths must be walked alone," observed Naythorn. "While I accept that it is my destiny to one day lead the white herd in the direction of the fixed star, I will not rush the departure of my band. There is more in Prow Mountain that needs to be done to make secure those that here stay behind. And until he has mined the blue gold, I will not separate myself from Captain Avalcar. I owe him that much. Without the gallant assistance of the Phoenician captain, and those few that came with him, I would not have triumphed in the *Battle of the Pavilion River*. In my delay, I follow the lead of Aneilee. Just as she will come to change and grow before regaining the white herd, so also will I."

"Hmph! Captain Avalcar," neighed the blackmane, "before you depart the pavilion and travel to the canyon of blue gold, I happen to think that there is something here to be done that requires the joining together of all of us."

The blackmane turned to Timidthy and Dansey, "Do not you two also feel a certain unease that we overlook something important? Tell me what is lacking. What in this hollow mountain requires now to be done?"

The boarling and the yellow wolf sat down before Naythorn. Anticipating more information to be shared, the two waited for Naythorn to neigh again.

"Until one more thing is accomplished," continued the blackmane, "my heart tells me that a timid boarling and a yellow wolf cannot this place depart. But what can that thing be?" Naythorn looked intently at the very smart boarling.

"Finding myself uncertain of how to reply," responded Timidthy, "permit me to think back to the beginning of our latest adventure. A recounting of what has been accomplished can help to identify what remains to be done.

"In Shining Canyon, Hammer and Lucars refitted our armor. We saw a vision of Captain Avalcar arriving at these shores. Next came a vision of the death mask warriors in pursuit of unicorn matriarchs and refugees walking into the basin before Prow Mountain. Chief

Bigclaws and the Forgotten People were called upon to help us battle the monster wolf Trike. Avalcar and Tristanbear arrived. The matriarchs raised a unicorn shield. Commanding countless wolves and painted warriors, Trike attacked. Then, in the nick of time a phantom specter came to end in our favor the fierce conflict. Following battle, Bigclaws was made to be high chief and Bashkeem was made to be governor. The columns of the pavilion palace began to be... rebuilt."

With his eyes and ears focused on Timidthy, a smile began to form upon Dansey's face. For a brief moment his lower jaw stuck out and his eyebrows began to arch. The wolf thought better, and replaced the beginnings of a clown face with the features of acute wolfly intelligence.

"From what Timidthy just recounted," yipped the yellow wolf, "much energy has been expended in travel, battle, and work that needs to be... *celebrated!*" That barked, Dansey started to chase his tail while yipping natural wolfly joy.

"Exactly right, Dansey!" exclaimed Timidthy. "After many hundreds of years of decay, the reborn pavilion insists that it be celebrated. And such a great and noble rebirth requires a... *very big party*. Naythorn, Avalcar, and Elianor cannot depart until the renewal of the pavilion is with ceremony marked."

"A great procession of unicorns, animal persons, and warriors is called for," interjected Bigclaws. "Ceremony and celebration will help the new citizens of Prow Mountain to take full ownership of this hidden canyon and the wide basin that lies before it."

"Hah!" exclaimed Hammer clapping hands together. "In the shadow of the pavilion palace I feel a sense of true contentment. It is to me a comfort that the momentous battle we fought outside this canyon did not change the set of one rock within the crumbled pavilion. Old stones piled on more old stones whisper to us that without the interruption of war, peace and tranquility can here persist for more hundreds of years."

"I know what you say, Hammer," answered Avalcar. "Neither you nor I found in Phoenicia the protected isolation that here exists. Yet, I am anxious to get on with my task of refining gold and returning to my ship. The soldier in me knows that not until I finish the task before me, can rest await. Governor Bashkeem, do you truly need me and my company to attend the festival of rebirth?"

"It seems that Captain Avalcar is very impatient to resume his work," neighed Naythorn. "Of course any dedicated sea captain wants as quickly as possible to get back on the water."

"Bashkeem has not answered my question," reminded Avalcar.

Elianor saw an opportunity to express the same wish for a hasty departure as had done Avalcar.

"Every day that I postpone my return to the white herd, I fear that another unicorn is to wolves lost. Now that the *Battle of the Pavilion River* has been won, I too want to depart tomorrow with intent to rescue the white herd. Left in the strong hands of Chief Bigclaws, Prow Mountain will be well-guarded."

"For my friend I will answer," said Bigclaws. "Bashkeem knows that right here and right now we witness something very complex and difficult to bring to happen. Both he and I know that if Captain Avalcar, Elianor, Tristanbear, and Naythorn help us to launch with rightness and solemnity the Pavilion Nation, a notable blessing will ensue to those of us that here remain."

"Look here," motioned Chief Bigclaws. "Regaining her strength, Aneilee stands."

"I will hear no more that the high escort is to remain behind!" exclaimed Elianor stomping a front hoof. "You are ever the spiritual guide of unicorn horses. If not with me, than you must with Naythorn return to lead our white herd."

"I have a new destiny to fulfill," answered the high escort. "The pavilion will be my new home."

After patting the neck of the high escort, Hammer commented, "If Dame Aneilee can here remain, then why cannot I stay and help the Forgotten People to become a great nation? I am every day made older. My legs will not much longer permit me to endlessly march across desert, plain, and mountain."

"Then, I will with you stay and be your helpmate," said Shawnee grabbing the hand of the master blacksmith. "As well as love the pavilion, I will cherish the man who now says that he wants to settle down."

"You *cannot* abandon me!" exclaimed Lucars in disbelief. "You and I, Hammer, are a team! We have many times saved each others' very lives!"

"Lucars," responded Bigclaws, "the founding of a nation is not easy. But, if I misstep I can count on those that with me stay behind. I can rely on Hammer, Shawnee, and Aneilee to help me confront cowardice, greed, and jealousy when they manifest themselves."

"My friends," offered Bashkeem, "a ceremony graced by the presence of Naythorn, Aneilee, Elianor, Avalcar, and Tristanbear will inspire desperate people to believe that their destiny is exceptional. With this nation begun with ceremonial unity and magical hope, a blessing immeasurable will come to the people that inherit Prow Mountain."

At the powerful words of Bashkeem, the heads of Avalcar and Elianor finally nodded in agreement. Their departure would not happen before took place a fitting ceremony in the pavilion palace.

Soon the contented Hammer and Bigclaws sat smoking rolled leaves of tabac.

CHAPTER 35

CEREMONY AT THE PAVILION

The sounding of drums began a festival of rebirth. Prepared to see something they had never before seen native men, women, and children filled every empty space to be found within the pavilion palace whose floor had been cleared and cleaned.

Head and tail raised high, Naythorn entered the pavilion's center aisle that stretched eighty paces long. The muscles of his legs and sides rippled with equine power, and the metal ribbons interlaced about his horn glowed a deep blue. The memory of the terrible fight that not so long past had taken place in the pavilion he now entered, the fight that led to the rescue of Rayalas who for the gift of his healing blood grew wings, added gravity to Naythorn's eyes. Upon reaching the three steps that mounted the raised dais, the blackmane turned to face the multitude, and then stood straight and still.

Mounted on Mistral followed Bashkeem. Those gathered in the pavilion cheered loud their governor.

Wearing a headdress whose brilliant feathers extended down each side of Seahorse, and hefting an axe in his left hand, Chief Bigclaws rode next. Upon ascending with Bashkeem the dais, the chief raised his left arm and proclaimed, "Ever loyal to our Governor Bashkeem, I protect and keep safe the Pavilion Nation!"

At that promise the cheer begun at the front of the pavilion spread quickly.

In perfect cadence with the beats of drums advanced side by side Aneilee, Elianor, Cabalblade, and Rainsnow. Midway down the center aisle of the pavilion the two stallions and two mares reared high, and for long moments balanced themselves with front hooves flashing. The horse and three unicorns moved to stand at the side of Naythorn.

The drum beats embraced a new rhythm. Entering the pavilion, Isabayas and Belfloralex walked ahead of young girls formed into lines, with the smallest in stature at the front.

The two unicorn fillies began to prance. When left front hooves together rose, the girls raised left feet. When right front hooves rose, the girls elevated right feet. Unicorn hooves struck quickly left, right, and again left, right. Once more the girls followed the steps of the unicorn dance. When the fillies reared upward, jumping girls extended arms above their heads. Mothers and fathers were enthralled by the pageantry of their daughters' choreographed movements. The dance ended; as the girls ran to find their families loud cheers engulfed the assembly.

Into the pavilion Lianvil led forward the human person contingent of the blackmane's band. At the sight of such a fearsome feline walking on hind legs only, the assembly quieted. Positioned on the left the island girl Alexzana called out *right, left, right, left, right, two, three, four...* To the call of the cadence Amaluna,

Shawnee, Marsand, Scarlet Point, Lucars, and Hammer walked in step.

Next came the yellow wolf whose display of tumbling captivated the throng. The family of five wild boars, bodies built stolidly to almost the same height and size, marched abreast of each other. Alongside a bison and cattle stepped two mountain sheep and two dogs. In noticeably disordered fashion Tristan and twelve bears ambled next down the wide central aisle.

The magical armor of Avalcar shined resplendent. On his right walked Princess Admira, Prince Ermal, and Cholo. On the captain's left came Prince Majit, Sulay, and Enos. Reaching the front of the pavilion, the company of Avalcar moved to stand with Tristan's bears opposite Naythorn's band. Avalcar joined Bashkeem and Bigclaws on the raised dais.

Grarring and howling like lions and wolves, next proceeded the young men and women warriors trained by Chief Bigclaws. Their acrobatic tumbling and spirited thrusts of axes, knives, and bows riveted the attention of the onlookers. A change in drum beats signaled the young warriors to find and join their families.

Featherspark and Webstir flew lastly into the pavilion. Each waterfowl carried one end of a long strand of braided flowers with a profusion of red, blue, yellow, purple, and orange petals. Above the raised dais hovered on wings the goose and duck.

"Come forward Master Hammer!" proclaimed Avalcar.

"You are called, so go!" ordered Lucars pushing his friend.

"Sergeant Hammerclaw," began Avalcar, "am I to understand that you have chosen to resign your post in Naythorn's band, and pledge allegiance to the Governor of the Pavilion Nation?"

"That is so. And understand, Sir, that my decision comes not without regret. As a sergeant under the command of Captain Naythorn, I lived the adventures of a lifetime."

"Hammerclaw, after your friends depart you will no doubt... be lonely."

"That, Sir, is assuredly so. I will miss them, everyone."

"And will you miss some more than others?"

"Yes... that also is so, Captain."

"Since that is the case Master Hammer, your friend Lucars... eh, Lucars come and join us... has proposed a solution to protect you from the despair of loneliness."

Lucars motioned for Shawnee to accompany him.

"Go, Mother," whispered Amaluna.

Shawnee and Lucars soon stood one on each side of Hammer.

"I captain a great vessel," said Avalcar gazing intently at Hammer and Shawnee. "While on a voyage, whether or not I am found on the deck of my barge, I have the power to perform certain legal ceremonies. Master Hammerclaw, today under the laws of *our* land I ask if you will love, honor, and cherish Lady Shawnee, and will you do this for the rest of your days whether in health, sickness, peace, or war?"

Lucars elbowed his friend to answer.

Hammer glanced wide-eyed at Lucars, widened his eyes even more as he turned to Shawnee, gulped, cleared his throat, and answered, "Yes, Captain Avalcar, I will be most glad... to do exactly as you say."

"Will you, Shawnee, bind your heart to the love of this man Hammerclaw, and with him make here your new home?"

"Captain Avalcar, I promise!"

"Then," continued the sea captain, "by the authority granted to me by my country of Phoenicia, and with Lucars as witness, I declare Hammerclaw and Shawnee to be... *married!*"

With ends of the floral braid still clenched in their beaks, Webstir and Featherspark descended to drape the strand of flowers about the shoulders of the couple.

Able to wait no longer Shawnee threw her arms around Hammer, hugged his neck, and kissed him.

It seemed that Hammer finally understood what had happened to him. More to himself than to anyone else he shouted, "By heavens, *I am married!* Married to Shawnee! This lady will make me to be the happiest man alive!"

Upon the placement by the two waterfowl of the string of flowers around Hammer and Shawnee, the assembled natives fully understood what they had just seen to happen. For many, the embrace of Hammer and Shawnee symbolized the joining together of two cultures to become one Pavilion Nation.

"Ahem, Captain Avalcar, may I have a word with you?"

"With the newly married gentleman of this realm," answered the sea captain moving to the lowest step of the raised dais, "I would be most pleased to discuss any matter."

"Without asking permission I before did something rather extraordinary... if I do say so myself."

Hammer reached into his cloak and drew out the cloth-wrapped crown he had recently forged of blue gold.

"Sir, etched into the recently discovered second doorwell of Shining Canyon, Lucars and I found a crown with a motif of a winged unicorn. Upon considering the engraving, I said to Lucars that the crown was a prophecy that was about to be fulfilled. The presence in our band of Isabayas, the only winged unicorn in the whole world, convinced me to make the crown. As I did not want to worry anyone else about this, the crown was by me quietly forged. Now it seems that this crown can today be made to fit upon the head of its rightful owner."

"Exactly so," replied Avalcar. "Your initiative, Hammer, was *brilliant*. Your timing is better than perfect. It will be our honor to officially crown the Prince of the Pavilion Nation."

The Prince

When Avalcar raised aloft the crown, throughout the pavilion no sound, not even a muffled cough was heard.

Avalcar motioned for Bashkeem, Chief Bigclaws and Princess Admira to join him on the raised platform, and for Isabayas to stand before the dais. After saying something in a quiet voice to Admira, Avalcar handed her the crown.

"Because Captain Avalcar knows how much I esteem all that Bashkeem has accomplished since the day that I, my sister, and two brothers first met him, the day when from a burning city he rescued us, I am this day privileged to make a coronation."

The princess raised high the crown and proclaimed, "Sir Bashkeem, the nobility of the leadership and loyalty you have given to Ermir, Resi, Ermal, Maroun, Majit, and myself, six princes and princesses of Troy and Phoenicia, is... *unrebukeable!* By the authority vested in me by the king that before sent many ships across the immense ocean to rescue the white herd, and by my brother the new Prince of Troy, I now formally crown Bashkeem to be... *The Seventh Prince!*"

Admira placed the crown on Bashkeem's head.

"Prince Bashkeem," spoke next Avalcar, "six princes and princesses of Phoenicia and Troy, whose lives you have forever changed, will long remain your fast friends. Now you, the seventh prince, ride forth and display your crown to your gathered people!"

"Hah! Seven is the most lucky number!" exclaimed Chief Bigclaws.

With a big smile and a nod of his head, Bashkeem acknowledged the chief's words. The Seventh Prince proceeded to mount Isabayas.

As the winged filly pranced down the center aisle of the pavilion, Prince Bashkeem held his neck and back perfectly straight and looked neither to his right nor to his left. Shafts of sunlight made the crown's blue and gold hues to glisten and sparkle. When Bashkeem unsheathed and raised high the magic sword he had received from the king of Phoenicia, Gallop glowed a brilliant blue.

Isabayas reached the end of the long aisle, turned, and trotted fast. With the seventh prince on her back she extended her wings, flew above the unroofed pavilion, and circled gracefully the spectators below. As he rode Bashkeem held aloft both his sword and crown. The winged horse returned to lightly land hooves. After dismounting, Bashkeem joined Avalcar and Chief Bigclaws still standing on the steps of the dais. When Prince Bashkeem raised his arms above the heads of his two friends, the assembly cheered loud.

"Prince Bashkeem, with your permission I have one more ceremonial duty to perform."

"Of course, Avalcar."

"Come, Naythorn Blackmane to stand before me!"

While he did not want to be singled out for attention, Naythorn realized that before so many attentive onlookers he could not disobey a direct order. The words that came next relieved his worry.

"Come Belfloralex and stand beside Naythorn! Lucars and Admira, come also to stand before me!"

Chief Bigclaws handed a box wrapped in a wool skin to Avalcar.

"Naythorn and Belfloralex, facing soon a long journey that follows the fixed star, the golden spirals and tips of your horns connect to the courage and beauty in your hearts."

From the box Avalcar drew out and held high two halters woven of blue gold.

"Brought all the way from Phoenicia, these are gifts from my king. In this very place these halters were long ago given to Briarburr, the first blackmaned unicorn, and to his noble companion the winged filly Peli.

"I will recount that before Briarburr came to this place, with the help of Peli he gathered the people of my land so that they could throw off the yokes of tyranny. Because Naythorn here made safe a refugee people, and because of the many brave deeds of Belfloralex, it is fitting that these two unicorns come to wear these sublime halters. The enchantment with which they were woven will make even more magical two horns now wound in blue gold. Wear these in honor of your distinguished forebears." Avalcar placed the finely braided halters on the heads of the two unicorns.

The Phoenician naval captain next held high a golden diadem.

"Admira, on the battlefield you were transformed from warrior to healer. A warrior takes, but a physician restores life. The healing power gifted to your eyes and hands saved many lives. I now pronounce you... *Lady of the Pavilion Palace!* Wear with honor and pride this diadem bearing the image of this pavilion. A thousand years ago it was given to Princess Maryeta, the heroine of the founding of Phoenicia, who in this valley also did great deeds."

Avalcar lastly drew from the ancient box two forearm braces worn to protect in battle.

"Lucars, by your many deeds of valor you have earned these braces engraved with the images of lions. They were long ago given to Prince Lyons, the brother of Princess Maryeta. Without the inspiration of that prince, the canyon of magic gold would never have been found."

Emptied of its precious halters, diadem, and forearm braces the ancient box disintegrated into dust.

Accompanied by a slow beat of drums Naythorn, Belfloralex, Lucars, and Admira turned and walked down the aisle of the pavilion. Aneilee, Isabayas, Elianor, Cabalblade, Mistral, Seahorse, and Rainsnow came next. Thereupon followed the bovines with two waterfowl balanced on their wide backs, the wild boars, mountain sheep, dogs, yellow wolf, and great lion. Absent Amaluna, Shawnee, and Hammerclaw the human persons in Naythorn's band walked next. Avalcar led Princess Admira, Prince Ermal, Prince Majit, Sulay, Cholo, and Enos. Tristan's bears closed out the departing procession.

Isabayas flew back the length of the pavilion, alighted by Amaluna and exclaimed, "Come with me!"

"Because Isabayas represents a miracle of life that must be grabbed hold," said Shawnee, "my daughter cannot refuse the offer to fly upon the back of the winged unicorn. You must, Amaluna, now take care of your brother Scarlet Point. Besides, now that he has left behind his best friend Hammer, Lucars needs someone at his side... to keep his thinking straight."

"But, how can I leave behind my mother? Tell me, *how?*"

Hammer touched the maiden's shoulder and said, "Daughter, for Shawnee's daughter is now become mine, know that every day that you two are apart I will take the best care of your mother."

With tears welling up, Amaluna embraced her mother. Hugging next Hammer she said, "I know that you will make my mother's days, every one of them, to go well."

Grabbing hold the mane, Amaluna sprang lightly upon the back of the winged unicorn. The two floated high above the columns of the pavilion, and after flew away.

The assembled natives had not moved.

Holding high his arms, Chief Bigclaws proclaimed in loud voice, "Let every man, woman, and child gathered here never forget that Naythorn Blackmane, Captain Avalcar, and Tristanbear made possible the repossession of the hollow canyon inside Prow Mountain!"

CHAPTER 36

EPILOGUE

"Can it be done?" inquired Prince Bashkeem of Hammer as the two studied a carefully drawn plan indicating the dimensions of stones and the heights of pyramid sides.

"It would be the greatest monument ever built in this land. Because they are pleased to not live in fear, and to here truly belong, those long ago known as the Pyramid People will readily lend their arms and backs to cut and move the heavy stones.

"Still there are many questions to answer. Where can be found a thick and level rock base to support a weight made by thousands of stones stacked on top of each other? Where shall be positioned the chief cornerstone? Can the foundation stones somehow be made to interlock with each other? What is the strategic distance that from the pavilion palace will be neither too close nor too far away, for placement of the pyramid? And, how can the construction site be best protected from attacks by enemy warriors and wolves?"

"Those are the needed questions to be asked," agreed Bashkeem. "You, Bigclaws, and I will inspect several likely sites to our east and south. Surely one place will be found that holds promise for the construction of a tall and mighty pyramid. By the way, Hammer, have you today seen Aneilee? When we tomorrow depart, I want to leave her here in charge."

"She awoke me in middle night to tell me that she was going to take a long walk to calm her stomach," replied the blacksmith. "Since then I have not seen her. Hmpf! Now that I think about it, her not returning strikes me as strange."

"When I need her most, Aneilee has a knack for disappearing," replied Bashkeem. "Oh well, it is not my place to give her orders. The high escort of the unicorns will no doubt soon come back to us. So then, we leave tomorrow at the break of day. Instead of the high escort, during our absence I will leave Calichay in charge."

"Good idea," responded the master blacksmith. "That will take his mind off the recent departure of his granddaughter Swiftdeer. Of course he misses her very much."

"She would not be deterred. But because she is so young, her decision to join Naythorn's band surprised all of us," answered Bashkeem.

"We have traveled many days. Can this, Bashkeem, be the place?" inquired Chief Bigclaws.

"It does seem so," answered the Seventh Prince nodding his head.

"Thank heavens for that!" exclaimed Hammer. "For too long we have been searching."

"This valley is well-hidden," continued Bigclaws. "My scouts can easily monitor who enters and leaves this place. And the rise of the interior plateau provides my warriors a good defensive position."

"The springs that flow plentiful fresh water to drink, will also supply wetness to lubricate the cutting of stones hewn from surrounding cliffs," affirmed

Bashkeem. "And there is no doubt that the soils in this valley will grow plentiful maize for the workers to eat. By the most direct route that extends over the walls above the pavilion, the distance from Prow Mountain to here can in five days be negotiated."

"Then we three are in agreement!" exclaimed Bigclaws clapping two big hands together. "This is the place where Bashkeem's impressive pyramid will be skyward built."

"Errr, Prince Bashkeem, how long will it take to build the huge monument that you envision?" inquired Hammer.

"I will have it to be completed in ten years... or so. The construction of the tall pyramid will for me have special meaning. You see, having myself grown very close to Olsi, I still mourn his loss in the battle against the monster black wolf. It was a blessing to see the highborn Egyptian discard his arrogance, and become transformed into a loyal and courageous first mate. The pyramid will for me represent a funerary monument to the brave young Egyptian that sacrificed his life to make the Forgotten People of his ancestral Egypt, once more to know freedom."

"Did Avalcar speak much to you about the loss of Olsi?"

"Avalcar's eyes told me how much that loss troubled him," answered the seventh prince. "A good field commander feels personally the death of each and every soldier under his command."

"Having myself lost in that battle too many young warriors, on that I will agree," responded Bigclaws. "For my part I remain amazed that the magic armor served to protect the trueness found in the hearts of every member of the band of Naythorn."

Captain Avalcar and Prince Ermal

"Based on the size of the big smile he wears this morning," observed Ermal, "I can only guess that Captain Avalcar is elated to be found again on the high seas in command of the Jenelisa."

"You are not wrong. I continue as well grateful that in my absence the crews readied perfectly our barges. For Prince Ermal of Troy everything has also worked out well. Transporting on their strong backs the blue gold sheets to the shore, the two bovines saved us much time and work."

"Master Buckwhite and Sir Taurington are three times stronger than any other bovine," declared Ermal. "And Marsand, Scarlet Point, and Alexzana did a marvelous job helping Lucars to forge the magic metal sheets destined for Troy."

"The days spent in Shining Canyon with Naythorn and his band were truly unforgettable," reflected Avalcar.

"I was much taken with Naythorn's conviction that the white herd will soon find their protective hold," added Ermal. "He neighed that the suffering of the unicorns and the near disintegration of the white herd fulfilled a fated requirement... that before they could find lasting peace the magic horses should become humbled, and grown in strength and wisdom."

"Hmph! I am happy to see Sulay once again made captain of his former barge the Sea Stallion."

"And I myself am pleased to captain our third vessel the Star Sheen," replied Ermal. "Which, by the way, I should soon be getting back to."

"Carrying blue gold sheets in our holds, on the day of our arrival at Troy Prince Ermal will be greeted as a hero."

"Captain Avalcar will be lauded as the true hero of the expedition that carried two unicorns across the immense sea," responded Ermal.

"But you do not seem as excited about the return voyage as I thought you would be," replied Avalcar,

"Of course I look forward to once again seeing my brother Ermir. However, in that regard I have one problem; he will not understand how I permitted Admira to remain behind. He will say that the fledgling kingdom of Troy has more need of her than does a blackmaned unicorn."

"Explain to Ermir that just as Cholo was made to leave behind his brother Bashkeem to the work of governorship, and Lucars was made to leave behind Hammer to the work of the forge, so you were made to leave behind Admira to protect and preserve the purity and goodness of the white herd."

"That, Captain, is the best way to frame it. The loss of Bashkeem to Cholo and their father, and Lucar's relinquishment of Hammer certainly puts my loss into perspective. Hmph. I wonder where now travels my sister. I want for her to stay safe."

"Let the prince worry no more about his sister," encouraged Avalcar. "Become a member of Naythorn's band, Princess Admira is living the adventure of a lifetime. She will no doubt come to play an important role in making at last safe the white herd.

"And Ermal, I am very pleased that Mistral and Seahorse now travel with Rainsnow, Elianor, and Cabalblade. I can imagine the excitement of the last two unicorns of Phoenicia upon sighting the white herd. For my part, I will be ever thankful that I fulfilled my goal of meeting the fabled blackmaned unicorn whose nobility I shall never forget. Thinking about it, I rank the blackmane as the greatest commander I have ever served."

"Greater than Admiral Zoumar?"

"Yes, Ermal, I would say even that. The difference is that Admiral Zoumar does not command powerful magic. Never have the odds of battle been so against a Phoenician general as they were against Naythorn in the *Battle of the Pavilion River.* You may disagree, but I believe that the miraculous arrival of the specter that ultimately undid the black monster Trike, had to do with the magic of Naythorn. The blackmane is a unicorn that will not by evil be bound."

"The magic gift of Mistral gives birth to mists," reflected Ermal. "Crimson's gift was to enchant the clouds with her visions. Perhaps Naythorn's gift is to unknowingly summon magical help in his time of need."

"That *has* to be Naythorn's gift," answered Avalcar. "That reminds me of other things magical. When the storm-tossed Zoumar found himself lost on his voyage back to Phoenicia, a strange rainbow with its top made to be a pointed archway guided the admiral to a safe harbor with beaches of pink sand. That rainbow renewed the hope of every sailor in the admiral's fleet. As his flagship followed that rainbow Zoumar instructed me to never forget that the magic of blue gold has to do with truth, that unicorn magic has most to do with love, that the magic of the Rayalas Borealis brings grace, and that the doorway rainbow brings heavenly hope."

"Truth, love, grace, and hope... those four words are indeed *magical,*" agreed Ermal.

The Specter Joined

Through another night trotted Aneilee.

Daybreak found the hooves of the high escort climbing a mountain far removed from the basin before Prow Mountain. Happening upon an indent in a rock wall that well-fit her horse body, she there slept through the remainder of the day.

The fall of night found Aneilee rested, fed, and in surprisingly high spirits as she traveled higher the mountain. A deep sky made resplendent with myriad stars authored a sheen of fragile light that felt magically soft, and that on a high place welcomed her presence.

"This night is precious," neighed the high escort. "I hope that he will here and now finally join me."

She did not wait long.

"You came, Aneilee, to find me."

"How does this night treat you?"

"For a being that cannot sleep or eat, I am enough well. But, through every moment of the day I suffer. You must help me to end my wretched existence."

"If you let me," answered Aneilee, "I will help you to transcend your existence."

"How is that possible? After all the evil that I committed, what remains of my heart is irretrievably rent. I am tortured by the images of the hurt and pain that I inflicted on countless beings, even on my friends. Silent voices persecute me. They will not allow me, not even for one night to cast away and disregard my former cruelty."

"Unicorn magic works breathtaking miracles," encouraged Aneilee. "I promise that a day will come when from your pain you are delivered. But first you will do hard things that bring healing to this new land, and all the while I shall be at your side to comfort you. I will guide you along the path that out of searing pain brings your deliverance.

"This is the first time I dare to receive your embrace. You could snap my horse body in two, but I know that you will instead permit my spirit to enter into your being and calm you. With me cradled in your grasp, you will finally tonight enter the realm of deep sleep."

Not so many moons past Aneilee could not have imagined herself to ever become gripped in the bosom of a fearsome specter. Still, the high escort of the white herd found herself to be surprisingly calm. As she waited for slumber to enfold her being, her thoughts came to focus on matters of innocence, goodness, and... evil. For almost her entire life the protection afforded by the white herd had permitted and encouraged her to be gentle and pure; that was no longer so. Made by the kicks of the once powerful Hoovefort to plummet off a high cliff, she had come to know the harsh pain consequent to unfathomable violence. Her own kind had cast her aside. In the *Battle of the Pavilion River* her gentleness had been profaned, and her hide had stained red. But, what from her former sheltered life had she really lost? And could she have gained even more than she had lost?

"I have finally come to know that gentleness unprotective of the blameless, is not benign," neighed softly the high escort. "Compassion undefiant of evil, is not kindness. While fleeting was my time of innocence, my redemption shall long endure."

Dansey Departs

The Shining Canyon of Spire Mountain had been left behind, and led on by Featherspark, Buckwhite and Taurington had returned from the coast.

Naythorn led northward his band, Princess Admira, Prince Majit, and the newly pledged Swiftdeer. The blackmane was only a little surprised to one morning find that the independent Tristan and his bear friends no longer trailed his band.

Long travel awaited before reconnection with the white herd. However, strangely enough the blackmane was not apprehensive for the safety of the unicorns. Again and again the stallion told his band... that with their help the white herd would in due time come to gain a hold that proffered the promise of long peace.

"Join with me, Lianvil," yipped the yellow-mottled wolf. "Let us fall back to the rear."

After walking some distance together the lion still had not spoken, so the wolf sat himself down and yipped what was on his mind, "I go to find someone that now needs me, or will soon come to need me."

"Find who?" grrrd Lianvil.

The open-ended question set the mottled wolf up for what he found to be a funny retort. The lower teeth of Dansey began to protrude forward and his eyebrows arched high in an incongruous grin.

"Find whom... is the correct form of uniform speech."

"Wipe that clown look off your face," growled Lianvil. "It is a serious decision that you now take. For a solitary wolf the wide world is a *very dangerous place."*

The clown face was replaced by features intimating keen wolfly intelligence.

"I am unprepared to leave Naythorn during what soon promises to become a very challenging and difficult time for him."

"No, Lianvil, on this journey I will travel alone," clarified Dansey.

After howling at the sky the wolf barked again to his feline friend, "Her solitude troubles me. Something deep stirs within her. With her, I should have stayed. Hmpf! I do not want to leave Naythorn's band, I like it here with you. *Yarroooo!* I will very much miss my best friend Lianvil."

"I will also miss the lone yellow dancer," grrrd the lion. "But, are you sure that you can find her?"

In answer to the lion's question, Dansey waved his tail about. Then Dansey began to chase his tail.

"Give to her greetings from the lion captain that before commanded Spire Mountain. *Rrrraarrruuurrr!* So then, my yellow-hided friend, until we meet again... *farewell."*

On paws made lightened the lone yellow dancer wolf trotted away.

THE END

ABOUT THE AUTHOR

G. D. Hanson taught at Auburn University and Penn State University. His academic degrees are from Dartmouth College and the University of Minnesota. He is married and resides in South Dakota and Costa Rica.